TOM HENIGHAN

The Well of Time

FONTANA/Collins

First published in Great Britain by
William Collins Sons & Co. Ltd, 1988
First issued in Fontana Paperbacks 1988

Copyright © Tom Henighan 1988

Printed and bound in Great Britain by
William Collins Sons & Co. Ltd, Glasgow

To my sisters:
Margaret, Helen, Mary Jo and Patricia

Acknowledgements

I should like to thank the many people who helped me during the writing of this book. These include: Barbara Hehner of Toronto, and Mic Cheetham, my agent, in London, both of whom offered specific and valuable advice at an early stage. Also my editors at Collins, Laura Longrigg and Rachel Hore, who critiqued, encouraged and guided with great skill. Also my friends Pat and Bill Milliken, who with their Ingrid-like daughters, Sarah, Erin and Emily, are closely associated with all the stages of writing, and provided a wonderful background of enthusiasm and joy. Much of the MS. was originally typed by Pierrette Meilleur, who took a gratifying interest in the story. Thanks also to my son Stephen for general encouragement and to my wife, Marilyn, who reads more fantasy more sensitively than almost anyone, for never giving up on this. And last but not least, thanks to Josh Beer, for telling me what to do with it.

In researching this book I have drawn on many scholarly and popular sources. These are far too numerous to mention, but, besides the sagas themselves, I should like to recommend the following, which combine imaginative insight with careful scholarship: *Gods and Myths of Northern Europe* by H. R. Ellis-Davidson (Penguin Books); *The Lost Gods of England* by Brian Branston (Thames and Hudson); *The Norse Myths* by Kevin Crossley-Holland (André Deutsch) and *Westviking* by Farley Mowat (McClelland and Stewart). (Despite the research, I have, of course, felt free to invent, modify and combine, as the story required.)

Contents

Widespread they stand, the Northland's dusky forests.
Ancient, mysterious, brooding savage dreams;
Within them dwells the forest's mighty god,
And wood-sprites, in the gloom, weave magic secrets.

Jean Sibelius: Superscription to Tapiola

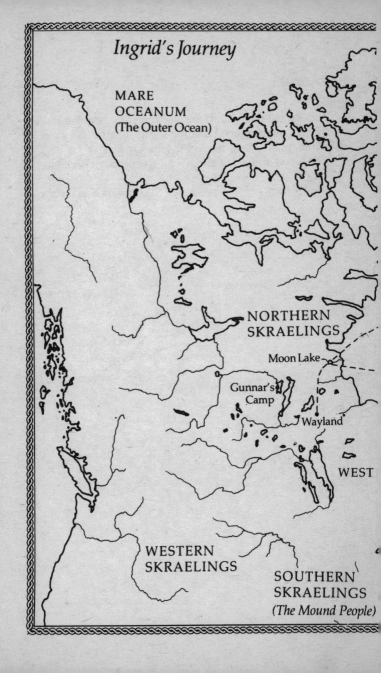

Ingrid's Journey

MARE
OCEANUM
(The Outer Ocean)

NORTHERN
SKRAELINGS

Moon Lake

Gunnar's
Camp

Wayland

WEST

WESTERN
SKRAELINGS

SOUTHERN
SKRAELINGS
(The Mound People)

PROLOGUE

How strange, to walk out after the evening meal, to slip past the houses at the edge of the village, to hear easy laughter drift from before so many fireplaces, and to realize that my story-telling days are almost over.

I, Skallgrim, of Eastland, a poet and an old man – of whom perhaps you have never heard, though some of my tales are familiar – I know now that I will never return to Wayland, that remote and wonderful village, from which I once drew my best inspiration.

Here, in comfortable Lokasenna, secure in the south Viking lands, I think of passions I witnessed, of stories I imagined, of the real north – of that magical north of my dreams. I make my way – slowly, for age has deep claims on the body – out past the gaunt poles, all that remain of the old stockade (it was pulled down some years ago, when peace with the Skraelings seemed assured) . . . I come easily, almost without thinking, upon the small clearing where my wife, Kara, lies buried. I sit on the large stone on which Grind carved a cross. (A cross! Yes, for the outward signs change, though perhaps not the feelings that create them.) I lean back to enjoy once again all the earth sounds, the night sounds: the owl's call, the fox's shrill bark, the chatter of crickets . . .

I look up.

Yet, despite the procession of stars, the shimmering freshness of the moonlight, there is something lacking, for only rarely comes a glimpse of that magic light, that breathtaking light, more beautiful than any star: the aurora.

And the sky seems almost poor without it.

In old age, I know, style should grow leaner, the truth should appear unadorned; and that is not a bad prescription for youth either. I have no wish to imitate the tricks and gauds of those who would make the craft serve a trivial purpose, to entertain idle schoolboys or impress witless merchants. My story cost me too much to discount it at such rates. But sometimes, as with the aurora, true magic surprises us, it shines forth, demanding to be seen, to be celebrated. With luck, it can even be drawn up, though by skilled hands only, from the deep well of time . . .

Now I have written it down, the whole story, all that I first told around the fireplace of Gunnar the bandit, in a place far north of here, an outpost really, further north even than Wayland, so many years ago.

I did not go to that nest of robbers voluntarily. I was abducted, carried away from Urd Lake, where I was quietly fishing, and mercilessly beaten when I refused to give the outlaws information on the caravans from Westland. (What did I, a poet, know of caravans and loot?) When we reached Gunnar's camp, they threw me into a rude hut full of goat-droppings, and left me more dead than alive.

That night, I was dragged before Gunnar himself.

He was a big man, past the prime of life, with very dark eyes and a round, strong face, that must have lost shape with age and indulgence. When he spoke – with a sly, controlled power – his thick lips curled visibly beneath his beard. I remember, quite clearly, how from time to time, he would glance around the circle, his face sweating a little in the heat of the fire that blazed close by the crude wooden dais on which he sat – was it I alone who noticed the slight air of contempt, touched a little by fear, with which he regarded his fellow-bandits?

'Well, poet,' said Gunnar in a loud voice. 'Since you know nothing of the comings and goings of trade, perhaps you might favour us with a story, something to entertain us here in this Thule beyond Thule. We may seem unworthy of your art, far too rough-forged for your liking, but I can assure you that we value the craft of the *skald*, of the skilled poet, and have often longed for a good tale in the old style to remind us that words can be more than curses or commands, or the dreary mumbles of the half-baked. Look into the fire, poet, and take your cue from the god Loki; let us see how your words twist old things into shapes new and strange.'

I had expected no mercy from such a man, and yet, when I heard his witty, supercilious and somewhat formal manner of speech, I could have shouted for joy. A way out of my predicament immediately suggested itself. Nonetheless, I was cautious. He might well be raising my hopes before turning me over to his rowdy drunken followers to be tortured or executed.

'Sir,' I addressed him, with as much panache as I could muster. 'I appreciate your interest in the art of story-telling and, indeed, I have seldom heard such elegant phrases of invitation, even in the best circles of the large towns of Eastland, but I am afraid that I cannot begin any tale suitable for your taste here at the fireside. Loki is deceptive, and might lead me astray in the telling. Besides, the fire, though dazzling and full of energy, soon burns itself out; or else craves an endless fuel. I am afraid any story told by the fire might begin in a brilliant deception, and end up leaving the taste of ashes in the mouth of the *skald* who speaks it. Therefore I beg your pardon and hope to be excused from a story such as you request.'

I stopped; a low murmur from the shadows, followed by a few outright jeers, made me wonder if I had miscalculated.

Gunnar held up his hand for silence.

'Poet, since you find the fire no fit source of inspiration, perhaps you will not shy away from demonstrating your feelings in a more concrete manner. It would amuse us, I'm sure, to see you take up Loki's challenge in hand-to-hand combat. In short, though I intend to hang you up on a branch till you sing for us, do us the favour of making your own way through the fire to the ash tree you see there. A man of such quick wit may be gifted perhaps with a shifty foot. March, or I'll have you skewered for breakfast!'

Now I was really frightened. At a signal from Gunnar, two burly outlaws moved forward and seized me by the shoulders, hurling me straight towards the fire – it was no timid blaze

19

but a huge roaring furnace of light. What followed I don't know, though my eyebrows were singed and I smelt fire in my hair. I tumbled forward and screamed, banged my jaw, then rolled away in the darkness, past the dais on which my tormentor sat guffawing, surrounded by the rest of that cruel gang.

I lay there moaning but was soon lifted by strong hands, and brushed down like a dog or a child. They swung me up in a halter, high up on a branch of the ash tree. While they were securing the ropes, Gunnar had climbed off the dais and regarded me for a while, his face like an apparition in the flickering firelight.

'Well, poet,' he chided. 'How does it feel to sit on the branch like an owl? Does your perch there, your height above men, bring a story to mind? Do you, perhaps, think of the great god Odin, hung up on the ash tree, staring down until the runes came into his mind?

> 'Do you know how they should be carved?
> Do you know how they should be read?
> Do you know how they should be coloured?
> Do you know how they should be tried?

'Or perhaps it is the Christ himself that you are calling on? As he himself called on the All-Father when he was hung up to die. How well does the old tree inspire you, poet? Let us hear from you now!'

What could I answer? I was choked up with anger and fear. In that instant I thought of the lost years, so fleeting; I thought of my own childhood in Eastland, of my time as apprentice to Ragnar, that fine smith; but I wielded the hammer rather badly and I hated the forge-fire. As an orphan without vocation I would have been banished to the mines, except for my strange gift of words. It had saved me, yet how had I used it? To get myself fine dress and women, to entertain fools!

A tall girl, dark-haired and shapely, approached Gunnar and handed him a silver cup overflowing with some foaming dark brew.

Seeing her, I remembered a trip long ago with a caravan, in the days when I was already a fop and a wastrel poet. I had met an old man in the woods who had told me where I would find a princess. He was a strange old man, with one blank, blind eye; his words were later confirmed by a lame pedlar. But, of course, I didn't then believe in the gods or in fate. I told myself I had come upon the princess quite by accident.

I spat out some blood, from a cut lip, looked down at the outlaws and cried out:

'This is a fine view indeed. I can see bald pates, and the smallness of big men. But, sir, though a story hangs in my mind, the tree does not serve it. I mean no disrespect to the gods in their perches above men, but though this tree is symmetrical, rooted and growing, though it takes firm hold of the earth, it is stolid, unmoving, the possible victim of lightning from the very heaven it aspires to. I cannot, with the best will in the world, sing out from this tree, though I have in mind a story that would greatly please you.'

Gunnar drank from the cup and tossed it away. 'Be hanged, then, poet, until morning. For warriors, there are pleasures more urgent than words.'

The bandit chief turned away, half-dragging his girl off into the darkness. A general lassitude seemed to settle down on the village. The fire went on burning, but no-one bothered to toss on fresh fuel. A few screams and some harsh laughter pealed out from under the branches of the nearby pine grove. A breeze rose from the distant lake. I swung gently in my rope sling. I had been beaten and burned and threatened with death, but I was still alive and, as the hours drifted past, my mind went on working, against fatigue, against darkness, on the germ of my story. I watched the fires die out and the stars move across the sky. At last, dawn came up from far beyond the clumped line of the woods. Then I slept.

I was awakened by the crowing of cocks and the chatter of birds in the branches above me. A few of the village women moved about their tasks in the clearing below. Some were gathering roots, others hauling water from the shining river that wound its way into the birch stand lying some little distance beyond the village.

The outlaws hauled me down later. I was too numb to feel fear, though they kicked me and dragged me through the village. The dogs started barking; children laughed at me and pointed. But now I had something up my sleeve!

Gunnar was waiting for me by the river, enjoying a late breakfast. I begged for some food and wine and with amused eyes he watched me devour the cold meat, bread and fruit, and gulp at the big jug. At last he leaned over and said to me:

'So our fine feathered bird has come down from the tree? I hope that sleep has cleared his brain and that morning will dazzle him well with the prospect of life.'

He tossed a large bone to one of his cringing dogs, then rubbed his big hands roughly together.

'Now, my friend, I have been very patient. You have refused the inspiration of the fire; you have declined to sing from the branch of the great ash tree that looks over our village. I give you one more chance, for I truly long for a story, a story such as only a good *skald* can make – for you see I have enquired of your reputation, and am patient because I have heard of your fame and your skill. *But my patience is at an end*. Look out on the river, and give me a story that will occupy all the remaining nights of the summer, or by the gods, I will have you thrown into the rapids!'

I was ready for him. I had found my story. As I swung high on the branch of the ash tree, I had seen it before me, as clear and as fragile as a breath of smoke rising from a village chimney.

'Sir,' I said quickly – ready with a speech I had almost memorized. 'It is surely a good sign that you have brought me to the river. I have loved the river since childhood. It seeks its way through the forest, shapes itself to the landscape, making a good sound, shimmering and changing, and often reflecting the light of day and the mysterious moonlight as well. The river offers us constant refreshment, both of body and soul, it carries us forward and, sometimes, in the still waters of its secret reaches, we see ourselves clearly. The river shall be my inspiration, for indeed I have a story, not only of seeking and finding, but of strange, fearful things that may rise from the depths of the water.'

Gunnar looked away, then back at me, with a sharp, wary glance. I knew I had touched on a sensitive point. Luckily, I had remembered hearing rumours that the outlaws drowned victims in the lakes in the dire ancient manner. Of course I knew, even then, from long experience, that my listeners were bound to my tales, not only by the visible cords of pleasure, but by the hidden ropes of fear and desire.

Gunnar swallowed a deep draught of wine. 'You'll begin your story tonight,' he said in a low sombre voice. 'We'll build our fire by the river, in sight of the ash tree. May Loki and Odin and the shining clear waters inspire you. There have been no sagas to cheer us since we settled this land. If your fare can equal our hunger, then your fortune is made. Now go off and rest and work up your art for the feast.'

And that was how I first came to tell the story of Princess Ingrid, I Skallgrim, an old man, who has written it down for you here, with the best of his love and understanding.

SKALLGRIM'S TALE

For there is another history that a people makes besides the externals of wars, victories, migrations and political catastrophes. It is an inner history, one that takes place on a different level, a story of inner events, experiences, singular guidance, of working and becoming mature in life's mysteries . . .   *Gerhard von Rad, Genesis*

In Wayland the Maiden
By the Wise One chosen
To overthrow his Wisdom.

> *from Skallgrim's Testament, Part the*
> *First, circa AD 1058*

The Coming of the Grey Folk

Bjorn the pedlar reached down into the cool shining stream and scooped up handful after handful of the clear and delicious water. He sputtered a little, and choked, the water ran on his beard, wetted his rough cloak and the neck of his bright ragged jerkin. With a frown and a sniff he stood up, wringing out his long sleeves and kicking a few stones and leaves into the water in testy ingratitude. An owl hooted nearby; he shivered and felt repentant, sorely tempted to cross himself, though he professed to despise the Christians and all their works. Nor could he forget that he was carrying a wide variety of precious herbs and cure-alls to Einar the doctor, who lived with his family in Wayland and was a staunch defender of the old gods over the religion of the Christ. Einar would not have approved of such an opportunistic invoking of the crucified one, probably fearing as well it might somehow pollute the good herbs and simples that Bjorn had gone to such trouble to collect for him.

With a sigh, Bjorn stooped down and took hold of his heavy pack, swinging it up on his shoulders, and jostling it about until it was comfortable. Then he clasped one end of his thick staff, touched the knife in his belt with his fingertips for luck and once again started along the narrow trail that led to the village of Wayland, still a full evening's trek distant.

It was late summer, though the night was cool, for which Bjorn gave thanks, and there was a fine, bright, full moon to light his way through the forest. The pedlar, who had made the journey so often, had no trouble, even when the going was hard, in following the slender markings that charted a path through the tall elms and birch, the beech stands and labyrinthine evergreen glades. He was adept at avoiding the worst places – the drinking holes of bears and wolves, the Skraeling hunting grounds, the impenetrable part of the bush. This time, he had been especially careful to stay clear of the great swamp-bogs that ran for miles around the margin of Skuld Lake. There, it was said, stripped broken fingers of trees poked up through a green ooze of mud and tangled grass, startled herons rose without warning and, at night, the shimmering swamp-fire burned with an intensity never before seen by common travellers.

Bjorn shivered, thinking of the rumours he had heard in the south about recent events in Wayland. Grey shapes, rising up from the mud, ordinary folk dragged away and never seen again, wolf-packs on the hunt, strange plagues of flies and grasshoppers that came down and caused sickness and ruin. It was all because of the millennium time, the Christians would say, the thousand years after the Christ's death, the time of the end of the world. But the millennium had come and gone and, unless those learned ones had counted wrong, which was always a possibility, there should be no more trouble. Not until Ragnarok anyway, the ending by ice and by fire.

A white moth fluttered up out of the darkness, and Bjorn spat but missed it. Sometimes he would help himself to the herbs and remedies he was carrying for old Einar, chewing or tasting them gingerly, though once or twice he had retched his stomach out afterwards. The pedlar respected the old man, though with some reservations. Einar was the only healer in Wayland, a wise cautious fellow with two strapping sons and four beautiful daughters. A good man, Bjorn had to admit, and yet, despite all his skills no match for Floki, the village headman, and his gang of thieves. God, how he hated that fat swine! Why, he had even dared to whip Bjorn in public for supposedly selling him short on some trinket – treating him as if he were a mere thrall, a slave, and not a free wandering trader! He spat again, viciously, just remembering it.

Wayland, although an outpost, over the years had become a thriving town, with as many as five hundred families and, if

28

the townsfolk had had any sense, they would long ago have slaughtered Floki and his three sons and his cousins and given Einar the power. But Einar was a peaceful man, not one to encourage such violence, and Wayland, despite its prosperity, was a strange place, set all apart on the edge of the great woods, surrounded by the big lakes and by Skraeling tribes who rode in great birch-bark canoes. The townsfolk, sad to say, knew almost nothing of Eastland and Westland, never mind Vinland or the home country. Most of them had never even seen the sea! In some ways they resembled the Skraelings almost more than the Viking races, and it was said that some of them intermarried with the birch-bark Skraelings or those who lived in the great mounded cities in the far south, an unheard of thing among the Vikings of the older settlements.

Still, it had to be admitted that they worshipped the familiar gods, and spoke the good old tongue and recited the sagas. And it was even rumoured that Einar's family, at least, came of a noble ancestry – that Einar himself was descended from no less a personage than Odin the Wanderer! Or, come to think of it, was it Loki the trickster who had fathered that family of healers and warriors and singers? But it couldn't be Loki, as Bjorn quickly realized, for Loki only gave birth to monsters . . .

Bjorn stopped for a while to relieve himself – too much damned water! He shifted the burden on his back, tugging irritably at his leggings. The pack was heavy, for although Einar's herbs were light, Bjorn never made a trip without bringing back special bracelets and gold from the far south – some of them probably taken from murdered Skraelings, but who cared about that? He got a good price for the skins he hauled down from the lakes, and from Wayland above all, and since he was not averse to dealing in shady goods, he made quite a profit on picking up gold and silver and trinkets fashioned of turquoise, which fetched wonderful weights of prime skins in Wayland.

While Bjorn stood there urinating, the bright moon sailed up from behind a distant high clump of elm trees, the shadows seemed to stretch and grow and interpenetrate, and a soft breeze rustled the thick leaves all around. There was a tramping and a snarling not far away, which caused the pedlar to hold his breath, and then, after a suspenseful silence, the cold mournful howling of a timber-wolf.

Bjorn looked nervously over his shoulder, pulling the strings of his trousers tight, and hurried away across a rough open track where the tall grass coiled up, bunched and glistening like matted silver in the moonlight.

He knew very well that the wolf-pack would not harm him; he was confident of his way through the forest, and yet somehow he had to admit that this was turning out to be the worst trip he had so far made between the older settlements to the south and east and the outpost of Wayland. First of all, he had narrowly missed being taken by a Skraeling war party at the Two Rivers Junction. He had had to climb a tall oak tree – no easy task, for the pack was heavy and he was getting on in years, his limbs stiff from all those nights sleeping out in the dampness of the trail. He had had to crouch for hours in the branches while the savages ate a meal almost directly below him – it was sheer torture! And while there was no longer supposed to be open warfare between Viking and Skraeling, he didn't for a minute trust his skin (or his skins for that matter) to a truce made by fat chiefs on both sides for their own purposes. There was still no certainty what would happen when stranger met stranger in the bush.

Then, the previous morning, he had woken up to find two yearling bear cubs nosing around in his pack – the first time this had ever happened to him. He did not stay to make his meal, but decamped at once, fervently hoping that the mother was not in the vicinity.

Now, as he looked warily around him, he found something about the moonlight that disturbed him. Maybe it was the great clarity of everything, the unearthly strange contours the light gave to each leaf and grass blade. Or perhaps, it was the rumours that were getting to him. Was it possible that there was something in the idea of the world coming to an end after a thousand years or so? Were the old gods angry at Floki and his greedy, cruel reign in Wayland?

Bjorn was no fool, and he had picked up many strange tales in his travels. Most of them, he knew, were just tales, stories to listen to and marvel at around a roaring fire. But some had a ring of deeper truth. It was said, for example, that long ago, certain victims, the chosen ones, were given to the ancient earth mother to ensure the fertility of the fields. (Even as the dead, he knew, were often burned in the long ships of the coast and the old country – sacrificed to Odin, they flew straight off to Valhalla.) The story went that, in the old country, long before the migrations, chosen victims were thrown into the bogs and that, when the Vikings came to the new land, the custom prevailed, though many denied it, pretending that the fields were so fertile that it was not necessary to propitiate the old gods.

Bjorn had heard a few times in Hallbera's tavern in Wayland the old settlers tell in a whisper of what they had seen: of men and women strangled and shaved and thrown into the great bogs near Skuld Lake, corpses sunk deep in the preserving mud until their very skin hardened into a semblance of leather. And at special times, when the village fell on evil ways or when the great mother sanctioned it, the grey folk, it was said, would come to life and creep painfully out of their unhallowed graves to walk the countryside, harrying the descendants of the first settlers, reminding them that they could not escape their dark past, or that even, in their pride and seeming sufficiency, they could not avert the wyrd-fate, the unfolding of destiny.

The pedlar stepped in under the silvery canopy of a great spreading beech tree and watched a fawn and a doe pick their way slowly across the open spaces between two deep thickets of underbrush. In the dark sky far away he saw a flicker of heat lightning, and reached quickly under his cloak to touch the small carved image of Thor he had pinned there, at the same time murmuring the spell he had learned as a child:

> Fire in the sky, fire by night
> Guide me safely home by your flickering light!

Having murmured this old rhyme under his breath, Bjorn stretched his broad shoulders, rubbed at his dark silver beard, spat, and moved on.

After a while he came to more water, this time to an even larger swift-running stream, one of the southern branches of the Ice River, and he followed the bank of the stream northwards, using the stars to take his bearings and picking up some landmarks that would have been missed by anyone but a traveller who had come that way many times. He was happy now to be trekking alone at night; the eeriness of the moonlight no longer disturbed him or perhaps the herb he had been chewing was beginning to work some magic on his soul. At any rate he was glad he had chosen, as he sometimes did, to avoid the hot trails by day, and that Einar's own specific against the mosquito bite (pine resin boiled up with citronella) seemed to be working better than the bear grease he had used in the past.

The stream led on, into a shadowy valley, where dead stumps poked up from the low-lying wetland. Bjorn recognized the place and grew even more pleased with himself. The night was far from over, yet he was only a few hours brisk trek from the outlying farms around Wayland.

He had made better time than he expected, and could have a sleep on the trail and arrive in Wayland quite fresh, ready for a good day's trading, and a long night of drinking and wenching. And here he smacked his lips greedily, warily, and let float through his mind a few images he would normally have suppressed while on the trail. Such thoughts were best saved until the real thing was close at hand – otherwise it was very easy to lose your concentration. He was one of those who had never been waylaid on the trail – it was all a matter of concentration. Still, the journey was almost over now. And thoughts were but thoughts . . .

He remembered, last midsummer eve, spying on Einar's daughters and some of the other village girls bathing in the Ice River. They hadn't expected a traveller from the south just then and he had enjoyed watching them for a while from a screen of bushes and scrub. One or two of the girls, though very young, were nice wenches, no doubt. Not quite fattened up enough for his taste, of course, hardly a real pair of breasts among all of them, but very lean and coltish for all that, toothsome enough certainly. That youngest daughter of Einar's, Ingrid, he thought he liked best, though she was barely seventeen. Not that she would cast a look at the likes of him. The finest lad in the village, young Thorkel by name, was in love with her, however much she might profess to ignore him. And not even Floki and his gang would dare take up with Thorkel, unless some night by ambush, that is. Thorkel was a wild one, with a quick temper and a crazy eye, and he had sworn to kill anyone that so much as glanced at young Ingrid: that threat cooled most of the hot bloods of Wayland. Still, there was no penalty for looking when you knew how to hide yourself properly.

The pedlar came on a place where the path narrowed and the dead, broken tree-stumps grew thicker. His pack felt heavier now and to lighten the load he began to sing, very softly, to himself, a little song he often used to introduce his herbs and simples, when he had a surplus and decided to try to sell them to the villagers.

> Aromatics, astringents
> Balsams, elixirs
> Infusions and lotions
> Even syrups and teas
> tinctures and tonics
> For I have them all. I have them all
> At a price that will soothe you . . .

And as he sang Bjorn recalled all the remedies he had tucked away safely in the driest part of his pack: alder bark for swellings and sore limbs, bayberry for soaps, birch bark for pimples and eruptions, borage for good spirits, horseradish for massage, lovage to take away freckles, sunflower seeds to help the digestion, yarrow for toothache . . . Some of the very rare herbs from the far south and west (bougainvillea, plumeria, sagebrush, yucca), he had bartered for, while most of the others, he had gathered in certain places at certain times of the day, according to Einar's instructions, so that the commonest plants might take on their true magical qualities. Of course it was really his own trade, his lively exchange of skins and of trinkets, that would make him a rich man. Yet who was to say that all the magical herbs that he carried for Einar weren't part of his good luck?

A loud splash and a beating of wings nearby startled the pedlar from these thoughts. He stood for a moment on the low grassy knoll where the path wound in among the trees; he looked out far to the right, across a tangle of splintered trunks, low rotting stumps and thick bush running silver at its myriad dark roots. The marsh seemed to suck down the moonlight, veining the black water with a sharp iridescence. Only a bird, thought the pedlar, a bird startled by some night prowler – a fox or a snake.

He touched the knife in his belt and waited for the silence to settle down around him. Then he heard a sound that made the skin on the back of his neck prickle sharp; he swallowed once, shivered and held his breath while he listened, not certain he could trust his own ears.

From the edge of the swamp, not far from where he stood, came a gentle oozing and gurgling, like the seeping of air through soft mud. The gurgling continued, then climaxed in a series of faint popping sounds, as if seedpods were snapping, or bubbles were bursting one after another in the darkness. There followed a churning and threshing about in the trees, as if great clumsy animals were beating a path through the woods. This went on for some time; Bjorn could not move, he stood rigid with fear, only listening, while the threshing and plunging continued. Then came a new sound, somehow more disturbing than the others: a low, steady tapping, a drumbeat as of stone against stone, a clatter that rose from the deep sighing woods and seemed to violate the virtual silence, so that Bjorn closed his eyes, afraid that some terrible vision would follow, that the trees would all topple, the swamp rise up and engulf him. But even as a half-suppressed scream rose hoarsely and died in his throat, the clattering noise stopped, a wind stirred the thickets; he opened his eyes on the calm breathing marshes, the moonlight.

Then Bjorn found he could move, and he ran, the great pack thumping down on his back – he ran out of terror, with lumbering, slow steps, as if chained in a nightmare.

The path wound on through the woods, he could see it. His heart pounding wildly, he ran on, avoiding the bare roots, the tangles, the clefts in the path and the low hanging branches. The pack thumped down on his back, knocking the breath from his chest – wheezing and gasping, he plunged on, then collapsed all at once on the soft turf – he could press not a single step further.

He rolled on his back, with his eyes closed, his staff clenched tightly in his right hand, and listened. The wind stirred softly in the leaves far above, nothing more.

He lay gasping, but little by little his breathing slowed down; he listened, as if in a trance, to his own panting breath.

A nearby twitter of laughter wrenched him up; unbelieving he lay on his side, pricked his ears like an animal. A guffaw rang out, then the banter of voices, a male and a female, quite human it seemed, a short distance away.

Bjorn rolled over, hunched down on his hands and knees. With quite sharpened senses, but a much confused mind, he crept warily forward, burrowing along through a scraggly thicket of brambles, parting the branches with care, inch by inch. The laughter and banter continued – it was somehow reassuring, yet he dared not stand up; sweat poured across his face and he wiped it away with rough, trembling hands.

At last he came to the edge of a wide, shaggy field. The trail, which skirted the field, lay on his right: at that point it wound along the marsh and disappeared, through a broad grove of birches, in the direction of Wayland. Now in the clear moonlight Bjorn could see everything: near the birches a big rough farm wagon and two tethered horses, stamping and pawing uneasily. Some distance away a small fire, still smouldering, and beside it two figures, a man and a woman, it seemed, clutching and rolling around in the grass.

Bjorn whistled a low sigh of relief and spat softly into the brambles: well, perhaps he had been a fool after all. Somehow he had lost control and changed in his mind the noises of love-play into strange, eerie sounds. This couple had come out from Wayland to make love in the woods, and taking advantage of their isolation, they had let themselves go. Bjorn smiled to himself; he could imagine what kind of games they had been playing.

Yet no sooner had he reassured himself on this point than a terrible doubt seized his mind. What he had heard before had not come from this field, nor from this direction at all. It was not the sounds of this couple's love-play that had frightened him – but something else, something quite remote and unfathomable. This pair, it seemed, had been too busy with each other to notice . . . But perhaps he could ask them.

With a grunt and a shrug of his big shoulders, Bjorn started to rise, then suddenly stopped and crouched down. The woman, for it *was* a woman, and quite naked at that, skittered across to the fire and jauntily cast a few sticks on the embers. The fire blazed; he gaped at her rosy young body and licked his lips. Then the man staggered up – a great hulking figure – and reeled along towards her. As he seized her, he bellowed; she screamed, and together they tumbled down in the grass.

Bjorn swore and bit his lip. There was no doubt about it; in the firelight for just an instant he had seen the round bearded face, the crooked nose and that sharp drunken leer – unmistakable. Floki himself, from the village, out for a night's sport.

Nor had his games changed, as Bjorn saw, lying there helplessly, beating his fists angrily together. Floki dragged himself to his feet. He staggered to the fire, plunged his hand in and pulled out a sharp glowing brand. Then he made for the girl; she swung at him wildly, shrank back.

'You scum, you fat worthless scum!' she shrieked out. With a vicious, quick gesture, he stabbed her.

She reeled back a few wobbling steps, then collapsed. Floki roared incomprehensible words and lurched forward.

Bjorn gripped his staff, fumbled for the knife at his belt. He saw that the girl was still moving, writhing grotesquely in the lapsing firelight. By the gods, he would kill the drunken bastard before he could do her more harm! His fingers closed on the knife; he started to rise, then stopped all at once, as if stricken.

Shadows had taken shape in the woods. A half-dozen figures rose up and came shambling from the trees, with stiff outstretched arms. Bjorn held his breath. They spilled out of the darkness where the trail ran right into the field. He watched them come slithering on, all silvered by moonlight, jerking and swinging their arms as they moved. He saw dark shaven heads, thin grey rope strands at the neck. In the moonlight, their skin shone like dark polished leather and their footsteps made soft, sucking sounds on the grass, as if the earth oozed and ran soft where they walked.

Bjorn felt his legs go – he collapsed in the thick of the bush. He had seen much in his travels, but now sheer horror riveted his gaze and, despite his hatred of Floki, he wanted to cry out, to warn him, but his voice stuck fast in his throat. He crouched there with clenched trembling hands, thinking, these were the grey ones, the undead, the victims come out of the swamp. Then the horses reared up, writhing and pitching in terror.

The dark ones moved forward, with blind, sweeping tread.

'Turn, by the gods, look around!' Bjorn whispered, and the drink-sodden Floki looked around.

For a moment the headman stood there. The fire flared beside him, and Bjorn saw his plump arms go up, the squinting disbelief in his rosy, glazed face. Whimpering loudly, the girl tried to crawl off, one hand pressed tight on her gashed chest.

The dark ones came forward, their cold stares unchanging, all rigid. The girl wriggled away screaming. Floki tried to run but tripped over her sprawling body.

Two of the dark figures reached out, as if groping for something unseen. Then the girl ceased her screaming and Floki cried out, his voice shrill and dreadful. Bjorn watched in horror as the man and woman were dragged inch by inch across the rough field towards the marsh.

No, no, no, something in him repeated in a flat hopeless semblance of speech. His throat was parched dry; sweat ran on his face and his hands. The horses broke tether and thundered away in the darkness.

The ghastly procession had stopped short at the edge of the marsh. Bjorn bent his head, unable to watch more. Then he heard a slow swish of steps, a soft lazy splashing.

When he looked up the marsh road was empty.

For long minutes he lay there, pressing his palms on his shut eyes, listening to the quiet sounds of the woods as if they were a mockery.

An animal terror possessed him, such as he had never known before. He sprang up, tossed his staff away, and swung the pack off his back, kicking his way clear of the tangling bushes, and sprawling out clumsily on the rough grass. In a few seconds he had torn open his pack and was scattering the carefully wrapped bundles in all directions. Of these he took the heaviest, thrusting them inside a few small bags he secured with a drawstring. He slung these over his shoulder, kicked his pack into the brambles and ran.

He ran in the flat, open spaces, scarcely daring to look towards the marshes. The trail led him into the birch stand; crashing through branches, he flinched, but kept on.

He ran through the darkness, his clothes drenched with sweat, his breath wheezing out in great gasps. Twice he stumbled and fell, the second time crashing down hard on a bare coiled-up tree root.

He lay there, frantically straining his ears for a sound, terrified lest he should hear some pursuit. But the woods behind him were quiet.

After a while he slowed down, casting a quick nervous glance behind him every few steps, not attempting to run. He could feel his wild beating heart steady down as he walked.

At last, as the moonlight slipped away and the sky crowded up with the late stars, he came out on the first of the farms outside Wayland. He felt bruised and half-dead, his legs shrieked with pain but his thoughts came apace now, his mind free from terror.

He must go straight to Hallbera's tavern and rouse the whole village – Floki's brothers and cousins might otherwise not believe his tale. But he would tell all, and offer to show them the place where the grey ones had come – so long as he did not have to go there alone or at night.

With a slow, heavy gait, consumed by exhaustion and still trembling, Bjorn came to Wayland at last. Dawn was just breaking as he caught a first glad sight of its white shining façades and its crowd of high chimneys that stretched above the swaying cornfields and the endless dark green of the forest beyond. In a few minutes he was banging for all he was worth on Hallbera's front door. From time to time he turned and looked nervously back down the road where it curved away towards the dark woods.

The Wanderer

Just one week after the townsfolk of Wayland had brought back Floki's abandoned cart and recovered the missing horses from the woods, a young farm boy, his clothes torn, his face scratched and his blue eyes sharp with terror, ran into the house of Einar the doctor at the edge of the village with yet another tale to set tongues wagging.

The boy, it seems, had been pursuing some deer at the margin of the forest where it bounded the Ice River, when he lost his footing and fell into a gully filled with brambles and loose stones. He was stunned but not seriously hurt, and was just recovering himself when he heard in the field above him a low chanting and singing, a number of voices raised in a language he barely understood, though he recognized the tone as solemn and mysterious and could pick up a few of the words – references to a journey, a storm, a passage from one world to the other. The boy crept cautiously to the top of the gully and peered across the meadows, and the sight he saw then sent a shudder of fear through his slight frame.

Ambling away from the spot where he crouched was a great crooked grey horse, its skin all shivering and wrinkled, its head bent, its tail jutting up like a stiff broom. It was no ordinary horse in any respect, and least of all in its legs – for the boy saw eight of them, and very human legs at that, full booted and stiffly marching, seemingly in time with the low rhythmical chant that grew fainter and fainter as the apparition made its way towards the woods.

Einar the doctor shook his head in warning at those who greeted the boy's tale with malicious and doubting laughter. It was true that no-one else had seen the creature, but had not Floki's clan themselves confirmed the strange story of Bjorn the pedlar – there were footprints, and herbs scattered everywhere, there in the brambles. In fact, as Einar affirmed with a sly glance, the two events were surely connected – Bjorn's encounter and what the lad had seen. And he added:

'The boy speaks truly but does not understand what it is that he has witnessed. Sleipnir, the eight-legged horse . . . an old ritual! There are some who would bring Odin or Thor, or the other ancient ones back to earth, hoping thereby to deal with the grey folk. But those who call for such as Odin the Wanderer may be surprised when his coming is not to their liking!'

Not everyone understood these enigmatic words, but Einar himself had occasion to remember them later.

Several weeks passed, and as the days began to shorten towards winter an unseasonal darkness descended upon Wayland. The sun itself seemed to have been swallowed up by some icy cavern at the horizon's edge. A dull yellow light smeared the sky; dark clouds, ominous with storm, rolled in from the north. Then the hearthfires became a refuge for all – anything for some happy, dancing light, for some warmth to set against the endless and gloomy days of the world outside.

And after some weeks, came more rumours and a few sombre facts. Strange shapes were seen under the trees where the deep woods skirted the town, creatures who moved both on four legs and two and who disappeared if anyone approached them. During the night, the real night of blackest darkness, the howling of wolves was heard, though no animals were discovered by the hunters who went out to kill them. And, worst of all, a strange fungus-like growth appeared one day in the stored hay crop and began rapidly to rot the whole summer's harvest. All the while, the days remained gloomy, and the nights were afflicted by the sickly semblance of moonlight, or else were given over to a darkness that was thick and impenetrable.

Floki's brothers and cousins, who had accepted the Christ only out of convenience, and were worshippers of the old gods by preference, looked in their travail to the ancient ways that the priest mocked. A straw man and then a young goat with its throat cut were found hanging in a barn belonging to the eldest of the clan. Certain runic markings, splotched with blood, were detected on stone cairns which had been hastily thrown together near the main path leading to the deep woods. No-one was certain if these were actually invocations, or sacrifices made to avert the doom which seemed to have descended on the village.

But early in November of that year all speculation ceased, for one night during a wild and terrifying thunder-storm, the year's worst, a strange and powerful figure walked out of the woods to change the life of every villager forever.

All of a sudden the weather had grown warmer, though it was not the usual golden Indian summer but a sultry, heavy thickness of heat which left the skies darker than ever, the air stagnant and almost fetid. Towards evening the wind rose suddenly and the storm broke in an uproar as if endless invisible troops of wild horses were raging and stampeding from horizon to horizon. Thunderclaps shook the very foundations of the houses, and lightning seared the streets with a brightness unseen in recent days in those parts. When the downpour was heaviest and flames hissed up from an old barn which stood on the outskirts of the village, a tall, bearded stranger was seen by a few surprised townspeople to step out of the shadows near the smouldering barn, and to walk with bold and commanding steps right down the middle of the main village street. A great blue cloak hid his figure but he seemed to be very long and lean, peering out from under a floppy-brimmed hat with a single eye which took in every detail around him with fierce and devouring attention.

By the time the stranger reached the main crossroads at the centre of the village, many faces were pressed against windows to get a better look at him. In the flashes of lightning that illuminated him as he walked, there came to many onlookers a moment of sharp recognition, as if some chord of long-buried memory had been struck by a sudden hammer blow. But the Wanderer paused only for an instant at the crossroads – then with the same bold and determined stride, he marched onwards through the pelting rain (which seemed hardly to touch him) until he reached Einar's house, a large white clapboard building with three chimneys which stood by itself at the extreme west of the village.

Again, only for an instant did the stranger hover, like some large dark bird, at Einar's threshold, before raising his staff and tapping loudly three times, demanding entrance.

By this time, many villagers were alert and anxious. They had not failed to notice the manner and dress of the stranger, his determined path to Einar's house, and they took in at once how the crack of his staff on the door seemed, perhaps not altogether coincidentally, to quiet the worst blasts of the storm. Although their curiosity was now at a peak, none of them, not even Floki's brothers and cousins, dared to intervene, so that when Einar's eldest son threw open the door and, after a moment of silent gaping, invited the stranger to come in, the street remained deserted behind him, a dark moist track gleaming fresh in the first clear moonlight of the month.

Inside the house, however, Einar himself showed no such fear or reticence as may have inhibited his neighbours. When his eldest son led their guest to the big fireplace where the doctor sat studying a book of herbals, Einar looked up sharply at the lean cloaked visitor and then motioned him politely to

42

take a seat. While Einar's two sons moved a huge oak chair into place so that the stranger could more easily converse with their father, the doctor's four daughters joined their mother on the large couch at the other side of the fireplace.

'You have come a long way in bad weather,' Einar said in a quiet, steady voice, after some moments of silence.

The stranger leaned on his staff, which, contrary to custom, he had carried with him right into the sitting room. They could not help staring at him, though later, when they all discussed it together, everyone seemed to have noticed, or perhaps seen or heard, something different. The boys remembered his fiercely insolent eye, and the way his knotted gnarled hands gripped his staff; the girls had observed that the visitor's clothes (which by rights should have been soaked through from the rainstorm) appeared dry long before the heat of the fire could have warmed them, while Einar's wife, Asta, declared afterwards that the stranger's boots, although worn, showed no signs at all of having been used on the rough roads of the countryside, and she insisted that as far as she could see, he might have dropped out of the sky on to their very doorstep. As for Einar himself, his fascination was with the stranger's voice – a slow, creaking, insolent kind of voice, as he described it, a voice that could hardly be contradicted, and which very few would have the courage even to interrupt.

And in fact no-one, not even Einar, did interrupt when the stranger began to speak of the hard times at Wayland, of the dark weather, the spoiled crops, the unwanted visitors, and of the sacrifice that had been offered in hopes that the old gods would take pity on the villagers. And everyone in the room remembered the stranger's voice when, as if summing up both his purpose in being there and his philosophy of things in general, he snarled:

'The gods take pity on no-one!'

For some reason this statement caused Asta, who had up until then sat as awe-struck as the others, to remember her duty as hostess, and she motioned to her youngest daughter

43

Ingrid, indicating that she should bring a mug of wine for the visitor.

Ingrid, obedient as ever, stood up, and at once the stranger's hooded glance came to rest on her.

There was a moment of silence, a pause, as the old Wanderer, his head tilted haughtily back, regarded the girl. Ingrid stood there, her tall form unbending, her blue eyes sharply fixed; then with one delicate white hand she brushed away a wisp of black hair, turned, and strode off across the room and through the doorway into the kitchen.

The stranger immediately turned to Einar and asked him what the girl's name was. At this point Einar, too, began to remember something of his social duties, and after pronouncing Ingrid's name, he started to introduce his family in a formal manner, but the stranger silenced him with a single sharp tap of his staff. They waited in nervous silence until the clattering of dishes in the kitchen stopped and Ingrid returned, carrying a small silver tray on which she had set a single mug of red wine, a few thin crackers and a slab of the best local cheese. Without any hesitation, she approached the stranger, curtsied politely, and knelt down so as to offer him the food and drink.

But to the family's astonishment the stranger immediately rose to his feet, standing full length above the girl and, when she inclined her head upwards, meeting his devouring gaze with an unflinching look, the Wanderer bent down slowly and raised her to her feet so that she stood almost face to face with him. Then slowly, he reached across and grasped the mug of wine with one bony hand, and putting it to his lips, took a single sip, without ceasing to stare at her with his searing and hypnotic eye. And as her sisters and mother watched open-mouthed, and as her father clasped the wooden frame of his chair, the stranger slowly lifted the cup on high and offered it to the girl with a gesture of long-accustomed courtesy and homage.

Ingrid drank, then took the mug on her tray, and knelt down against the foot of the great oak chair.

The stranger tapped his staff three times quickly on the

floor and the girl's head sank slowly down on the seat of the chair, her eyes fluttering one, two, three times, before they shut. The tray clattered and a little stream of wine, red as blood, touched the stranger's boots.

Einar started to rise.

'Sit down, fool!' snarled the stranger. No-one had ever called Einar a fool before then.

'What I have to tell you may not be heard by your daughter,' the stranger addressed him, ignoring the terrified women on the couch, all of whom were struggling to overcome their paralysis and go to the assistance of Ingrid.

'To you, on the other hand, I will speak bluntly,' said the stranger in a voice more lofty and insolent than ever. He held Einar's attention with the power of his single, riveting eye.

'You, more than most others, may understand how things are changing, how the old ways are passing minute by minute, dissolving like mist in the sunshine of a new day. No-one, not even the most ancient powers ruling earth and sky, can alter fate. Yet to my eye, to my one good eye for whose surpassing vision I paid very dearly, there appears to be, not an endless unfolding, but a great wheel that turns round on itself. The new gods will disappear and the old gods return in new guises. You above all should keep faith with this truth, Einar, for you are no ordinary man, but are yourself descended from the ancient ones. Your family, Einar, was given from on high a precious and terrifying gift, which is the power to affect in a profound way your neighbours and the world around you as you work out your own personal destinies. And yet, to your shame, you have forgotten the responsibilities of such a gift – you perverted this power by allowing your village to come to evil ways. You temporized and excused, you hesitated to take action, you permitted evil and folly to rule Wayland!'

The stranger raised his staff above the floor as if he would bring it down with a crash, but he held it fast, suspended in the air. He stared for a moment at the unconscious girl. Einar started to speak, but then hesitated, coughing roughly, as if he were choking on the half-formed words. But the stranger ignored this and continued.

'I have been summoned, not by you, which would have been proper, but by the churls of the village, and in a ritual as befits such numbskulls, the very ones who brought so much of the present evil to pass. Yet their case is hopeless; they are incapable of a single noble action. It is your family, Einar, that has the power and, even as your family must accept the blame for this sad decline of the community, it must be ready to offer its energy for the recovery of what has been lost. That is why I have come to your house and ignored the others. You are of my own line and your failure is my failure. Now it is time to make good use of the powers you have been granted.'

Einar bowed his head slowly; the others hardly dared stir. They wanted to help him, to reach out, but the eye of the stranger was cold and forbidding. And after a moment of silence he continued in the same solemn tone.

'There is only one hope now for Wayland and its people. I have decided it here. Your daughter, the youngest, must be sacrificed, if necessary, for the good of the village. She must venture alone to the far north, to the wilderness where none of your people has ever dared to go before. Though the quest be fearful, she must seek for the new light. She must find the elixir of power that will restore the village to a life without terror. If she succeeds, the grey folk will be driven back to the swamp-bogs and will never return. But if she fails, or dies on the quest, none of you will mourn her long, for you and your whole village will perish, and be lost in the darkness of your own making.'

Half-rising from his chair, Einar shook his head in protest and began to speak, but the stranger thumped his staff hard on the floor. The house itself seemed to jump all around them, the furniture bumped, the kitchenware clattered, the fire roared up the big chimney.

'Not a word! Not one single word!' commanded the stranger. 'It is all of you who must ask the youngest for this sacrifice. It is you who must convince Ingrid that this was no dream and that there is still hope for her, for you and for your village. I have been called and this is what I have to tell you, but I will not return . . . And now I take my leave!'

With that, the stranger swung round so that the great cloak flared out, and the edge of it brushed lightly against the chair in which Einar sat speechless. A black scorch mark appeared all at once, ingrained at that very place, but the family simply sat there in a dazed silence, as the stranger strode boldly out of the room, and eventually, out of the house, though the door made no sound when he passed through it, and none among the townsfolk who still kept watch from a distance saw him depart.

But Odin's wild companions did not vanish. On the very edge of the town, where the woods ran close to the near fields, the howling and low muttering growls of wolves could be heard through the night, and a housewife drawing her shutters on a lonely farm a few miles from the Ice River saw a pair of ravens flap suddenly out of the mist and disappear in the shadows under the trees.

As soon as the stranger had passed through the doorway of the room, Einar leapt from his chair and crossed to where his youngest daughter half-reclined, apparently in a peaceful sleep. Taking her in his arms, and with the assistance of his sons, he set her gently down on the big couch, as Asta and the girls made way.

While some herbal tea and apple brandy was being prepared, Einar gently massaged his daughter's wrists, and in a few minutes the girl opened her eyes. She looked round her with a surprised air and said anxiously:

'You know I never faint. Even when I fell out of the cottonwood tree and broke my arm I didn't! Where's the old man gone to? There was something I wanted to ask him.'

Einar smiled to see his daughter all of a sudden herself again, and handed her a very small glass of brandy, tempered with herbs.

'Drink this,' he said gently. 'You'll feel better, and we'll talk about our visitor.' His voice was calm, but seeing his wife's sombre expression, as she hovered solicitously by, he felt a shadow pass over his mind.

47

When he retired to bed that night, Einar lay a long time next to his sleeping wife, staring at the ceiling and making plans for the following day. In the morning he announced that a family council would be held that night. Then one by one he took his children aside and spoke a few serious words to them, asking that they prepare themselves for the evening's meeting with some thoughtful consideration. To Ingrid he said only that the meeting concerned her and a sacrifice she might have to undergo for the family and the village, and that she would be called upon to make the most important decision of her life that very night. Einar then took Asta for a long walk across the Whispering Meadow (which was reputed to be a place of good counsel in the worst of times), while Ingrid decided that if such serious business was at hand, she must prepare herself in her own way, so she hiked off to the Ice River, and spent the day in her canoe, a glorious day full of wind and water, clouds skimming the high heavens above her and the song of birds in her ears.

It was the first clear and wholesome day in weeks and with winter coming fast she was glad to enjoy it to the full. The sudden fine weather seemed to reflect the happiness she felt in her heart when she realized that her father, and in fact her whole family, needed some great sacrifice from her. Of course she had decided, at once, to give of herself freely and with joy, so that by the time she joined the gathering that evening her eyes shone, she was in high spirits, and the meeting almost threatened to turn into an occasion for hilarity, until Einar himself appeared.

Einar and Asta were sunk in gloom about the singling out of their youngest daughter for a trial which would have daunted the bravest man in the village, and the villagers themselves had proved highly suspicious of the visit of the Wanderer to Einar's house. As Einar and Asta returned from the Whispering Meadow they had been accosted by Floki's relatives asking for a full explanation of what had transpired between them and the Wanderer. Was there a secret pact to spare the family at the expense of Wayland itself? Had the family been warned to depart from the area at the earliest opportunity? What messages of wisdom, if any, had the familiar, ancient guest passed on to the sorely tried townsfolk?

To such questions Einar and Asta could only give evasive and partial answers, though they attempted to be reassuring. Everything would become clear in a few days, they insisted. Of course they knew in their hearts that if Ingrid refused to make the journey that the Wanderer had prescribed, they would never compel her nor allow the townsfolk to intervene; indeed, they almost hoped that she would refuse to believe them when they told her the true import of the Wanderer's words. Einar, while making his preparations for the evening, reflected bitterly on the special cruelty of the stranger, who had placed the burden of this news on them and who had set up the possibility that their beloved daughter would see herself as nothing more than a sacrificial victim in the ancient manner, destined to atone with her life for the nameless wrongs of the past. And how unjust of the Wanderer, who seemed to blame him for not reviving the custom of the blood-feud. For if he had intervened against Floki, enlisting his own sons and Thorkel, for example, what would the result have been but bloodshed, revenge fights, the worst of the old ways? He shook his head sadly and went to join his family with a heavy heart.

When Einar entered the sitting room, the chatter and bantering of the children stopped. They noticed that he was carrying, not only the great brass candelabra that formed the setting for the family's most formal meals, but a small goat-skin-wrapped parcel, which none of them had ever seen before. Einar set the candelabra down on the great oak table, and Asta began lighting the candles. As she carried the taper from the fire across the room, giant shadows danced on the stark white walls. Soberly, the children took their accustomed places at either side of the table. Asta brought tea and honey cakes and a small jug of brandy for the men.

After they had all eaten a little and taken a few sips of drink, Einar cleared his throat and started to address them.

'My dear wife and children,' he began, speaking in the formal manner he sometimes adopted with them, 'We all know that at this time of troubles for our community, our family has endured a visit from one of the ancient ones to whom our forefathers prayed. There are mysteries yet in this world and we have not sought out the burden that has been placed on us; nor is there point in asking ourselves why we have been honoured (and cursed) by the appearance of that blue-cloaked stranger who presides over the dead and yet wanders on human paths with ravens and wolves for companions.

'We only know the upshot of his visit. Our own daughter, Ingrid, inexperienced though she is, has been chosen by the Wanderer himself, or by the Fates that rule all things, to go on a journey that may save us all from the curse of the grey folk that lies on our village. It was characteristic of the wiles of the stranger that he should not ask our dear Ingrid directly to undertake this terrible task, but should force those who love her best to lay the burden on her. I have requested that you think about this carefully, and I have decided that none of us has any right to ask for this sacrifice that will in the end probably yield so much bitterness to all. Hard as it is, the choice must be Ingrid's alone, and if she refuses the Wanderer's injunction, we will never mention his visit again in this household.'

Having made these observations, Einar paused, and cast a most searching look at each of them around the table, but he had not so far, nor did he at that moment, look directly into the eyes of his youngest daughter.

Ingrid, however, spoke up at once. 'Please tell me what it is I am to do, father.'

None of them could fathom her blithe and almost joyous manner. They did not realize that it came from a boundless depth of resignation to the will of fate, and out of a powerful love for each of them singly and for the family as a whole.

Her father was slow to reply, for now indeed he searched her face with a glance full of love and sorrow and, at last, almost of understanding. In a few words he conveyed the message of the Wanderer, and explained that on the assumption that she might well choose to go, he had asked each member of the family to give her something of extraordinary value to help her on her journey.

Ingrid, for the first time almost sombre, bowed her head slowly in acquiescence.

Her father drank deeply of the brandy in his mug and began to unwrap the goatskin parcel.

Only Einar and Asta knew what the parcel contained; the children looked on with eager attention as their father set aside the skin and an inner wrapping of soft lamb's wool. A moment later their gasps and exclamations filled the room. For there in front of them, gleaming in the firelight and candlelight, sat a silver cup the like of which none of them had ever seen. Very gently, Einar raised it up, polishing it a little with the lamb's wool, and then he set it down again so that the children could begin to take in the intricate carvings that covered it – warriors on horseback; soldiers in rows blowing long, wolf-headed horns; a strange, stag-headed figure holding a serpent.

At the sight of such wonders even Lina, Einar's usually taciturn eldest daughter, could not contain herself. 'Tell us what it is, father!' she demanded in her deep, singing voice, before the others could open their mouths.

Einar's ageing eyes glowed fiercely in the flickering light. He touched the precious vessel with the ends of his fingertips, and looked around the table.

'Booty!' he announced with a sharp laugh. 'Our ancestors were warriors, remember, not farmers and herdsmen. It was captured in a great battle against the Celts, the ancient people, then lost, and discovered again by your great grandfather in Iceland.'

The harsh note of pride in their father's voice surprised the children. From their earliest years they had regarded him as a healer, as one who hated all violence, forgetting that in him, as in themselves, something of the old Viking freebooter still endured.

'Ingrid,' Einar said in a voice much softened. 'You have chosen the hard way of the journey, to bring back a portion of the magic light from the far north, so that the village may be saved from destruction. This cup, a sacred cup of ancient times in which the wyrd-light may be content to rest, is my gift to you as you leave us. Take it from my hands and with it my kiss and my blessing.'

Ingrid rose slowly and came around the table. Her father held up the cup and with a deep and shuddering sigh placed it in her hands. As her fingers closed around the shining metal a tremor ran through her body, she staggered a little, but caught hold of herself in time to take her father's kiss. She wanted to throw her arms about him, to hug him to herself but her desire not to let the cup fall prevented her from embracing him freely.

She leaned over and kissed him passionately on the side of his mouth. Then she returned to her place at the table, cradling in her hands the precious vessel, which gleamed and sparkled as her tears fell upon it and into it.

No-one said anything for a while, as Asta fetched more brandy for Einar. Harald and Eric, the doctor's two sons, looked around gloomily. They knew their turn was next and indeed Einar signalled them almost at once to make their presentation.

With much shuffling and stumbling of phrase, as they unsuccessfully sought to keep a tight rein on their emotions, the brothers presented their gift.

It was an old whistle covered with runic carvings which they had found on a fishing expedition to the far north of Skuld Lake. Although they had cleaned off the caked green mould that encrusted the object and the whistle shone with a deep copper lustre, no sound seemed to be produced now when it was blown. For a long time it had hung on a buckskin cord above the bed in their room. Ingrid accepted the whistle and immediately put it around her neck, bowing her thanks to them and remembering with some guilt how deeply she had coveted the whistle when she was a child.

Harald and Eric sat down, casting shy and solemn glances at their youngest sister. Einar cleared his throat. Lina, Helsa and Kristiana rose and embraced their sister in turn. Then

Lina fetched from the large chest in the corner something that looked like a heavy grey blanket and set it down before Ingrid.

'This was to be your birthday present, made by the three of us. Take it now, dear Ingrid, for your journey and may the gods protect you and bring you back safely to us.'

Ingrid slowly tumbled out the fabric, and saw that it was a grey homespun robe, thick, strong and plain, proof against chill nights and bad weather.

'We finished it this morning when father told us that you were almost certain to go,' Lina said, her deep voice slightly hushed. 'We pray it will keep you warm always and protect you.'

Ingrid looked at her sisters. There was Lina, dark-haired and beautiful, though not so tall and strong as Ingrid, and Helsa and Kristiana, blonde and fragile as china doll princesses, despite all their fondness for riding and playing at sports. Once again, the sisters embraced, and more tears were shed.

Asta, deciding things were getting out of hand, got up and gave the fire a vigorous stir with the poker. She threw on some chunks of cut wood, and poured another measure of brandy for Einar. Then she fetched a very small wrapped parcel from the cupboard on the other side of the room and brought it to Ingrid.

'Sometimes the oldest things are the best things,' Asta told her youngest daughter, then added, with a smile, 'Though it isn't always true of people. Your father has given you the cup of grandfather Hannes, the most precious family treasure; your sisters have given you a cloak such as a young girl of ancient times might have worn. Now I give you the cardamon cake I made last year at midsummer. You remember, Ingrid, how I wrapped it up with my own hands, after following the recipe your grandmother first gave me when I was your age. How time flies past, it's hard to believe! You must take other food with you – we will pack it all, Ingrid, your sisters and I – but this cake is very special and, if the gods allow, it may feed you when all else fails.'

Hearing these words Ingrid could contain herself no longer;

after solemnly kissing her mother, so as not to disgrace herself in front of the family she turned quickly and strode from the room. In the hallway, however, she started running and fled up the stairs to her little attic bedroom. There, she collapsed on the bed, tears rolled down her cheeks, but she stifled all sounds with her hands, so that the family would not hear her crying.

Downstairs, Einar and the boys were beginning to argue, taking out their feelings in a storm of petty quarrelling over matters which none of them cared anything about. Finally, Asta broke in and put the question that was secretly disturbing them all:

'But when does she have to leave?'

No-one said a word, for they all realized at that moment, as if for the first time, that they were losing Ingrid.

Two Meetings

She moved swiftly across a blanketing silence of snow. Wrapped in light furs, protected against the chill of the day, she poled and coasted along the frozen margin of the lake.

She had been at home on skis since childhood and now her skill served her well, as she raced along the edge of the trees, seeking always a straight path through the vast evergreen forests that stretched away endlessly towards the north.

No breath of wind stirred under the low and sullen sky. Her quick and occasionally anxious glances took in the flat expanse stretching far to the east, Skuld Lake with all its teeming life struck featureless by winter. She soared between boulders, and skimmed across the tufted crest of a ridge stripped of its burden of snow. A sombre beauty was every-where: in the gleam of ice, in the cleft of a frozen stream, in a brown jutting arm of deadwood angled against the pines, in a line of crows flung suddenly shrieking from the white, powdered scrub.

It was hours, seemingly, since she had last stopped to rest, and inevitably to cast a sad glance over her already vanishing trail, faintly imprinted on the land she had passed over. Her energies aroused, she refused herself the luxury of another stop, but her thoughts drifted back, to the previous night spent in old Rinta's cabin on the Ice River, to the moment when she passed the boundary of the town and struck open country – and intermittently too, despite her inner resistance, to the stiff and tense moment of parting from her family and from Thorkel, whose tight jaw and sadly drifting manner betrayed his helplessness before the loss of his closest friend.

During her fitful sleep of the previous night and in the long silence of the morning's trek, she had had time to realize that something had disturbed her about Thorkel's manner: it was not the strong and bold friend of her childhood who had said goodbye to her, but someone rendered passive by events, an uncharacteristically crushed and chastened young man, who barely managed a furtive embrace as she turned for the last time to try to stir him from his lethargy.

Now, as she swung easily around an outcropping of dead trees, rising like a staked-out maze from the lakeside, she pulled her thoughts back from that disturbing memory, and rehearsed once again her plan of action.

It was a vague, almost hopeless strategy worked out with her brothers and her father in the hectic days preceding her departure. As the stranger's words had grown faint in their minds, the scepticism of the men had deepened, and they had agreed that to fetch the very source-light of the northern sky might be impossible; the Wanderer had spoken in riddles, surely, and of goals that applied only vaguely to a task that must have a secret meaning and dimension. What Ingrid must do was to venture as far north as she could, to pass beyond the customary trails of the village hunters, and to hope to find there, on the very edge of the known lands, a sign that would betoken that the gods had relented in their persecution of the village. Then and only then would the grey folk return to their swamp-graves; and Ingrid might yet grow up in a Wayland restored to its primal happiness.

As she sat, sometime later, making a lunch of various dried fruits and bread, her head resting on the thick bulk of her backpack, she tried to calculate exactly how far she had come from the village. It seemed probable, judging by the few landmarks she had noted that day, and based on the information she had received from her father, that she was now fully three-quarters of the way along the west shore of Skuld Lake, and only about two hours ski-trek from the last hunter's shelter that the Waylanders had set up on the very edge of the unknown lands to the north.

Soon, she would enter that true wilderness, the dark lands, and stand with no human person between herself and the great emptiness, the Ginnungagap of the old tales. Surely then, she would see everything in a new perspective, and she would know what to do.

For some time her thoughts drifted into the future, into the far north, only to be tugged back by memories from the past – and she heard her sister Lina's laugh shatter the still air, her father's commanding voice, the slamming of a door in the house with three chimneys. Soon her eyes closed, her head sank down and she slept.

The voices continued, louder and louder, as she stirred and untwisted herself from sleep. A face seemed to float down from the sky and gaze at her from only a few feet away; she saw it through half-shut eyes. Something told her she must bestir herself, pull herself into full consciousness, but her body was lazy and placid; she rolled over and her nose, mouth and cheeks became buried in a snowdrift. Lazily, she stretched out one arm to get her bearings, and turning as she did so, she felt at her fingertips the hard unmistakable contours of a boot, implanted firmly in the snow.

With a yell of alarm, she jumped to her feet. The sleep fell from her eyes like a veil.

Before her stood a red-cheeked giant in furs. He grinned at

her and ran one hand through his mop of white-blond hair with a familiar gesture.

'Thorkel!' she cried, puzzled but happy to see her friend looking so much himself.

'I thought I would never catch you,' he said. 'Don't you ever think of rest?' He smiled at her and stepped forward, holding her at arm's length.

She surveyed him quietly with her measuring eyes. 'I'm so glad you've come to say a proper farewell,' she said. 'Won't you share some food and drink with me? You must be very hungry.'

He had set his skis next to hers, leaning on the trunk of the giant bare elm beside which she had camped. They sat face to face, braced against their packs and looking at each other with serious concern.

'It was foolish to go to sleep without a fire or shelter,' he told her. 'You might have got frostbite, or worse. It confirms what I feared, that you cannot possibly make this trip by yourself.'

She turned her head slightly, knowing his criticism was just. Far away at the edge of the distant woods she saw a white rabbit bob up, scurry, then vanish. She turned back to him with a withering look.

'I can take care of myself,' she said haughtily. 'It isn't cold enough to get frostbite. Have some bread and cheese and shut up.'

Thorkel rubbed his blond beard and gazed at her in perplexity. Then he began to laugh, and the laughter took hold of him – he could hardly contain himself. She could not help laughing too, to see him like that.

'You're certainly amazing, Ingrid,' he ventured, with a sideways look. He picked up a little handful of snow and tossed it away. 'Everyone knows you're very beautiful, but only your friends realize that you're also as wilful as sin and at the same time as erratic and fluttery as a butterfly. There's no hope of trying to reform you, that I know.'

She was happy to hear the part about being considered beautiful and the rest was tolerable enough, though not quite so accurate, she hoped. She fed him a few raisins from her hand.

'I'm going with you,' Thorkel said. 'It's the only way we can be sure you'll get back all right.'

She stared down at the snow that was melting slightly under their boots.

'It's the only way,' Thorkel repeated. He scrambled to his feet, pulling her up as he did so. She made no resistance, but stood looking squarely at him.

'How is everyone – the family?' she asked in a trembling voice.

He started to smile. 'I only left this morning at daybreak,' he protested. Then, seeing her unhappiness, he went on: 'They were all so sad to see you go. When I told them I was coming after you to join you, they felt much better. Your father said to tell you not to worry any more about Floki's relatives. Some of them fled the town, leaving just after you did; the others I swore I would challenge if they stayed. They, too, are gone. Perhaps the gods will spare the village now . . .' Ingrid bent away from him and started to put on her skis. She would not dare let him catch a glimpse of her expression at that moment, but her voice came strong and clear.

'It's too late for that. I must go on – alone,' she said, reaching for her pack.

'I won't let you. I'll come after you.'

'I won't speak to you then. I'll never speak to you again.'

'This is foolishness, Ingrid.' He spoke as if he were losing his power over her. 'You mustn't do this.'

She tied up her pack slowly, then swung it, with an effort, on to her back.

'Tell my father, my family, that you found me well,' she said.

She stood there, tall and straight, looking at him with her calm blue eyes. With one hand she brushed a loose strand of dark hair under her cap.

'Ingrid,' he said, and took a step forward, then hesitated. 'Ingrid, don't go yet. I've got something I must tell you.'

She had started to turn away, now she stopped and looked at him expectantly.

'I didn't want to mention this, but perhaps it will make you change your mind. Back there, at the south end of the lake, where you skirted the swamp-bog, I followed your tracks. Your father told me the plan was that you should stay as far away from the swamp-bog as possible. I was only a few hours behind you – perhaps not so much. Yet I found other tracks following yours.'

She took a deep breath. 'Ski tracks, you mean?'

'Not ski tracks, Ingrid. The tracks were made by those who walk without skis – or shoes of any kind. They were made by the grey folk.'

She stood silently for a moment, staring down at the white crusted snow.

'The tracks veered away after a few miles,' he went on. 'But they didn't circle back. They went west and north. They might be trying to cut you off near the outpost huts.'

'In that case,' she said, plunging her poles in and giving a sharp, sudden shove, 'they will have to hurry. As you know, I'm one of the fastest skiers in the village.'

She moved away from him with a few swift strokes, then suddenly circled round towards him. He stood gaping at her, as she stopped, just out of reach.

'Well,' she said, when he hesitated. 'Do you want to kiss me goodbye or don't you?'

He kissed her on the lips with closed eyes, and she felt her comfortable, half-mocking intensity dissolve for a moment in the warmth of his encircling arms.

'Guard yourself, Thorkel,' she whispered. 'And don't follow me.'

She knew he could not help but watch her, and she imagined herself becoming a small speck, a mere dot on the horizon of dim grey light. When she finally looked back, he had disappeared in the greyness, and she could only hope that he had acquiesced to her wish and begun the long trek back to Wayland . . .

During the next few hours the wind came up strongly and the sky darkened.

Ingrid's pace slowed down to a weary trudge; her pack felt twice as heavy as before – nearly as heavy as her thoughts. Occasionally she stopped to listen, and once or twice cast apprehensive glances at the wood where the trees grew thickly, making an almost opaque screen of shadows that shifted as she moved.

As she struggled onwards, feeling increasingly bleak in both body and soul, slowly, inevitably, the countryside changed its character. She found herself on higher ground; the land rolled away slightly to the east, and she could begin to sense the sweep of the great north crescent of Skuld Lake. Ahead, almost due north, were a series of ridges, strewn with great boulders which lay mottled with frost; they shone a mouldy grey in the faint light. Farther to the west the woods seemed to flow together like a green smear on the gathering darkness. In this country she felt isolated and, despite the gloom, too highly exposed to the sight of hidden eyes; at the same time, it was a relief to put some distance between herself and the thickest part of the evergreen forest.

The wind continued to blow, the cold seemed unrelenting. She had to stop and cover her face with a fur mask. On and on she trudged, her arms and legs pumping away in mechanical rhythms, her mind gone as blank as the landscape.

She moved forward steadily, but almost as if she were sleepwalking, and at last nearly touched the side of the hut before she saw it, a log house only a little larger than a very large horse stall. It was a moment before she realized why the sight of this crude building gave her so much joy. For the first time in hours, she had encountered in this bleak landscape something unmistakably made by human hands.

Seeing the familiar runic markings carved deeply into the door gave Ingrid the sense of a last, fragile connection with everything she had known since childhood. This was one of a series of outpost huts built by hunters and trappers from Wayland. Here, from the time peace had been established with the Skraelings, the Waylanders had camped and stored food, skins and game, while they made an occasional foray into the unknown wilderness to the north and west. Beyond here lay the region of mystery, the territory of the unknown powers of the northlands.

In the last glimmerings of the faint, yellow light of the day, she began to take possession of the hut. As the wind caught and tore at her fur sleeves and leggings, numbing her fingers and face, which she had uncovered for the work, she struggled to make her way into the tightly shut cabin. She dug through the snow, then from her pack she drew out her grandfather's hammer, stamped with his own mark, and knocked out the carefully set pegs that secured the heavy cedar door. With the point of her hunting knife she worked the edges of the door until the frost relented, and she was able to swing it back on its hinges and enter.

The inside of the cabin was musty and cobwebbed. A sharp odor of skunk made her wary and the darkness seemed full of faint scurrying. It took her a long time to get a fire lit; she was tired and still numb with the cold and her hands worked clumsily with the flints, which felt like icicles at her fingertips. At last she got a small pile of shavings ignited, and the cabin flared up with sudden shadows. The sight of the bare wood chinked round with anciently applied smears of mud, made her heart sink. In one corner, cradled in a pile of rotting skins, lay the bones of an unknown animal, a tiny white skeleton picked clean by time and marauders.

Quickly, to avoid any danger of fire, she transferred her light to two candles drawn from her pack and stamped down the smouldering shavings until they were ashes. Then she lay back against the hard ridged walls of the cabin, closed her eyes and rested.

For a short while she dozed there, opening her eyes a little later to find her candles almost burnt down, feeling herself hungry and ready for real sleep at last.

She piled some of the useful treasures from her pack round her, the precious gifts of her family remaining safely wrapped inside, and feasted on dried venison, bread and few sips of brandy from the carrying jug.

She blew out one candle, set the soft part of her pack under her head and wrapped herself in her grey homespun as a blanket.

She lay there and her eyes grew heavy staring across at the flickering shadows on the walls. Outside, the wind moaned and belaboured the loose shingles of the roof. She knew that she must sleep, but the very thought struck a tension in her, sharpening her mind to every wayward, random sound. The clapping and banging outside became a series of catches of breath, as her nerves tensed and her ears magnified the slightest noise. She tried hard not to think of Thorkel's parting words about the tracks that seemed to cross her trail far back near the village. She did not want to imagine, but began to imagine nonetheless, a slow stalking carried on through the night, lurching soul-less things afoot in the snow, coming closer and closer to where she lay helpless and already terrorized by the mere possibility of such contact.

At last she could stand it no longer and resolved to get up. Anything was better than waiting there in the glimmering half-light to become the victim of those shadowy night-things. But then she thought of the cold outside and of her weariness, and of what course she would take in the morning and in the middle of such thoughts, quite unexpectedly, she fell asleep.

In the dream she had it was suddenly summer. She was paddling her canoe across a swamp of green slime that stretched endlessly away through a landscape of giant ferns, vast rotting trees and creepers that overhung her path and brushed her cheeks and forehead as she moved. Suddenly, in the water just ahead, arose a great beast, one such as the dragons she had heard tell of, with great teeth, fiery-breathing nostrils, and horns and scales the colour of sunset. She was startled, attempted to get to her feet, and upset the canoe. In the next minute she was pulled down into a swirl of black water and, reaching out in sheer terror, felt her fingertips viciously stung, as if by lightning.

She awoke with a shudder, hot with the sweat of her nightmare. The cabin was silent, its skin of thick darkness seamed with mysterious silver. She had that strange feeling which affected her sometimes after a fitful sleep, that while her eyes had been closed the whole world had transformed itself. She felt now that the very air around her was composed of new elements, beams of light flickering in through the tiny chinks of her cell.

No longer frightened, but in awe of the cold crystal silence, she struggled slowly to her feet. Slipping into her boots, and wrapping herself up loosely in her homespun blanket, she crept slowly across the floor and, after a moment's hesitation, while she listened with fast-beating heart for sounds that might betoken danger, she pushed open the door of the cabin.

For a moment she stood there, her eyes opening wide on the scene that lay before her. The wind had died down, the clouds had blown clear, and the sky was a radiant darkness, a black sphere of glittering moonlight and stars. As she breathed the chill air, the fast-swelling moon, far above, stunned her with its gleaming presence. She shivered from the roots of her hair to her feet. High in the west, she saw the familiar constellations, great Thor marching onwards in a blaze of fire, and white sparks whirling down from Freya's spindle; while all around her the hard snow itself seemed softened to lacework by the starlight.

Ingrid stepped slowly, warily, out of the doorway, as if almost fearing to jar on the perfect and crystalline silence. She turned and peered over the cabin's low roof, towards the north. Her eyes opened wider.

Dancing and trembling, the aurora's green light gathered there against the darkness, bright webs breaking and flaming, dissolving, reshaping and swirling up into luminous curtains. That wild dance of wraith-light, pitched between deep sky and earth, yet belonging to neither, seemed to sweep down with intricate energies and capture Ingrid's very soul as she moved with slow and dreamlike steps out and away from the cabin and on to the open space of the ridge.

Never had she seen the lights so restlessly bright, as if they signalled a violence of tenderness enacted in some far range of the sky. Yet they touched her, struck deep in her mind; she suddenly wanted nothing more than to shout and to move, yet she dared not – it would have destroyed the perfect stillness she felt there. So she waited, receptive, watching the endless play of light, and thinking how wonderful, how impossible it would be to draw down and command that energy, to capture even the smallest part of it.

Then in a whisper, she spoke, for the first time openly, the deepest wish of her heart.

'All-Father, Wanderer, help me! Our village has need of that light.'

She stood there for a few moments, her eyes shut, her fists clenched tight, her mind fixed on her wish. Then she walked very slowly back to the cabin, pulling her thoughts away from the distant unreachable sky.

Inside, she was no longer fearful. She wrapped herself up in her cloak and let her head sink down on her pack, knowing that for the present the world outside was free of all threat. It was a pure world out there, pure and inhuman, without the shadows she knew could stalk even the brightest human hope.

Ingrid drifted down into restless sleep. And in the morning, sunlight piercing the chinks of the cabin woke her with merciful slowness and ease.

Her first thought on waking was that she was terribly hungry. I'm going to cook a good breakfast, she promised herself, trying to warm up her toes by wriggling them inside her blanket.

She sat up, yawned, stretched her arms, and pulled her pack wide open so that she could choose the best part of her rations to make a feast with. She bent down and, peering closely, almost nearsightedly into her food stores, she brought out a bit of dried beef, some vegetables and a small bag of wild rice.

In an excellent mood, head high, and humming a comical love song she had learned as a child, she marched out of the cabin.

The day was brilliant and splendidly clear and the cold air glittered around her. How promising everything looked in the sunlight!

She turned round. Almost within arm's reach, a creature pawed and swayed, eyeing her with its large dark eyes as it hung back, nervously edging away from the side of the cabin.

It was a reindeer, the animal the Skraelings called caribou, and she had never before seen a live one so close. She waited for it to bolt, her heart beating fast, though she reminded herself that it was harmless, a living creature, and a beautiful one, with upraised antlers and a thick brown body that stood out sharply against the white curve of the snow.

Slowly, Ingrid backed away. The reindeer's sensitive gaze followed her movements with interest. She retreated carefully, letting her mind take in the details she had missed in the excitement of the first glance of discovery. She saw nothing to indicate that the animal had been pursued by either man or beast; it must have walked up to the cabin at its own pace, for the faint imprint of tracks stretched back to the woods, a regular line strung out to the edge of the evergreens.

When she stopped and bent down to scoop up some snow to be melted for cooking, Ingrid half expected the reindeer to shy, but it merely snorted softly, and took a few slow steps, moving its hooves in that shovelling manner that seemed to indicate that it was pawing for food.

'Are you hungry then, caribou?' Ingrid said aloud, and suddenly laughed at the sound of her own voice. Still the animal stared at her, bending its large head down, so that the mane on its throat bunched. Is it going to bolt now? Ingrid wondered, but although she was a full thirty feet distant by this time she could almost feel how it settled back on its hooves, turning its head and withdrawing its gaze, as if it were suddenly sure of her.

When she had packed as much snow as she could in the cooking pan, Ingrid took a few steps back towards the cabin. The animal looked up at her but did not shy away as she slowly approached. When she was within arm's length and the branching antlers stood up before her, bone clean except where the last patches of fuzz clung, she could feel the caribou's warm body, and on an impulse reached out and laid her hand gently on its brow. The animal quivered and stamped like a horse, its eyes shining brightly close to hers. Then to Ingrid's utter amazement, the great bulky animal half plumped down right beside her, rolling its back sideways a little, and then suddenly stretched out again, stamping and swinging right round, so that its antlers lightly brushed her coat.

'Why, caribou, you're half tame!' Ingrid burst out in her surprise, and dropped her snow-filled pan on the spot. The animal bent at once and licked at the snow in the pan. Ingrid pulled off one of her mitts and rubbed the caribou's back, feeling the dense warm coat under her fingers, making contact with the sway and motion of the heavy shoulders.

On an impulse, she took firm hold of the caribou's mane and reaching with one hand around the animal's neck with the other swung herself quickly and easily up on its back.

At once she knew that the animal was meant to bear riders. It buckled just slightly beneath her, swaying and stamping as if to adjust to her presence there, and responded at once to the slight pressure she applied from her knees. They moved together, reindeer and rider, across the shining snow, as Ingrid took hold of the mane and the beam of the antlers, and after a few steps turned them back towards the cabin.

Ingrid almost shouted with the joy of her discovery. She urged the caribou about and it responded, tramping and dancing, until at last she noticed that her mittenless hand was growing numb in the cold, and that one of the large hooves of the animal had plunked down hard on her cooking pan, bending it hopelessly out of shape.

Quickly, she swung down from the caribou's back, half-expecting even now that it would take fright and bolt away across the trampled snow, but when she had descended, and stood there for a minute gazing at it, she knew that it had no fear of her and would remain. She watched it watching her as she retreated slowly into her shelter. Inside the cabin, she lit a small fire and began her cooking – though it was not the fancy meal she had planned for, but a simple one of fish and rice. While she ate, she kept peering out through the doorway, watching the caribou, which was grazing nearby, pawing and prodding the snow and uncovering the hidden fresh shoots from the hardpack.

She had to take hold of herself now, and consider the meaning of this meeting. An idea was forming in her mind, one that would involve a complete change of plans and would require that instead of pursuing her journey as she had agreed with her father and brothers, she would take a new direction of her own.

The arrival of the caribou, she felt, could be no mere accident. The creature had wandered out of the woods, not in panic or as part of a regular migration, but because it was destined to serve her. She had simply to look at its patient and docile manner, at its all-but-articulate glances and movements, to realize that it must bear some connection to her quest. Besides, it had arrived in the sunlight, after a night in which she had been granted a clear vision of the northern lights she was seeking. It had welcomed her as its rider and seemed to be eager to go on with her, even to carry her off north in the very direction she wished. This was a time, surely, to trust to her fate, to believe that the All-Father or the spinners of destiny had arranged things for the next stage of her journey.

By the time she had swallowed the last mouthful of her morning stew and warmed herself with a few cups of herb tea mixed with apple brandy, she had settled on her plan. After scattering the ashes of her fire in the snow and tramping them down, she went to work on her pack, rearranging the contents and removing from the recesses of the leather satchel a couple of strong skin bags, a coil of rawhide, and the large needle she had so often used at home for all manner of stitching and repairing of leather.

She worked quickly, for despite the sun there was a bite in the air that suggested cold weather all day. While she worked, from time to time she spoke softly, almost naïvely, to the caribou as one would to a child, and her voice seemed to soothe and charm the animal, which gazed at her gratefully, almost as if it could understand every word.

'We're going on together,' she said. 'You've come especially for me, I feel it! Oh, I'll do everything I can to make the journey easy for you . . . If only you'll help me now, dear caribou, I promise that you'll get home too . . . There are terrible dangers' (and here she lowered her voice and glanced quickly around) 'things that lurk in the woods. But together we can escape them. I know we can!'

Ingrid got up and went over to the animal, gently stroking its brow and its thick hairy muzzle, while it looked at her quietly with its mild brown eyes. She had finished her sewing and now slung the completed, joined rawhide rope around the animal's neck, while her pack, divided into two large leather satchels, and joined by another strip of rawhide, she set across the animal's strong back.

Then, very reluctantly, she took her much loved skis and stacked them in the cabin with the poles, after which she carefully secured the heavy door, setting the pegs back in tight so that the next visitor, possibly even herself, would find the cabin quite snug and ready for use.

After she had finished, Ingrid bestowed one last, fondly lingering look on the cabin which had given her shelter; then she turned, and climbed up on the caribou, which stood steadily and strongly under the weight of the girl and her pack.

Ingrid took hold of the improvised reins and urged the caribou forward towards the dark line of trees that stretched away as far the eye could see. She breathed a single word in the animal's ear: 'North.'

In the Forest

Sunlight lay heavy on the firm, crusted snow. The path wound its way through the forest. For hours they had followed the hidden bed of the river between the dark, spreading evergreens – pines, tamarack and spruce – that hemmed them in and forced them forward along a margin of shifting shadows.

Several times Ingrid had pulled them up short, stopping to listen to the low howl of the wind in the branches above her, half expecting to hear some familiar sound that might indicate that she was not alone in that wilderness of trees. But each time she dismounted and stood there, gently patting the caribou's hard-worked back and shoulders, the woods seemed to thicken with silence, or else the distances echoed with gusts that made her shiver to think of the oncoming night.

As the day waned, she felt her spirits sinking. Perhaps it might have been better in the long run to have trusted to her own skills, to have strapped on her skis instead of accepting this strange, rough mode of travel. Now her fate was partially in the care of the beast that carried her and, although the animal seemed willing, almost determined, to serve her, she still felt awkward perched on its back, and wondered how long she could ride without falling off into the snow from sheer exhaustion. At times, grabbing wildly to prevent her satchels from slipping away and being trampled under hoof, she realized that the uncomfortable, steady motion, the sameness of the sights before her, had lulled her into a kind of somnolence, that her mind was drifting down into waking sleep; and then she had to stop and recover herself, for she could not afford to relax in the middle of these unknown woods, in which all the skills and alertness she possessed might be needed just to stay alive.

It was, as she calculated, about two hours before sunset when she dismounted from the caribou to rest for a moment under the shelter of a great, spreading tamarack, whose branches interlocked on all sides with those of the more common jack pines. As usual she spoke a few words of explanation and encouragement to the animal, snuggling up to the beast's rough mane, touching its antlers and addressing it, almost as if she felt she could make it speak to her. The caribou bent its head, accepting her contact, its breath steaming in the cold air, its front paws lifted to chop at the snow.

Ingrid took a few steps up and down the path, more than ever aware of the thick, crowding bush which obscured all but a narrow swathe of sky.

Peering into the depths of the woods, as she had nervously done through the day, Ingrid saw the ghostly scrub, grey among the tree trunks, and the dark-needled branches above; but the path kept on winding away, so that it was impossible to guess what lay beyond the next curve or what might be happening even a short space back through the bush.

Ingrid hesitated, opening her mitts to breathe a frail warmth on her palms, watching the caribou nibble at small plants it kicked free from the snow with its hooves. As far as she could tell, they had nearly reached the end of a long valley, through which the hidden streambed twisted and meandered. At the last rise she had noticed a pair of hills beyond which the land seemed to flatten, though it was hard to be sure of such things with no real point of vantage, and the endlessly deceptive tricks of the light on the trees and the snow.

She had been looking for a likely place to make camp, hoping for a clearing in which she could improvise a makeshift shelter of pine boughs, proof against wind and the possibility of snowfall at night, but ever since noon the path had been narrow and at some points the stretching branches had brushed at her elbows as she rode.

Sunset was imminent; she could not afford to go much further; on the other hand she felt that she could not camp at this spot. It was far too enclosed, without offering any real shelter, and in fact her caribou already seemed restless and was turning towards her now, with the semblance at least of impatience, stamping its hooves, moving a few steps along and then bending its clumsy head around with almost a questioning glance.

Ingrid felt desolate. Thoughts of her family assailed her; she had a clear vision of her father at their hearthside, of her brothers skiing their favourite paths by the river, of her mother and sisters singing an old ballad of Iceland as they walked back from the church. The terrible reality of her aloneness lay heavy upon her, like a weight of air. She walked back mechanically to where the caribou grazed, and stood for a minute half-paralysed, staring with hopeless eyes on the deepening gloom of the woods.

Just then a cry sounded, a long piercing howl that echoed back on itself, like a note held forever in the icy sky. There followed, from all sides, an eerie chorus of echoes, a fugue of disembodied voices that quivered across the valley, like a dirge of shadows.

That cry, for infinite seconds, transfixed her. It was as if she had been suddenly suspended in a block of ice, so that her mind chilled and all she could see blurred suddenly without changing its shape.

Her hands shook; she groped for the caribou's reins. The silence rushed up from all sides. The dying sunlight lent no comfort.

Ingrid struggled to hold the animal steady. Trampling the snow underfoot in its terror, it failed for the first time to respond to her touch and command. She grabbed at its mane and somehow got up on its back. They lurched ahead in a ponderous motion.

Ingrid whispered encouragement; she sensed rather than saw the wild roll of the caribou's eyes, and felt the uneven thump of its stride. Pine needles beat at her elbows, she hung on as the path twisted sharply. The dull crunch of hooves and the sound of her own breath reassured her. She drew up her shoulders and sought to take charge of the terrified animal.

A sudden blow on the side of her head sent her reeling. The caribou slipped away from her leg grip; she crashed in a tangle of branches. The beast plunged on down the path and disappeared.

She lay on her back, groping with body and mind for a sense of her hurt. Pain flashed through her elbows and shoulders, her head throbbed. One mitten came away blood-stained from a scratch on her neck.

She blinked up at the dark-needled branches; snow inside her furs made her shiver. Gingerly testing, she started to pull herself up, clawing and poking at the thicket of boughs. The caribou was nowhere to be seen.

Shaken, but seemingly uninjured, she got to her feet on the edge of the path. All around her, the woods lay silent and empty. After some moments, her head cleared and she was able to discover the source of her accident: a huge rotting pine log half-fallen across the trail, notched in the high branches of a neighbouring tree. Straightening up suddenly on the caribou's back, she had struck herself a glancing blow on this obstacle. She had been very lucky, she decided, that the wood was half-rotten.

But where was her caribou?

In the terror of losing it, she ignored the flashes of pain that beset her. To be left alone in these woods, without food or a mount, to be deprived of the precious objects she carried – that would mean a quick end to all her hopes.

But even as she moved in sudden panic along the trail, pressing her mittened hand on her aching elbow and neck as she ran, a second long-drawn-out cry pierced the gloom of the valley.

With a wild glance at the shadows coiling and multiplying under the trees, she took flight, hurtling herself down the path in the grip of a panic that made her cry out as she ran.

Slipping and sliding, she fell to her knees on a soft patch of snow, but scrambled up and ran, dodging both thickets and logs, until she collapsed, quite breathless, a full mile from where she had started.

Her eyes closed, she lay back quietly in the snow until the relentless cold made her stir.

She opened her eyes on a sudden new thought. The wolf, she remembered, the wolf is Odin's companion.

Slowly, she got to her feet. It was nearly dark now below the topmost level of the trees, and the path ahead was dissolving into the woods that surrounded it. Ingrid raised her hands in the manner of her ancestors and breathed a silent prayer to the god of lost souls and the homeless dead. Her fists seemed to close on an invisible staff. She felt strength come flowing back to her limbs, and her mind take hold in the old way. She ventured a few steps forward, and then a few more, until she was walking on at a steady pace. She knew she must find the caribou before the wolves did.

The darkness in the treetops all around her sank down to meet the darkness of earth. Moment by moment, Ingrid had to stop to reassure herself that she had not wandered away from the path. It was impossible, in the gloom, to attempt to follow the caribou's tracks; she could only stumble on, calling softly to the animal, while peering helplessly down at the unreadable markings in the snow.

At last she approached what seemed to be a sweeping curve in the path. She made her way forward, her mittened hands brushing the pine needles. She stared ahead, stopped in perplexity. Past the screening wedge of the branches the trail seemed to vanish, swallowed up in a shadowy undergrowth thicker than any she had so far encountered.

She walked forward, her heart sinking at each step. Was this the end of the path? Was this the point where the wilderness swept over everything, leaving her no way out of its tangle of darkness?

She could move neither to the right nor to the left and, as she tried desperately to free herself from the thicket, she found that she was hemmed in by a crisscrossing network of boughs spun tightly together in a way she could not at first fathom.

It was only when she stopped struggling, forcing a calm on her heart, slipping backwards and making herself survey the imprisoning tangle with care that she saw what it was: a number of huge pine trees had fallen down across the path and formed a barricade so thick that even a rabbit could hardly have crept through it.

The caribou could not have gone this way; either it had not followed the path at all, or it had been forced to circle away, into the deep woods, where the darkness made pursuit impossible.

Ingrid bowed her head under the weight of this knowledge. She felt her resolution falter. Without the caribou she could have no fire; she might freeze if the temperature fell, or else be devoured by the wolves that would seek her out in the darkness. She could neither stay where she was, nor continue. She closed her eyes and attempted to choke back her fear, but terror constricted her throat. She reached up a mittened hand to loosen her fur scarf.

It was then that she remembered her brothers' gift, the carved metal whistle that hung on a cord at her neck. This was all that remained to her of the gifts of her family. How useless it was to her now, that treasure she had longed for through childhood, a mere toy!

She buried her face in her cold mittens, helpless.

Then a sudden, wild hope drove her into action. She tore at the wraps at her neck, twirling her scarf off. Shivering, she reached inside her garments and pulled at the cord of the whistle. It swung in the darkness before her like a key made of copper.

At her lips it was strangely familiar; she had tested it a few times in Wayland, and then forgotten it altogether. Her father had told her that it was too high-pitched for human ears, but that she should be careful of what might come in response – though in the village nothing ever had. Now she blew the whistle hard, piping out a shrill summons of which she could not hear a note.

Desperate, she blew the whistle again and again, until at last she tumbled down in the snow, exhausted, not by the effort of action, but by these repeated expulsions of her vital breath.

After a few minutes she got to her feet and continued the piping until her cheeks ached.

She waited, straining her ears against a soft moaning undertone of wind, listening for the sound of hoofbeats, the thud of heavy paws on the snow, the breaking of branches.

Nothing.

She hunched down into the spreading tangle of the fallen trees and waited.

For some minutes she attended to the low murmuring voices that sounded persistently near her, beside her. Was it only the wind in the trees that she heard?

The crack of a branch made her start up. She stood, sharply attending in the darkness. The crunch of feet, the swish and rustle of branches – there could be no mistake: something was approaching at a steady pace, moving straight towards her down the very path she had followed all day.

She felt the muscles of her body tense; her eyes searched back through the gloom of the woods encroaching on the path. Her thoughts swam in shadows; nothing was visible.

Then a vague form detached itself from the gloomy background and seemed to move towards her. That upright shape was no wolf. She strained hard to see it.

'Caribou?' she cried out, in a voice half-choked and tentative.

The crackle and rustle grew louder. Her greeting sounded faint in her mind. Another shape surfaced from that near pool of blackness. Then another. The path swarmed over with hunched shapes, all moving steadily towards her.

Ingrid clawed wildly at the tangle of bushes behind her. The boughs struck at her face as she twisted and shouted. One more minute, said her deep mind in the darkness, one more minute of panic and everything will be over.

She tore herself free of the tangle and ran stumbling and crying into the woods.

She ran hunched and low, bursting through the branches with half-closed eyes. A whiplash of needles struck at her, snow stung her face. Slipping and stumbling, she fought her way through the trees to the top of a cleared ridge and collapsed there.

The sound of her own wild breathing possessed her; how long she had been running she did not know. She dabbed at her sweating face with a mittened hand.

Dim shapes detached themselves from the shadows at the bottom of the low hill. She stared at them, hypnotically bound to them, unable to scream. They moved with relentless, awkward precision, blending together, then detaching one from the other, like a swarm of giant insects, advancing.

Ingrid crawled to her feet, she felt helpless and dazed, her body floating weak, yet bound to that stone, unable to take one step in the crusted snow.

She turned round. A face hung in the air, a smooth face dark as leather, wrinkled and frozen, regarding her. In the eyesockets, nothing. A twist of stiff rope at the neck, and two arms coming round, bone thin, to embrace her.

Her scream stuck in her throat, but she ran. She covered the clear space in a few wild, sliding steps, and went crashing in among the trees where no shapes were. Lunging forward, she beat her way through the resisting branches. As she moved, the face moved with her in her mind. She saw the thin strands of the man-creature's hair, the wrinkles on forehead and cheeks, the veins standing out on the stretching hands. She felt herself drawn back into those arms to which the odour of the embalming swamp still clung like the perfume of death. She remembered the knife at her belt. Anything was better than to let herself be taken by the grey ones. But to be carried away, dead, into the darkness, to be dragged down into the swamp hell, to be forced to walk, forever, with the living dead – her soul cried out against this horror, and she ran, struck at and battered by branches, and then, unable to run further, she lay down in the snow, shivering and gasping for breath.

She closed her eyes against the horror and listened.

Silence . . .

And then, from beyond the near line of trees, a soft crunch of footsteps.

Ingrid struggled wearily to her feet. She leaned on the trunk of a tall pine, peering anxiously through a tangled skein of snow-capped branches. Shadows moved where her trail made a gash in the still forest.

Higher up, where the woods bunched thick on a near ridge, more shadows stirred in the gloom.

And ahead, the trees closed in, making a darkness her glance could not fathom.

They were cutting her off! She must run while she still had space and breath.

She sprang down the slope, dodging the trunks and using the branches to swing herself forward. It was dark now, so dark that she ran without seeing, out of instinct and terror, stumbling and repeatedly smacking her shoulders and arms on the thick boughs.

Within minutes she found herself thrashing and tearing at a hopeless, stiff tangle of branches. Desperately, she sought to claw her way through, but only wound herself tighter and tighter into the mesh of the trees.

She felt her legs pinned, and she panicked, kicking and tearing at the branches until at last, bruised and frightened, she managed to wrest herself free, collapsing back on the snow, and staring around her with a dim, uncertain feeling of recognition that slowly took hold of her mind and senses.

When Ingrid dragged herself to her feet and looked around it came to her, a sudden awareness that she was facing north, peering into an extended tunnel of shadows that stretched away between the sloping hills. She had circled the impassable blockage of trees and now stood on the other side of the barrier, yet she had been trying with all her might to claw her way back through that wall to the place where she started!

The grey folk had driven her up through the woods and then back down to the path. Even now she could hear them, thrashing and tearing the trees as they came in pursuit.

Wearily, Ingrid plunged away into the darkness. Her best chance, she knew, was on the open space of the trail, where her speed would serve her well. But it was too late now, she had exhausted herself too quickly, and they would catch her, coming on with their steady, unstoppable tread.

And when she saw the hulking form ahead in the path she knew she no longer had breath left for flight.

She lurched forward in dream-like abandon, reaching down slowly to find the long knife strapped at her waist. Her fingers closed around the hilt and she drew out the weapon. Her mittened right hand held the knife away from her body, blade upwards.

The darkness in front of her exploded in motion. She swung out the knife to slash crosswise, but a sharp blow sent her reeling. She fell back, rolled across the path and struck a snowbank. A trampling and plunging of hooves passed her by.

She sprang to her feet, choking snow, and hurled herself forward, reaching out in the darkness.

Her fingertips brushed against a familiar, shaggy mane; with a joyful cry, she swung herself round, as the plunging beast settled. Scrambling, she dragged herself up on the animal's back. Her hands reached down for the familiar, improvised reins. She found them and also the saddle bags as tightly strung there as she had left them. The caribou snorted, danced forward. Ingrid felt her body tighten as they moved off together. Hopelessness fell away like a husk.

She urged the caribou on, taking heart from the strength of its eager, fresh stride; weary, she clung tightly, desperately to the animal's neck.

Ahead on the path, a clattering rhythm arose, as if axes were striking again and again on dead trees. The caribou's shambling gait did not alter, but Ingrid felt herself tensing, as she strained to pick out the source of the sound.

The repetitive tapping fell on her mind with unnatural force. For days she had heard only the sighing of the wind, the shifting and stirring of the forest, the rare cries of birds, and tonight the terrible howling of the wolves. But this hollow clatter bore the menace of something intended, a signal directed at her from the darkness.

She sank down on the caribou's neck, whispering low soft

words of encouragement, shutting her ears on the sounds that grew louder and louder. The animal plunged on, oblivious, steady.

Ingrid sensed rather than saw the steeply rising cut of the land: black trees furled like grim sails against a grey gloom of sky. They moved through a cave-like darkness, where common shapes melted and shifted.

The noise became terrible, falling around them unceasingly. Ingrid remembered the sound of a rat once trapped in their pantry at home, its rabid tapping of teeth or of claws on the hardwood. She struggled to shut out the memory, to close her ears on the lunatic drumming around her.

She became aware all at once of a general movement, of dark shapes fluttering there on the edge of the path. The black shifting gloom pressed upon her, as if the trees themselves had lurched a few steps forward.

Ahead of her, figures rose up on the path. They shone, sleek and menacing, creatures born out of the slime, and their arms moved and clattered – as Ingrid saw to her horror – arms striking arms in mechanical fury.

Not once did the caribou hesitate, though Ingrid, shrinking away from the sight, tucked her head like a child in the curve of her arm, and desperately clutched at the animal's mane as they plunged on. They crashed straight into the ranks of the menacing grey folk.

Ingrid stared, horror-struck, as arms groped like crab claws, arms that were human down to the finishing detail, with every twist and fold of stiff clothing visible, and veins etched clear on the back of those stretching hands. Real faces gaped at her, the faces of men and of women blinded by darkness, gone rigid and perfect as statues cast up by the earth. She saw the long curving lines where their throats had been carefully slit, wrinkles of pain on their brows, capped heads wearing blindfolds, domed like beehives, eyesockets staring at something beyond her.

For the first time the caribou shied, and Ingrid felt herself sliding off-balance, her left hand's grip on the mane torn away. Her right foot crashed to the earth, and she swung up,

79

clinging fast to the animal's neck. They blundered and pitched through a mêlée of bodies. A woman's grey face, with lips half open, and round sightless eyes, from which a blindfold had slipped, stared up at her. The woman's fine high forehead reminded Ingrid of Asta.

Odin, she thought, these were once our people.

The caribou, with pounding hoofs, broke free of the throng. The path closed behind them in shadow; silence engulfed them like a presence. She clung to the animal, staring with dazed eyes at the forest that lay before her, that moment transfigured by a shimmering light. She rode on for long, anxious minutes. The snow glittered sharply. Low glowing hills stretched away. Ingrid forced a look back – all trace of the grey folk had vanished. She had come out of the valley at last, and the clouds, fast dispersing, had uncurtained the far sky.

They drove on, relentlessly. Ingrid's mind slowly unfixed; her hands ceased their trembling. Again she found power to take stock, to search round her. Directly ahead, some miles down a slope quite uncluttered by trees, lay a round shining mirror of starlight, a vast lake, deep frozen by winter, and polished by winds until the surface shone like an ancient shield.

She pulled up, turning once more to cast an uneasy glance at the dark forest behind her. Then with a sigh she swung the caribou forward, towards the place of which she had so often heard, and sometimes dreamed – a place without menace: Moon Lake.

Moon Lake

The caribou ran with a stiff-jointed lumbering grace. Ingrid, exhausted, hung on. Faint winds twirled snow across patches of ice. Dark gulfs like crevasses flattened then vanished beneath her.

She had swung the caribou down from the rimmed shore, away from the forest, plunging ahead on the thin snow, across the welcome abyss of the ice-covered lake. Here the air was very fresh; light glittered around her and Ingrid stared, dazzled.

Though her body felt pummelled and listless, she hoisted herself more firmly aloft on the animal's back, then leaned down to whisper soft thanks to her faithful companion. If only the caribou could speak – what it might tell her about its escape in the woods, just before it returned to her! No obvious marks suggested a struggle, yet the cries of the wolves had been ominous, and the clutching hands of the grey folk must have stretched for the animal. Had the caribou come in answer to her desperate whistled note; or had the whistle brought instead – those others? Shuddering, Ingrid remembered the faces, not the vague ogre faces she had feared but the fine-chiselled half-*human* faces pathetically raised to her.

The caribou plunged along steadily. Swaying down on the animal's back, Ingrid drifted in and out of a furtive half-sleep, her body rocked to an incessant rhythm. She sank at long last, through many swirling dream-shapes, to childhood, a small dozing figure curled in the straw of a farm wagon. Voices floated around her, stray words that refused to settle in sentences. One voice seemed intimate, precious – she heard the sensible straightforward tones of her mother. The voice said she must move and waken!

Ingrid slipped sideways on the flanks of the caribou. She made a wild grab at the reins, and pulled herself up straight. Her hands felt numb in her gloves, and her feet throbbed.

The caribou reined in at the pressure. Wide awake, Ingrid stared at the bright lake. She leapt down from the back of the animal, warming her hands and her legs to life by a frantic jumping.

She looked again, taking in the sharp change in the landscape. A steep low ridge ran down from the near hills and jutted out like a barrier. She must have been asleep for some time, for left to its own will the caribou had skirted close to the eastern side of the lake and come in almost under this low spur of landfall.

Ingrid stared up into the dark tree-clad slopes. In the starlight and faint moonlight everything seemed peaceful and glittering. Yet she wondered, with a slight shudder, whether she would ever again be able to trek through the forests with a firm heart.

She led the caribou forward across the hardpack, talking to it aloud, and patting its muzzle. In the distance, somewhere beyond the out-jutting landfall, she sensed that the sky had flared up – but perhaps she imagined it because of her new angle of sight, framed as it was by the ridged spur.

The woods were farther away than she had imagined, but after a while she came near them, and looked hard for a place to camp. But either the trees spread too widely for shelter, or else the gashed hills fell steeply to lakeside, and she was forced to walk onwards, following the out-jutting spur back to a point where it stopped, perhaps half a mile from the shore.

At the very tip of the landfall the trees grew more thickly, and as she approached she began to think it might be there she should camp, if she could.

It took some minutes for her to reach the very end of the ridge, for in fact it twisted and folded away, so there seemed no clear point at which she could say she was north of it. She considered cutting in under the trees several times, for the land looked approachable, but now the fact or illusion of light led her onwards: a bright distinct glow that seemed to rise from the roots of the trees, as if something flared up in the rock marrow, igniting the snowbanks to a spidery glimmer.

Then, finally, just beneath the cloven mass of a dark gleaming boulder, she did turn the landfall.

Turned it and stood there unbelieving. There lay a second landfall creating a bay in the lake, and in that bay stood a cabin, with ice-walls glowing fiercely in the grey frosty night.

Ingrid had never seen anything like it.

The cabin stood spacious and foursquare, a log-buttressed structure with wood-framed windows laid right in the ice-walls. Above the steep roof, apparently shingled with bark, fat coils of smoke flashed pink in the darkness.

The girl clung tight to the caribou's neck. Vaguely, she remembered the tales of the far-away Skraeling huts, domes made of ice blocks that sheltered the wild folk in winter – but these were mere stories, which few of the Waylanders believed. Yet here was a whole splendid cabin of ice-blocks, snug-built and safe on Moon Lake, with no sign of the Skraelings at hand.

Ingrid led the caribou forward. Apprehensive, but very tired, she knew she must seize this chance for a shelter, come what may. If this was an outpost of the Skraelings, she thought she might try them with presents, seek out their assistance, and trust them to help her. It had not gone well between the Waylanders and the Skraelings before this, and the wild folk might treat her with anything but kindness and hospitality, but in any case, her chance of escaping them here on the lake seemed minute. To approach them directly would be best, might be, in fact, her only hope.

Slowly, and with one or two pauses, in which strong doubts assailed her, Ingrid made her way to the cabin. The caribou trailed along, docile, loose on the lead, but she sensed (or had she imagined?) its nervous alertness. She patted the animal, and whispered reassuring words, then dropping the reins a little way from the cabin, she stole up alone to one of the lighted windows, and peered in.

The brightness dazzled her eyes, but what she saw cheered her: sleek skins pegged up on the snow-packed walls, a bundle of branches stacked in a corner; on a table nearby a bowl full of leaves and pine needles; and on one side, only partially visible, a huge wooden bed, piled with furs. Everything glowed as if with light from a hidden fire.

Ingrid moved cautiously, blinking in the darkness, along the front of the house. She stopped at the massive wooden door, on which, with infinite patience, someone had carved an elaborate five-pointed star.

Could this be Skraeling work? Ingrid asked herself, puzzled. The design might have been done by someone from Wayland itself. A faint hope rose in her heart – if only this were an outpost of her own people!

She crept on, marvelling at the trickles of light that ran like bright veins through the ice-wall. The caribou wandered in close to the house, stamping restlessly. She waved it away with a gesture and leaned over to look through the other large window.

A woman sat at a low, crude table, carding wool. She was bent slightly forward, and Ingrid saw clearly her fine golden hair, and her white fingers flying across the dark wool. Behind her, as if in a well-stocked pantry, rose shelves crammed with bottles, and to the woman's right, on a large wooden chest, there burned a single large candle.

Ingrid whirled away from the window, pressing her body flat on the ice-wall. Her pulse pounded wildly.

The woman had suddenly looked straight up at her, and Ingrid, struck by her beauty, had been unable to move, but had stared gaping back into those dark blue and questioning eyes.

Before she could gather her thoughts she heard the click of the latch and saw, as the great door swung inwards, the snow flare with light. A charming voice called to her, in the purest Icelandic:

'Please come in before the cold does. You must have travelled a long way on a frosty night.'

Ingrid hesitated, and then walked slowly to the woman,

who stood smiling and beckoning. The girl slipped into the room and waited, quite speechless. The woman shut the door and carefully latched it, then turned back to her.

Almost immediately, there was a scratching and pawing outside.

'My caribou,' Ingrid said, feeling awkward.

A flicker of annoyance passed over the woman's fair face. She unlatched the door, and Ingrid went out. She struggled a little with the reins and satchels, feeling the woman's impatience behind her. In a few minutes she had retrieved her possessions, and whispered some encouraging words to the caribou.

'We'll feed the animal later,' the woman said curtly, as Ingrid re-entered the cabin. The woman waved her across the room to a place by the brisk, glowing fire. Once again she seemed pleasant, almost gracious. 'You must first rest and eat,' she told Ingrid. 'Afterwards, there will be time for conversation.'

Ingrid threw her satchels down by the fire and collapsed beside them. She felt the tension already begin to let go of her body. The fire was very warm; even so, Ingrid felt, it would take hours to thaw the tips of her toes and her fingertips. Already, she had almost forgotten the luxurious comfort of a real house.

The woman at once became busy unwrapping small parcels of edibles – meat and fish, and cheese, and various dried roots and tubers. She stood beside a high table set near the large wooden bed that Ingrid had seen from the window. The interior of the cabin formed a single room, with the bed at one end and the bottles and various implements as well as bright piles of wool and cloth at the other. The fireplace was set in the centre, and candles and a small lamp provided the only other light, so that the translucent walls flickered, far in their depths, the wood floor shone brightly and various metal pans and utensils glittered with uneasy glamour.

As the woman busied herself with her preparations, Ingrid watched her, quite spellbound. She must have been about the age of her sister Lina, or perhaps a bit older, Ingrid decided, and it was hard to say which of the two might be considered more beautiful. But while Lina, despite her dark hair, was a soaring daylight beauty, the woman, blonde as she was, seemed all earthbound and shadowed. Her green woollen dress, which clung tightly to her slender but voluptuous form, was cinched with a yellow silk cord, like a monk's. Her hair, arranged in long braids, bore the lustre of clean burnished gold. Her eyes were the deepest blue Ingrid had ever seen. It was the woman's face, however, in its subtly shifting moods, which marked her as special. Already in the first few minutes of meeting, Ingrid had noticed that the woman's blithe and reassuring smile could give way in an instant to an expression that was utterly different. The exact nature of this secondary expression, Ingrid might just then have found hard to define; but with those instincts that sometimes serve us in the first moments of meeting, she detected a coarseness behind the beautiful demeanour, and a sharpness of suffering etched in the noble lines of the face.

When the woman had finished preparing the small tray of delicacies, she poured out a mug of fine apple brandy, offering both food and drink to Ingrid, who meanwhile had removed her outer garments, and lounged, quite in bliss, by the fire. Ingrid expressed her delight at the feast, and began to eat greedily, watched all the while by the woman, who sat on a hassock nearby, staring down at her.

When Ingrid had devoured most of what the woman had brought, and refused more, her thoughts went out to the faithful caribou, but the woman, seeming to anticipate her concern, brought forth a bucket full of grains mixed with greens that she had prepared with Ingrid's supper.

'You would like to feed the animal yourself, I'm sure,' said the woman. 'Wrap this cloak around you and call to it from the door. It will come to you, and you can talk to it so that it will not desert you before morning.'

Ingrid put on the fur cloak and picked up the bucket of food. It was so cold when she opened the door that she wondered how she had been able to endure it. The caribou was nowhere to be seen, but when she called a few times, its familiar lumbering form came out of the shadows. It approached the house warily, a fact Ingrid could not account for, but at last the animal thrust its head deep into the bucket of food and began to eat. Ingrid spoke a few words of reassurance, telling it to stay near until morning. The beast looked up at her, almost as if it had understood her words. She closed the door carefully and latched it as she had seen the woman doing.

The woman helped her off with the cloak; as she came near, Ingrid could smell the fine scent of musk in her skin and her hair.

'My name is Glimir,' the woman said, with a smile. 'You will want to sleep soon, but first tell me something of yourself and why you are travelling late in such country.'

Ingrid sat warming her hands by the fire; she avoided Glimir's glance by pretending to be engrossed in the flickering flames; and meanwhile she tried hard to think what she should say to the woman. Though she had no experience in the matter, it seemed to her unwise to explain too much, until she could be sure of her listener.

Almost as if she sensed Ingrid's hesitation, the woman rose and went to the large wooden bed at the far end of the room. She began to toss the fur wrappings back, and to fuss with the coverlets, talking to the girl as she worked.

'Of course, you must be very tired. A night journey in winter is no small thing, even with a caribou for company. Perhaps you don't want to begin at the beginning. But at least tell me your name and where you come from, my dear.'

Ingrid, disarmed by such gentle solicitude, told Glimir her name and a few things about her family. As she talked, a likely story formed itself in her mind. She explained the plight of her village and said she had taken a vow to make a pilgrimage to the far northlands to atone for whatever fault had caused the troubles in Wayland. Pointedly, she said nothing about the visit of the Wanderer, and she could not bear to mention her encounter with the grey folk, or even to bring up the matter of their incursions on her village.

'You were lucky my husband Mord decided to build this

cabin for the winter!' the woman laughed, after hearing out Ingrid's tale. 'A pilgrimage is all very well, but your village must have been desperately anxious to please some god, sending so young a girl on such a trip. There is a difference between a pilgrimage and a sacrifice, Ingrid.'

Ingrid noticed that the woman used the terms of the old religion; she found the slight tone of mockery in Glimir's voice disturbing.

'Will your husband come back this evening, then?' Ingrid asked. She was anxious to learn more about the woman, but cautious.

'Oh no, by no means,' Glimir told her, with an ingratiating, pleasant smile. 'He has gone further into the wild lands to seek skins and pelts, and to trade with the Skraelings. He will not return, possibly, until spring. Men on their own do not like trekking in winter, though young girls seem to find it quite possible!'

'Is your native village close by then?' asked Ingrid. 'I have not heard of a village in these parts, or anywhere near here.'

The woman finished making up the bed and came over to offer Ingrid more brandy, which she accepted with a nod and drank. She could feel the liquor beginning to warm her, and was happy.

'I don't imagine you would have heard of my village,' said the woman. 'It lies north of the land of the Skraelings who build high places and are ruled by the Great Sun. It is far to the south of here. The town is called Lokasenna . . . But I see you are an eager brandy drinker as well as a trekker. Would you like more? No? Then I suggest that we both sleep. It is very late, and the sun shines early on the lake.'

Ingrid stretched her arms, yawned and groaned at the stiffening tug of the muscles. She had come a long way and wondered if she were not almost past sleep.

Glimir seemed to surmise at once how she felt. 'If you are to rest well after such a journey, you must relax. Put on this night robe and I will let you sample some of my precious balms.'

She tossed Ingrid a light-woven garment from a peg near

the night table. Then, as Ingrid changed before the fireplace, Glimir busied herself at the far end of the room, mixing a potion from her bright coloured bottles.

When the liquids were blended, Glimir studied the result, then poured a milky white substance into a small flask and carried it over to where Ingrid lounged on the rugs. As the woman bent down, Ingrid could see little points of firelight sharpen in her deep blue eyes. Glimir said nothing, but setting the flask to one side, took Ingrid gently by the shoulders and turned her. The girl felt herself moved and arranged by Glimir's strong hands. The pungent smell of the balm made her dizzy.

Although Ingrid was inclined to be shy with this strange and commanding older woman, massages and common bathing were usual in the village, and she took the ritual as a matter of course. She felt Glimir's hands move with expert skill to shift off the night dress behind her, and the deep pressure of her strong hands applied first to her back, and then to her thighs, calves and feet. In a short while, Ingrid's eyes closed, and her muscles relaxed. She hardly remembered how the skilled hands turned her body and worked down from her shoulders to soothe her. She found herself dozing, her breasts tingling, a faint scent of almonds sharp in her nostrils.

She was not sure, she might almost have been dreaming when a voice commanded her, with the softest insistence, to rise up and walk to the bed. She felt herself move, supported by strong arms. The lights seemed to blaze up then die out. She was pushed down and collapsed in the feathery blankets. Vague noises and faraway flashes of light struck her senses. She imagined that she heard a woman's musical voice singing near her. Then darkness, the deep-scented, long-falling darkness of sleep.

In childhood, Ingrid had sometimes awakened at night with a feeling of strangeness, not knowing quite where she was, and once or twice this had occurred at the end of a nightmare, and Asta had come to her with sensible words and had calmed her. But even in childhood it was seldom that Ingrid could not quickly distinguish her dreams from the waking reality or from visions that lay in wait in the borderland world between day and night.

Later, however, as she rested in Glimir's fine bed, an odd fancy seized her. She imagined she sat up straight out of sleep and saw the whole room glowing faintly in the light cast by the dying fire.

Nothing stirred, and yet there was something strange there, which came about as she stared at the ice-wall beside her. Slowly the ice seemed to shift and to lose in one place its misty translucence. Little by little, as the ice cleared and grew quite transparent, Ingrid found that she could see outside. There, in the pre-dawn starlight, the snow lay white and peaceful, the lake stretching away in a frosty glitter to the dark-mantled hillside beyond.

For a long time Ingrid stared and seemed to hold that unmoving landscape in her mind's eye. And then, far off in one corner, under a bank of far trees, a tiny shape gathered. It gathered and shook itself, swinging slowly up on the ice of the lake, until it moved forward with a brave, steady shamble.

Ingrid could not stir and barely breathed as she watched it grow larger and larger, approaching with great bounding steps. For almost at once she had recognized it, a white bear, come out of the forest and heading straight for the cabin.

Ingrid wanted to turn and to wake up Glimir at once (for it seemed certain now that she could not be dreaming). But when she tried to move she found that she could not; her body was fixed in the place where she sat and she could not shift it, try as she might. Now a panic began to seize her as she saw the bear bounding closer, coming straight for the clear bright space of the ice-wall. She opened her mouth and tried to cry out a warning, for she feared not only for herself and Glimir, but for the caribou, which would surely be killed by the beast. But she found to her deepening horror that she could not utter a sound, that her voice was denied her – she was helpless there and unable even to close her eyes on the terrible sight.

The bear came in closer and closer. She could see claws, the fixed sharp gleam of its small eyes, its teeth bared and menacing, set in a red gash of mouth.

Ingrid sat there in horror, unable to move, as the bear stood up at the wall, and with great sweeps of its claws began to tear at the packed ice, its fierce eyes fixed in malevolence on her. An explosion of ice flakes made a shower on her face. Ingrid could not even scream.

Then, suddenly, she felt a stirring beside her. All at once she was free and turned to find Glimir's upraised naked form on the bed, fur blankets falling across her like a quickly shed skin. Ingrid saw with a shock that Glimir's fixed gaze was as sharp and as terrible as the bear's.

'*Helgrind! Helgrind!*' Glimir cried, in a voice shrill as an eagle's.

A slow fall of white flakes dissolved on the girl's lap. The great flashing form of the bear tumbled back through the torn sheet of ice. Ingrid started to speak, but Glimir's chill hand touched the back of her neck. Her eyes closed, the power went out of her shoulders and arms, and she sank down in darkness.

Conjurings

Slowly, very slowly, as if climbing step by step up a steep mountain path, Ingrid awakened from sleep. The warm spicy scent of the coverlets, the dark cosy bed, the pleasant hiss of the firepot, almost convinced her, in the first stretching moments of consciousness, that she was safe at her grandmother's home outside Wayland. She rolled over, yawning, aware of a lingering stiffness in her buttocks and thighs, though that too was pleasure, a sharpening of muscle that gave her a sense of the body's reality.

91

The high roof sloped down in sunlight. Dust beams danced in the space of the rafters, the walls gleamed ice-white. Ingrid sat up with a jarring sense of displacement. The events of the night siphoned back.

She slipped out of bed, her feet touched the cold floor. She saw that her clothes had been laid by the fire, where a large black pot hung steaming and bubbling. She tiptoed across the room, stopping only to cast a quick glance at the snowbound lake through a window, then began quickly to dress. Light blazed into the room, patterning shadows; birds scuffled and sang at the chimney. Ingrid tugged at her boots, anxious to get outside, though the room was so pleasant.

The unlatched cabin door swung open. Smiling and pale, Glimir entered, her blonde hair loose-fringed with light. She was holding, in one mittened hand, a small bundle of pine needles. Ingrid scrambled to her feet, her searching glance fixed on the older woman.

'Good morning, my dear,' said Glimir, turning back to latch the door and to set the pine needles down on a table. 'I see the fire is still burning. Good. Shall we have food then, and talk?'

An anxious thought made Ingrid stiffen. 'My caribou – ' she began, but Glimir, pulling her furs off, reassured her.

'I have already fed the animal. It's safe and well, Ingrid, and you need not fear for it – whatever you may be thinking.'

The last phrase conveyed to Ingrid that Glimir had no intention of ignoring the events of the night. The girl knew at least that she could raise the matter directly, or as directly as she dared, for there was a kind of awe in her mind about Glimir. The feeling annoyed her, for there were few in her life she felt daunted by, but Glimir was one.

'You look very lovely, today, Ingrid,' Glimir told her when they sat down a few minutes later to a breakfast of porridge, dried fruits and milk. 'The rest here overnight has done you much good. I hope you will stay with me a little longer.'

Ingrid knew that if she did not speak out boldly, she might learn nothing from Glimir. 'When you went out gathering just now,' she asked, 'you found no sign of – other travellers.'

It seemed to Ingrid that Glimir smiled with a special smile of private amusement.

'As you shall presently see,' she said, 'the morning is as clear as a newborn's eye. Were you expecting someone in particular?'

Ingrid had tried hard to suppress all thought of the grey folk; thus when Glimir next spoke, she started up, visibly shaken.

'I have heard that the grey folk have once more come out of the swamp,' Glimir said quietly.

'What – what do you know of the grey ones?' asked Ingrid, controlling her voice with an effort. Her hands trembled slightly, and she pressed them tightly together in her lap.

'I should think you would be the one to tell me about them, Ingrid,' Glimir continued, unblinking. 'Is it not Wayland they threaten, and you who are chosen as victim?'

Ingrid rose to her feet. She stared down at Glimir, at the woman's cold eyes, at her quick slender fingers. In her grey woollen dress Glimir seemed frail, quite enveloped by the red cloak she had put on before breakfast. Two silver brooches fastened the cloak to her dress, a neck-ring of silver twined serpents at her delicate throat.

'Who are you, really, Glimir?' Ingrid demanded to know, peering down from the height of her anger. 'How is it that you have heard about the grey folk? And – this I insist that you tell me – what happened last night while I slept? I remember a dream that was terrible – and more than a dream!'

A shadow passed over Glimir's face. She looked suddenly much older, a woman worn out by thoughts. Slowly, she rose and, stepping forward, pressed herself close to Ingrid, who started to shy back. The girl felt herself gently embraced, Glimir's full body against her. Glimir leaned forward and touched Ingrid's cheek with a delicate kiss.

'If only you could love and trust me,' she whispered. 'You are beautiful, Ingrid, a strange swan-like girl, but a warrior too. You must tell me your story, the truth of it. Only then can I help you.'

Ingrid disengaged herself from the woman's embrace.

93

Feelings of pity for Glimir were mixed with a wariness – with a certain revulsion. She allowed herself to be led to the fireplace, where they sat down together.

'How is it that you know of the threat of the grey folk to my village?' asked Ingrid, coming back to her question. Now that she had seen that the strong Glimir could be vulnerable, she had hopes of a clear answer.

'Such news travels fast in the wild lands,' Glimir said, looking down at the silver rings on her hands. 'Sometimes the Skraelings visit this cabin – only yesterday a few Skraeling hunters arrived to trade for medicines and charms, and they told me of the return of the grey folk . . . and also that a warrior maiden was abroad in the deep woods . . .'

Ingrid's eyes widened at this reference to herself, but Glimir continued without pause.

'As you see, I am not helpless here in my cabin. I have means to avoid the grey folk, even as the Skraelings do. In Lokasenna I learned a great deal of magic. That is how I was able to turn back the white bear. You were right, Ingrid, in thinking that what you saw in the night was no dream. The bear has taken to prowling, and grows in rage when I repel him, as my magic enables me to do. He wants the honey I have stored in great quantity for my husband's return, but he shall not have it. I assure you, he shall not!'

As Glimir rose to throw a log on the fire, Ingrid saw how her rings caught the light.

'What kind of charm did you put on me with the balm, Glimir?' Ingrid asked. 'Why was it necessary to do such a thing?'

For the first time Glimir seemed confused and embarrassed. She looked away, guiltily eyeing her bottles. Then she spoke in a low, sad voice full of feeling.

'To be truthful, it was a love charm, Ingrid. Because you are so beautiful, and I have been alone for a long time.'

The girl blushed in confusion. She was glad that Glimir seemed not to notice and simply carried on talking and staring distractedly past her. Ingrid knew how deeply she missed the womanly warmth of her sisters and the strong delicate care of her mother; she tried to recall if anything shameful had passed between her and Glimir but she could remember little enough of the previous night.

'It was necessary to make you sleep at my will,' explained Glimir. 'I knew the white bear would come and did not wish you to be alarmed. Your own strength of mind ensured that the spell would not hold, and so you witnessed what I wished to spare you.'

Glimir pushed back a few loose strands of her hair; she was smiling and bright featured again, so clear eyed and fresh she seemed at that moment to be closer to Ingrid's age than to that of her elder sisters. Rising, she fetched two fine stone goblets from a shelf and poured them both drinks. She handed a goblet to Ingrid, who accepted it warily.

'Not a potion, dear Ingrid,' Glimir assured her, 'but simply some excellent raspberry cordial to help you on with your story.'

Ingrid tasted the drink and found it delicious; when she blinked at the sharp sweet taste of it, she caught a glimpse in her mind of bright berries in snow. She drank more and it seemed to her that the cool liquid so soothed her that all effort was overcome and that she longed to speak.

She began at the beginning, as she knew it, and from there unfolded the whole history of Wayland's sorrow, leaving out nothing, neither her meeting with the Wanderer nor her flight from the grey folk through the forest. From time to time, as she spoke, Glimir's gaze sharpened and fixed on her, but at those moments she felt even more anxious to continue, and soon her voice seemed to be something apart from herself, a soft throaty whisper purring on as the fire crackled and hissed and the birds went on singing in the sunlight.

When at last she had finished, the girl lay back with a sigh and Glimir, with ritual care, rose and removed the goblet she had constantly refilled as Ingrid unfolded her story.

Then the older woman stretched out one hand, and helped Ingrid to her feet. When she spoke, her voice took on that close-pressing, intimate tone that somehow made the girl uneasy.

'You know the grey folk cannot harm you here,' Glimir told her. 'Not while you are under my protection.' She paused, holding Ingrid in close scrutiny. 'You have been sorely tested, but there may be worse trials to come. Later, you must show me the cup your father gave you. That is what I need to examine, if I am to help you. For the time being, Ingrid, let me warn you about one thing. Do not be tempted to blow the whistle I noticed last night hanging about your neck. That can only bring trouble. But now, Ingrid, do not gape at me so gloomily. Let us both go outside and see how brightly the morning shines, even after the darkest night.'

Ingrid eagerly welcomed the suggestion. She felt Glimir's presence like a weight – she needed to breathe and to think. Yet as they pulled on their outer garments, the furs and the wrappings, they joked like two schoolgirls, and a few minutes later burst from the cabin as if the darkness between them could be dissolved in the spirited sunlight.

Outside, the first thing that struck Ingrid's eye was the caribou, standing motionless, not far from the door, the sweep of the white lake behind it. She ran to embrace it, throwing her arms around its great, thick neck and rubbing the hump of its back with her mittened hands. Its dark eyes, more soulful and expressive than ever, looked into hers. She saw in them a kind of recognition, then, as the animal twisted and danced out of reach, a wariness.

'Caribou?' Ingrid asked, wondering.

Glimir approached, her cold breath steaming in the air. The caribou backed off, its head lowered just slightly, its gaze fixed tight on the women.

'The animal was frightened by the bear,' Glimir said in a flat, knowing voice, 'but it has not been injured. It will stay near the cabin and you shall feed it well. The rest here will do it good, as it does you good.'

Ingrid looked at the beast, at its quivering nostrils, its wary, bent head. She had the distinct sense that it had backed away at Glimir's approach. The older woman's mittened hand touched her shoulder.

'Come, Ingrid, there are things I want to show you.'

She felt herself pulled away, drawn out into the flashing white loop of the lake. On both sides, but at some little distance, the green clad ridges pincered in towards the cabin. As they walked on, and Ingrid looked back, the icy walls of the shelter seemed to melt away into shimmering brightness of air. If she blinked even harder, she imagined, the cabin might vanish altogether.

'This is the first thing I want to show you,' Glimir said quietly. 'It is a place to fish, and sometimes – to see beyond winter.'

At their feet was a hole several inches in circumference, drilled deep in the ice. A little cloud of steam perked up there, as if from the bowl of a pipe.

'Bend over and look closely,' Glimir suggested. Ingrid turned to her companion doubtfully, but the woman only smiled and pointed to the ice. The girl knelt down and peered into the little cauldron of steaming vapour.

'Tell me what you see, Ingrid,' Glimir asked from just above her shoulder.

'A white cloud-like smoke, but ice-cold on my cheeks,' Ingrid told her, watching the ragged wisps break and dissolve in the air.

'Look closer, and tell me what you see, Ingrid,' Glimir said, from a space that seemed airy, more distant.

Ingrid stared even harder at the white-coiling vapour.

'I see shapes, vague shapes beginning to form in the ice-shaft.' And, indeed, the hole in the ice seemed to have grown wider so that Ingrid, peering down, looked into a pit of shadows.

'Look closer, much closer, and tell me what you see,' came the voice of Glimir from a great distance, faintly, just reaching her ears.

Now as Ingrid stared down, the white drifting fumes cleared, and she saw first a clear surface, as of unruffled waters, and then, even deeper, the sharp green of summer, a vague patch of field focused at last to a boundaried space. She saw stone walls and markers, a spreading orchard, the yellow and blue points of wildflowers, little needles of colour almost hurting her mind after all the blankness and the whiteness of winter.

Then the voice of Glimir again, this time deep inside her, commanding that she look even closer.

Ingrid looked and saw herself standing at the edge of the field. She was wearing her favourite blue summer dress and her hair was bound up and coiffed with a silver comb. Beside her, taller even than she was, stood the Wanderer, the blue of his cloak matching hers. Ingrid looked on with sad pleasure, feeling the tears run on her cheeks as she contemplated this summer image of herself, so tall and straight in the sunlight. Then with a shudder she noticed the thin rope gently twisted around her neck, one end of which the Wanderer held in his left hand. She could almost feel that rope now tightening and tightening on her neck. Both she and the Wanderer moved, as she saw, towards the shore of the lake that lay just beyond the stone wall and the orchard. They walked with slow, ritual steps, the Wanderer leading her on.

The voice of Glimir, inside her, demanded to know what she saw.

But Ingrid plunged one hand down into the ice-hole, her fingertips curling inside her mittens at the cold shock of dampness. She gagged, wrenching upward, a pressure snapped like a cord at her neck.

'Glimir!' she cried out, her mind springing free of the vision. She felt herself circled and held in the woman's embrace. She opened her eyes and blinked at the glare of the lake; slightly dizzy, she rested her forehead on Glimir's right shoulder. A few minutes later, Ingrid stood face to face with her companion.

'I'm afraid of your world, Glimir,' she said. 'I must leave this place tomorrow.'

Glimir stared at her dreamily. 'I'm not sure what you have seen, Ingrid. I admit there is magic in the air here, but I do not fully control it. You must believe me when I say that I want to help you.'

Ingrid looked down at the still-bubbling ice-hole and shuddered. 'Nevertheless, I must go on,' she said. 'And if you help me I know I will have a better chance of success . . .'

Glimir stretched out a mittened hand. 'Come, I must gather herbs that lie under the snow in the woods. Do not trouble yourself about the things that you see here. The walk will do you good and I shall show you how to survive on your journey, when all else fails.'

They wandered across the lake into the woods, where Glimir indeed procured a few herbs, digging through the snow with a stick made from deer antlers. The girl looked on with mixed feelings: the woman was being kind to her, clearly, explaining something of her craft, yet this only served to remind her of the trips she had made with her father, and a kind of homesickness overtook her.

The shadows had begun to gather in the trees when they started back. The strain of the past days weighed on Ingrid. Would she ever be able to continue her journey? The longer she stayed with Glimir, she believed, the more she would lose the will to go northward.

As they approached the cabin, Glimir stopped for a few seconds to search the horizon.

'The lights will be very bright this evening, Ingrid,' she explained. 'Perhaps something extraordinary will happen.'

They entered the cabin, which seemed gloomy and dark after their long walk across the ice. Ingrid started to pull off her furs, but Glimir stopped her.

'You will feel better after a hot bath,' Glimir told her. 'Drink a little brandy and then come outside. There is some feed in that wooden bucket for your caribou. Give it to the animal while I prepare the bath-hut for us.'

While she was offering grain to the caribou, Ingrid noticed how Glimir had stirred up the fire near the bath-hut. Puffs of white smoke curled in the clear air, joining the ghostly white wisps that floated up from the roof of the cabin. Dreamily, lazily, Ingrid strolled round the side of the building. The sun gleamed deep in the ice-walls; the bay stretched its bright light before her. And there, slashed deep in the hardpack, clearly visible all around her and disappearing only in the blanket whiteness of the farther lake ice, were the heavy scorings and paw marks of a foraging animal.

Ingrid bent down and examined the tracks, then turned to the cabin, which loomed up a few feet behind her.

The bear must indeed have come charging straight across the lake, only to pull up at the wall of the cabin – held there no doubt by the power of Glimir herself, stopped at this very point by a magic that snuffed out its animal violence in seconds.

Ingrid fixed her gaze on the wall of the cabin, just above where the tracks stopped. She could discover no sign of the cruel slashes and rips she had seen the bear's paws making in the ice. The wall looked so smooth, not transparent but full faceted and glittering, like the rough pond ice she had skated in childhood.

She stretched out her right hand towards the wall, waiting for the cold shock of contact to pulse through her mitten. But her hand met no surface; it went straight on into space, as if there were no wall, as if she had probed an invisible niche in the ice, as if there were nothing solid to touch.

At that moment she heard Glimir's melodious voice calling her from the front of the cabin. Quickly, she pulled her hand back, as if it had been pinpricked, then reached out again, and this time, with Glimir's voice raised anxiously in the distance, her mittened hand struck the cold, solid facing of ice. Sheer terror possessed her, then she breathed again, sharply took hold of herself, and refusing another trial of her senses, ran without thinking away from the spot, round the cabin, and straight into the arms of the waiting Glimir.

Glimir's Brooch

'Come, Ingrid, the hut is ready now,' Glimir said, and led the girl towards the rough wooden shelter, which stood a little apart from the cabin itself. Ingrid could feel her heart beat fast at the woman's very touch. This is an uncanny place, she was thinking. I must escape, I must escape soon.

The cabin was well sealed and snug and, having pulled the door shut, Glimir at once began to undress. Mechanically, Ingrid followed her example. She was now really fearful of Glimir's powers and did not want to be literally naked before her. Glimir, however, chose to ignore her hesitation, treating it as mere shyness. Urging and chiding in a motherly fashion, she once again succeeded in putting Ingrid at her ease. Yet at the back of Ingrid's mind, like an image repeated forever, a hand reached out for a wall that was no longer there.

When the two women stood naked together, Glimir began to pour small cups of hot water on the fire-heated stones, and a thick steam rose up. Little droplets of water gathered on her neck and face and her skin shone. Ingrid found the older woman to be as beautiful naked as she had seemed fully clothed. She envied Glimir's full breasts, rich and shapely, and the pleasant voluptuous curves of her body. She felt herself by comparison to be too thin and muscular, though she knew that the men of Wayland admired her, and in Glimir's glance now she felt admiration, and even devouring enjoyment, which frightened her.

After a while, when the air was thick and steamy, Glimir picked up a pine cone from a shelf and began to rub it vigorously over Ingrid's shoulders and back. The rough, searching motion, at first almost violent, took on a sharp rhythm. Ingrid sat down on the small bench-board, while the massage continued, then, at Glimir's insistence, she lay full-length. The massage continued around her body, and after a while Ingrid relaxed. She could feel all the muscles in her body lighten.

Then it was her turn to massage Glimir, which she did, at first with great hesitation, almost as if she feared that the other's body would vanish at her fingertips. After a while, however, stimulated as she was by Glimir's obvious pleasure, all her doubts about the other woman began once again to dissolve, and she found a deep satisfaction in the way her hands travelled around her body. For some time they both lay relaxing, and Ingrid fell into a kind of sensual daze, so that when Glimir at last got up and with tender affection, embraced her, she submitted.

For a while they clung together, then Glimir pushed open the door, and with a deep sigh and a few muttered words which Ingrid did not understand, she swung in a small bucket dripping with snow and splashed it mercilessly all over them.

Ingrid howled at the punishing cold. Quickly accepting a tossed cloth from Glimir, she dried herself thoroughly, then pulled on her clothes. After a brisk and heady run across the snow, they tumbled, invigorated but quite out of breath, into the cabin.

Glimir made herb tea and drew Ingrid with her to the fireside, where they sat silently contemplating the flames until the older woman, in a voice somewhat formal and serious, said:

'Now, Ingrid, I think it is time to show me your father's cup.'

Ingrid had pulled open her satchels and quickly changed into the comfortable grey homespun her sisters had woven as a gift for the journey. Carefully, she lifted, from its place in her pack, the small lamb's wool parcel containing the cup, laying it to one side while she waited for Glimir to finish combing out her hair.

Glimir had put on a pure white robe that was bound at the waist by a thin silver cord. On her breast she had fastened a large round brooch of polished silver, a gleaming eye that attracted Ingrid's curious gaze.

Now, setting her comb aside, Glimir leaned forward and with an eager gesture indicated to the girl that she should unwrap her treasure. Slowly, and with fingers that trembled ever so slightly, Ingrid removed the soft wrappings.

The cup shone brightly in the flickering firelight. Glimir stared at it for a minute, her blue eyes fixed on the wondrous object; then, muttering a few incomprehensible words under her breath, and making a quick gesture with her left hand, she took hold of the vessel.

Glimir turned the cup round and round in the light. Her fingers ran over the stem and the base and slowly around the lip of the vessel, as if she were reading its language of figures by touch. Ingrid stared at the carvings that seemed almost lifelike – it was as if they had been animated suddenly by Glimir's probing fingertips. She understood, for the first time, the figure of a man or priest, seated in ritual pose, holding a great snake in his left hand, and a silver snake bracelet in his right. On his head he wore the antlers of reindeer or caribou. A caribou pranced by his side on the right. A wolf danced away on the left. A mandrake root pattern filled up the spaces between. Other animals reared and plunged on the face of the cup; bulls knelt under the knives of grim celebrants; jaguars and antelopes, a winged horse and a dolphin whirled to the left and the right. Warriors on horseback, soldiers with long wolf-headed horns continued the pattern; and in one place a giant figure of a man or god held a poor victim ready above a cauldron.

Turning and turning the cup in her hands, Glimir's bright gaze focused inwards, as if she were reading a message projected inside her by energies drawn to her mind through her sensitive fingers. After a while, she relaxed – slowly, she set down the cup, and like a celebrant concluding a ritual, she quietly laid her hands on her lap, and looked up at Ingrid with a sudden and disarming smile.

Ingrid knew by now she was Glimir's own thrall. The woman had powers that Ingrid was unable to resist and,

worse still, that she did not want to resist. She felt some of
the heavy burden of her quest thereby lightened: after all,
how could she master a world controlled by such beings as
Glimir? It was foolish of the Wanderer to have chosen her,
foolish of her family to have thought she could succeed in
helping the village.

'Now that I have seen the cup, I can tell you some of the
secrets that lie behind your journey.' Glimir leaned forward,
with a narrowing gaze. 'I can tell you, Ingrid, how you can
succeed in saving yourself and your village – how you can
destroy the power of the grey folk.'

Ingrid thought of the face of the woman in the forest, the
face of the lost woman, so like Asta's. 'I am here to listen,
Glimir,' she said in a low voice.

Glimir picked up the cup and pointed to the image of the
victim, to the cauldron stamped on the precious silver.

'The Wanderer has told you that in order to save your
village from the grey folk, you must seek out the magic light
in the far distant northland. Your own father gave you this
cup in order that you might catch the precious north light
that, men say, flashes down on the earth from the shields of
the Valkyries. You thereby would atone for the deeds of your
ancestors, who, like the makers of this cup, cast victims into
the swamps, in order to ensure that the great mother would
grant them rich harvests. Now this ancient cup shows part of
the sacrifice, animals and men offered up, as you see, but *not*,
Ingrid, *not* to the mother.'

Glimir held the cup higher; her voice seemed to gleam like
the silver.

'Where on this cup is a sign of the mother? Where is the
healing image of woman? The swamp and the cauldron prove
nothing. The mother wants seed and not blood. It is Wodenaz,
Wodan and Odin who demanded the sacrifice! It is he of
many shapes and disguises, the deceptive one, the father of
war and the warrior who demanded the blood rites of victims.
The Wanderer himself gave birth to the grey folk by his
sanction of battle! Ingrid, you have been deceived and you are
on a quest that can lead you only to further deception. You

104

have been duped by the man-gods and rulers, to serve as a victim, atoning yourself for their great crimes and cruelties.'

Glimir, in all her bristling magnificence, rose. She took hold of her cincture belt, staring down at the cup with a look of pure scorn and aversion.

'The ancients dared to accuse the mother and to dishonour her symbol by setting such things on this vessel. Our people have accepted these lies by taking the cup as their own. But the true lore is different. The victims were offered to Odin, some before and some after the terror of battle. It was done in the old days, and in the first battles with the Skraelings. There was no peace and no mercy, but only the glory of war, and the promise of joy in Valhalla.'

Ingrid, stunned by Glimir's words, drew back. It seemed to her that her world had spun round, that in a flash a reshaping of all she perceived had occurred, throwing most of her precious truths into question.

Ingrid whirled around and walked away from the fire, towards the great wooden bed. She leaned back on the bedframe and desperately pondered, averting her eyes from the other, until she heard Glimir relax with a long sigh. She looked up to see the woman sink down slowly by the fire, her blonde hair falling lightly askew on her shoulders. Glimir sat there unmoving, her head in her hands, as if the force of her accusation had drained her.

Ingrid knew then in her mind, and at the pit of her stomach, a terror as great as any she had experienced in the wood. If what Glimir said could be true, then her father was false, her traditions a lie, the intent of the Wanderer evil – all had somehow conspired to make use of her womanhood, to make her a part of the cruelty they secretly lived by.

But as soon as this thought formulated itself in Ingrid's mind, she could see that such an idea could not possibly be the whole truth. She had her own experiences to testify that her father was a healer not a slayer. It was true he had gloated a little when showing the cup, but did not everyone have in them a pull to the opposite? Did not the healer himself sometimes find himself tempted by violence, destruction? Glimir's version had truth in it, but not the whole truth.

Not the whole truth, that was the thought that Ingrid must cling to, despite Glimir's unknown and terrible arts of persuasion, despite her strange magic, the power of her glamour and womanhood. Ingrid knew that her awe of Glimir had something of love in it, that she was powerfully attracted to the magic of Glimir's bright beauty and lore-wisdom. She felt drawn to her person, but now that the woman had begun to reveal herself, Ingrid might find ways to subvert her, to escape from her power.

Ingrid moved across the room to where Glimir sat, and reaching down, slowly raised her to her feet. She embraced the other woman tenderly, holding the cup in one hand as she buried her head in Glimir's soft, scented hair.

'If I am not to save my village as the Wanderer told, then what must I do to escape the terror of the grey folk, to set those poor victims to rest until the end of time?'

Glimir drew Ingrid to the table bench, where she sat with one arm around her, while each laid one hand on the cup, which glittered between them in the firelight.

'The cup must be returned to the mother, Ingrid,' Glimir told her softly. 'You must quest not for the light of the sky-father, but for the fire of the earth-mother. Far away, very far away, in the ancient homeland of our people, is the volcano called Nerthus. It is there that the cup must be destroyed, offered as a sacrifice to the great mother, who will then take the victims of the All-Father's wrath to herself. When you throw the cup of your own free will into Nerthus, the grey folk will return to the swamp, and the curse on your people will be lifted.'

Ingrid stared down at the figures on the shining cup held between them. Glimir's words bore conviction, but there were things engraved there that she had not explained. The mysterious snake-forms, the stag-heads, the cauldron. What could the cauldron mean but the mother? Surely not everything evil came from the father-side. And Odin was powerful, magnificent, no more evil than Glimir. Ingrid rejoiced in her heart because the woman, by revealing herself, had given her a new reason to try her own powers. Not even Glimir understood all the lore of the world, but on the contrary, she was herself burdened and fearful. Perhaps she could be won by Ingrid's love to a less unjust vision of the Wyrd-path.

Gently, Ingrid secured the cup from Glimir and set it on the table. She took Glimir's right hand in her own, and softly caressed it, as she said in a low voice:

'What you say, Glimir, explains much, but it does not explain everything. Is it not true that the things of the mother, the swamp and the lake, sometimes devour us? I have loved and still love my father, and I revere the Wanderer and cannot accept that he is evil. I have seen with my own eyes the mystery of the lights and I must explore that mystery further. I do not know how to save my village from the grey folk. I do not know if I have such a power. But I know this, Glimir, that I am beginning to love you, and do not want you to deceive me any further. If you will help me, as teacher and companion, there will be hope for success.'

Having spoken these words Ingrid turned to Glimir, whose hand she had felt growing rigid as her speech unfolded in the stillness of the room. Glimir's eyes were fixed on the farther wall, where the deep glow of sunset burned blood-red in the depths of ice. Glimir did not turn her head, but Ingrid could feel her shoulders trembling.

'You are still bound up with the past, Ingrid. But the past you accept is an illusion!' Glimir's voice seemed to stretch out, faintly quivering, like a fragile branch.

Ingrid stood up and turned to face Glimir. She too, rose to her feet, her deep blue eyes burning.

'I cannot accept what you say as the whole truth,' Ingrid said. 'Together, perhaps, we can find the real truth.'

Glimir's gaze was unyielding.

'Ingrid, look at my brooch,' she said in a voice flat and pitiless.

At once on her guard, Ingrid struggled, fists clenched, against the temptation to obey.

'Ingrid, dear, look.'

The shift of tone caught her. Ingrid, surprised, found herself staring directly at Glimir's round brooch. What beautiful silver, she thought then, such fine silver. Her thoughts drifted away, her fists clasped harder, then opened; her hands fell to her sides.

The brooch seemed to come at her, as if she were bending her head to a white flower; or as if a flower had come flying upon her. She could not shift her gaze from the brooch, which was no longer a brooch, but a round silver eye, or a wheel. She had known it was that from the first, she remembered – an eye or a wheel.

The eye was a silver point in the darkness, then larger, as large as the whole world.

'Keep your gaze on the brooch, my dear Ingrid.' She heard Glimir's voice from a distance, but there was no need to say that: there was nowhere else she could look. And she saw the eye move slowly around her, so slowly. It circled her once, then again, then a third time.

The eye stopped and she stared in upon it. The eye was a wheel full of living beings, pure silver, but visible shapes, shapes of people, of women.

The women were naked, and beautiful – of all ages and conditions, but noble and upright. They walked boldly forward, their eyes clear and shining, some tall and slender, some short, some fat with a fine sleek precision. They moved on a green plain in sunlight, and some carried weapons – long spears or knives – while others held implements – spades, hoes and rakes – and some trundled bare blooming children. And Ingrid saw that there was something familiar in all this teeming diversity, something that shone out of each – the confident glow of a courage she felt in herself. But the sky suddenly darkened, and another scene floated to view. And Ingrid looked and saw women, on a blackened, burnt plain, all trembling and bent. There were the bruised hurt bodies of women who had been beaten by men. She saw women, mere children and grandmothers among them, attacked and thrown down, assaulted or raped. She saw strong women turned into beasts of burden, and beautiful women made to dance or sing naked while men looked on leering. She saw brave women in childbirth, screaming and groaning. She saw them bite off their umbilicals, and shake and beat their stillborn children, vainly attempting to stir them to life. And there was something familiar in this too, the desperate fear of subjugation by men and by life that she felt in herself. All this glowed there, in the bright whirling silver.

Then the wheel spun again, only faster, relentless; it roared like a white-hot cinder straight at her face. Ingrid screamed and fell down in darkness.

Frost

She awoke, as it seemed, bound high up in space, the wind roaring past her, howling up from a black pit beneath. Wrapped tight in her cloak, she felt her limbs stretch like roots in a bedrock of shadows. Her body swayed sickeningly downwards; the ice came in furious blasts, hurt her eyes. A dizzying draught pitched her upwards. She might have been lashed to a branch stretching over a precipice; or swung from the mast of a ship, flung helplessly down, then hauled back, just in time, by the recoiling motion.

She tried hard to peer through the darkness, but now her eyelids stuck fast, and she felt a new terror of vertigo. Try as she might she could no longer open her eyes. It seemed she was swinging, suspended, in a bottomless shaft. She could hear, endless fathoms below her, the great wind start up, then rise, sighing, as if through a thousand torn branches. She gathered her will and tried to force sight on her eyes. The icy wind punished her face, choked the cry in her throat. Her thin cloak flapped like a sail.

Again, she gathered her strength, desperately straining to see – if only to see – in the blast of the maelstrom. The wind spun her round and round like a frail, tattered leaf.

A third time she summoned her will, felt the power form a single knot in her body, the energy gather within her, until, rising up her spine like a fountain of light, it burst forth in her mind like a flood. The darkness split open, like the bole of a felled tree. Strange lightning crackled and shivered below her. Sweet dew touched her lips like a well draught.

No sooner had she tasted this than her body was lifted, as if by a giant hand, from the void and the darkness. She lay on her back staring up at the swirling night sky.

A great arc of green fire stood up between zenith and landfall, light molten and flowing in stark ghostly runes. Through these shapes, the stars gleamed like bond marks. Ingrid saw all that shivering light as the folded hem of a curtain that at once concealed and betrayed the infinite darkness of space.

Feeling her helplessness, then (for her eyes alone seemed to move at her will), she breathed a silent prayer to the All-Father, bleakly aware of the landscape that held her: a ring of snow in which she lay frozen and rigid, propped up to gape at the blank dazzling lake and the hills.

Gone was the cabin, its ice-walls, its fire – no sign of the structure remained. It was as if it had never been. Yet Ingrid knew that, in place of that circle of snow, there *had* been a cabin, a sheltering roof she had shared with the beautiful Glimir. An illusion shared is reality, Einar had told her. Yet now Ingrid suffered a thought more profound: when trusted reality wavers, the mind's truth itself seems illusion. Ingrid felt herself caught in a world without boundaries, where things flowed together, where a hand could pass through a wall.

It was long after midnight, and dawn was still far away. A time when the human soul is least in possession of the earth. The wild green light of the sky cast a lurid glow, flickering across the low hills, glimmering in the depths of the lake ice.

Ingrid could not move, but her gaze encompassed a wide

110

sweep of landscape and sky. Not far away lay her satchels, ransacked and tossed down, the contents scattered here and there on the ice – faint scattered patches in the circle of snow. Had Glimir found what she wanted? Or had the fearsome white bear ravaged all while she slept?

Sadly, Ingrid thought of her caribou. There was no sign of the animal; Glimir had doubtless lured it away. Yet how could it help her when she herself lay there all powerless, only able to look out and breathe, and vaguely to take note of her body?

Despair shut Ingrid's eyes and she slept. She awoke, casting wildly for memory, for bearings – the relentless march of the stars proved the onrushing hours. Soon dawn would announce itself.

Again, Ingrid struggled to move but she could not. Her limbs had been bound by the spell Glimir set there. She tried not to think of the brooch, or the suffering figures that writhed on the wheel . . . Ingrid closed her eyes between heartbeats; she felt the sweat on her forehead, the chill of the dew on her cheeks.

She was aware that if she lay there any longer she must die. She imagined the chill taking hold, gently dulling all pain, until deep sleep, falsely soothing, should carry her down into darkness. She feared that she was already sinking, unable to save herself, possessed by the cold.

Yet her body felt warm and protected – could this be the last stage of all feeling? She looked now, as if for the first time, at the grey homespun cloak that enwrapped her. It lay like a fine meshed cocoon round her lower body. She could feel how it wound up and around her propped shoulders, how the cowl pressed tight on the crown of her head, luckily folded back so that her view was nowhere obstructed.

Now she realized that all the while she had lain there, she had taken its warmth quite for granted. At the same time, something strange had occurred, so strange that at first it eluded her perception. Even now, struck as she was by the truth of her inner conviction, she doubted. Yet a part of her mind kept insisting, until at last, she could doubt it no longer.

Slowly, imperceptibly, most of all while she slept, the cloak

111

had been growing about her. It had lengthened and thickened and spread out to enwrap her inert, helpless body. Slowly, the grey homespun had thickened, like a new snakeskin fashioned in sleep, like a fine fur gifting her body with warmth to survive through the night.

Ingrid vaguely recalled a dream-sense she had that her body was rooted in earth and was growing. Something had protected her, even under the cold green fire of these skies, and she thought of her sisters – of how they had fashioned this cloak for her journey, no fancy cloth, but the plain homespun wool of their ancestors, made at the standing-up loom in the house with three chimneys. Was it their own unspoken love that had worked such a miracle? Or – and Ingrid's heart sank at the thought – was this another deception of Glimir's, who seemed to take wanton, grim pleasure in working her trickery?

Glimir's magic made Ingrid feel helpless; and now Ingrid fought off the fear that this, too, was cruel trickery – to leave her at last, in such comfort, until the grey folk or the wrathful white bear should find her and finish her.

But she would not give up. She attempted to raise herself, to cast off her life-giving, unasked-for skin. But she could not make her will work to serve her. Tears of frustration ran down her cheeks, until at last, her emotion all spent, she felt herself drift into sleep.

Out of that sleep, from time to time, she gazed with unseeing eyes at the blank, brilliant sky. Her senses kept touch, almost as if something deep in her mind feared to lose hold of the shifting night.

And much later, as it seemed, her consciousness quickened; it was not simply the rush of the breeze on her cheeks, or the knowledge she had from a glance that the sky had perceptibly brightened, but the stir and the flutter, the discordant shrill piping, around her. She opened her eyes wide on the bright scene before her. Four or five white-throated sparrows had landed inside the circle of snow and were busily probing the cast-off objects strewn here and there with her satchels.

Ingrid slowly blinked away the last traces of sleep. The morning was luminous and clear, with the hooded brilliance of sunrise – every notch in the snow rife with shadow. She was sharply aware of the slow climb of the sun far away in the east, a warm presence close on her cheek, light blazing up in the trees on the distant ridges.

As the sparrows darted and probed in her belongings Ingrid was roused to a finer awareness. She could almost feel their small beaks like pinpricks on her skin. Their endless dance seemed to weave in and out of her consciousness, like the notes of a song rung new every moment in the vivid air.

Immobile and helpless, Ingrid could only admire the persistence that drove the small birds again and again to the satchels, their hunger alerting them, holding them close to the precious objects that Ingrid herself could not reach.

Time passed, the birds fluttered and danced there, until at last, for no reason Ingrid could easily fathom, a stir of fresh energy seized them, as if an invisible presence had whirled them up in a frenzy of quarrelling joy.

The birds seemed now to be moving and circling one point, their target a small ragged parcel cast off from the satchels, which they flew at with quick darting motions. The shrill piping racket grew louder; the flurry of their wingbeats became a frenzy. Then, suddenly, down from the sky, from beyond Ingrid's sight-range, a plump, croaking raven descended, and landed a few feet away from the gyrating sparrows.

Cruk! Cruk! said the raven – its shaggy throat bristling, its head cocked to one side. It looked like an arrogant shadow, strutting across the snow.

No sooner had the raven alighted, than the sparrows, as if stung by something presumptuous in the manner of the intruder, flew at it, whizzing and darting about the head of the larger bird, causing it, with a few flapping wingbeats, to remove itself further from them, though it leapt all the closer to where Ingrid lay watching. Immediately, the sparrows resumed their attack, and the raven retreated. Ingrid could see that the small birds were already raiding the cast-off parcel, simultaneously striking at the retreating raven, and gathering bits of food from the folds of the cloth.

The skirmish continued, bringing the hapless but stoical raven closer and closer to the point at which Ingrid's grey homespun cloak lay like a blanket around her feet. Suddenly, Ingrid understood what it was that the sparrows were feasting on – nothing else than her mother's own cardamom cake, in process of being demolished before her very eyes, plundered minute by minute from the familiar, wrapped parcel that Ingrid could now see lying cruelly exposed in the snow.

Horrified, Ingrid opened her mouth to cry out, but at that very moment the raven, having reached a point just short of her cloak, leapt up, and once again harried by the sparrows, flew straight at the girl's face.

Instinctively, Ingrid closed her eyes. Her cry stopped in her throat. She suddenly choked, her mouth full of crumbs. The whirring wingbeats went past her, brushing her forehead and making her scrunch up her eyes, though the confused flapping and the shrill cries trailed off far beyond her.

She opened her eyes just in time to see that the indomitable sparrows had returned full of joy, to their plunder. With a shiver of disgust she realized that in passing one of them had dropped a few crumbs of her mother's cake, which had fallen into her open mouth and stuck in her throat. A very few crumbs, for the taste was nothing more than a faint irritation, a reminder of her need for a drink, for some food that was real and substantial.

With an effort Ingrid swallowed the dry bits of the cake. The raven was gone now; it must have flown far off across the frozen reaches of Moon Lake. The sparrows went on with their forays.

Ingrid began to feel cheered by the unceasing energy of the birds. Again and again they darted and fluttered around the little parcel of cake, quarrelling and feasting, piping their high-pitched, varying notes. It was impossible to begrudge them the food, so vigorously did the birds go after the treasure. The girl found herself smiling across at them. She wished she might, if only for a second, hold one of the tiny things in the palm of her hand, just so as to enclose there all that stirring, quick life. Inside her homespun she felt her

114

palms quicken at the thought, her fingers coiling and uncoiling.

Her fingers coiling and uncoiling. Slowly, she slid her arms from the cloak, wriggling and turning her body, the stiff anxious motion giving way to a wild flailing joy, to a hoarse cry of release, as she leapt away, tugging and bracing, her fingers shocked by the sudden miraculous contact with the snow.

Ingrid wrenched herself up and pulled the cloak free of the snow, crawling away on her knees, as if she were imprisoned in an awkward, huge sack.

Frantic with joy, afraid to stop dead on the snow, she crawled clumsily forward, as the startled sparrows scattered before her. She scrambled across to the small ravaged parcel and raised it straightaway to her lips, biting through the ragged edges of cloth and tasting the half-frozen spicy portion of cake, now indeed her salvation.

She sat for some moments, feasting, half-choking, shaken by sobs of relief and wiping her eyes with the backs of her hands, feeling with every dry mouthful the power of self-movement return as a low hum of pleasure that made her whole body sing with sheer thankfulness.

When she had devoured all the bits of the cardamom cake she felt stronger and surer of her own newly fledged movements. Attempting to rise, she pulled hard at the sides of her cloak, felt her moccasined feet touch the hard ground, and stood up, a little unsteady, but with a short-breathed prayer of thanksgiving to Asta for her wonderful present.

Ingrid looked around at the shining, bare lake. She stood almost in the middle of the snow circle, among her scattered belongings, watched the sparrows winging unsteadily off, flitting from rest point to rest point on their way to the distant woods. Nothing else moved. As the sun climbed higher and higher, the new day poured itself out on the ice.

Ingrid spontaneously stretched out her arms and murmured a short prayer of thanks to the gods. In her mind she was uncertain what power had preserved her but she felt favoured by chance in a way that went beyond accident, and she was grateful, deeply grateful, for her gift of life and movement.

Quickly, she set about collecting the contents of her ransacked satchels. Her first concern was to put off her homespun and dress in more manageable clothing. Still folded and fresh in one satchel she found both inner and outer garments to suit her – shirts and leggings and a good buckskin jacket, a hat and her mittens, all chill to the touch but warming as she moved quickly in her fevered wish to be off. She wrapped her cloak up carefully, and packed it away, took stock of her food, and her fire-implements, and began to tie up her satchels. Then with a sudden shock she remembered that she had not seen her father's silver goblet among the things left to her by Glimir. She stopped, felt the numb helpless grief that accompanies the loss of prized things, but nonetheless turned out her satchels, as if the treasure might somehow be hidden in the folds of the bags.

She gave up at last and sadly acknowledged the obvious. Glimir had stolen the cup while she lay oblivious, helpless. She had taken the cup and left Ingrid to die. Glimir was her enemy; despite her seeming affection, Glimir wanted only to foil her quest, to forestall her. How could Ingrid go on without the precious cup? How could her promise to her family and to the Wanderer be fulfilled?

She reached down for her flask, and after warily sampling the contents, she drank. The brandy was warm in her throat, but her heart felt chilled as she started away, the satchels strung round her shoulders. Perhaps now it was time to return, to seek help, to look to her father, her sisters – to Thorkel – to join in her search. No one could blame her now for turning back, she knew that. Yet she also knew that her gaze turned instinctively north, that her steps bore her that way, towards the forest, in the direction of the trees and thickets she most feared.

As she trudged on, however, her thoughts returned fleetingly to her life in Wayland. She remembered many things, but in particular a certain skating race of a few years before in which she had lost to a girl she should have beaten. When the

116

race was over, she had taken the result with a good grace, but in her heart she had said: We shall see who comes out best next time, Astrid, we shall see.

As Ingrid made her way across the little frozen inlet where so much had befallen her, and from which she was so anxious to escape, she murmured to herself, (and, in spirit, to one other) the same kind of challenge: We shall see who comes out best next time, Glimir, we shall see.

Harg

Ingrid struggled along, skirting the pinewoods that crowded down to the frozen lake-margin, stopping now and then to adjust the straps of her satchels, shifting the clumsy burden that punished her back and her shoulders as she trudged through the snow.

In a very short time the brightness of the day had faded, though the air had grown warmer, and the girl found herself sweating and shivering by turns in her warm buckskin clothing. For the space of an hour she had stopped, built a fire, cooked her meal, and rested, meanwhile anxiously searching her mind for a plan that would give her desperate trek some hope of success.

As she stared into the fire's dying embers, and watched the mist rise up from the lake in great swirling billows that swallowed the peaks and the forest, she thought how the landscape itself seemed illusion, dissolving in luminous clouds, as if Glimir's spell continued to work wherever Ingrid might choose to direct her steps.

In vain had Ingrid searched the near shore for a trace of Glimir's path. The woman was shaman or witch; if she did not wish to be followed, there was no way to track her. But

Ingrid must find her and recover the cup to carry out the will of the Wanderer.

Yes, she would be faithful to the dream that had come while she lay under Glimir's spell, a dream Odin himself must have sent – for like him she had felt herself swinging close to death, but secure on the world-tree and able to taste the sweet water of Mimir's well of wisdom, a well that enables those who drink from it to read the secret runes of the sky and the earth. She felt privileged to share in the thought, in the memory of the warrior god; she would need all her strength, all the wisdom of the gods, to win to the end of this journey, to bring back the gift of light to her village.

Yet Glimir, too, haunted her. There had been truth in the woman's words, a plea on behalf of all women, on behalf of the helpless, for whom Ingrid had heard no-one else speak. And had she not felt, in Glimir's warm embrace, something magical, something healing? She could not hate such a woman, despite her treachery.

Ever thicker the mist had come down, until the birches stood together like the lodge poles of a roofless, vast house. Ingrid wondered how far she could walk in such weather. Underfoot, there was melting, the ice growing slippery. She longed for the sight of her caribou; at the same time, she feared what Glimir might have done to the animal that had served her so well.

In the early afternoon, her path swathed in mist, she rested beside a small stand of pines. She lay cradled against her satchels, dozing and dreaming, yet fearing to sleep – still haunted by the events of the previous night, and determined to keep close control of her own mind and body. Yet despite her firm will, she did drift away, her head sinking down, her feet stretched out in the snow.

When she opened her eyes, the focus came sharply, as if her senses had meanwhile alerted her mind to some subtle intrusion. She jumped to her feet, not knowing at once what had disturbed her. Behind her, thick mist hid the woods; she listened but heard nothing more than a slow dripping of water, a snapping of banches, released from the cruel ice.

Then slowly, she directed her gaze at an angle across the ice, searching the thick folds of the mist for an alien shape. There was nothing – only the hardpack all dented and blistered, the line of the shore swallowed up in a feathery chasm. She looked higher, and stopped, her hands clenched tight at her sides.

What she saw was impossible, madness. Unafraid, she ran skidding towards the apparition, her knees slammed down on the ice, she went sprawling.

She jumped to her feet, but the shape had not moved. It hung like a trophy, a dim creature of mist, rising ghoulishly above her.

Awe-stricken, but suddenly calm, she walked closer, her glance searching upwards.

Hung high on a bare branch, wreathed round in thin swirls of mist, was a horse – or the ghost of a horse – which seemed to be dissolving as she looked, its skin wrinkled and drooping, its eyesockets empty, its legs stringy as dried meat. The trunk of the old ash on which it hung, anchored on a low rise, had been hidden by the mist; now she saw the outline of the tree, just visible on the near line of shore.

Ingrid had the strange fancy that the horse had floated gently down through the mist and been nailed where it landed, that its flesh had almost fallen away, that the crows had plucked out its eyes. Sightlessly, with the branch serving as backbone, the creature stared out at the lake. White ribbons of mist, like smoke, curled out of its belly. Its tail jutted stiff as a brush.

There were few horses in Wayland, and none, Ingrid thought, had been hung up in sacrifice. She remembered the strange eight-legged creature first seen before the arrival of the Wanderer in the village. The eight-legged horse, steed of Odin.

Ingrid looked anxiously round. Had Glimir set up this thing to keep off the grey folk? Afraid to walk under the horse, the girl circled away, edging out from the bank, staring up at the hollow eyes with a shudder.

The ice opened up and she fell, with a half-throttled cry, into killing cold water.

She swung out her arms, seized the jagged ice lip – which came away in her hands. She was caught in a trap-hole. She kicked out, splashing and churning the water, flinging the icy slush back in her face. She choked and her heart pounded wildly – she seemed to be sinking. She screamed and by sheer force of will bobbed up in the slush – then slipped down, almost under. The water came through her mittens. Her teeth began chattering, her fingertips numbed.

From a distant past moment, she remembered some words of her father. She groped at her belt for her knife; her fingertips clumsy, unfeeling, and somehow got hold of the handle. She prayed the knife would not drop in the water, took hold, tugged it out. She had strength enough in her fingers; they closed tight round the knife.

She could feel the water come in on her legs and her belly. A few minutes more and her body would freeze from the soaking. She leapt like a frantic diver at the jagged ice edge, her arm swung up quickly – she brought the knife down on the ice.

Slowly, she stretched out her body, pushing her belly up high. Using the knife point as anchor she tugged herself forward. Her shoulders came over the lip. She heard the ice cracking beneath. She hung there, her feet tipped down in the hole. More ice cracked beneath her. She pulled out the knife, swung it down on the ice as she slipped. The ice went on cracking beneath her. She pulled herself forward. She sprawled on the lip of the ice, her shoulders and chest flat. Once again she swung up the knife. The point held. She pulled herself forward, her legs inched up on the ice.

Her breath came in gasps, she sprang ahead jubilant. She was out of the ice-trap.

She knew what to do then, if only there was time. She ran for the bank, slipping down on her rump, shoving frantically forward. Her feet touched the edge of the land. The trunk of the ash tree towered above her.

She found a soft run of thick snow, where she flung herself

120

down, rolling over. She was gasping and choking, but determined. She twisted and writhed in a mad dance. No water came in on her body. The snow must be soaking up moisture. She rolled over again in the soft drift.

A man stepped out from behind the thick ash trunk. Ingrid stopped there as if paralysed. The scream died in her throat. She sat there with gaping eyes, her jaw hanging down.

'I am Harg,' said the man, coming towards her.

His dark eyes were the saddest Ingrid had ever seen. He was of medium height, stooped, but not old, with a short dark beard and dark hair. He was dressed in black skins and he wore a black fur cap. His face was craggy, his features sharp cut.

Ingrid snapped out of her trance, scrambled up.

'Your hands will freeze,' the man said. He stepped forward. Ingrid backed off and then stopped, held there by his unsmiling eyes.

The man came up boldly, seizing hold of her hands. He tore off her mittens and examined her fingers. Then he pulled at his fur jacket, exposing a white tunic. With a few quick twists he unfastened the tunic strings. He took Ingrid's bare hands and pressed them flat on his chest, squeezing her hands tight against his warm skin.

They stood eye to eye. Slowly, the blood rose, both in Ingrid's hands and on her cheeks. His eyes were alive with a flecked yellow fire. She felt his soft skin at her fingertips.

After a while, he let her hands drop, and went about fastening up his clothes.

'Your fingers will not freeze now,' he said in a low, clear voice, then stood back rather stiffly; as if the close contact had widened the distance between them. Nonetheless, he spoke kindly:

'My fire is not far off,' he told her. 'You must come there and dry your clothes.' He turned round and started away. Ingrid stood speechless, but at last murmured after him that she must fetch her satchels. He followed her to the cache, hoisted the bags on his back, but stooped after one or two steps, as if listening.

A faint distant clatter could be heard through the mist, like the rattle of dice on a board. Ingrid stood shivering; her eyes searched the shrouded dark woods.

'This is unhallowed land,' Harg told her grimly. 'We must go to the valley at once – there are things in pursuit of you or of others. I have heard them for some days, and followed their tracks, but so far I have seen none, only Skraelings in flight through the forest. You must not be afraid, though. There I have very strong magic; here, like you, I have only my knife.'

Harg moved away, shifting the pack on his shoulders. Had Ingrid detected a faint smile on his lips at those last words? He must have been watching while she pulled herself out of the water. Very well then, he would know of her strength as well as her foolishness. She brushed at her coiling damp hair. But of course he was not really very handsome – just gloomy – and barely the same height as she. For some reason she thought of Thorkel, with his blue eyes and his big hands. Poor Thorkel! How jealous he'd be if he saw her now.

Harg walked ahead with quick wary steps, now and then stopping to listen, peering through the mist. They circled the ash tree; the horse seemed to melt and float in the air as they passed. Soon it was hidden from sight. Thick mist swirled around them, but off through the gaps Ingrid noticed the rise of the land – steep cliffs to which a few stunted evergreens clung, dark forests on all sides unfolding.

They had entered a valley struck deep in the near ridge. As they moved from the lake, Ingrid felt, or imagined, the land closing in, the gentle, soft sighing of branches, a darkening texture of air. But Harg went ahead at an easier pace; he cast no more glances behind them. Soon they came on a path where Ingrid saw footprints. For a moment she wondered if Harg had companions, though something about him seemed solitary. There were animal tracks on the path, large claw-marks.

Their way angled up through a forest. Clumped snow dripped gently from branches. Icicles glittered and crackled. Harg stopped on a clearing, by the side of a huge fallen birch tree. Pitching her satchels, none too gently, down into a snowbank, he looked round at Ingrid.

'A short rest,' he explained, almost apologetically. He motioned her to a seat on the birch trunk. She brushed off some snow and perched there. From his belt he removed a small flask and unplugged it, then offered it to the girl. The drink was delicious, tasting of berries and honey. Harg took a mouthful and put away the flask. The smell of his coat had an animal sharpness, but she thought of the white skin beneath.

They followed the winding path through the woods, crossing at one point a gully spanned by a log bridge. A few crinkled summer leaves had seeped to the top of the snow; stiff weeds sprang untidily out of the banks. Harg marched relentlessly onwards. At last they came to a place where the trees thinned out, and the mist drifted off into space; there the land fell sharply away on one side, while the path stopped dead at a facing scooped out in a cave-like entrance. In the furthest recesses of this tunnel-mouth, Ingrid thought she detected a faint gleam of light.

He led the way in and she followed, a little warily. It was a large cave, the lowest part of the roof being several feet above her head, yet Ingrid was immediately taken by the warmth of the air and the feeling of cosiness there, despite the sweet, rank smell that vaguely disturbed her. Underfoot, there was damp earth, loose stones, scattered diamonds of ice. As they moved forward, the way became clearer. A fire had been built at the junction of passages, thin smoke rising up through a narrow roof-cleft to the world outside. Harg set down Ingrid's satchels and attended the dwindling fire, nursing it back to life with wood chunks drawn from a stacked pile. As the flames crackled up, the girl looked around in the cavernous darkness.

On one side a large, roughly circular space formed a chamber. Cut pine boughs lay under a frame bed, skins sewn together and attached to some rope lengths, and these in turn lashed to four stout poles driven into the earth. A few weapons gleamed on the wall – a sword and a broadaxe hung next to a large wooden shield, which was painted in various colours. There were satchels laid out on crude shelving, small tools and a half-dozen bottles, unlit candles set up in niches and, opposite Ingrid, over the black gaping mouth of a deeper recess, a beam strung with dried meats and herbs. Next to the woodpile, beyond the blaze of the fire, yet another passage, a narrow one, wound into darkness.

'I will go out for a short while,' Harg said. 'Take off your damp things and spread them near the fire. If there are no dry clothes in your satchels, borrow some of mine from the pegs there, underneath the broadaxe. When you are dry you may want to rest for an hour. There is no danger here while the sun shines.'

With that he turned and hastened back through the tunnel. Ingrid had many questions, but she swallowed them all with a shrug, and began to strip off her clothes. It was a relief to stand by the fire in freedom and nakedness, stretching her body in the welcome heat, knowing that she belonged only to herself. Harg, so hidden and strange, had helped save her. She was drawn to him, yet she was also a little fearful, and was glad to have a few moments free of his presence to collect herself.

Hastily, she ransacked her satchels and pulled out some clothes. She began to dress quickly, having spread her damp things by the fire. She longed for a mirror, but could not find a clear surface there to examine her face. She shrugged her shoulders and fluffed out her hair with her hands.

She could not stop thinking of Harg. The feel of his skin was still at her fingertips. She looked at her hands, blushed, and picked up one of her satchels. She carried it across the cave and set it down next to the staked bed. She lay down on the bed, which was firm and yet yielding and fitted the shape of her body. Harg's bed, she thought, the bed of a hunter. She lay back at ease there.

Once or twice on her journey, in moments of quiet contemplation, she had asked herself whether the Wanderer had chosen her just because of her youth and her innocence. The old customs had sometimes required that a virgin take part.

Ingrid sat upright, staring down at her body. Harg's sword gleamed on the wall near the bed.

Slowly, she climbed to her feet, crossed the chamber. Reaching up, she took careful hold of the sword, tipped it slightly. Her blue eyes stared back at her, anxious yet clear; she smiled, rolled the hilt, making crinkles of light on the polished blade. She turned back to the fire, humming a song she had learned from her grandmother.

Ingrid threw a few chunks of wood on the fire. She did not feel in the least like a rest, but paced the length of the chamber, impatient for Harg. When he failed to appear, she pulled on her cloak and went after him.

Outside, the world seemed spacious and cool. Through a gap in the white layered clouds, she looked down from the cliff. Rough tops of pine trees speared up through the mist. A faint yellow dappling of light streaked the sky at the hidden peaks.

Ingrid quickened her pace down the path, wondering if she should call out to the man, who seemed to have vanished from sight. She was troubled: for she needed his company. She longed to find out who he was, and whether he might be willing to help her still further. *There is no danger here while the sun shines*, he had said. But the sunlight would not last forever.

She had nearly decided to cry out for him, when she saw him, slumped down at the foot of a birch tree. She ran forward, thinking him injured, then pulled herself up a few feet away, gazing down at his bent, stiffened form.

Something stopped her before she cried out. He lay there, his shoulders hunched down, his black hat askew on his head, his arms hanging loose at his sides. He was snoring a little, his face wan and white – cat-napping it seemed, quite exhausted to judge by the dark smudging circles underneath his closed eyes.

Ingrid gazed at him tenderly. He looked so frail and so helpless, yet more handsome than she had at first thought, only a small fringe of whitening hair betraying his age or his burdens. She sat down beside him on a few of the boughs he had spread there to rest on, and waited.

After a while, he stirred, groaning as if in a nightmare. Ingrid reached out to touch him and wake him, but before she could do so, he leapt to his feet with a cry, his eyes opened wide and he stared at her crazily, as if he might suddenly leap and attack her. Then she cried out in earnest, calling his name till he startled and woke from his dark dream and knew her.

'I did not mean to sleep,' he explained, getting hold of himself with an effort. He started away up the path, but she saw how his hands trembled.

Walking back to the cave, he had no more to say. He busied himself at the fire, then lit candles in the various niches. He placed some of the candles in the dark narrow tunnel that opened out beyond the fire. He carried some spruce boughs from the circular chamber and laid them out on the floor by the candles. Then he piled skins on top of the boughs, stripping the place on the wall where they hung. All the time she watched him, but he ignored her, avoiding her eyes. Finally, he took a long wooden pole from the floor beneath the place where the weapons hung and began to pry at a great stone that lay to one side of the main entranceway. Groaning and struggling, he at last succeeded in moving the stone a few inches.

Ingrid looked on, growing angry. 'If you would only tell me what you're doing I could help,' she said in a sarcastic voice.

Frowning, he tapped the staff on the floor. 'Help me, then,' he muttered softly, and again applied the lever to the stone. Ingrid put her mittens back on and began to push. After a while they had moved the stone almost to where the candles burned just beyond the fire. Only the downward incline of the floor made it possible. The passageway in which Harg had laid out the bed was now almost blocked off from the rest of the cave.

'I don't understand,' Ingrid said, when the hard work was finished. 'Must we lie separated by a stone?'

'Later,' Harg waved off the question. He pointed to the far wall with an awkward gesture. 'There is food there, and pots and a goatskin of water. Perhaps you could cook for us?'

He looked so comically doubtful that Ingrid laughed. She went about making a meal, stopping now and then to ask Harg where this or that item was, happy to lose herself in tasks that recalled so many pleasant days of her childhood. It surprised her that even the thought of her dear home in Wayland could not make her sad at the moment.

She concocted a stew out of dried meat and vegetables, sprinkling in herbs, and passing hot water to Harg, who stripped to the waist to wash while she worked. She cast a few glances at his white gleaming skin as he bent near the fire. She noticed the long scar that ran from the base of his neck down his back, opened her mouth to remark on it, but decided to wait.

Harg pulled on his shirt and a clean jerkin, then a light fur jacket. He looked handsome and fresh, Ingrid thought. While they waited for the stew, they drank more of the honeyed cordial from a carved drinking horn. Then Harg took a small instrument like a flute from one of his satchels and began to play. The music echoed softly in the distant dark corridors. He played, as she expected he would, several very sad melodies. They fell on her ears rather strangely, and he explained that he had learned them from listening to Skraeling chants. He recited a Skraeling song for her in the Icelandic tongue.

> This forest is not thick enough to hide
>   my shame.
> With my axe I have built a shelter, with
>   my arrows found meat.
> But evil spirits are waiting,
> Their cries break open my dreams
> And by day I am afraid.

When he had finished, there was a silence between them. Ingrid had many questions to ask, but she felt he would speak to her, for he looked at her tenderly, as if begging her understanding in advance. She got up at last and served the meal.

When they had feasted sufficiently they sat by the fire. Harg took a long drink from the horn and then said quietly, without looking at Ingrid: 'You are strong, and beautiful as well. It is out of selfishness that I keep you here, though I should have let you go on your way. It is possible you could have escaped the grey ones – but there are things that cannot be escaped.' He looked at her with his sad eyes. 'Perhaps you would tell me your story.'

Ingrid knew she could conceal nothing from Harg, that she was incapable of doing so. She began with hesitation, seeking for the right words, but she told him everything. From time to time as she spoke, he made her stop and asked a few questions. When she told, finally, of her encounter with Glimir, Harg could no longer sit still. He paced the cave by the fire, staring down at Ingrid with sharp, angry eyes.

Ingrid finished her story, then, she too, stood up, and watched as Harg walked the length of the passageway, stopping at the threshold to cast an anxious glance at the fading day.

'It is time,' he said, hurrying back. 'You must make your preparations for sleep. My own story can wait for the morning. But I will tell you this. You must sleep there behind the stone, which I will roll across the tunnel that leads into the mountain. There is nothing beyond your bed that can harm you, but you must be protected from what may come from outside, when darkness falls.'

Ingrid's trust in Harg had stretched to its limit. She hesitated. 'You want me to sleep there, walled in behind that great stone, with the darkness behind me, with all the dark things of the mountain free to crawl up through the tunnel to reach me! O Harg! I cannot!'

For a moment she thought he was going to kneel to her. 'I beg you,' he whispered in a frantic, choked voice, looking back over his shoulder at the tunnel's entrance. 'I beg you to, Ingrid, and I swear by the All-Father that no harm will come to you if you do. If you refuse, then not even Odin himself can protect you.'

Ingrid turned away with a sinking heart; the panic in his

words was beginning to affect her. She knew she must do as he asked, though she was in terror at the prospect. Then she felt his strong hand reach out and take hold of her wrist, very tenderly.

'I will give you my axe and my sword. I will give you the staff in your keeping. With those you can dig your way out, for the stone will not cover the passage completely. If anything happens to me, you must leave here at once, but only by day. You must not think to travel by night on this mountain.'

Ingrid stared blankly at him. 'But you told me the grey folk were prevented from coming here. You swore that your magic was potent. What are you telling me now? I must know what it is I should fear!'

'It is not the grey folk who will come here. It is – wild beasts.' He hesitated, then continued, in a half-choked voice. 'I cannot protect you from them, Ingrid. I am cursed to wander each night on these hills – to hunt what I can. I must go out in the woods before night falls.'

Ingrid took Harg's hand in hers. Pity welled up in her heart. Then a deep troubling thought made her ask him:

'It's Glimir who has done this to you, Harg – tell me, is it not Glimir? I saw you shudder at the mention of her name. She has put you under this spell.'

Though she felt his deep misery, Ingrid could not stop. 'She has done it because she loves you, Harg. Tell me, is Glimir not your lover? That is why she has done this – because she is your lover.'

Harg looked at her with eyes full of pain. 'No, not my lover,' he said, 'my sister.'

Cave

She lay hunched in darkness, expectant, uncertain, her mind stretching out to each sound. A few feet away the fire crackled softly; from a distance the low moaning wind sang. Shadows flickered and ran on the rough sloping walls, the roof scaled away into glittering peaks.

Never had Ingrid's mind been so clear and attentive. Her senses seemed magnified, focused – she felt to her fingertips the faintest trickle of water run off from the melting ice, her glance fixed each weave of the shifting shadows.

Sleep was impossible and after a while she threw off the skins that enwrapped her and sat stiffly there in the firelight, smelling the pine scent, feeling the dampness creep up from the depths of the cave. A current of air touched her cheek like the brush of a cold hand; she shivered and climbed to her feet.

For the third or the fourth time that night she fed wood to the fire from the small pile she and Harg had stacked up beside her pine bough bed. Then, warmed and cheered by the blaze of new light, she wandered to the back of the cave, and stood gazing down into darkness where the passage twisted away into the heart of the rock.

What might lie beyond in the coils of the cave, she feared to imagine; just to stand there and listen to the faint, disembodied howling that sounded in the depths of that darkness, tested her nerves to the utmost.

She had been a fool to let herself be shut in here, for she could not sleep, and had nowhere to run from attack. Next to the boulder, at the cave mouth, staff, sword and broadaxe stood propped against a large stone. Ingrid hesitated only a moment; then she started across the cave, determined to take action, to free herself and go in search of Harg. She must know at once the hunter's whole secret; only then could she trust him – and herself with the feelings she had for him.

Three steps across the cave, however, and Ingrid pulled up short. A low growl, harsh and menacing, rolled from the cave-mouth, from the other side of the stone.

Ingrid stood still, her fists knuckled tight. The weapons gleamed a few feet away in the firelight. In the sudden, sharp silence the girl held her breath.

A sound at the back of the cave made her whirl – there was nothing – the crackle of ice. Then the whining again at the cave-mouth, still closer. Ingrid stepped forward to within a few feet of the stone and reached for the broadaxe.

A great paw came down at her out of the darkness. She screamed and fell back, two small vicious eyes bore upon her, a snout and sharp teeth, the cave-mouth exploding with violence.

The white bear lunged at her, whining and snarling. Its paw swipe had missed and curved razor claws flailed the air. She lay sprawled and helpless; the air stank of terror and violence. The weapons went clattering down out of reach.

She wriggled away on her back, calling 'Harg! Harg! Harg!' in a choked, hopeless voice. Above her, the huge boulder rocked as the beast swarmed and howled at the entrance. Ingrid cried out as her hand touched the edge of the fire. She jumped to her feet and ran towards the back of the cave. The snarls of the bear seemed to follow.

Blindly, she stumbled in darkness – reaching out, felt the cold rough walls at her fingertips. She dared not look back, but flung herself forward with an unsteady, desperate momentum. She suddenly tripped and went down, sprawling hard on a shelf of cold rock.

She lay there, as the cries of the beast rose to fury behind her. The great boulder, viciously struck, rang the floor at her elbows; she shoved herself forward, as if by sheer will she could break through the stone walls to safety.

She crouched in a small niche of rock, pressed tight in the

damp clammy crevasse. The howling continued. Her thoughts raced in terrible sequence. Harg must be dead. Glimir had used him to trap her. Now she was left to the bear . . . or saved for the grey folk . . . but not while she could still use her knife. Her right hand came down, in search of the knife hilt. Her fingers brushed the cold stone, touched something that moved; she pulled back.

Ingrid screamed and sprang to her feet. She felt, through her body, the shudder of contact with cold scales, the uncoiling slithering enemy. She jumped back, aware of the whipcord that struck her, of the sharp sudden motion beside her.

The snake coiled away in the darkness. It hung like a glittering thread on the lip of the stone, then, as she screamed, disappeared.

Losing control, Ingrid fled. Without thinking, she ran through the cave to the fire. She picked up the flaming wood and began hurling the smouldering brands at the bear. Howling and snarling, the beast rocked the boulder. Then Ingrid remembered how Glimir had faced it. The words sprang at once to her mind.

'*Helgrind!*' she cried. The bear hung there, frozen. She leapt forward with a smouldering brand in each fist. The beast was gigantic. She faltered, then pitched both the firebrands at once.

'*Helgrind!*' she cried and ducked quickly forward. Her hands closed on the hilt of the long sword. With an effort, she aimed the sword upward and jabbed.

The beast roared in pain, toppled back. Ingrid edged slowly away. The boulder stood up like a rampart.

She heard the low squealing and growling diminish, but kept her eyes fixed on the boulder – on the unmoving darkness. The wind sighed softly in the tunnels behind her. The sword fell out of her hands. As the tension broke on her body, she collapsed on the floor – relief came in low, sobbing gasps. She felt the first pain in her right thigh, a brutal, sharp stab, unexpected. She rolled over once; the pain seemed to spread out in waves through her body. Fists clenched, she started to rise, then hunched down, as if cradling her pain. It raked her again and again. She could stand it no longer and lay helpless as the fire and the cave seemed to spin ever faster. She felt herself pulled down to darkness.

Coming to, she remembered how the great hollow space boomed with sound: the shuffling and scraping of stone, the trickle of water, the groans and cries of a man. She accepted her agony, tried to speak when she felt herself moved and then carried. She remembered, as if through a thick web of shadows, a hunched powerful figure that bent to her, tearing her clothes with rough fingers. Then the pain sharpened, wave after wave racked her body; she thought of the snake, tried to scream, but unconsciousness seized her.

She felt herself lifted. They were bearing her off to her funeral. Lights broke in darkness; it might be the canopied sky. She imagined the whirl of the planets, the movements of stars. The aurora eluded her; nothing ignited its shimmering light, but a great roaring heat swirled up to consume her; her body seemed to be melting away in a furnace that roared ever higher. She let herself melt in that dark fire and slept . . .

Ingrid opened her eyes. Harg looked down at her tenderly.

'At last,' he said in a low voice, and reached out to wipe her damp brow. The touch of his fingers was soothing. He leaned back, all haggard, dishevelled. His eyes were intense points of light. A strong fire roared close beside them.

Ingrid felt weak but alerted; she could measure the span of her body, was aware of its calm, breathing motion, of the gentle stir of her limbs. Only the vague and intimate pain at her thigh gave her pause to remember.

'A snake,' Harg told her. 'A snake in the cave, where I found you. I drew out the venom. Your fever has lasted two days. You must drink this, then perhaps you will sleep.'

He held up a cup to her lips; the potion tasted vaguely familiar. She knew she could not possibly sleep now; her mind and her senses were knife-sharp. She would just close her eyes for a minute . . .

She opened her eyes to find Harg there beside her.

'You've slept through the day,' he said quietly, 'Perhaps you feel better.'

In his voice was a note of anxiety. She pulled herself up, though he protested, pushing her gently back in the soft, swinging bed. She refused to lie down, but sat stiffly poised – light-headed, but determined.

'Are you going to starve me to death?' she asked, making a wry face. A great, relieved smile dawned on Harg's perplexed features. He sprang up and busied himself in one corner of the outer cavern, while Ingrid lay gazing at the fire and at a single beam of sunlight which drilled in on the rockface from the afternoon world.

Harg came back with a platter of bread and sliced meat and Ingrid ate heartily. By the time she had finished, Harg had ready a bowl of hot soup, which she sipped, feeling moment by moment much stronger.

Having taken her soup, Ingrid rose. For the first time she noticed she was wearing a shift that was not hers. Harg must have undressed her when he dragged her out of the inner cavern.

'Whose dress is this?' Ingrid asked, with a ripe blush. Her fingers smoothed out the fabric.

'You should not be walking about,' Harg told her.

'Turn around,' Ingrid commanded. She steadied herself, taking hold of a ledge.

Obediently, Harg turned away. Ingrid pulled up her shift and examined the wound on her thigh. It was ugly and red, smeared with white ointment, and the sight made her wince. She staggered across to where Harg stood, and took hold of his arm.

'Is this Glimir's dress?' Ingrid asked. Harg averted his gaze, saying nothing.

Ingrid shoved free and went slowly, unsteadily forward.

'You must rest now,' Harg told her.

She moved to the passageway and peered into the cavern in which Harg had shut her up. A low fire burned there, casting light on the walls and on the boulder, now rolled to one side. A few ragged scraps of her clothing still lay by the fire. Two metal stakes, trailing chains, had been driven deep

134

in the earth and stone floor. Harg must have fixed them there while she slept.

Ingrid felt suddenly weak. She walked slowly back to the fire. Harg helped her sit down, stretching out one mittened hand to assist her.

'The bear,' she said, with a shudder, 'The white bear – you killed it?'

Harg shook his head, murmuring softly, 'I could not, though I saw the blood on the sword.'

There was silence between them. Harg seemed unwilling to speak. Ingrid leaned forward encouragingly. 'Harg, you must tell me your story.'

The hunter's gaze seemed to bend back inside him, as if he were seeking some answer still hidden in the thickets of his mind. Ingrid saw the strain on his face, how he nervously brushed at his beard; his dark troubled glance made her sad. She leaned over and kissed him.

'I cannot . . .' the hunter said brokenly. 'I have put you in danger.'

Ingrid took his bare hand and caressed it. 'Tell me everything, Harg. Fate has brought us together. You must trust me.'

Harg stared gloomily in the fire. He shrugged his shoulders, as if with a deep resignation. He began to speak, at first in a low, halting manner, then his voice grew more steady. From time to time, as he talked, Ingrid stopped him with questions.

'Lokasenna is the name of our village,' he told her. 'It lies far to the south, but north of the land of the Skraelings who build high places and are ruled by the Great Sun. My father was Ragnar, son of Thorleif, and my mother was Sirit. She was a beautiful and much desired woman, though she died giving birth to my sister. Our village is not like others of our people, for most often we live in peace with the Skraelings and exchange with them many goods as well as lore and all skills of the craftsman. While still young I learned Skraeling songs, and to shoot with bow and arrow, as well as other things from the tribes. In our family, besides myself, there was only Glimir, a few years younger, but gifted with visions and knowledge and learned in the ways of the seeress. She was beautiful, like her mother – as you have seen – and trouble came of it.

'While she was still a girl many men were in love with her, though they also feared her magic, and kept at a respectful distance. There was one exception, however, and scandalous, for this was a half-Skraeling youth, named, in the language of his people, Coyote, who also possessed the gift of vision and magic. Now despite the friendship between our folk and the Skraelings you will realize that no inter-marriage is possible, and contact between boy and girl is forbidden under the strictest penalties. Despite this, the young man who is called Coyote, the product himself of a shameful union between Skraeling and Viking, and an outcast, became the lover of my sister.'

Harg's words trailed away; Ingrid sat there in horrified silence. She was thinking of Glimir, her own age perhaps, at the time of this clandestine love.

'My father knew that Coyote had dishonoured our family. He led a small party of warriors in search of him. Though the boy was an outcast from his own tribe, the Skraelings were aroused by this foray. A battle resulted and my father was killed. Such was the end of the trust between our village and the tribes. Glimir fled with Coyote. I vowed at once to find them and take vengeance in the name of my father.

'For over a year I pursued them. Their magic was strong, but my skills as a hunter were great. I followed them up river, across the lands of the herds, through the forests. I was driven on by despair. The thought of the Skraeling with my sister was goad enough, and I knew that my village would be waiting to hear that our honour was satisfied.

'I, too, became an outcast, forever in search of the quarry, hiding myself from the warrior parties of Skraelings; sometimes stopping for news at one of our villages, but always under suspicion, a young man consumed by revenge. I grew old too quickly, with no friends and few women to cheer me, yet I would not turn back.'

Grim-faced, Harg rose, to pile up some wood on the fire.

When he sat down Ingrid asked quietly: 'But you found them? At last you did find them?'

'Glimir I found first. It was late in the year, the forests were sunset red, golden, the wild geese were flying. I came to a lake with a waterfall – far to the south of here. A small hut lay in a clearing of birches. It was silent there, except for the roar of the water; no sign of a fire. I crept towards the hut from behind, afraid of some magic. Then I saw her, at the front of the hut, by the lake. She sat alone and unmoving. How my sister had changed!

'She was beautiful still but a deep frost seemed to lie on her heart. Her eyes had grown cold and her mouth had set hard in grim lines. She made no effort to harm me or thwart me, but slowly came back to herself, as if awakening from a trance. The more she awakened, the more separate I felt from her. I took her cold hand and we entered the hut.

'I built up her fire and we sat there. She took nothing to eat or to drink. At last I asked her about Coyote and she told me he was gone – he had left her two days before. He was not coming back.

'I did not question her further that day. We slept in the hut and I watched her for most of the night, for I still feared her magic. Next morning at last she told me her story.'

Harg was silent. A few red flickering beams of the sunset touched the far wall with dim fire. 'It's late,' the hunter said quietly. '. . . And . . . I cannot continue.'

'Please,' Ingrid whispered. 'It will be better if you tell.'

Harg closed his eyes; he was silent for a while, then told the rest quickly, almost in a whisper.

'Glimir had borne a child of Coyote's; it was a little girl, but she died. Coyote tried to abandon Glimir then, and she was tempted to kill him, but for the sake of the child's memory she did not. On the day I arrived she must have decided to pursue him. How she degraded herself for that buck! Of course she finally tricked me – my sister is very clever. She ran off to join her lover, and I followed, full of anger, but I was days behind them, having finally woken up from the

137

drugged state in which she had cast me . . . At Moon Lake I finally caught up with them.

'It was a bleak and grey day; the lake ice had firmed for the winter. I walked out on the south shore and found them both waiting, standing some distance apart from each other, Glimir off to the right of her lover. I had prepared myself well for their tricks – made my plan. I would neither go close enough to look in their eyes, nor listen at length to their voices. Even so, as I approached I nearly broke my resolution, for it seemed to me then that they both looked very helpless and desolate – a trick, no doubt, to confound me. When I drew as close as I dared, I stood still, took my bow off my back and readied my sword and my axe.

'At that moment Glimir began speaking. I listened a while to her words, though I did not look in her eyes. She told me she loved the Skraeling, even as she loved me, and that they intended to part no more. They wanted my forgiveness on behalf of my father, and then they would take their leave, forever, if that was my wish. She spoke some further deceitful words of that kind, but I ceased to listen, because I was watching Coyote, being careful of spells, taking measure.

'He had changed in the years since I had seen him in Lokasenna. He was grim-faced, with only a slight hint of the shifting smile that marked him as trickster and thief. His hair was ragged and long, and his buckskins were tattered and dirty. He no longer stood like a warrior, though a warrior he had been, shaman though he was, but he hunched his shoulders a little as he stood there, as if he were trying to cast off a burden.

'I decided then that the time for talking was over. I had nothing to say – all this was clearly a plan to deceive me. I had made up my mind long ago and I sprang at once to the kill.

'I ran sideways across the ice, for I knew the surface in front would not hold me – it was part of their trickery I had seen through at once. As I moved I heard Glimir screaming and saw her run towards Coyote. I doubled back towards them and slung my axe on the ice towards the Skraeling, whipping

138

it round on a thong I had made for the purpose. This strange tactic caught him by surprise and he tumbled, just as Glimir came near. I think she would have put her arms round him to protect him from me, but when he fell he caused her to fall too. She skidded some way on the ice. That was the chance I had waited for. I called on the name of Odin and attacked while the Skraeling was helpless. His bow and arrows lay on the ice; he had only a knife. I struck him through with my sword before he could join hands with my sister. The blow struck his neck and killed him at once. I never knew why he made no use of his bow.

'I, too, fell on the ice from the force of my blow. I lay there in joy and sang the praises of Odin. Glimir ran to the Skraeling and raised the terrible keen over his body. Dancing beside him, she seemed to rise from the ice. When she turned to me her face was transformed. I could not bear her look, nor could I turn away from it. She came like a hawk at my face and I closed my eyes in darkness and helplessness.'

Harg was silent for a moment. Shadows had gathered around them; the fire blazed up as the hunter kicked at a log. Ingrid stared at him, clasping her hands together, unable to speak.

'There is not much more to the story,' Harg said in a voice barely audible. All energy seemed to have left him: he cradled his head in his hands.

'After the battle, Glimir worked magic on me. Because of her spell, what it made of me, I could no longer return to our village. Perhaps I did not want to return any more. I found this valley, while she had stayed nearby on the lake, all alone. From time to time we see each other, from a distance. We have not spoken once since that day. Now perhaps you will know why the name of Odin, why the deeds of men, are hateful to her – and why she sought to detach you from the will of your father and brothers.'

Harg stood up, turned away. Ingrid climbed to her feet, drew him back, gently forcing him round till he answered her look.

'I am sorry for you, Harg,' the girl said in a low voice,

139

feeling her sadness deepen as she gazed into his burning dark eyes. 'I am bitterly sorry – but Harg, there is yet more to tell.'

'I don't want your pity.' He pulled away with an angry shrug.

'Give me your hand, Harg.'

Ingrid took hold of his mittened hand, drew him back.

'What is it that Glimir has done to you?'

His eyes shifted, uneasily. He started to push the girl back, but Ingrid, with a swift motion, peeled his hand of its covering. Then taking firm hold, she turned up his palm.

Though she knew what was there, the girl bowed her head at the sight.

Harg crumpled down on a rock ledge, and covered his face. Again, the red raw wound on his left hand was hidden. He sat there, refusing to look at her, trembling.

'I know what you are, Harg, but I . . . want you.'

The words came in a whisper. Harg sat unmoving, like stone.

'I want to stay with you – tonight.'

So I have said it at last, Ingrid thought. She knew that the man was at once the source of her terror and her comfort. But Harg did not look at her.

She went to him, knelt down, wrapped him round with her arms.

White Bear

Ingrid shivered – for the weather was colder – then huddled back in the cave mouth. Her skin was still damp from her bath; Harg had refused to help her, though she had massaged him with oil, combed his hair out. She insisted the rites be fulfilled; there was no one to officiate, so she took on the duties herself, preparing her man for their love-night, everything happening as if the great terror which lay on her heart could be banished by following the rules she had known since childhood.

Harg, inconsolable, had stood by the fire, a condemned man. She knew by the hungry look in his eyes that he wanted her, as she wanted him, but his way of dealing with terror was different from hers: he had tried to send her away, then seeing she never would go, he begged her to come no closer to him than the threshold of the inner cave, where he lay now in chains and awaited the nightly doom of the sunset.

The sun sank, barely touching the far cliffs. Ingrid leaned on the rockface, weighed down by her sadness. This was her bridal night, but what had Glimir's anger made of her bridegroom? If Harg had ever been joyful, all that had dissolved when he struck the blow at Coyote. Now he and his sister were locked in a terrible struggle and Ingrid's journey had carried her into that darkness where brother and sister had long ago lost themselves. Closing her eyes, the girl stretched out her hands to the sunset, and murmured a prayer to the great Freya to allow her to walk through this terror and rise up with the sun as a woman who nursed the seed of her man in her.

Going inside, Ingrid slipped into Glimir's white gown – it was all that Harg could provide her with. Silently, she breathed a second prayer: that great Thor might grant her a handsome warrior son. Then she bent down and took a handful of dried seeds from a bowl on the rock shelf and tossed them into the fire.

She thought suddenly of her family and of the strangeness of this ritual without mother or father, and a bleakness assailed her, though she struggled against it. She found the small dagger Harg had set by for her, and drawing it out of its fine leather sheath, gently touched the glittering point to one fingertip. A small drop of blood came; the rest she let fall in a cup full of the berry drink Harg had set by for her.

The fire hissed but the cave walls reflected no more sunlight. A low stifled moan from the inner chamber told her that

141

Harg's trials were beginning. Her heart beating fast, she crept through the narrow opening.

Harg lay stretched out naked on the floor, his arms and legs drawn back by the chains. In the firelight his whole body shone – the sweat ran off him, and his head tilted up, as if he were staring at some terror suspended above him. His chest heaved in rhythmical spasms.

Not far from the man, the fire crackled softly; the cave walls receded and closed. Ingrid held back; her fingertips brushed at the boulder. The white bear had stood where she stood; and the snake had slid out of the depths of the cave. Yet a slow-drifting calm seemed to weigh down her body – too heavily.

Then she knew that Harg must have added a drug to the potion.

Anger took hold of her; she would not be spared the least of his terror. She turned round and stumbled along in her haste to the junction of passages. There she bent over and made herself vomit the drink. The glimmering darkness whirled round her but she would not go under. She tore the dress from her body and rolled on the cave floor; stones cut into her skin. She staggered across to the cauldron, feeling a black point spread out in her mind. But she splashed and slapped at the water, dousing her face and shaking her head till her vision came clear. Painfully then, with wide out-stretched arms, she made her way back to the cave where Harg lay. There she stood shivering and exhausted.

Harg's cries tore at her senses. In her panic she had dropped the knife. He had wanted to save her, to arm her or put her to sleep. Her man did not trust her! She crossed the floor slowly, her eyes fixed upon him.

Harg's body stretched out, lean and muscular, strands of loose chain wrapped around him. She could see in the firelight the black hair at his armpits, and his skin shining darkly with sweat. Slowly, his head twisted back, as if some force inside him were turning him over. His eyes remained shut, but a soft gentle moan sounded deep in his chest, issued forth despite the clenched white teeth and the drawn lips. The

142

chains at his ankles and wrists rattled. Ingrid crouched over him, laid her head on his chest, ran her fingers along his hot, roughening skin. She lay full upon him, the throbbing life of his body possessed her, a sharp pulse took hold; she felt herself cradled and swung, and she held on – her fingertips ran on his back.

She felt the man twist underneath her. He writhed as if casting her off, but she clung to him. The sounds from his throat became high-pitched, ferocious. In glimpses she saw how his body seemed struck into light by the fire. The hard, sweating man spread beneath her. His skin shone dazzling white – yet not skin now but a thickening fur that bunched against her body. Then he opened his eyes and she looked into two small blank orbs; his teeth gnashed and snapped at her face. A loose end of chain flung out by one powerful paw struck her arm.

'Harg!' Ingrid screamed, but the white bear mocked 'Harg!' in a guttural growl; its red tongue lolled out, touched her cheek.

Ingrid lay terrified in the arms of her lover. She had lost herself there, had become a mere thing to be snarled at, or torn. She was quite helpless now, and the rub of his fur, the smell of his body, disgusted her. She pulled back in horror from the jaws that snapped at her throat.

At the same time she felt a violence within her, an anger, the strength of her body on his, the desire to have done with her girlhood, to fight for and capture her pleasure. She swung her fist round and struck the beast's nose till he howled. Then she reached down, seized hold of its member where it pressed on her stomach and wielded it into her, guiding and striking with sharp plunging strokes until warm blood ran on her belly, and a black flood first of pain then of pleasure swept through her limbs, half engulfing her mind in a storm of blurred images.

She saw the grey folk coming after her with outstretched stiff arms. They surrounded her and engulfed her, pulling her down into darkness. Black mud ran in her throat and choked her, and in her terror she could not even cry to her father.

She sat then in Einar's lap, helpless. He stroked her; blood ran trickling across her thighs. Village boys came and made fun of her, pointing at her bloodstained clothes. Thorkel shook his head in disgust. Glimir smiled slyly and kissed Ingrid's breasts.

Ingrid felt herself lifted and cradled by the strong arms of her lover. She opened her eyes – it was no longer the white bear but Harg who lay with her, inside her. She leaned over and kissed the dark hair on his chest. He looked at her gratefully, tenderly. She unwound a full length of snapped chain from his body.

'I love you, Harg,' she whispered, brushing the white-streaked hair off his ear. She stretched her long body beside him and he came to her tenderly, with a clear, soft light in his eyes.

They walked by the half-hidden river, in the heart of the valley. Night rushed towards morning, the air was bell clear, and Ingrid leaned close to her man.

They came at last to a small rough-hewn shelter of logs, set near a boulder, where the blank river curved between snow-drifts. From out of a dark recess, Harg took a skin bag enwrapping a blanket of fur. He set this blanket down in the shelter on a low bank of logs, and they drew it around them as they sat there. They felt the chill of the night on their faces, but their bodies were warm, pressed together, wrapped round by the fur.

They sat there for some time, feeling the power of the dazzling sky, in which the aurora had begun to flare and glitter, then Harg began to speak in a low voice, half turning to the girl, who took off one mitten and caressed his beard with her hand while she listened.

'Ingrid, this is true happiness, to be cured at last of Glimir's dark spell. I think I am free of it, I am sure everything is changed now. It was terrible, it came like a nightmare and held me. Each morning I remembered the rage and the terror, and pictures returned to me: raw scenes of pursuit; all the blood-lust and killing. Sometimes, when I woke up, there was blood on my face and my hands. Once or twice I found bodies of deer or of caribou, all mangled and torn. And sometimes I seemed to remember that in my rage I sought out Glimir, to kill her, but found her magic too strong – like a wall of ice that confined me.'

Ingrid reached down and held her lover's hand in a tight grip. Fearful thoughts lurked at the edge of her mind. She refused to confront them.

'I could not endure the thought that I should hurt you,' Harg continued in a slow, soft voice. 'From the first moment I felt that I knew you, that we were meant to be lovers. I wanted to help you, to save you from the grey folk, but I was afraid you would leave me if you knew the truth. I tried to protect you; I even hoped you might kill me rather than leave me alone with my curse: for I knew that the curse had a fatal truth in it. I could never escape it alone.'

Ingrid turned to him. 'What do you mean, Harg?'

The man bowed his head. 'I gave way to my animal rage when I killed the Coyote. Glimir made sure that I knew the full weight of that crime, for she made me a predator. I became what in a moment of rage I had chosen to let myself be: a killer by nature, but without the clean need of the animals. Only your love could save me from that.'

'You told me your story, and I felt sympathy for you, Harg. Already I desired you as a man. Then when I saw the wound on your hand I understood everything. I knew that I loved you, and would die rather than leave you, though I was afraid of you. I wanted no potion to let me sleep through your agony, and no knife to defend myself from you. Oh Harg, take me again here and now, with the lights making the sky wild. I long to make love without terror!'

They stood up together and the fur blanket fell at their feet. Harg stooped down and brushed the edges clean of snow. He kicked away the logs and spread out the blanket in the niche of the shelter. Ingrid lay down on the blanket. Harg looked down at her with loving eyes. He crouched and they fumbled with the folds of their clothing, laughing and teasing each other. He made love to her there and she responded and urged him along till their cries mingled together and filled up that space of the valley.

They dozed while the fur held its warmth but at last the chill drove them up. The lights had faded away and faint, barely tangible hints of the dawn struck their senses. A shift in the pattern of darkness, a soft brush of wind, the call of a bird – Ingrid looked all about her with fresh dazzled eyes, and listened for new sounds of night with sharp eagerness.

But Harg put his arm round her waist and drew her close to him. 'There are things to be done before sunrise, Ingrid. Your quest is no longer a lonely one. I have powers that can help you, now that you have freed me from my sister's curse. First you must give me the whistle you wear round your neck, the gift of your brothers, you told me . . .'

Ingrid looked up at him doubtfully, and Harg smiled and continued: 'For a young girl you trust very little. Perhaps it's better that way.' Then he added: 'The runes on the whistle have power to call up things from the water. It is a sure signal to the grey folk, and safer by far that you throw it away. I will find a place in the ice and give it back to the water.'

Without a word Ingrid removed the whistle from the strand around her neck and handed it to him. She followed as Harg walked up the riverbed; he stopped now and then to test the ice, then at one place bent over and with his knife hacked out a space. Carefully, he laid the whistle in the hole, then spread some loose ice over it.

They walked back under the stars to the river hut. There, Harg stopped and turned to her, as if sensing her feelings. 'We must make plans together,' he said. 'It is time to think of your journey. The source of the lights is still far. You are the chosen, the daughter of Odin, the Wanderer. We will go on together, if you wish, and find our way to the goal.'

Ingrid pointed north, towards the dark hills and beyond. 'But what lies that way? Is it only darkness and ice?'

Harg shook his head. 'No, just north of here there are Skraelings and, beyond that, who knows? The people of the ice. Somewhere north and east, as you know, lies the old homeland of our people.'

Ingrid protested. 'But Glimir has the cup of my father. And I know now, for she has made me see, that the cup reveals part of the mystery.'

'It is not Glimir who has the power of choice but you yourself. Only if she succeeds in winning you to her own way of thinking can the cup be cast into Nerthus. She cannot do it herself. Sooner or later she will have to give you the choice.'

Ingrid drew back; the enormous weight of her quest lay upon her almost as a physical burden. Harg took her hands and pulled off the mittens, then gently kissed her cold fingertips.

'Before we make plans there is something you must witness, if you have strength to.'

She looked at him questioningly.

'I can show you Wayland itself and your family and how everyone fares, though not at the moment of seeing.'

Ingrid's heart leapt at the thought, though his strange phrasing puzzled her. To see her mother and father, her sisters and brothers, the houses, the village itself! Oh, if she could only make contact, could speak to them, what strength she might draw from the moment!

'I have power only to call forth the images,' Harg told her. 'I cannot draw our time and their time together. What you see may not be the present, but a moment in time past or future, or even a moment of what might have been. For I can bring to the surface only what lies at the deepest source of your own knowledge. What you know of your family is more than you yourself realize. Do you have the courage to face up to it now?'

Ingrid knew that whatever the consequences she must make this contact. She bowed her head solemnly, and Harg drew her to him and pressed his lips to her hair.

'Come,' he said, taking hold of her hand. 'We must act while the moonlight and starlight favour us.'

After stowing away the fur blanket, he led her down to the riverbed, right out on the snow-bedecked ice. They followed the winding bank south a few miles, while Harg from time to time stopped, and brushed away snow from the hardpack. At the same time he kept looking up at the round moon which dipped in and out of the clefts of the western hills. They at last reached a point where the river twisted to bring the moon into sight in a gap of the peaks, its light flung down a long stretch like poured molten silver. Here Harg stopped and, measuring quite carefully, cleared away part of the snow in a circle. Then he polished the ice surface briskly with the sleeve of his coat. Finally, he took a small instrument like a sundial out of his pocket and set it down in the centre of the circle, driving it into the ice there. Slowly, he walked round the circle, as if reading the depths of the light, then stopped and marked a spot on the circle's circumference, facing into the moonlight.

'You must stand here,' he told Ingrid, and she stood where he pointed.

'. . . A thread of light will unwind as you look. You must turn your gaze slowly around, circling the peg and following the thread that unwinds. When you find it, hold on, and fasten your gaze to it. It will wind you away to the edge of the circle. Then, if Loki the trickster is willing the sights will appear.'

Without hesitation Ingrid turned her gaze to the peg. Right beside it, held fast in the ice, lay a small knob, or spindle, of light. As she stared, this light began to move, and she followed it round as it circled the peg. Ingrid fixed her gaze on the light as it turned in ever brighter, widening circles . . . Then her heart jumped as a vision of neat white scrubbed houses appeared, Wayland in summer, its chimneys ranged on the blue sky. Only something was missing – the streets lay empty of people, no wagons or horses crowded the main square, the doors were all shut up and boarded. Ingrid looked closer: there, on the very edge of the town, was her own dear house with three chimneys, but the windows loomed blank, no fire in the kitchen, and the front door nailed shut and hung with a great black cross. Then, down the street at the blacksmith's, a door opened, as if thrust out by a mighty

148

hand. A few figures emerged, gaunt men and women, thin and half-starved, wrapped round in worn, ragged clothes, their heads bowed as they bore along a small wooden palette, on which the tiny shrivelled body of a child lay – and Ingrid peered closer but the scene drifted off. And she gasped to see swarms of the grey folk emerge from the fields on all sides and blunder and lurch towards the town, crushing down as they moved the few scraggly rows of corn, and snapping the bare twisted branches of fruit trees as they tottered on past.

But this scene, too, faded in darkness. And then Ingrid saw Einar and Asta, and reached out to touch them – for it seemed they were close enough – but her hand passed right through them, and she cried out as they drifted away.

Ingrid could stand it no longer and she cried out. Harg held her tightly in his arms. 'I did not think it would be easy,' he said quietly. When she had stopped trembling they got up and followed the line of the bank towards the hill path. The darkness pressed close and Ingrid peered anxiously into the thickets.

'You said the grey folk could not come into this valley?' she asked, circling Harg's wrist with her tight-gripping hand.

'It is not likely,' he said, and she saw the grim set of his lips. 'I set up the horsehides, which work powerful magic to fend off intruders.'

Nonetheless, Ingrid breathed easier when they had passed through the pines and come out once again on the open bank. Not far ahead they would turn up the hillside. As they walked, she fought away fears that had entered her mind with the images raised in her trance. Harg had asked not a single question about them. She would tell him what she had seen when they lay under the blankets together. Her mind was in conflict – for the idea of sleeping with Harg gave her pleasure – it flooded her senses; yet her fears for her family gnawed at her, and she wondered if she and her lover should not return to Wayland together. She would ask Harg about this – in a little while.

They turned at last up the hill path. The sky was lighter, thought Ingrid, sombre light-grey filtering into the dark-blue, though the stars still burned bright all around. With the moon out of sight, the hillside seemed gloomy. They stopped at a faint sound, as of branches snapped at a distance. Merely the wind or a snowfall, or an animal stalking, thought Ingrid. But Harg took her arm and detained her – he signalled for silence and they listened together. Ingrid shivered, remembering night in the forest and the long cry of wolves, but now there was silence, except for the rustling of branches behind them, back by the pine grove it seemed.

Harg bit his lip. Ingrid started to speak, but something new caught her attention. She pointed up high on the hill where a dazzle of light flared out from the rocks.

'Look, Harg! What is it? The sunrise?'

The man gazed up, and was silent, then turned back with a face full of woe. 'The cave!' he cried, and sprinted away up the path.

She stood there a moment in shock, then followed on the heels of her lover, who had pulled out his knife, and moved off without once looking back. But Ingrid was fleet and stayed close, scrambling up through the bushes, into the evergreen forest, to the place of the birch tree. There Harg for a second had paused, but when he saw Ingrid immediately behind him, he leapt forward at once. They came to the gully spanned by the log bridge. Ingrid breathed heavily, Harg's shoulders heaved; she could hear how he gasped. They paused just a moment there, gazing up at the flickering light on the treetops beyond them. Once again, Harg leapt away, kicking and scrambling across some fallen branches, then bounding away up the path.

They raced through an alley of trees – but at last they broke out, coming straight on the bare rocky ledge where the cave lay. The whole place was flooded with light, a furnace of light pulsing out from the cave mouth, wild lurid light on the rocks and the straggling bushes, light flung back from the snow in a glare that blinded them suddenly.

They stood there together, gasping, unable to speak. Heat blasting their faces, they strained to see what hung burning in the mouth of the cave.

Ingrid was the first to move, for something familiar tugged at her, led her. Second by second the fire seemed to die down. She edged a little closer, then heard Harg behind her, his steps and his warning.

At the same moment she saw the dark hanging shape, staked up like a victim, like a haunch for a feast, and she raised her arms, screamed, and ran forward.

It was the caribou mount, to her unmistakable, though its throat had been slit from ear to ear and its body half-consumed in the bonfire.

The Sacrifice

The caribou's head hung in air, tilted up, held fast by a stake and a rope, while the fire-blackened body fell away in a ruin. The sweet odour of charred flesh was sickening. Her hands touched the hot smoking body. She screamed with the pain and leapt back.

Ingrid licked at her hands and plunged them down in the snow. Then she felt Harg's strong grip at her shoulders; he lifted her bodily and carried her off to a sheltering rock ledge. She lay on her back, while Harg rubbed her fingers with snow. A trickle of succulent juices from the meat ran in her throat. Ingrid closed her eyes and shivered with a guilty pleasure. She felt that something sweet and poisonous had touched her lips; she nodded with drowsiness.

Some minutes passed, a sudden crash startled her. The caribou's head had fallen down into the fire. Slowly, with hesitant steps, she walked with Harg towards the blaze. Her palms burned as if salt had been rubbed into the raw flesh, but she made no effort to disengage her right hand from her lover's tight grip. The pain seemed to soothe her shocked senses; it drove away the sweet taste of flesh that she loathed and yet wanted.

They stood together, watching the flames lick up round the head, which had fallen down at an angle and lay singed with black soot. The antlers rose up like a broken lyre; the eyes seemed to melt in their sockets. The cruel wound in the throat glowed with a thin rosy flame.

Harg took hold of the antlers, then changed his mind, pulled away. Ingrid followed him back to the edge of the firelight.

'It's better that we leave it so,' he said, and reached down to recover the knife he had dropped there. He handed this weapon to Ingrid, and warning her to be on the alert, made his way into the cave. A few moments later he returned, carefully stepping around the bright fire.

Despite the heat, Ingrid stood shivering. 'It was Glimir,' she said in a flat voice, without looking at him.

Harg bowed his head and said nothing. He led her away towards the trees, into darkness. They walked for a while and Harg kept looking behind them, his hand held firm on the hilt of his sheathed knife. The fire was dwindling fast in the cave mouth. As their eyes grew accustomed to the darkness, they could see the first signs of the dawn – a smoke-grey sky that swallowed the stars one by one.

'When the fire burns out, we'll go back,' Harg said. 'No-one can stop us from being together.'

Ingrid was surprised at the passion in his voice. Her longing for Harg seemed all at once to have slipped away from her. She felt cut off from the simple joy she had known by the river. Half-ashamed, she drew her man back and pressed a fierce, hard kiss on his lips.

'It was Glimir who did this,' Ingrid repeated. 'She hates me; she will not let us be lovers.'

Harg did not answer.

If only the tears would come now, Ingrid thought, but her heart felt like ice. She imagined how Glimir must have lured the caribou away and controlled it, how she had waited and watched, thinking the white bear would tear Ingrid apart in its passion. But now they were lovers, and Harg was saved from Glimir's dark magic. So, in her fury, she had given them this.

'We must rest and then act,' Harg said in his grim way. The shadows were back in his face, Ingrid saw.

Slowly, they circled the fire. It was only a thing that lay there now, and Ingrid took care not to look at it.

Traces of hot greasy smoke hung thick in the darkened cave-mouth. Ingrid crouched in the passage while Harg built up the fire. Only then did she think to look to her possessions, but hearing Harg's sharp gasp, she turned and saw for the first time how Glimir had hacked their bed all to pieces with Harg's own sword. And there stood the weapon, plunged down deep in the floor, transfixing the skins that Glimir had torn away from the bedframe with her own hands.

Ingrid sank down, unable to speak. Harg examined the frame and the skins of the bed, then with an oath gathered the broken and slashed bits in his arms and carried them out to the cave-mouth. She knew by the fresh flare of light just where he had thrown them. He returned and, with an effort, plucked his sword out of the floor and bore it across to the passageway, just beyond where their new fire lay. Using the weapon itself he made some signs on the earth there, then lay the sword down so its point faced the entrance. Ingrid watched him, thinking with numbed mind what force of hatred had been needed to drive the sword through their bed right into the half-frozen earth.

Without a word, without so much as a look at Ingrid, Harg conducted a meticulous search of first the outer and then the inner cave. He examined the food stocks and the implements, set his weapons in order (for in seizing the sword Glimir had upset the broadaxe and shield), then unrolled some new bedding and spread it out on the floor. Ingrid sat watching, feeling cold and forlorn, then she forced herself up. She searched through her satchels, but nothing of hers seemed to have been touched. As she laid hold of the familiar things brought from Wayland, desolate images rose in her mind.

153

Harg, seeing her turmoil, came over and turned her face up to his, kissed her, and held her.

'You have saved me with your courage and love,' Harg said with a quietly drawn breath. 'Glimir cannot accept that we should be happy, but her power can be broken. Let us rest now – we are safe here – and talk later.'

Carefully, gently, then, Harg began to undress her. Ingrid, feeling the touch of his hands, bowed her head. She lay back, somehow removed from her own tense excitement. Her body responded, but her mind was preoccupied, distant. The blanketing skins, and Harg's body too, were cold and uncomfortable. His fingers seemed rough on her breasts; he entered her quickly, with sharp stabbing motions and she remembered the knife he had given her, the one she had lost in the cave. Had Glimir found it and taken it away for her own magic purposes? Ingrid started to speak but Harg's moans prevented her; she felt her body respond to him, the pleasure take hold. But her mind seemed to drift into space, unconnected to the glow at her thighs. At his climax Harg roared out his pleasure; his hands clawed at her back and her buttocks. She writhed and responded, arching her body and shrieking, but her mind cried out 'Animal! Animal!', and when finally, his hot sweating body lay inertly and heavily pressed against her, at the back of her faint drifting consciousness she stiffened with fear and hostility.

For a while then she dozed, faintly aware of the hours creeping by, feeling his body twist and untwist in the half-light. At one point she dreamed she had fallen out of her cave, into warm, bubbling water. Something brushed at her foot, a rat snout thrust up, and she tried to scream but choked on the foul tepid water.

Darkness ensued, but somewhat later Ingrid opened her eyes. The smell of cooked meat seemed to fill up the cave; Ingrid rolled over, blinked away sleep. She was hungry. She forced herself up. There stood Harg by the fire at the cave junction, bent over the cooking pot, attending to breakfast. But Ingrid turned away. How could she eat ordinary food now, how could she sit down with the man who had let her poor caribou die? Men, powerful hunters, might kill and carry food to their women, but sometimes the food stuck in their throats, the rich juices poisoned their womanly hearts. Ingrid saw everything so clearly now. She had been initiated; she loved the sweet poison of the caribou's flesh, the rich blood of the sacrifice, but it was Harg's fault. He had led her to this knowledge, to this evil pleasure . . .

She groaned and sat up quickly. What was happening to her?

'Was it not you that killed the caribou, Harg?' She spoke without thinking; the words simply spilled out.

The man gazed at her in astonishment. As he took in the sense of her accusation, his glance fell, and he twisted away, looking frail and used up and uncertain. Then he answered her, in a voice that came from a distance:

'At night, there was always the killing – but not clean, like a sacrifice. By day I hunted with spear or with Skraeling bow. It is Glimir's intention to upset you by this trick. It was she who slaughtered the caribou – do not doubt. She is the princess of lies and illusions. We must not let her interfere with our love, Ingrid. We must plan to defeat her.'

They dressed and ate breakfast together in silence, but from time to time she found Harg's sharply questioning glance turned upon her. Ingrid swallowed little of the savoury gruel; but she drank honeyed wine, and at last got up to relieve herself.

She walked through the passageway into the bright chilly day. Outside, Harg removed his guardian sword and stood watching her. A few wisps of cloud floated high over far distant hills. Green forests lay round her, all spangled with sharp golden sunlight. The snow was immaculate white.

At the cave-mouth the black ring of embers lay heaped up with parts of the carcass: white bones stuck out, and a few blackened twists of the hide. The antlers had toppled down into the thick bed of ashes.

Ingrid's mouth watered at the odours of the singed meat. An impulse possessed her. Harg had gone back inside, and she stooped to the ashes, and scraped and clawed there for bits of cooked flesh. What she found she crammed in her mouth, feeling suddenly ravenous. The sweet taste of flesh seemed to make her veins sing. She craved more and more, and her digging grew frantic. The ashes ground in her teeth like rough sand, her mouth and her fingers turned black.

At last she was satisfied, her belly stuffed with the succulent meat. Staggering up, she moved off, following the footprints she and Harg had made the evening before. She spat out a mouthful of ash as she walked, and saw it was flecked with bright blood. Perhaps she had cut her mouth on a caribou bone.

On the way back, just in sight of the black ring at the entrance of the cave, she stooped down to the soft snow, which had drifted thick near the split trunk of a half-toppled tamarack. She plunged her hands down, twisting and scrubbing until the small patch turned dingy and grey and her fingers, scummed over, went numb with the cold. Quickly, she lifted the snow to her face and rubbed hard. She wiped her mouth dry on her jacket.

She stood there, the chill of the day creeping into her bones. She fought off a feeling of shame; how would she justify her carrion hunger to Harg?

She flung the snow down with a quick angry gesture. Her feelings swelled wildly. Why should she justify herself at all? She hated Harg's past now, and resented Glimir's claims on his love. Glimir had shown her the truth – that Harg was a spent man – all his emotions played out in the past. She had been a fool to enter his sordid, dark world. Harg could give her no pleasure; she did not feel free in his arms.

As Ingrid stood there in pain and confusion of thought she saw Harg emerge from the tunnel. He looked at her anxiously, seemed to control himself, waited. Slowly, she walked forward. As she approached, she noticed at once how he stared at the stains on her face.

She stopped a few feet away and returned his sharp gaze.

'Is something the matter, Harg?'

He said nothing, but turned and walked slowly back into

the cave. She followed, surprised at her own calm indifference. Her voice had sounded quite brazen.

Inside, he bent to stir up the fire. 'We must talk,' he said without looking up at her. She began to wash the stains off her face, first tossing her jacket away on their improvised bed. On an impulse she pulled off her jerkin and shirt and began scrubbing her shoulders and breasts. Out of the corner of her eye she saw how Harg watched her.

She sang a few verses of an improper song she had learned from her brothers, massaging her nipples meanwhile with the palms of her hands. Harg took a heavy step towards her; she stopped singing and faced him:

'Do you want to make love again, dear? Or are you already tired out?'

The man winced a little as if she had touched him with knife point.

'You're not yourself, Ingrid. You have broken the tabu as Glimir hoped you would. The foul meat has poisoned your mind.'

A slight thrill of fear touched Ingrid at these words; but something within her made light of the feeling. She knew that nothing Harg said could convince her. The men made the laws, set up the tabus and the women could only obey. It had always been so, but need not be so any longer. She reached out towards Harg, shifting her hips with provocative, insolent playfulness.

'You must purge yourself now of the carrion,' Harg said, and stood there with set jaw, regarding her.

'Are you afraid to make love to me, Harg, is that it? Or would you prefer your dear sister, Glimir?'

Harg lunged forward, swinging his arm. The flat of his palm struck her cheek. Jarred by the blow, she reeled sideways. Her anger came storming up and she screamed at him:

'Go lie in the earth, old man, where you belong! Your flesh stinks worse then the caribou meat. I've never loved you and I'll never be your lover . . . You're a beast! That's what I found you and that's what you remain.'

Ingrid backed off, her cheek stinging still; she was shocked

157

at the words she had found in her mouth for him. He had turned ashen white, pale as the first morning sky. His face remained drained of all light. Pride checked her impulse to reach out and touch him. She huddled at one side of the cave, and quickly pulled on her clothes.

Harg sat down by the fire and for a long time did not cast a glance her way. Ingrid began to gather her things up, to pack up her satchels. She felt as if something were driving her on to a place where she had not thought to go; to be forced there was pleasure at some depth of her mind – she did not know why. She only knew that to love this man's body again would be death for her.

'You must not go, Ingrid,' Harg said, shivering by the fireside. 'I will not let you go.'

'Will you kill me, then? Otherwise you will not stop me.'

Harg slowly got up and went to the wall where his weapons hung. Ingrid watched him with faint trepidation. Now comes the terror of force – a voice seemed to say in her heart – the man's ultimate threat.

Harg stood wielding his broadaxe, his piercing glance fixed on her face.

'No, Ingrid,' he said coldly. 'I will not kill you.' He dropped the axe suddenly, stepped forward, and reached out to her. But Ingrid trembled out of reach. Then he said in a quiet voice. 'If you mock me or thwart me now I will not hesitate to kill you. And then I will kill myself, for I love you.'

Ingrid sank down on a ledge and listened with bowed head.

'If you will not allow me to free you from the spell of the tabu there is nothing to help you. For I cannot force this cure on you. Glimir has won for the moment. But I believe we may yet win, for the power of Odin is with you, a power far greater than Glimir can draw upon.

'I intend to let you go now. I see I must do so. You will go north, I know, but the poison will make you a madwoman; an easy prey for the Skraelings.

'Once you have fallen into their power your chances of winning the light may be lessened. But there is one hope – a Skraeling shaman who may help you. His name is Birch Tree

158

– it is a name that may save your life, so remember it. As for me, I intend to go after Glimir. Oh, do not smile, Ingrid, I am not in love with my sister. I shall recover the cup from her, if I can, and bring it back to you. I will find you, wherever you are . . .'

Harg paused, picked up the axe, raised it high; Ingrid shrank back – but he swung it down hard and smashed a stone outcropping to fragments. 'Let it be as the fates will it!' he shouted in a voice loud and terrible, a voice Ingrid had not guessed that the quiet Harg could muster. Then, dropping the axe where he stood, he whirled round and strode out of the cave.

Ingrid did not move, though her hands trembled uncontrollably. She knew that whatever need had bound her to Harg had been struck into dust. A man full of strange moods, he had lived in a world of beast madness that was frightening and dangerous – never could Harg be the pure man of her dreams.

A cold wind breathed in the cave, and the fire glittered up. Ingrid went to the wall where Harg had hung up his sword. She tipped down the blade and examined her image in the bright, polished metal. How her skin shone – it was almost transparent! How cold gleamed her eyes, like moonlight trapped in blue crystals! There was nothing animal there, nothing that stank of the flesh – she was a princess, a princess of glittering light! A woman with power in her soul and no longer a girl.

Idly, she let her hand dangle down, touching herself where the man had possessed her. She remembered her long knife hidden away in a satchel, found it, and buckled it on. What was it Glimir had told her the Skraelings had called her? A warrior-maiden abroad in the woods!

Though no longer a maiden, she felt herself pure now and stronger than ever.

All that remained was to pack up the food for the journey.

She cast a glance once around the cave chamber – how gloomy and hateful it seemed to her suddenly. Her throat tightened – how hungry she felt again. An idea came to her mind. She slung on her satchels and slipped out of the cave.

There lay the circle of ashes; but they had been shifted, she could swear it: she dropped her pack and bent down on her hands and knees by the black ruin. Fiercely, she dug in the ashes – if the man had removed the life-giving food she would kill him! Black lumps flew up as she scratched away, soot scummed the fresh snow. In the midst of her frantic digging, Ingrid caught sight of a strange shape some distance away in a tree. It seemed to float down from the split, angled beam of a half-fallen tamarack. She climbed to her feet and walked slowly towards it. She saw that Harg's tracks preceded her.

Bare antlers rose over a fire-blackened skull. Beneath hung a haunch of charred meat. She thought: he has set them up there to torment me.

Ingrid shrieked and ran forward. She jumped and grabbed hold of the antlers and skull, which were lightly bound to the trunk. She flung them away: they came separate in air and clumped down with a soft muffled crunch in the snow.

She dug at the cold haunch, scooping mouthfuls of sweet flesh. As soon as the food touched her lips a wild hunger seized her. She tore off huge, soft strips of the flesh and devoured them. The hunger possessed her. She pressed her mouth to the dark haunch and gouged out meat with her teeth. She had come near to choking, and her stomach retched at the food; then she fell in the snow, spewing the last indigestible morsels.

She lay there panting and coughing; the cold seemed to run in her bones. At last she pulled herself up. Light-headed, dizzy, she drifted back to the circle of ashes. All around her cold light gleamed up from the snow. She could see the blue veins stick out on her wrists.

She must be off on her journey, but she could not live without meat. Painstakingly, for her body seemed built out of feathers, she managed to stuff one part of a satchel with most of the remaining flesh from the carcass. But the faster she worked the colder her hands grew; and her teeth chattered violently, steadily.

As she started the trek down the hill she felt better. She did not look back even once. Minute by minute Harg seemed to fade from her mind. She passed down the hill, over the log bridge. A rabbit scuttered away in the forest. The day was so dazzling – the sky such a rare blue – that even the shadows that lay under the pine trees were luminous. The snow, slightly crusted, crunched under her boots.

She came down to the valley and followed the riverbank north in its windings. She passed the rough hut where she and Harg had made love. The snow was not thick here and she trekked fast, as if to make sure that the icy fist in her breast would not open. Yet, slowly, that chill from the centre spread out; she walked faster, tried to quicken the warm blood she still felt in her veins. She sweated and shivered by turns, yet the cold held her fast in its grip.

After some time the face of the land changed a little. The frozen riverbed narrowed; hills pressed in close; stunted trees poked from high shining rock clefts; early afternoon sunlight struck the cliffs to fire. Making her way round a jagged spur of rock, Ingrid stepped out on a broad plain where the riverbed wound through a vast forest of snow-bedecked pines. There, some distance ahead, rose the tops of dead trees – elm, beech and birch – betokening a swamp. Beyond it, as far as she could see, the forest stretched north.

She turned, and saw, high on the hillside behind her, skewered out on a long branch, the grotesque stiff form of a guardian horse-skin. It was a twin to the one she had seen on Moon Lake, just before meeting Harg. And beneath this one stood Harg himself, watching her, staring down from the height of the cliff. She shivered at the sight, as the memories came rushing back, then she bent down, and plunged straight ahead, down the near slope, towards the spot where the riverbed slipped into the forest.

She trekked on under the trees, surprised at the darkness, the gloom there, but grateful too for the light, for clear runs where the riverbed, wearing only a bare crust of snow, lay open to the blue sky.

A beautiful lightness of soul came upon her. It was the

meat, she felt it in her blood now. She wanted to dance through the trees; she accepted her fate. She could not really die – with death she would float away free of her body, go where she willed, return to her village. Just to be near her family, not even to touch them, but to float in the clear air – that was all she wished for.

Ingrid walked on, the afternoon dwindled; the shadows grew deeper in the scrub-tufted snow that lay under the trees. An hour passed, and when she looked up the sky was no longer blue: a great scudding cloud mass seemed to smother the forest. The air had grown chilly, a slight wind stirred the top branches. The snowdrifts made her progress more and more difficult.

Step by tired step then, she felt her packs become heavier. While the sun shone, she had not noticed the weight. But slowly, a chill crept over her body – for a while the hunger had stayed it – but now it came back, opened up in her chest like an ice flower, ran in her veins like chill water; her lips turned blue and her teeth chattered. Again she was hungry, and she thought of the meat, knowing full well that a tabu was broken, that Glimir had tricked her, as Harg said – but she hated Harg more than ever. She felt the cold at her thighs, in her legs; her toes were numb with it, and her fingers. Only by eating more meat could she warm herself; but later, she knew, the chill would possess her.

Then she sensed all over her body a strange prickling of skin, a shivering cold as if ice crystals were forming in her pores. At the side of her face she felt the caress of a movement; and she blinked as her eyesockets swelled up, as if she would burst into tears but could not, so drained of all feeling did she feel.

She could not go on, her body was trembling and strange. She let her packs fall in the snow, but her clothes themselves were too heavy. She zig-zagged along, then pulled off one mitt, and saw to her horror how her hands sprouted dark hair. She cried out, touching her chin, for hair grew all over her face, and dark locks fell down to her shoulders.

Around her the woods had grown dim; a strange light

touched the snow. The wind howled in the treetops. Ingrid felt ice drops come down in a shower; then the skies seemed to open, the rain pelted down. It struck the branches and snow and ran off the needles; the underbrush rattled; in a few minutes everything shone with a coating of ice. Ingrid slid forward; she looked out from eyes that were rimed thick with ice, a blur of green and grey shapes seemed to threaten. She stretched out her arms, tumbled down. Her clothes were unbearable now; they clung to her body like a mottled dead skin. She tore at them viciously. First her hat, then her jacket, her tunic, her shift and her trousers. She threw her boots off and ran.

She was naked at last in the snow, her body all covered with thick hair. She tried to cry out; something tore at her throat, and passed through her lips – unearthly shrill howling. The pain in her eyes was unbearable.

She ran now, fully naked in the heart of the storm. She ran blindly through mazes of dead trees, by instinct avoiding the trunks. Wrung by a sharp pain that was almost pleasure, her mind lapsed. The ice shower pelted her body. Close by she heard with a magnified sense the padding of feet; a snarl sounded somewhere behind her; she felt without seeing the red eyes of timberwolves. A low howl pursued her, then was swallowed by silence. She ran, a blind thing, along one side of the river.

On the opposite bank, near a long line of cedars, sat a boulder, all glistening with fresh ice. Beside it, two figures moved in the snow.

She approached them, hag-like and hideous, with wild streaming hair. She shrieked, and the sound, neither joyful nor sorrowful, made the figures stand still in their tracks.

She ran closer; they waved their arms; one shouted.

It was strange, how every word came clear, though she understood nothing:

'Go, quickly, my son – tell the village. A Windigo comes to destroy us!'

Windigo

The black creature shrieked as it staggered along towards the hunters. The older man stared aghast at what seemed a swollen cadaver; it crossed the stream and lurched towards them.

His son saw, by contrast, a thing made of flies, all shifting and buzzing and gathered in air in the shape of a slim girl.

> *The Windigo is coming –*
> *Ice demon, storm demon,*
> *Black hair sprouts from its body,*
> *Its blood is made of ice!*
> *Hear its dreadful scream*
> *And lose your manhood,*
> *For it feasts on human flesh.*

Shigak, the elder, remembered this lore well; he was the first to tear his gaze free of the terror. He cried out, then swung round and clouted his son on the back. The Buck slid away on his snowshoes. The old man sprang towards the nearest boulder and hurled the dead rabbit, part of the day's kill, straight in the Windigo's path.

Shigak scurried on past the boulder and made for the near line of cedars. He did not dare look at the Windigo, though its wild shrieks pursued him. Behind him, he saw his son moving with great speed down the riverbed; then he came on the cedars and, seizing hold of a slippery branch, pulled himself into a low tree. He climbed for a few frantic moments, then stiffened, and wedging himself at an angle between the trunk and a branch six feet from the ground, he closed his eyes and pressed his mittened hands tight on his ears.

Some hundred yards distant, at a bend in the river, the Buck stole a look back. The black creature seemed to have paused near the boulder, but Shigak was nowhere in sight. The young man gave a cry and threw himself forward, risking a fall to gain speed. The village was four miles away and he still had to skirt the last of the treacherous swamp-land.

Through a maze of dead trees, he careened along, watching with care for the soft ice. A faint trail led straight through the heart of the pines. There the glissade of ice gave way to a powder; the snow-shoes took hold and he pumped his way forward. On this run he would lose half a mile but the footing was sure.

As he stroked forward he cast more than one anxious glance at the woods on both sides. Had anyone known that the Windigo was coming? His uncle, Birch Tree, had been talking for days with the other members of the Midewiwin, the seers of the village. The young men believed that their elders feared a raid of the grey folk who haunted the lands to the south, and that Birch Tree had set up his conjuring tents at the southern edge of the village to do magic against them. No one expected a Windigo to strike from the south; yet somehow his uncle had known better.

The Buck strode along, the hiss of his shoes strong and steady. He did not believe that the creature had taken his father; Shigak was known in the tribe as the wiliest of men; he had powerful protectors, though Birch Tree's magic was greater. Only Birch Tree could stop the Windigo from destroying the village. And the Buck badly wanted to help him.

Recently Birch Tree had told him he was destined to die young; and he wanted to do some great deed before that day came. He was still a youth, but though he was not very tall, his muscles were perfect, his body the fleetest and strongest, almost, in the whole village. Already he had taken some scalps, killed his first moose, and slept with many of the village girls. He had spoken once at a council and the old men had listened.

From behind him came a wild shriek, like the cry of a child being murdered. It was the Windigo's voice: now the whole village would know of its coming; his news would make little impression, for the timid would already be stricken to panic and seeking to run off to safety, while others would sit by the dwellings and hope for good magic. The honour due to his run would be lessened.

So be it, thought the young man, and slid and half-rolled down the hill. At least he would reach the camp before the creature attacked. It was only a short way now, on the well-known path through the maples. He swept along through the scrub bush, between huge, scarred trunks; bare branches leaned from the darkening sky. He felt his legs tightening for the first time and his breath quickening at the last gruelling effort, but minutes later he came straight on the village, a scattering of domed huts lying between the bare wintry grove and the faint hollow that marked the curve of the river.

Now a new sound struck his ears – a long drawn out wailing, the crying of children, shouts and complaints, and he saw that the camp was already in chaos, men and women running about, beating their breasts or screaming out imprecations and pleas for a miracle. The darkness came on apace and the wind swirled up from the river; the tent skins flapped wildly, the long poles swayed in the sharp gusts.

The Buck stopped to pull off his snowshoes. He saw Amik, a noted young boaster, collapsed near the lodge of his father, his handsome face twisted in fear, while his sister bent over him wailing. So much for his manhood, the Buck thought, and glanced the length of the village, where snow-swirls kicked up by the wind enveloped those who had fallen down helplessly to await their destruction. He must find Birch Tree at once and prepare the defence – there was no time to waste. As he hurried towards the tents at the south end of the village, he wondered if Shigak's wives had already run off and if Happy Tongue would remove her spell from the Way-Michi-Gooshi – though even that muscular giant could hardly stand up to a Windigo. Besides, his uncle would have to approve of his release and his uncle would have no time for such thoughts at the moment.

'Where is your father?' a familiar voice asked at his elbow, and at the same time a sturdy figure appeared in his path, taking hold of his arm with a firm grasp. The Buck half-turned to greet the lithe, nervous Wabooz, and pressed Mang's arm in return. A nearly naked child crawled out of a dwelling a few feet away, followed by a terrified anxious mother. The three men stood together, a calm little circle in the midst of a swirl of chaotic activity.

'My father sent me here,' the Buck announced quietly. 'We met the Windigo in the woods. It is a terrible fly-plagued creature but it has the shape of a woman.'

Wabooz laughed grimly. 'Perhaps old Ningig created it because the girl with the bracelets rejected him in favour of you. Did the creature show any interest in devouring you especially?'

The two younger men laughed but Mang, the war captain, shook his head in disapproval. 'Wee-sa-kay-jac, the trickster, makes jokes but first sets a trap for his enemy. Birch Tree sent us to find you. Are you running off at the mouth or helping to stop this?'

He waved his hand at the scenes of confusion around them. An old man sat wailing and beating his breast by one dwelling; another wigwam had collapsed, as a family struggled to gather belongings and flee. Children, disturbed by the din, clung to their relatives, screaming. The chill, mournful cry of the Windigo seemed to ride the wild gusts that tore at the tent skins and sent the smoke flying in short, choking downswirls.

'Let us go, then,' said the Buck and turned his face into the storm. The other two followed.

Bending forward, they moved with all haste in the teeth of the wind. Their cheeks stung with the ice, their eyes smarted, but they saw how the whole south end of the village lay empty before them, the dwellings deserted, though one, set back from the rest, sieved flames and poured out white smoke where someone had slashed through the skins. As they swept past, the sinister hissing of ice meeting fire struck their ears, and they shuddered despite themselves as the cries of the Windigo rose up from the riverbed directly before them.

'Birch Tree is there,' shouted Wabooz, cupping one hand against the din of the storm and pointing ahead. Three tiny conical tents had been set in a triangular space by the riverbend and the wind howled around them, lifting them nearly away from their anchoring poles.

But the Buck saw at once how strangely the tents swelled, a wind from the inside stretching the rough skins to bursting. The willow hoops, slender and frail, caught between contrary forces, seemed ready to split; the poles stood up off the earth; tiny sparks flew out of the roof holes.

'Birch Tree has told us to heat up the stones; he has taken his place in the rear tent. He wants you to wait by the centre mark, there just behind the other two tents. You will be the bait, young Buck. May the good spirits protect you! So farewell!' Mang wrapped his friend round with a rough hug, Wabooz turned away without speaking, but raised one arm in a gesture of triumph belied by his grim, set face.

'Heat the stones well,' the Buck said – ritual words of bravado. But his courage came near to failing him. He longed to run after his friends, who slipped swiftly away: there was surely much more they could tell him. With an effort he checked himself, watching their bent forms drift back towards the village. The Windigo shrieked, but at that moment the Buck heard the spirit of Tindat, his dead brother, speak in his heart. Was it only the wind? The sparks flew up from the conjuring tents. He saw where the mark had been placed in the centre – that was his post.

He pulled his fur coat tightly around him – the hunting charms still hung there, impotent now, for he was the hunted. Yet the medicine bag at his belt gave him courage. He suddenly thought of his father, caught a glimpse of a grizzled old man hunched up in a cedar . . .

The Buck waited nervously, his eyes fixed on the small tribal bag with the talismans. The storm rose in furious gusts; ice-needles flew in his face. Around him he heard now his uncle's untiring chant and the rumble of spirits arising from

168

deep hidden spaces. The three tents sparked fire, each one a bellows of voices.

May the beast not appear, the Buck prayed, may the soft ice devour it; but at that moment the blinding white space of the riverbed disgorged a dark speck. The Buck hated spiders and had once as a child nearly fainted at the sight of the spider-spirit peering out from a moonlight tangle of white web. Now he felt his knees buckle, his power of movement give way, as he saw how the dark thing swelled up, like a huge black boil that would burst and spill poison upon him. He had no manhood left and he knew it; in his thighs, in his loins, was a pitiful trembling and weakness. Any second, he feared, he would fall where he stood, for the closer the beast came the more that his manhood seemed ready to leak away in the snow. What has happened to me? he questioned himself with a new bitter power of reflection. It was not like this in the woods. Tindat, do not look on me now!

The Buck closed his eyes, clenched his fists tight. The scream of the Windigo held him.

A few seconds and terror and pride drew a look. He saw the Windigo shudder and lurch towards him through the snow. Each step bound the Buck still more helplessly fast where he stood.

The creature came staggering; the ice shone on its dark, grizzled skin, on its rough coat of hair. Red eyes stared out at him, eyes full of terror and malice. The shrieks were like fingernails grinding on shells in his brain. He saw lips that were twisted and swollen, gashed, bleeding raw.

The Buck felt his legs slowly crumple beneath him. He sank to his knees, his arms drooping down at his sides. The creature came closer, almost even with the two forward tents; they roared near to bursting with a din of wild voices. Sparks flared up from the tent peaks, blew off in the cruel, howling wind. Behind him, the Buck heard his uncle's voice bellowing out from the third tent. He wanted to run away, to draw out his knife but he could not.

The Windigo stopped in its rush as if struck by a stone axe. Hurled back, the coiled beast collapsed like a fir tree shivered by lightning. Force lines, visible fire-sinews, leapt through the air from each tent, and the Buck crawled back in a space that was bounded by shimmering light.

He wriggled away, nearly blinded by fire; his mittened hands pawed at the snow. In glimpses he saw how the Windigo reeled at the boundaries, screaming, uncertain, like a beast foiled of its prey.

Voices roared from the prayer tents. The Buck wriggled back, then turned, crawled a short, desperate space on his hands and knees. He was only a few feet away from the third tent; it twisted and spewed light, shaking and flashing, like a skin full of storms.

Close to the barrier, the Buck tried to rise. His body felt drained of all power, his arms and legs heavy, as if buried beneath stones. He crouched there, unable to pull himself up, while the skins of the tent shook fire and the air a few feet from his face opened fissures of light.

He was helpless, enclosed by the light, half-dazed and unable to free himself. The voices around him, the screams of the Windigo, seemed to blend in his mind like a spell that contained him and bound him. He could not crawl up to the barrier; he could not turn back. He tried to seize hold of his thoughts, to focus on Tindat. The air rang with silence.

Then, with an effort, he turned round. The barrier fire had quite vanished. The Windigo came at him, a black thing that ran with a sinuous gait. Its cold grieving eyes wept; its blood-spattered mouth was trying to speak!

Shock made him helpless. Then a firm hand touched the back of his shoulder; he moaned and collapsed where he stood. A small figure in the robes of a shaman stepped past him. Two outstretched bare hands pulsed with light.

The *wabeno*! the Buck thought, his terrified glance focused up, the fire-carrier!

The Windigo loomed over Birch Tree, who waited. The creature stretched out its arms. Then the shaman too raised his arms and held up the full, glowing coals. The Windigo stopped in its tracks, its eyes shining blankly with fire.

The shaman moved closer, reached up, and with a sharp

sudden thrust held the glowing hot coals very close to the Windigo's eyes.

The Buck pushed his face down in the snow and covered his head with his arms. A scream seemed to shatter the air all around him. He flinched at the odour of singed flesh.

Slowly, the Buck raised his head; wet snow ran over his face.

His uncle crouched there, like a tiny, fierce bird. Beside him, a dark form stretched out. The Windigo had been dazzled, felled by his uncle's bright magic, yet the Buck feared to go closer; he pulled back, hands trembling, and the scream still found echo inside him. On the white snow, a few feet away, two small glowing lumps hissed.

Then Birch Tree got to his feet. At the same time, a voice called and the Buck, startled out of his daze, whirled around. Wabooz and Mang hurried forward, carrying blankets and a large tunic made of rough caribou skin. They nodded to the Buck, then hesitated, stopping a few feet from where Birch Tree awaited them, their eyes fixed on the strange form lying prone on the snow.

The shaman regarded them, saying nothing, though his almond eyes narrowed to slits. Slowly, he raised his wrinkled hands, and extended them, palms turned up, so that Wabooz and Mang saw the fire-blackened skin. Mang did not move, though his gaze narrowed; Wabooz shifted his feet.

Birch Tree stood back and gestured commandingly. The two braves stepped carefully forward. With eyes half averted, and heads held stiffly away, they began to wrap up the creature in the tunic and blankets.

It was sunset. The storm had passed on and the village lay calm in its wake: a child cried; one wigwam still smouldered and a few, stripped by the wind of loose skins, sat like hollow hives in the twilight. But most fires still burned and, as the procession advanced, a straggling array of the villagers moved between the tents to line the main path. They stood there in silence, with round staring eyes, or mumbled the charm

171

words under their breaths. Many hands reached down for the medicine bags, and a few women held their children away, as if something evil and threatening had come into their midst.

When at last they reached the appointed dwelling, the Buck saw how well Wabooz and Mang had prepared things. Red hot glowing stones lay in the fire close to the door of the sweat lodge, a small hut some twenty feet away from the wigwam chosen. A boy stood tending the fire, Mang's young nephew, and as his elders approached he stepped back, his eyes filled with awe at the sight of the Windigo.

Then the Buck saw how Amik, the boaster, had joined the procession, as if he were hunter or conjurer. He walked behind Mang, his head proudly held, until Mang finally saw him, and with a withering glance sent him back to the edge of the hushed crowd. Mang and Wabooz came forward with the thing wrapped in blankets. The watchers all seemed to catch breath while the two braves carefully lowered their limp burden so that Birch Tree could reach out and take hold of the blankets. The three men, pushing and pulling, got the Windigo into the hut. The Buck stood by at the entrance, well in front of the crowd. He could see straight into the tent and he watched as his uncle gently unwrapped the creature.

Using stout sticks, Mang and Wabooz were rolling up stones from the fire. The hissing and sputtering that followed drew some faint cries from the watchers. The two braves paid no attention, but with great skill moved five or six of the bright, glowing stones into the hut, leaving the white snow at the entranceway scorched with dark embers shaken off from the fire. Then they handed the waterskin in to the shaman, who pulled the entrance flap tight.

Almost at once a deep chanting began; a hissing noise followed, and thin wisps of steam drifted up from a few small flaws in the tent skins. The chanting continued, with new voices coming, and rhythms that pushed at the anchoring poles. Wabooz and Mang stood with the Buck; their faces relaxed all at once and Wabooz nudged the Buck in the ribs.

'Why not just kill the creature now that it is at our mercy?

Does Birch Tree have something in mind? Has he confided a vision to you?'

The Buck shook his head. Whatever his uncle had known, he had spoken nothing about it outside of Midewiwin. And Buck had not seen any other members of the sorcerer's group since early that morning, when he had left to go hunting with Shigak. As he searched the circle of onlookers with a careful glance, he confirmed his suspicion that Birch Tree had sole magic control of the Windigo. Then he remembered his fleeting sense that the thing was a female. He wondered if Birch Tree would use the prisoner to restore his failing virility. It was common for sorcerers to use magic for love-power. Even now Happy Tongue tried spells on the Way-Michi-Gooshi, to make him fall in love with her. And he himself had been made to fall in love with some girls by means of magic. Yet Birch Tree, he felt, was too old, he did not care about love any more.

A cry from the circle of faces around him brought the Buck back to the moment. Though the chanting continued its drone-like unceasing music, the tent-flap was moving, a hand reached out from a thick cloud of steam. A small, gnarled hand – Birch Tree's hand – was thrust out of the tent, tiny fingers clasped tight to a length of black hair. Mang ran at once to the entrance, took the hair from the shaman and waved it about for the onlookers to see. A half-suppressed tremor of elation ran through the whole group at once. With a cry Mang slipped across to the fire and threw the hair in. It flared up at once, disappeared. The volume of the chanting increased; the tent flap was drawn, and again the crowd waited, alert now and eager, caught up in the shaman's performance. A few minutes passed and the tent flap opened again – the shaman's hand was thrust out; Mang took more hair to burn. This happened several times over. Each time the tent flap was closed the water was poured, and steam bellowed out from the sweat-lodge. But the stones inside, as it seemed, were fast losing heat, and soon the entrance dispensed only thin, trailing vapours. Then the Buck, from his clear point of vantage, could at last look into the tent. As the flap was pulled back once again he saw Birch Tree's wrinkled round body bent over, all naked in thin steam, and behind him – a sight that made the young brave catch his breath – the naked white limbs of a girl who lay propped helplessly up at the back of the tent.

The Buck looked quickly from Mang to Wabooz, but neither had shared his fleeting vision – for Mang was busy again at the fire and Wabooz watched the war captain work with his typical quiet approbation, half-mixed with amusement.

Once again the tent flap was pulled shut, and the chanting began, a sun song describing the heat of creation. The Buck knew some of the words, but they drifted away from his mind – he was thinking of a body so white as to be made all of moondust. Birch Tree had conquered the cannibal spirit but where had the strange maiden come from?

The Buck shivered gently in the sharp cold of evening. A restlessness took hold of the audience. A child began crying and was quickly hushed up; a village dog barked a warning. A few glances turned nervously south, towards the riverbed.

Then the tent flap opened again and the hand of the sorcerer held out the tunic that the beast had been wrapped in. The alert Mang moved forward. For the first time Birch Tree had to speak his instructions, though the Buck could not hear his faint, croaking words.

Mang lifted the tunic away from the tent, holding it carefully at arm's length, and growled a few words to his nephew. The boy jumped to stir up the fire, and in a few minutes a roaring blaze lighted the circle. The Buck felt the warmth reach out, touch his face. In the background the barking continued, and he heard a few shouts.

With a quick motion Mang threw the tunic on top of the fire. For a moment the flickering flames dimmed away, then as the skin kindled suddenly, a new blast of light shot out, and shadows leapt through the space round the blaze.

Sounds of confusion arose from the edge of the crowd, out where the wigwams rose up in the darkness. Voices were raised and a few of the watchers craned round to see what was the matter.

At the same time, the tent flap opened once more and a murmur passed round the circle. There in the glittering firelight stood Birch Tree, a small figure struggling to hold up a burden wrapped round in a blanket. He shouted, and Mang and Wabooz both ran forward to help him. They took hold of the blanket, which slipped down revealing the face of a girl whose skin gleamed as soft-white as the snow at her feet.

Confusion seized the crowd. A shout greeted the sight of the girl; at the same time Birch Tree made sharp frantic gestures. The two braves lifted their burden and bore it across to the dwelling nearby.

The Buck started to follow, but a roar just behind him and the sound of a well-known voice brought him up. He turned to see his father, angry and threatening, push out of the crowd and make his way to within a few paces of where Birch Tree stood.

Shigak turned from the sorcerer back to his son, then with his eyes on the gaping village crowd, he pointed to a raw, red wound, still ragged and bleeding, that ran the whole span of his left cheek.

'The Windigo attacked me, but I repulsed it by means of my magic!' the old man cried out. 'I demand, according to the law of the tribe, that the beast be destroyed!'

Horrified, the Buck looked for an answer to Birch Tree, but the shaman at that very moment swayed and fell heavily in the snow at the front of the tent. With a cry the Buck ran up to the spot where his uncle lay motionless, took hold of his shoulders and turned him. His eyes stared wide open; he seemed rigid with cold. Frantically, the Buck began rubbing the old man's cheeks and his fingertips.

Discoveries

She heard voices, faint echoes of sentences spoken so softly she might have imagined them, after listening with shut eyes for so long to the steady, muffled strokes of her own heartbeat.

Those voices had been murmuring in the background, it seemed, for a long time, when she finally noticed the odd thing about them; that while they sounded queerly enough in her consciousness, and no single word of her own tongue did she hear, she in fact understood what the speakers were saying.

The sensation was strange, so strange, that she did not at first even bother to follow the meanings exactly. She let the quaint airy sentences flow in her mind; and wriggled down even more snugly under the rabbitskin blanket. She wished to be covered, protected, for her memory had failed her; she felt vulnerable; she had not the slightest idea where she was. She could not remember her name.

When she opened her eyes, though, very little surprised her. Perhaps her mind had already noted all these things. She saw the inside ribbed roof of a domed space of skins – at the apex was sharp blaring sunlight, and the thin curling smoke of the pit-fire drifted up. For a while she just lay there and stared at the ribbed roof. She felt strange, but most comfortable: and every passing moment brought further delight and a clearer awareness of the place where she was.

The voices were some distance off, just outside the space where she lay. As she raised herself up, she could see, near the deep central fire-pit with its shimmering pot, clay vessels and cooking trays, set out on a cedar-bark mat. A few wooden ladles and spoons stuck out of a small birch-bark bag (a *mockuck*, her memory told her, she had no idea how), while on the far wall two pairs of snowshoes sat next to the piled up blankets and robes. There too were three larger *mockucks*, all patterned and bright, made to hold the dried food – meat, rice and fish. All this looked so tidy and neat, it made her feel happy, as if it had been laid out especially to give her the pleasure of waking up with domestic things of a simple but obvious grace there in view.

In the same spirit of foreknowledge and ease, she reached out and helped herself to a small brown cube from the tray set right next to her sleeping mat: it was a cake of maple sugar, which somehow she knew would be delicious and healing – and so it was.

For a long time the sweet juices ran in her throat. Then she lay back, closed her eyes, and with slow careful steps, going from point to known point in her mind, she tried to bring back from the vague shifting landscape of memory the knowledge of just who she was.

Mostly, what she remembered seemed far away, distant, but clear in its outlines. She was in motion, running across the fields in the sunshine, or slipping as if by magic, across the crust of the snow; she remembered a day on the river in summer – she was swimming, and her sense of her own naked body in the water had pleased her. And the faces, she remembered the faces – but this was more painful – for they came at her teasingly known and familiar, and she could not quite manage to give any one of them names. She remembered (it must be her family) lovely, stern faces, warming quickly to laughter – at festival, holiday: the surprises and raillery. There were other faces too, intense and mysterious, and a house came to mind, one where sunlight on bright days honeyed the wood into mellowness, where in winter the wind rattled the boards and made everything creak like a ship.

She drifted towards sleep. She heard, vaguely, a conversation from outside. A deep, strong young voice said: 'Will she have taken the food yet?' And the hoarse worn shrivelled-up voice of an old man answered: 'She has taken it now and will rest. When she wakes, you and I will begin. I too must rest now, so leave me.' Then someone pushed the skins of the entranceway back. She heard the muttered groan of an old man, a log flung down on the fire.

Warmth, sheer warmth wrapped her round. Then came darkness and dreams and in one of her dreams she lay all alone in the snow, under the wide-spreading branches of an ancient oak. She lay there all shivering, propped against some square rough-skinned object, a sack or a saddle. After a while she noticed that worms crawled all over the saddle, and she jumped back, at the same time pushing the object away with her hand. But when her hand struck the surface it crumbled, dissolved – no saddle but a large rotting haunch of foul meat. And she ran through the snow, screaming wildly.

She opened her eyes; she was safe in the rabbitskin blanket. A young man leaned over with bright, anxious gaze; he held her, cradling her easily with one arm, his fingers massaging her shoulders and spine. Carefully, he helped her lie back. She felt dazed yet relaxed, staring up at his handsome smooth face. His fine skin gleamed in the light, darker than hers: he had prominent cheekbones; his dark wavy hair swept back in two loose braids; a blanket of soft fur, joined at the neck like a chasuble, hung over his broad chest. Shaking off her surprise, she propped herself up on an elbow to recover advantage, and he smiled at her, showing his white, wolfish teeth.

'I am called the Buck,' the young man said slowly.

Ingrid understood perfectly, but for a moment she was powerless to reply. A curious feeling took hold of her; she thought that this meeting had happened before. The young man was no stranger; she knew him. Long ago she had wakened to find him; long ago he had told her his name. His lovely, clear humorous gaze, his strong coiling body, his rich smile, were familiar. And she felt at ease in the strangeness of not knowing why this should be.

She sat straight up, feeling weak and lightheaded; her dream came back to her and she shuddered a little. The light in the tent was rich gold; she knew it must be near evening.

178

Beyond the fire-pit she saw a small, white-haired figure, curled up on a mat, the face hidden from sight. The young man followed her glance, put a finger to his lips in half-mocking admonition, and said in a soft voice:

'Birch Tree is still sleeping. He is a *wabeno*, and saved you from the evil spirit of the Windigo. He is tired now; the power is nearly gone out of him. He is my uncle.'

The young man spoke rather carefully. It was as if he chose his words so as not to offend her. When he pronounced the name 'Windigo' she suddenly smelled, from the clay pot that sat in the fire pit, a simmering stew – but the smell of the meat turned her stomach. She choked back her nausea and said to the young man: 'Could I have more of the maple sugar?'

This request seemed to throw him into confusion. He gaped at her, cast a look back at the sleeping *wabeno*, reached across to the small tray, where little squares of the sugar were piled – then hesitated. She found this so comical that she laughed; and he laughed too, picked up a square, held it up to her mouth. She took it between her teeth, made a face; he shook with laughter, and trying not to make too much noise, laughed helplessly, out of control.

Someone pushed open the tent flap; a current of cold air made the fire flicker up. A girl came in, her heavy robe trailing over a *mockuck* on the other side of the fire. She cast a quick glance at the laughing pair (Ingrid felt the glance was for her) then bent down over the stew-pot, and with a large wooden spoon helped herself to the food.

The young man, finally suppressing his laughter, greeted the new arrival with a dignified air. She sat down on a mat on the other side of the rabbitskin.

'I am called Happy Tongue,' she said, with something of the shyness of the Buck. She had a round open face, with high cheekbones, and glossy dark hair that was pulled back in a single long braid. 'Are you the sister of the white creature, the Way-Michi-Gooshi?' she asked, addressing Ingrid, but at the same time half-turning to the Buck. Her voice had a high-pitched musical quality that made her name seem appropriate.

'She speaks but she does not remember,' the Buck explained quickly. 'The Windigo took some of her memory.'

Once again the word 'Windigo' caused the girl pain. She sat there in silence, deeply troubled. She felt so completely at home here; yet she knew she was not like these others. A word hung on the edge of her mind: the *Skraelings. Can these be Skraelings?* she asked herself. The Skraelings, the wild folk, yet something in me is like them, though my skin is much whiter than theirs. *Have I become one of the wild folk?*

A soft groan issued forth from the sleeper on the other side of the tent.

The Buck stood up with a quick, cat-like grace. He exchanged a glance with Happy Tongue, who seemed at that moment to have slipped into some gloomy reflection. Then he said to the women:

'We must wake the old man now. Only the grandfathers can help us. Shigak is angry, the clans are divided. It is time to take counsel.'

Happy Tongue bowed her head silently and stood up. She crossed to where the old man lay and bent over him. She crouched there, just watching; the old man turned over. The Buck went to the pit fire and drew off a few spoonfuls of hot stew in a bowl. He handed it to Happy Tongue, who sat there unmoving. After a while the old man opened his eyes. He groaned once and covered his face with his small, gnarled hands. Finally, he sat up.

From her place on the other side of the fire the girl watched him closely. He was the strangest looking person she had ever seen, a tiny old man with a face all wrinkled and yellow, a white sketch of a beard and moustache, and two piercing dark eyes that seemed to run over with light. He moved like a man in perpetual pain, whose every slight movement required a firm act of will. He did not at first turn his head, seemingly wrapped up in his own thoughts and in the act of awakening, but accepted the hot stew from Happy Tongue, taking a few small sips with half-closed eyes. The girl stood back and the Buck stooped down to help the shaman rise to his feet. Slowly, they came round the fire, and the old man settled in a place a few feet away from the foot of the rabbitskin blanket. He looked at the girl intently with his strange liquid eyes.

'So, you have come to us at last,' he said slowly, clearing his throat and speaking in a slight creaking voice. She looked at him shyly, wondering at his words. Once long ago, she remembered, someone had told her a story – one about strange elvish creatures, neither humans nor gods. She thought of them now, of their strange powers, as the old man leaned over and took her right hand in his hands, studying it as if he could read her thoughts from this contact.

'We have been expecting you for so long,' he continued. 'I have often thought I would die before you came to us. But the grandfathers willed it should not happen so. And now you are here.'

She waited. He let go of her hand; a fit of rough coughing took hold of him, shook his slight frame. He recovered from this, sat back regarding her. After a while she felt she could speak.

'I . . . I do not know why I am here, grandfather. I do not remember. I do not even understand how it is that I can speak to you . . .' she broke off, her voice catching sharply as her feelings welled up.

Ashamed, she held back her tears, swallowed hard, and continued. 'Please help me . . . please tell me how you knew I would come here.'

The shaman's face clouded. 'That I cannot tell yet, but do not be afraid, you will know in good time. I will help you and you will learn the truth. But first,' – here he turned to Happy Tongue, who stood on the other side of the fire – 'you will go and fetch the Way-Michi-Gooshi, the white creature, to us. Bring him with good speed but do not come into the dwelling. Wait until the Buck or I come out to you. And, daughter,' he added in a voice strung tight, 'do not speak to him by signs on the way.'

Happy Tongue listened impassively, then rose and slipped out of the tent. With an effort, the old man turned back, seemed to gather up strength. The Buck sat perfectly motionless, his eyes on the girl.

'You are one of the new people, my daughter,' the old man said, waving his hand, as if suggesting a land far away beyond where the village lay. 'Your language is not ours, nor your gods. But I too come from afar' – he waved his hand feebly as if to indicate a direction just opposite to the one he had previously indicated – 'and I have learned to speak with the tongue of the villages.' He paused for a minute, cleared his throat and went on. 'Still, it is different. Your speech is a gift of the spirits, conferred on your tongue for a short time; mine grows out of the root of my mouth.'

The girl could see how the Buck was pondering this distinction. But the old man continued. 'You have been chosen for great things, girl, and the spirits have tried you accordingly. It was my task to save you from evil. It has weakened me terribly; in any case I have not very long to live. But there are things I must explain to you, my daughter. Shigak, an elder of the village, of the Wolf clan, which is also my clan, Shigak, the father of the Buck, claims that while the evil spirit possessed you, you attacked and injured him. He claims he drove you away and captured the things that you carried, that you struck him and wounded him. Do not be afraid, daughter, but it must be said: Shigak wants you destroyed for the good of the village.'

The girl stared at him. She could understand nothing of this. She felt a vague terror, though the old man's calm reassured her. She knew nothing of Shigak. Was it possible that in some fit or in fever she had somehow attacked him? How *could* she be sure, now that her memory had failed her, when all her efforts to pull up the past delivered no more than a blank space full of shadows and ghosts? She bowed her head sadly; she could not bear to look into the shaman's bright, knowing eyes.

In the silence she felt her cold fingers caressed by a warm, gentle hand. The Buck had reached out to her, without saying a word. She shivered a little, refusing to look at him. But she knew Shigak's son did not think she was guilty.

After a few minutes the old man spoke to her again in the same low, quivering voice.

'In three days you must appear before the council; there your fate will be decided. But do not be afraid, because I will be able to help you. If the decision is favourable you will be given back your possessions, which are now in the dwelling of Shigak. Then I will tell you how I had news of your coming in the shape of the Windigo.'

The shaman watched the girl carefully as she took in his words. The Buck had removed his hand from hers and sat back rather stiffly. They seemed to be waiting for something; then someone scratched at the entrance flap. The two men exchanged glances. The Buck rose and carefully helped the old man to his feet. They slowly circled the fire, then the shaman turned to the girl with a final admonition.

'The person who is here may make your soul dizzy. Do not let it fly out of your body. You know the feeling, after the heated stones grow cold and you run from the tent and plunge right into the cold water. It makes you come to yourself, and your body starts singing. Take the plunge now, daughter, and learn how to sing once again.'

The old shaman might have been wearing a mask, so wrinkled and remote did his face seem, stretched close to a smile. He turned then and spoke a few words to the Buck which the girl could not hear. The young man pushed back the flap and stepped out of the tent. There was a moment's pause; no-one appeared. Then came a few booming phrases in a language that sounded strange to the girl's ears, but only for one fleeting moment – it was her native tongue.

A huge blond man squeezed in through the entrance, thrust up his body to full stature, and peered suspiciously into the dimness. The shaman stood motionless, shivering and drawing his heavy robes around his frail body.

The newcomer started to speak: the girl moved – he saw her, hesitated, then with a step and jump cleared the fire. 'Ingrid!' he cried out. His cry seemed to set the tent shaking.

The girl shrank away, pulling the rabbitskin blanket up over her shoulders. She saw the man, at arm's length, stop short;

the eagerness died in his face. It came back; he took hold of her shoulders, gazed deep in her eyes.

'Ingrid! It's Thorkel,' he said in a full, solemn voice. 'Are you all right? What have they done to you, girl? You know me, surely you know me!'

His hands dropped down to his sides. He twisted around, as if to question the shaman, who stood silent but watching with interest. The blond man's fur cloak fell back; the girl saw a flash of green jerkin.

Ingrid, she thought, my name is Ingrid. Something shifted in her mind – as in the spring of the year a whole sheet of ice might suddenly fall from a window. She saw a world blurred but familiar. That world had been there all along, so close she could have reached out to touch it – yet she had not known how; she had forgotten the gestures, the words. Now slowly the names were announced, and her lost past rose up, second by second more visible, like a peak rising out the mist, standing clear in the sunlight.

She remembered the village, *her* village, and the house with three chimneys. And the baffling but sharply etched faces, each now had a name, and with every name came a rush of connection – she was Ingrid, Ingrid of Wayland – what a wonderful thing!

'Thorkel!' she cried, and sprang from the blanket to embrace him. Thoughts of her family, her journey, were flooding into her mind; she felt the rough blond hair and beard of the man on her face. He was tousled and shaggy and at the same time more haggard than she remembered, but she did remember and could compare, and she was happy to see him. His honest blue eyes and rough awkward manner brought her back to herself – to the girl she had been. She felt stronger and at the same time more vulnerable.

'For a minute I didn't recognize you,' Thorkel said, holding her at arm's length. 'With your dark hair and wrapped in that blanket you look almost like a Skraeling!'

How could she explain? There was so much to tell and so much she could not possibly tell – not to Thorkel.

'I lost my memory,' she said. 'These people found me and

184

took care of me. Perhaps I had lost my senses. The grand-father' – she pointed to the shadowy immobile figure of the shaman – 'helped me, and brought me here. He wanted you to come because it would make me remember . . .'

Her voice drifted away. She was following her own path back through the woods, back to the cave she had shared with the man. She thought, too, of the woman, of her tender, deceitful embrace, and she shivered. The dark woods held a secret; Glimir had tricked her, but she could not remember how she had come here.

'These *people*, as you call them, are screaming devils,' Thorkel broke in on her thoughts. 'After you sent me away I intended to return to the village. Despite your brave talk, I wanted to come after you with some others, to help you. But I met a small band of these savages and, though I killed one of them, they took me. They carried me here through the woods, and by means of magic made me their thrall. I hoped to escape – but they have hidden my weapons and my skis. Now I see they have captured you in the same way – but do not despair – perhaps together we can escape. It is so good to see you, Ingrid.'

Once again they embraced. She held him at arm's length and looked at him. It was the same old Thorkel, a bit ragged and desperate looking, but with the familiar honest blue eyes. How little those eyes could see of her now, of her own secret heart! From his corner, the shaman still watched them, and she said quietly in Icelandic:

'We must not think of escape, Thorkel. These people are not savages as you imagine. It is hard to explain – I know you will think it black magic – but I understand them. I mean I understand their language, their feelings. I cannot think of them anymore as just Skraelings, mere savages.'

The man looked at her in astonishment. 'They have bewitched you for certain, Ingrid. You cannot believe what you are saying.'

'I do believe it. I am speaking the truth. Not only do I understand the Skraelings, but I have met others of our kind and have seen wonders such as we heard of when children, but never thought to witness. I intend to go north, if I can, as the Wanderer deemed I should. I have learned to question much about the gods. I am confused and full of doubts about what is the truth, but some things I know. By magic I have looked at our village. Great sadness is destined to come, but I must go on as I can. There is no question of trying to escape.'

Even as Ingrid spoke, and saw how Thorkel's expression grew darker and darker, with a part of her mind she was desperately struggling to find her way back through the thickets of memory. Minute by minute she recovered a part of herself, but one puzzling darkness remained. She had left Harg behind and lost her way in a storm: then come out of the woods to this village – all *that* she remembered – but why would the details not come?

'You say you have seen our village, Ingrid, that you can speak the Skraeling language. How can I accept such things? How can I understand this talk of the gods and the future?' Thorkel looked at her sadly. 'But now I remember that you were always different and strange, even as a child. This journey and the magic of the Skraelings have affected your mind. When we are on the trail and heading back for the village, you will recover yourself. We have only to keep up our spirits and wait for the spring; then we will have the chance we need to escape!'

Ingrid felt anger come suddenly. So Thorkel, this impulsive young oaf, would not believe her! She stood up and addressed words to Birch Tree in the tongue of the Skraelings.

'Grandfather, I have just remembered something. The man I stayed with in the valley beyond the woods, he mentioned your name. He told me that I should try to find you, that you would help me!'

The shaman circled the fire very slowly. Thorkel looked at him hopefully, as if he expected him to settle the raving girl back in the blankets. But to the young man's amazement, the shaman opened his mouth and spoke in a like tongue.

'That is the man who walks like a bear after sunset. A witch put a curse on him. I met him once at the edge of the valley; he begged me for magic to take off the curse, for he knows the tongue of the Skraelings, as you do. But I was powerless to help him.'

'The curse has been lifted – I did it!' Ingrid said proudly. Then remembering how she had taunted Harg and then left him, and seeing the shaman's sharp eye upon her she fell silent.

'My daughter, I know that you ate of the meat,' said the shaman. 'I know that you left him.'

Ashamed, she nonetheless threw back a question. 'How could you know that?'

'I cannot say now. In good time all may be told. I am glad you remember, that your mind is your own. Now you may speak alone to the Way-Michi-Gooshi. Perhaps you can calm his rough soul.'

The old man raised his voice in a hoarse, brief command. The Buck appeared at the tent flap, entered, and offered the shaman his arm for support. At the same time he cast a glance first at Ingrid and then at Thorkel, who still sat open-mouthed at the babble of talk between Ingrid and the Skraeling. Ingrid thought she detected in the Buck's look a gleam of pure jealousy. Thorkel, she saw, felt the look of the Skraeling, and clenched his fists at his sides.

Thorkel stood up to his full height, glaring after the men as they stepped through the entranceway. When he turned, Ingrid saw the confusion in his eyes. Gently, she laid hold of his cloak, drew him to her. She kissed him lightly on the cheek.

'We must talk, Thorkel, there are things that you must try to understand.'

They sat face to face on the blanket. The man shifted uneasily, looked away with a frown.

'I see the Skraelings have worked their magic on you, even as they have on me,' he said in a quiet voice. 'But with you they have gone further. You must remember, Ingrid, you are a Viking girl – you belong to your village. We must try together to turn our minds against this devilish magic. We must return to Wayland and rid it forever of the curse of the grey folk. Nothing else matters.'

'You know that I must go north at all costs – otherwise there is no hope for Wayland. Why do you talk of returning?'

Thorkel looked round the dwelling, leaned forward eagerly, and said in a whisper. 'I have a plan. I have worked it out carefully. If by some magic you have learned the Skraeling way of speech, so much the better.' He took a deep breath and went on. 'I must tell you, Ingrid – do not be angry with me, for it is not my fault – the Skraeling girl, the young girl who brought me here to the tent, she has fallen in love with me.'

He looked at her anxiously, awkwardly, blushing a little. But Ingrid only smiled and, relieved, he went on.

'I'm glad you understand. After all, she has never seen a Viking before! But I have thought of a plan. My skis, my axe and my sword the Skraelings have yet. They make no weapons of metal, they do not know skis, and to them our crafts are mysterious, magical. Unfortunately,' – and Thorkel blushed even deeper – 'I lost my chance to make use of this. When they captured me and brought me here, they put me in a contest against one of their own – I think he is one of their leaders, a strong, wiry devil – and he beat me.'

Ignoring Thorkel's crestfallen look, Ingrid asked, with a stir of excitement: 'Not the young man who was here in the tent and led the old man away?'

Thorkel threw back his shoulders. 'That whelp! I could crush him with one hand. Just let him try!' His fist came down hard on the blanket. He closed his eyes and drew a long breath as if enjoying the fight in his mind. But the feeling passed by, his gloomy expression returned; he continued: 'No, it was another one, a sturdier one, whom they call Mang. He beat me three times at wrestling, but I swear the girl had done magic on me. She is ignorant and thought I would come to harm. The third time, he put his hand on me I felt myself powerless and she led me away to her tent; she was happy, it seemed, for though I lost my weapons of iron, she found I had others.'

Ingrid could not help smiling. How simple this man was.

188

Harg floated into her mind and the Buck, too, for some reason. She blushed.

Thorkel, coming to the point, did not notice. 'Don't you see what is possible? These Skraelings are mere savages, but they have powerful magic. The girl loves me and would follow me. You are able to talk to the old man. Why not offer them gold, weapons, all that we have back in Wayland, to come with us, to help us escape? With those two to guide us we could get to the village, and then use magic against the grey folk. These devils know more about the spirits of the lakes than our priests know. Even our gods are not at home in this country. If the Skraeling magician will assist us we can not only escape but bring help to the village!'

He sat back as if exhausted by his own eager plans. Ingrid tried to conceal her astonishment. Was it possible Thorkel was so out of touch with reality? Did he not know that the grey folk could only be dealt with by those who had brought down the curse on themselves? She decided it was impossible to try to convince him; he would only assume she was under some spell of the Skraelings. But his words had given her an idea; perhaps there was a way of defeating the anger of Shigak, of winning back her possessions, of freeing poor Thorkel and herself! She must go north, she must find Harg and seek his forgiveness; and with his help win back the cup from Glimir. Perhaps there was a way!

'Well?' Thorkel hung waiting for her opinion of his plan.

'Are you sure your skis and weapons are still in the village?' Ingrid asked.

'Of course. That devil Mang has brought them out once or twice and they all stand around gaping. I think they are afraid to use the weapons, and the skis they have no sense to try properly. They have snowshoes better than ours, so they have no use for them. What crazy thing are you thinking now, Ingrid? I can see by your expression that you have a plan of your own.'

'I will tell you in a minute, Thorkel. And I am going to ask you to allow me to try it, and to help me. If it doesn't work, then perhaps we can talk about yours. Right now, since I know the Skraelings much better than you, I see problems in your plan. And I think – please don't be angry, Thorkel – that I have a better one.'

Thorkel was shaking his head in a token resistance, but Ingrid could see that, as usual, he would give in to her wish. She leaned across, and looked at him with wide open eyes, then said quietly:

'Still, there is one thing you have not mentioned, Thorkel, since we met, and it is a subject even more important than plans of escape, or your hopes for our village.'

Thorkel looked baffled. 'And what could that be, Ingrid?'

'You have not told me whether I am still as beautiful as you used to think I was.'

There was a silence. Thorkel stared at her. Ingrid sat there enjoying his confusion. At last he became aware of her sly smile.

'Of course you are not serious.'

'Of course not. But, come, tell me anyway.'

Thorkel sat silent for what seemed a long time, then, having struggled to find the exact words he told her:

'You are more beautiful than ever, Ingrid. I thought so after the first few minutes with you. But there is something changed in you, too – I saw it right away, but how can I name it? Perhaps it is that you look like a woman now, not a girl, or perhaps some kind of trust has gone out of your eyes.'

The Village

Happy Tongue came to the tent early the next morning to help Ingrid dress.

'Birch Tree wants you to walk in the village,' she explained, standing back, in her shy way, behind the glowing fire. 'I was to take you but the Buck offered to go with you instead. He will be here shortly.'

Soon Ingrid had climbed out of the rabbitskin blanket and, after walking about a little to get the feel of the earth again, she put on the things Happy Tongue had carried with her – and carefully aired by the fire – moccasins and leggings and a tunic with baggy cape sleeves. Finally, the Skraeling girl slipped a delicate bone-necklace around Ingrid's neck and helped her on with a thick robe that soon began to warm her.

Happy Tongue stood back and looked her over; she seemed relieved when Ingrid stopped shivering and a faint red glow came into her cheeks. She started to turn, as if to circle the fire, but Ingrid caught her sleeve gently. 'Can we not talk for a minute?' she asked, stepping around Happy Tongue and squaring her back against the entranceway.

Ingrid wanted to ask the Skraeling girl about Thorkel and the Buck but she hardly knew how to begin; she knew she must go carefully, for fear of offending her in some way.

'The Buck will be here soon,' the Skraeling girl said, as if reassuring herself, or voicing a wish.

'You have power over my clan brother, the one you call the Way-Michi-Gooshi,' Ingrid ventured. 'Do you not fear his wrath, then? He is a person with powerful allies – spirits who might help him. How is it that he walks unbound in the village?'

Ingrid was sure she detected a slight blush on the other girl's dark cheeks at the mention of Thorkel.

'It is Birch Tree's magic,' the girl said, as if she were stating the obvious. 'It was powerful enough to save you from the Windigo and it is powerful enough to hold the Way-Michi-Gooshi here.'

'But the magic, what is it?' Ingrid asked. 'How does it work?'

Happy Tongue looked at her strangely. After a pause she said: 'Only the chosen ones know the magic, the members of the Midewiwin, or those who might join. I know nothing about it.'

'Is it forbidden to women?'

Again, Happy Tongue gave some thought to her answer. 'The powers are not forbidden, but women may not join the Midewiwin.' She started to move around Ingrid, to get to the entranceway, but stopped. 'Is it true,' she asked suddenly, the words spilling out quickly, high pitched and fluttering. 'Is it true, as Wabooz says, that you come from a tribe where the women cut off the men's penises, where everyone has weapons of iron and no one smokes?'

Ingrid was taken aback, but thought quickly and answered: 'The first thing you say is not true. Surely you know it, since my clan brother shares your blanket? You could not be in love with him if it were so. And you are in love with him – is it not true?'

Happy Tongue bowed her head.

'Then do not worry, Happy Tongue,' Ingrid assured her, 'for my clan brother is not my lover. And if Birch Tree and the elders allow us to go away from the village, the Way-Michi-Gooshi would choose to take you with him, if it was your wish.'

The Skraeling girl's round dark eyes narrowed, then widened. 'And the Buck would come with us too, since he is in love with you?'

Ingrid shivered a little in her loose, heavy robes. She started to ask Happy Tongue how she knew this, but stopped. It was obvious – and she too was drawn to the Buck – who could say why these things happened? Perhaps there was magic behind them. She ignored her fast-beating heart and continued:

'The long snowshoes – the sticks-that-walk-in-the-snow that you took from the Way-Michi-Gooshi – where are they?'

Ingrid heard soft, padded footsteps behind her. There was a scratch and a tug at the tent flap. Happy Tongue's expression changed; she seemed to catch herself out of a dream.

'Where are they? Tell me quickly?' Ingrid insisted. Happy Tongue slipped around her, murmured the single word 'Mang' and pulled back the tent flap, just as someone outside did the same. The Buck's smiling face appeared at the entranceway.

'Are you ready to walk with me?' he asked Ingrid politely.

192

Minutes later, she stood somewhat uncertainly in the glare of the day. It had been dark in the tent and she squinted at the white remote sunlight, which seemed to have little power to warm up the chill air. Around her the domed roofs of the wigwams plumed smoke. Dogs barked and the voices of children were everywhere. With a shy look the Buck took firm hold of her sleeve.

'I must take you to Birch Tree, but first you must walk through the village. The people will see you and know that the Windigo spirit is vanquished. Only then can the council deal well with you.'

Happy Tongue had drifted away between the tents. The main village track lay before them. Despite the cold, there was activity everywhere. Some women were busy removing a large skin from a rough wooden frame. A group of children were sliding down a snowbank, howling with laughter as they flopped on and off the thin birch-bark square that conveyed them. Hunched into furs, a small party of men on snowshoes moved towards the woods. A woman struggled along, hauling a sledge piled high with fat bundles. At last they came to an open space, where the white frozen river curved under the trees. A long, high frame like a tunnel of ribs rose above them, and two men were busy piling skins all around at the base. They looked up, their eyes fixed on Ingrid, then they shouted a greeting to the Buck. He waved his hand in an answer, and led the girl round the half-finished structure, and back towards the clustering tents of the village.

'It is the council tent,' he explained. 'They are building it now, so that my father can be heard before the elders.'

Ingrid wondered at the Buck's matter-of-fact manner. 'Does it not make trouble for you, that your father should hate me and condemn me?' she asked.

The Buck did not look at her, but answered softly. 'It is my father's right to defend his conduct and manhood. I think he hid in the woods and fears that someone should say so. He is jealous of my uncle and does not wish him to have all the credit. Besides,' he added after a short pause, 'I am a man

193

too, and can have my own opinion. An evil spirit possessed you and now it is gone. I think you are very beautiful.'

'Are you not afraid that I will cut off your penis?' Ingrid could not resist saying it.

He turned to her sharply, his eyes full of fire. 'That is a joke made by Wabooz. I see you know that, because you are smiling. You are making fun of me, then!'

He stopped in his tracks and stood face to face with the girl. Even drawn up to his full height he was a few inches shorter than she was, but seeing his handsome features set in a look that was serious, and passionate, she softened, reached out and touched him gently with one mittened hand.

Their rapport was broken by children, who ran up in a troop from the tents, danced around them and chanted, 'Windigo! Windigo! Who is the Windigo?'

The Buck started to shoo them, but Ingrid prevented him. 'It is because of you,' he explained. 'They are playing the Windigo game.'

The children stopped chanting and stood round in a little loose group. A tall boy held out a bundle of sticks. One by one the children drew lots, and one child, a plump little girl, was set apart from the rest. In disgust she flung her stick away then marched herself glumly to where a dead pine, with brown sickly needles, made a bush in the snow. The girl slipped in among the branches and waited. As the others came near, the girl stuck her head out through the branches and screamed. She twisted her features, and contorted her body, shrieking and raising her small arms as if she were wholly demented. Then she sprang out with a terrible shriek and took hold of the first child in line. A wild wrestling followed, as the Windigo girl sought to drag her victim away through the branches.

Ingrid looked on, at first gladly, then, little by little, anxiety seized her, a sharp surge of nausea welled up. By the time the Buck drew her away she was trembling, hardly able to walk.

'I'm sorry,' Ingrid said in answer to his questioning look. 'It was something I thought of when the children were singing –

that little girl's face . . . Was I really so terrible? Perhaps your father is right. Perhaps I did harm him.'

The Buck shook his head. 'You did nothing. It was the spirit that went into your body. Someone did magic against you, but Birch Tree has more powerful magic; he has saved you from your enemy. You must not be afraid.'

He led her away, between the dwellings, towards the main village track. Despite his brave words, Ingrid struggled hard to force her thoughts back to her time in the woods. She remembered Harg on a cliff looking down at her, a terrible hunger, then darkness. Nothing else. Glimir had tricked her, she knew that, but she too was at fault. Whatever the Buck said, she knew that.

Nonetheless as they walked, she stole once or twice a sideways glance at the young brave. He was simple and handsome, and he worshipped her – it was evident every time that their eyes met. His devotion made her feel helpless, and generous, unlike Thorkel's, which had no real power to affect her. If only she dared . . .

'Do not brood!' the Buck said, stopping all of a sudden to chide her with a friendly command. She narrowed her eyes, made a face, then started away very fast. They came out on the main track, moving so quickly they stirred up a dog which jumped from its place by a wigwam and barked at them furiously.

Two men came forward on snowshoes and greeted the Buck. One, very slender and tall, with a nose slightly crooked, and sharp gazing eyes; the other, his blunt features anxious, who moved with a lithe grace, though his body was sturdy and powerful.

'Birch Tree is awaiting the white girl,' the tall man said, looking at Ingrid with eyes that were wary and mocking. 'He rests in his tent, but already the village is amazed at his magic. To turn such a terrible creature into a being so harmless – he has great power indeed!'

Something in the man's tone and manner made Ingrid dislike him. She burst out – 'Who are you, whose tongue is no sweeter than his face, who are you to call me a terrible

195

creature, or even a harmless one! You might be mistaken for a young man, yet you crawl along on your snowshoes like an ancient. I will attend the shaman in good time, never fear!'

The Buck pressed her arm like a vice. 'Pay no attention to the girl's speech, Wabooz, she has been upset by the children. We are on our way to Birch Tree at this moment.'

'Her words are as bold as the Way-Michi-Gooshi's,' said the other man, addressing the Buck, 'but she is as skinny as a heron, and I think not half so graceful. As a woman she should learn to hold her tongue when men speak.'

'I think you must be mad,' Ingrid shot back, ignoring the Buck's frantic gesture, 'I am glad you have not used the sticks-that-walk-in-the-snow for firewood. Please take good care of them for me, for with them I shall teach the braves of the village a lesson they will never forget!'

She spoke the last few words over one shoulder, for the Buck, shocked at her demeanour, was dragging her off bodily. She heard a low buzzing of laughter behind her, a gruff ring of male scorn that she remembered from childhood. It enraged her.

'So these are the fools who fear for their manhood!' she cried out, as the Buck shoved her along past a small group of gaping women, whose whispers began as she moved on. Some boys playing snowsticks nearby stopped to watch.

'You will ruin everything if you go on,' the Buck pleaded. 'You have already offended Mang and Wabooz; now the whole village will think you are possessed again by the Windigo spirit. You must keep your mouth shut and walk proudly!'

Ingrid was struck by the man's desperate tone. With an effort she swallowed her rage and walked quietly beside him, though in her mind her plans had grown firm. She would show the village what a Viking girl could do! She would make them forget that they had seen her at the mercy of terror and darkness!

They circled the dwelling where Happy Tongue had dressed her a short time before. For the first time Ingrid became aware that it was placed almost on the edge of the encampment, and that just opposite it stood another isolated wigwam. She looked across at this second dwelling and there, in the entranceway, she saw Thorkel.

He was standing perfectly still, unnaturally still, as if frozen in place. Yet his glance measured out, as it seemed, every step Ingrid took with the Buck towards the edge of the forest beyond. And something deep in that glance, the sense of a bound rage and hatred, made Ingrid catch her breath, pause, and glance sideways. The Buck, she knew, must not see; controlling herself, she walked on and, at the same time, in a matter-of-fact voice asked a question:

'I want to know about Birch Tree,' she said quietly. 'Why is he so different from the others of the village? He does not look like one of the people at all. He wears a beard like the Vikings, though a skimpy one; his eyes are not round like yours, but elongated, almost the same shape as elm leaves.'

The Buck pursed his lips in a kind of relief, as if she was starting to come to her senses at last.

'Birch Tree is the strangest man I have heard of,' he said, just as another wigwam came into sight, at the edge of the woods, some short distance away. He spoke as they moved towards it steadily. 'He is not really the brother of my father – far from it. As a baby, they say, he was found at the foot of an oak tree, strapped to a cradle board, staring out at the world with his odd eyes and singing quietly to himself. They would have killed him then, but Nialig, the old woman who found him, warned against it – perhaps he was sent by the spirits, she told them, or by the ancient people who came over the sea, as a gift to the tribe, as protector. So he was adopted into the Wolf clan and quite soon showed the powers of a shaman. Later his fame spread to all of the villages. He has great knowledge and was the teacher of Tindat, my brother. Birch Tree told me that I will die young, even as Tindat did. But I am content.'

By the time the Buck had given this answer they had moved far past the tent where she had seen Thorkel. She was struck by the strange words that he spoke. She looked at him sadly, but could think of no reassurance, for she believed in destiny, even as he did.

They walked on in silence until they had reached the small wigwam that sat in the shelter of a grove of tall pines. A thin wisp of smoke from the dwelling climbed up through the trees and disappeared in the flat gloomy sky. The Buck stepped forward and scratched at the tent flap, and the voice of the shaman bade Ingrid come in. The young man pulled back the flap and the girl stepped into the tent.

The figure of the shaman seemed to rise through the smoke like a wraith. Except for one pile of furs and a few pairs of snowshoes the tent seemed quite empty. She could hear the steps of the Buck as he walked away through the snow.

'Daughter, I see you are tired,' the old man said in his quivering voice, 'though the fire I put back in your eyes still burns brightly.' His own eyes were warm, unrelenting. She nodded. Yes, the walk through the village had tired her; her body had not yet recovered from its nameless ordeal, yet a kind of strength was still in her.

The old man breathed deeply, half-closed his eyes, and went on. 'You are a chosen one, for the mark of the serpent is on you. You have fought for the soul of the man who walks like a bear; the Windigo spirit has been unable to destroy you. It was intended that you should come here, the spirit that is in you wished it so.'

Ingrid shook her head slowly, not in protest, but in helplessness before his words. 'But what should I do, grandfather? I have thought of a plan, but how do I know it will work to the good? There is a terrible burden upon me, and I do not even remember how the Windigo took me. The village children play games and make fun of me. I'm frightened, but I want to remember!'

The old man raised his right hand to stop her. 'Patience. There are things that are hard to remember; they are hidden for a purpose. When the time comes, they will be made clear to you. Now you must recover your strength, for there are ordeals to be faced, and you will need it. I have brought you here to reveal something to you, a simple story. I cannot tell the whole of it now, but neither can I wait, for there is great danger to come, and I am not sure what time remains to me. When the story is complete you will understand many things: why you have come here, and how it is that you know the speech of the village. Listen!'

Ingrid folded her hands in her lap and waited, and the shaman took up his story.

'Long ago, when the Buck's father, Shigak (that man who wishes to kill you), was much younger he fell in love with a girl. He was handsome then, and a skilful hunter, and the girl was the most beautiful child in the village. Her long hair was raven dark and her eyes were like those of the young deer, her skin was as smooth as a mink fur – it was a joy to see how she moved. So when the time came, Shigak took her to wife, and she was his favourite. At last she swelled up and gave birth to a man-child and he was called Tindat. She had another son later and he is the one whom we know as the Buck.'

The old man paused, cleared his throat and continued.

'Tindat was a child on whom the good spirits smiled. He was as beautiful as his mother, but manly and strong. He could speak and sing chants while he still crawled. When he first walked he killed with his bare hands Genay-Big, the fierce serpent. He became a great hunter, and his dreams were most powerful of all; very soon he was accepted into the council of the Midewiwin. He had great medicine and he taught the whole village new things. From him we learned for the first time the speech of certain animals, how to walk in the forest when the night-sun is away and never get lost: how to command the great birds of the storm. Everyone in the village loved him, for he was kind and full of humour and could understand their thoughts in an instant and help them. No one loved him better than his younger brother, the Buck, who followed him about, and to whom he taught many skills of the hunter; and to me Tindat came now and then when the spirits laid puzzling dreams on him. I gave him what advice I could. Then one day he told me he was destined to die young, and the Buck, too, and I knew it was true.

'The next winter – it was only two winters ago now – a

199

sickness came to the village brought on by an evil spirit invoked by some enemy. It was a fever and quaking that took hold of its victim and would not let go. The shaking tents and the sweat baths were useless, all magic failed, the village seemed doomed. But Tindat determined to save us and he fasted and prayed. Afterwards he walked out in the woods near the village, barefoot in snow, and called to the evil spirit to meet him. Three times he walked around the village calling to the spirit to come out and fight him. At last, the spirit came, in the shape of a black bear, and pounced upon Tindat. They wrestled together, the night-sun gave way to the day-sun, and still the two fought. At last the power of Tindat prevailed and the evil spirit fled. The village was saved, but Tindat was mortally stricken. He died, his hands and feet and his body all covered with wounds, but his eyes clear and shining. Then among the people there was thanksgiving and mourning together.'

For a moment the old man was silent; Ingrid heard only the crackling of the flames in the fire-pit between them.

'After we laid the young man to rest, prosperity returned to the village. We moved to this valley, where the hunting is good, the rice blooms not far away, the maple sap runs in the spring. The skill and courage of Mang have meant much to us; the Buck is our joy; nor have the good spirits failed me – but there is more to my story.'

The shaman raised his right hand for silence – Ingrid had started to ask why the Buck, too, had to die. She caught at her words, fell back, and listened.

'Shigak's favourite, the mother of Tindat and the Buck, had fallen ill during the time that the village was threatened. She too was saved by the action of her eldest son, but after his death she lost spirit. Shigak noticed how every day she grew colder, more and more remote, how the cold settled down in her eyes. One day, as he touched her, he felt the ice forming under her skin. He was sure she was becoming a Windigo, and was determined to kill her. The Buck was away with Mang on a war party. With Shigak's permission, I went to her for I felt I could help her. But the coldness took hold more

200

and more; it seemed that an evil spirit had power in her heart. At last, as she lay there in the grip of the cold, she told me her secret. She told me the reason that Tindat was destined to die, and why the coldness had seized her. Shigak, it seems, was not the father of Tindat. She had deceived him and given herself in secret to another man, but by stealth she hid this from Shigak. The Buck indeed was his son; but Tindat was the son of another. This was why the evil spirit had come to the village.

'I knew then that my magic was powerless to help her, for some powerful spirit hated her for her beauty. I went away and left her in the dwelling of Shigak. That night, in terror of the Windigo, he led her away to the woods, took his long knife and killed her. The body was buried in darkness. A few knew the truth and they were sworn to silence. Not many have mentioned her name since that time. The Buck still believes his mother died of the fever. I think Shigak hates you because he thinks that the spirit of the woman he killed inhabits your body. He believes you have come to destroy him. I know he is wrong but I cannot tell him, for another has sworn me to silence . . .'

For some time Ingrid sat without speaking. She could almost hear her own heart beating fast in her body. So she was bound up with these people, as if in fact she were one of them, as if in fact some spirit of the village possessed her! She shuddered, thinking of the Windigo games of the children – what *had* she become? What would Birch Tree demand of her? He sat there now with bowed head, his eyes closed; he had seemingly finished his story. Yet more was to come, the most important of all; why must she wait to know what would become of her?

'Grandfather,' she said, and paused, while he opened his eyes, raised his head, and looked at her steadily, silently. 'Grandfather, are not men cruel who would kill their wives when the Windigo spirit possesses them? For men, too, become Windigos, they too become cold, do they not? I am in darkness now, grandfather, help me!'

For a long time the shaman said nothing. He reached back

in his blanket and drew out a long stick-pipe, lit it with a splinter from the fire and sat there smoking, not looking at Ingrid. She watched him for what seemed endless stretched minutes. Finally, he looked up, his strange liquid eyes on her.

'It is not cruelty to kill a human possessed by the Windigo,' he told her, 'but a mercy. But better still is to drive the evil spirit out of the body. Whether man or woman it matters not. Better to drive the evil spirit out of the body!' His voice cracked a little in its hoarseness.

'As I have done for you, child,' he added softly, and put down his pipe.

Ingrid bent forward. She felt close to the old man now, close for the first time not only because of what he had told her but because of a secret they shared and he could not name or describe. And it was he who had saved her, with mysterious arts. So she had courage to lean forward and whisper:

'But what is to become of me, grandfather? Am I to go on like this in darkness and ignorance, not knowing how I can help myself or my people?'

The old man shook his head slowly. 'It is not good to know too much about the future. But I can tell you this: you are destined for great things, you too have the gifts of a shaman; you have great power to love. And you will love many times before you grow old. But a mystery always remains; some things are held in the hands of the spirits. It is like the story I told you, some missing pieces rise up to haunt us.'

As he spoke his tiny figure seemed to gather there in the gloom. 'I told you about Shigak and Shigak's wife and the beautiful children. I told you about the death of Tindat, and how he was not the son of Shigak, but I did not tell you who his father was. That man's name was Nangabi. He is dead now, Tindat's father – but the man had one other child, a son, by his own favourite wife. That son is the half-brother of Tindat, though only I know it. His name is Amik, and he too is famous in the village, for he is a boaster, a coward and a scoundrel. That is how closely related good and evil may be, my daughter. Now I have told you all I can tell you. You must go and let an old man have rest.'

Ingrid started to get up, and at that moment heard footsteps outside. As if in response to some secret summons the Buck had come back for her. She rose to her feet and bowed to the shaman, then pulled at the flap and stepped out of the tent. The Buck stood there waiting, a few feet away, his face bright with wonder and welcome. Ingrid took a single step, blinking her eyes in the dazzling grey light. She said nothing, but on an impulse leaned forward, close to the young man, and brushed his soft cheek with her cheek.

The Council

Ingrid stood stiffly alert; the dwelling's ribbed skins stretched around her. The fire roared; a monotonous drumming continued; from time to time a low chanting sounded. She closed her eyes in order to break contact with the sharp stares of the men who sat in judgement on her: the tribal council.

Then she remembered that the Buck was sitting only a few feet away, just behind her, and the thought made her open her eyes. She did not dare crane round: sullen faces carved from dark wood gaped at her, faces with eyes like holes burnt in dark wood. These faces seemed quite empty of feeling, but the green incised lines at the temples, the white lines etched on the jutting cheekbones, gave them an air of hallucinatory power.

Because she could put names to a few of the faces she felt better, though the nightmarish sense still persisted, that her judges were carved wooden idols stirring slowly to life. She had to remind herself that the scrawny bent figure on the other side of the fire (whose skewering gaze never left her) was Shigak, the Buck's father, her accuser. Beside him was Mang, all shoulders and discipline, wearing his daubs with an air that seemed to hover between pride and contempt. Out of the corner of her eye she could see the man called Wabooz, inwardly sneering, his lips curled, his head tilted back, as if her actual presence was distasteful to him.

No-one had told Ingrid to stand at attention, unmoving, to hold herself stiffly, to face her accuser. But that was the way they had placed her, when the men had filed in from the village. Their procession had streamed into the lodge, leaving the women and children standing there in the crisp, clear morning, whispering or complaining, watching the prisoner take her place in the circle of judges, as if she had done this many times before, or rehearsed it.

Now the long pipe was brought out, each man in turn holding it there to admire, cradling the feathered, streamered stem in his hands before drawing a mouthful. As it passed around the circle, a chant soared up once again, and Ingrid recognized Birch Tree's hoarse, broken song, at the far right. The drumming and singing continued. At the open end of the tent a child cried out briefly, then was silent. Time passed, then all at once the drumming ceased, the chanting voices were hushed. No-one actually turned, but heads angled towards Shigak, who stared at the fire, then slowly climbed to his feet.

He waited a while, as if gathering thought, then raised his head but did not meet Ingrid's bold glance. When he began, his voice came softly at first and the silence around it expanded, as everyone went rigid in stillness, straining to pinpoint each word.

Shigak spoke first of the gods, of the spirits, of the past of the tribe. There seemed in his speech no obvious goal, yet Ingrid detected a motion, a direction, as did all the others, for there was not the least sign of impatience, no stir or strained air that suggested they wished he would get to the point. Finally, when the old man had spoken for some time, he looked Ingrid full in the face. His dark eyes glittered narrowly, and the final words of his speech cut through the silence.

'Once, not many months ago,' he said, 'Tindat, my son, saved the village. He wrestled with and chased off the evil

204

spirit which would have destroyed us. He gave his life for the people. We have good hunting, and rice stocks and sugar because of that. Then it was my fate, and the fate of my son, whom we know as the Buck, to deal with a new evil sent by some enemy. It was Birch Tree's magic that tamed and made human the Windigo. But the Buck and I were the first to give warning. All was foretold by the dreams of a few, but only I and the Buck saw the Windigo approaching. We know the worst of it, the horrible things that we saw. I know that the Windigo came at me, though I fooled it by magic and it ate the flesh of a rabbit, not mine. But it struck at me and would have killed me. And it will kill all of us, if we do not strike first, if we let ourselves be fooled by this creature standing before us in the semblance of a girl!'

When he had finished speaking, Shigak remained standing. Ingrid drew herself up; she fought against the panic that came upon her at his words. He was asking for her death! But why couldn't they see it, why didn't they rise up and condemn him? Couldn't they see him for what he was, a dried-out old carrion, a beast of prey! Long ago his soul had been emptied of all feeling; now he was taking revenge upon her because a woman had hurt him!

The crowd at the entrance stirred and whispered. Shigak sat down, his face composed tightly, his hand trembling a little as he reached for the council pipe.

Everyone's attention had shifted, however, and Ingrid sensed that someone had stood up behind her. Very slowly, she half-turned.

It was the Buck, who was helping Birch Tree to his feet.

At the sight of the brave, all dressed up and painted, Ingrid's pulse quickened. The young man looked up; they exchanged a brief glance: an energy seemed to possess her. The Buck sat back, lowered his eyes. Birch Tree brushed at a white wisp of beard. He stood there unsteadily, the sharp, painted lines seemed to swallow his face – the withered, worn face of an idol.

A young boy emerged from the darkness, and led Ingrid a few steps away from the fire. Her back was now turned to the entrance; the two rows of men she had almost fully in sight. As the boy piled wood on the fire and the flames leapt, faces shone luridly then vanished in the gloom at the rear.

Ingrid kept waiting for Birch Tree to speak, but Birch Tree did not speak; he stood there, head sharply inclined, peering out at the assembly until at last with an almost imperceptible nod he set in motion a series of quite diverse actions.

A number of speakers arose, each one in his turn, and offered brief judgements. At the same time, a soft chanting sounded from the darkness at the rear of the tent. And Ingrid could feel how the crowd at the entrance fell back; there was shuffling, and a few murmured voices, a stir of cold air that brushed feathers and cloaks like an invisible hand.

First the man they called the Owl climbed to his feet, a very round fat man, with thick lips and coldly inquisitive eyes. He suggested that the prisoner be kept in the village and guarded until the Moon of Flowers; only then could they be sure that Birch Tree's magic had been successful in driving away the Windigo.

The elder called Ningig stood up, with a face all wrinkled and fallen, and said the girl should be sent away at once and, under penalty of death, never be allowed to return.

Then it was the turn of the oldest man of all, whose name she knew was Saginay. He could barely get to his feet and, when at last he did, he spoke in a high-pitched incomprehensible squeak. All listened politely, while, through painful, choked silences, the old man delivered a few meaningless phrases.

And others unknown to Ingrid rose and argued, each in his own way, that Shigak must have his vengeance.

At last the redoubtable Mang spoke. He stood there, with arms folded, sturdy and broad as an oak, the firelight glinting on his forehead, the high-cut roach lock parting his skull like a red-dyed plume, a long feather thrust out behind. After a few preliminary courtesies, he said bluntly:

'This girl is dividing the men of the village. It is a thing unheard of by our fathers, and there is only one solution. She must be sent away. I value Shigak's honour, and I respect

206

Birch Tree's magic. But the welfare of the village demands that there be no division on her account. I propose that she be delivered, under guard, to the south, that she be taken to the Great South Lake and left there so that she may rejoin her people. As for the danger that she might return and do harm to the village, there is an answer. We must hold the Way-Michi-Gooshi for sacrifice to ensure that she does not return. We must keep possession of whatever is hers and his in order to have some power to do magic against them. I ask whether this solution is acceptable to all parties.'

As Mang sat down, there was a stir among the listeners, Ingrid looked hard at the Buck but the young man evaded her glance. *This is the price he has paid to go with me*, she thought. Then she remembered what Thorkel had told her the day before.

On the previous evening, at sunset, Happy Tongue had appeared unexpectedly and led her through the camp, close to the tent where the Viking lay in confinement. The village girl had stood by, nervously waiting, while Thorkel came out, clear eyed but trembling, and embraced Ingrid. His manner was desperate: 'They're going to kill me!' he told her. '*She* overheard them. The one they call the Buck has agreed,' he added with a snarl of contempt. 'He wants you for himself and will do anything to save you!' At that moment Wabooz had appeared at the edge of the pines, near the place where Ingrid had spoken with Birch Tree. Happy Tongue had made a few signs before Thorkel; he blinked as if stunned; she shoved him back in the tent. Quickly, without looking around, she led Ingrid away from the spot. Refusing all conversation, Happy Tongue had disappeared almost at once. That night, as she lay in her tent, Ingrid had thought of Thorkel's words. The Buck had said nothing and she did not believe that the boy would deceive her. Ingrid had her own plan and if it worked Thorkel would be saved – this she told herself over and over before drifting into sleep. Thorkel's wild fears would soon be quieted . . . Now as she stood there before her judges, attempting to make the Buck look at her, she knew that Thorkel had spoken something of the truth. The Buck must have wanted to save her; and to strike a compromise to protect the honour of his father, he had been willing to sacrifice Thorkel. The Viking's hatred for the village was clear to them all. But how could Birch Tree have agreed to this?

Ingrid turned her attention to the old shaman. He stood just as before, all wavering and frail in the half-light, his head bowed, his arms crossed as if he were trying to hold himself up by means of his own stiff embrace. Slowly, the resonant chanting which had continued during the speeches faded away. The old man cleared his throat, unfolded his arms, and started to speak.

It was a long speech, delivered in that hoarse, croaking voice, so familiar to Ingrid that she almost imagined she had known it from childhood. The old shaman spoke slowly and deliberately. Like Shigak, he began by mentioning the gods and spirits of the tribe. Then he spoke of the past, of his own life and what he had learned of the world; of the village, of Tindat, the time of troubles and the young man's sacrifice.

It was clearly intended that this should arouse thoughts in Shigak, but Ingrid could see not a flicker of movement on the face of her accuser. (Nor could she catch the eye of the Buck, who sat there with bowed head as if turned into stone.) As Birch Tree worked along towards the end of his speech his voice gathered strength.

'We are all under the power of the grandfathers,' he reminded them solemnly. 'Many ideas are proposed, but what is the will of the ancient ones who determine? No one seems able to say.'

He let this thought hang in the air; then continued: 'What is the story we can tell of Shigak and the Windigo? That Shigak met the Windigo and gave warning to the village. That magic and cunning enabled Shigak to escape with his life. But why would the beast have attacked him and gone away hungry? This is not the way of the Windigo. Surely the ravenous beast would have finished its meal? Unless Shigak by means of his arts got away. And perhaps in the fight or the flight scratched himself on his weapon, or on the branch of a tree . . .'

Birch Tree paused and gazed, not at Shigak, but sideways down at the Buck, who sat with bent head. Ingrid followed his glance; the young man looked up at her quickly, then turned away. Shigak sat grimly, arms folded.

'We must return to the will of the grandfathers,' Birch Tree continued. He paused and drew breath, his head tilted back, his eyes half-closed. 'I have had dreams, which cannot be told yet. I warned of the Windigo's coming; I drove the evil spirit away. The guest brings more than herself to this council; she comes at the will of the grandfathers, to change all our lives here, to enter our stories. We must listen and then judge the best course of action.'

There was a silence in which Ingrid became aware of the slow shifting of bodies around her; she watched as the Buck stood to help the old shaman sit down. Birch Tree folded his arms and stared into the fire. The Buck did not look at her. Yet she knew it was her turn to speak.

Ingrid hesitated, then stepped forward, and began in a strong voice: 'I am a Viking girl,' she said, 'born in the Viking lands south of here, but closer to Skraeling lands than other Viking settlements. My home is called Wayland.' After all she had been through, the naïve cast of her simple declaration almost made her smile, but she caught herself up and continued.

'I have come a long way, because my own village suffers a terrible trial. I am on a journey to bring help if I can.'

She looked round the impassive faces, sensing the Buck's glance but not answering it.

'By magic I was tricked and transformed into – what you call the Windigo. I remember little or nothing of that. It was an enemy that did it, but I was at fault too. I did not want to hurt anyone; not any one of you. I remember only getting lost in the woods, then waking in a dwelling with my memory blanked out. It was thanks to Birch Tree and the man from my village, the one you call the Way-Michi-Gooshi, that I remembered anything at all. I still do not know how I am able to speak in your tongue.'

She paused, sensing their interest, and continued:

'I do not remember harming Shigak or anyone else. I myself, the real person I am – the person I want to be – intends harm to no-one.' (She looked directly at Shigak, whose glance refused to meet hers). 'I want to leave the village with the Way-Michi-Gooshi. I want his freedom as well as my own, though we may well go in different directions.' (She noticed how the Buck raised his head and looked at her with interest.) 'I think Shigak's accusation is mistaken, and I intend to prove it. Among my people, a woman may have power to rule if she takes it. I think your warriors are no match for a Viking girl!'

A murmur of protest, like a half-suppressed cry, rolled around her. She raised her hand for silence, obtained it, and continued:

'I intend to prove that I am innocent by the following means. I now challenge the swiftest young brave of the camp to a race in the snow. Three times around the village, and if I win I am to go free, and so must the Way-Michi-Gooshi, together with all our possessions. If I lose, I will forfeit all that I have, including my life, if Shigak is so cruel as to demand it! The braves will use snowshoes, while I will walk on the sticks you took from the Way-Michi-Gooshi. Now why do you all sit there like carved men? Are none of you skilful enough to take up the challenge?'

The assembly fell altogether silent; no-one moved or responded, and she wondered for a few fleeting seconds if perhaps without knowing it she had lost the knack of their speech. Then several things happened at once: Shigak's thin lips trembled, and he nodded, as if in fateful assent; Mang swayed visibly as if ready to spring up. Wabooz sneered and laughed; the Buck stared at Ingrid with round eyes of disbelief.

Birch Tree gathered himself as if he would rise, and the Buck moved to help him. At the same moment Wabooz stood up and said in a quivering, clear voice:

'I accept this girl's challenge.'

Another brave rose in the shadows at the rear of the tent. A voice said, 'I also.' Ingrid peered into the darkness and recognized Amik, the half-brother of Tindat.

Birch Tree, swaying a little, stood there and held up his hand. Then he saw that the Buck wished to speak, and he nodded, and waited with half-closed eyes, as if in sad patience, while the young man declared himself.

'I will compete against this girl and even give her advantage, and still beat her. No girl is faster than I am at such a race!'

Ingrid smiled and bowed her head. She was thinking how he had wanted to sacrifice Thorkel to make her his own! Well she would show them all, these conceited young braves! With Thorkel's skis on her feet she would leave them behind in the cold.

Remembering Birch Tree's strange words about fate, about the grandfathers, she looked to the old man for some sign that what she had done was the right thing. He stood, leaning down on the sturdy arm of the Buck, and his glance swept round the council. A strange piercing sharpness had come into his gaze, but he bestowed not a glance on Ingrid. He waited and, when no further challengers rose to declare themselves, he raised his right hand. A shiver of expectation seemed to run through the group; then, as if at a silent command all climbed to their feet, the grim Shigak clearly visible among them.

The meeting was over.

I have taken my fate in my own hands, Ingrid thought. Uncertain, she moved a few steps in the direction of Birch Tree. The path was clear, no one tried to stop her. Then she saw that the shaman had bowed his head and, as she approached, she heard him murmur, to himself, or perhaps to one not visibly present, 'So be it.'

The Contest

The day of the race began sunny, a dazzling blue-white at the smoke hole. Happy Tongue came with Ingrid's clothes, her Wayland clothes, warmed at the fire and familiar – tunic and jerkin, a well-worn light buckskin, her leggings and mittens and boots, and a cap for the cold. For a moment she hesitated, then decided to wear the bone necklace that Happy Tongue had given her. Breakfast was rice cakes, fruits and nuts, and a mouthful of stew. She ate slowly, while the Skraeling girl watched her.

At last she took up her skis, checked them carefully, adjusted the thongs, tried them on, then removed them. They were Thorkel's of course, but luckily he was only a few inches taller than she was. And the skis she knew from the past. When they were younger and had raced in the village Thorkel had bragged of how those skis had been made by his grandfather, Rig, from the choicest aged birch, edged with hickory. Once, when she was only fourteen, she had actually outraced Thorkel, so that she had been allowed to try them. That was the beginning of his admiration for her.

She cut a small plug of wax with her knife, heated it at the fire, then rubbed it well into the skis, scraping away the excess with the knife blade. She slipped a few spare pieces of thong into her pockets, bundled the skis and the poles in her arms and followed Happy Tongue from the tent.

Outside, she put the skis on at once and they moved away at last to the starting place. Looking around she wondered if something was wrong, for no-one in the village seemed to pay her much attention. Children looked up as she passed, but men strolled by without so much as a glance and women greeted Happy Tongue without taking notice of Ingrid. It was just their way, Ingrid told herself, not the Viking way – to be aware without seeming to; of course they knew of the contest.

Ingrid stood in a little clearing in the centre of the village, waiting for something to happen. A dog barked nearby and two boys, hauling a great stack of wood, shouted orders at each other. A woman picked up a skin from where it lay stiff on the snow and set it up over a frame. Then a few men came out of a dwelling, saw Ingrid and stopped. They waited, impassive, unsmiling, their fur robes pulled round them. Others appeared from between the near wigwams, Wabooz among them, looking anxious and solemn, but sleek in light leggings and jacket. He had discarded his moosehide boots, and wore moccasins set in his tapering snowshoes.

Laughter made Ingrid turn round. There was Amik the boaster, dancing and swaying, swinging his scalp lock with a crazy toss of his head, thrusting out his buttocks obscenely, and humming a tune.

Anger took hold of the girl. 'I see there are two women in this race,' she said loudly, swinging her ski pole up like a lance. Amik stopped dead; a sharp silence followed, then came a burst of quick laughter from the men. The young brave's smile curdled; he shuffled away without replying.

Happy Tongue touched Ingrid lightly on the shoulder. Mang and the Buck were approaching from the north end of the village, with the Owl, Ningig and a few of the other members of the council. They moved forward on snowshoes, without conversation. As they came near, others slipped out from the rows of the tents. Soon there were twenty or thirty men of the camp milling round in the space. Ingrid could see how the women stayed back, pretending to work round the dwellings, while casting quick glances at the group. Young boys came and stood respectfully back on the edge of the crowd.

When the Buck stopped a few feet away, Ingrid tried to capture his glance, to read what she could of his feelings, but he kept his eyes well averted, and seemed to have endless

213

words to exchange with Wabooz. They were both very nervous, she thought, while Amik seemed eager and aggressive.

Mang stepped out from the group that surrounded him and without raising his voice gave instructions. Three young men stirred to motion, hurried off and returned bringing axes and pegs, which they hammered well into the hard ground, three side by side and one a good fifty yards back of the others. So the Buck plans to make good his boast, Ingrid thought to herself, and she started to protest, but stopped herself, and instead tried a short practice run on the skis. She must let him do as he wished, she decided: it would serve him right if he lost by the distance he had yielded. She only wished they would start soon, for she found her arms and legs growing tight with the tension; the concentration she had on the walk from the dwelling was gone. Nor would the Buck look at her; he averted his eyes and talked to Mang, as Happy Tongue slipped past them, and stood on the edge of the circle.

Clouds billowed up in the clear morning sky. A drumming began on the edge of the crowd; there was a parting of bodies. Shigak walked solemnly out, wrapped round with a chasuble vest, and resplendent with feathers and ornaments. His expression was masked by the bold strokes of red paint on his cheeks; in one outstretched bare hand he held a wriggling, live rabbit. He stopped at the foremost three peg marks, addressed a few words to Mang, then raised the rabbit aloft. The drumming went on in the background; the crowd quieted suddenly.

Shigak drew a long knife from his belt and with a quick practiced gesture, cut the throat of the rabbit. Blood spattered down on the snow. He held the rabbit up by its ears, shaking more blood on the snow. At the same time he murmured a low, singsong chant; it was barely audible over the drumbeats.

When the blood had stopped gushing, Shigak cleaned off his knife on the snow, and slipped it back in his belt. He walked straight to where Ingrid stood and held up the rabbit. He let the blood run over the fingers of his right hand, then with that hand he reached out and touched Ingrid's left cheek. Seeing her flinch, he merely grunted, twisting his lips in

214

contempt, then turned swiftly away, and walked back through the crowd, which closed in behind him, concealing him.

The drums stopped abruptly. Ingrid stood trembling; her legs had gone rubbery. She felt the warm smell of blood on her cheek. She had been afraid that Shigak would kill her – she, afraid of that old man! She looked up and at last caught the eye of the Buck; he gazed at her with something like pity. Around her, a clamour arose; she could see the men holding up their fingers, in animated conversation, haggling and betting. They were wagering on the outcome of the race!

Mang took his place a few feet in front of the peg-marks. Amik and Wabooz strode up and stood facing the leader. Dazed, Ingrid hung by and watched them. Mang, it seemed, was addressing her; still, she did not move – all strength seemed to have left her. Then a hand touched her shoulder, she turned; it was the Buck. At a slow, steady gait, he moved back towards the rear peg, a long space behind the others.

Ingrid struggled over to where Amik and Wabooz stood waiting. She could see that the men were enjoying her discomfort. Amik played with his scalp lock, laughing softly and crazily under his breath; Wabooz lounged sullenly by. All at once she saw their bodies go tense. She looked up at Mang who jumped back waving his arms. The two braves sprang away; there was a roar from the crowd. The race had begun.

Ingrid was caught in her tracks. Mang gestured emphatically, then with a shrug of his shoulders, stood back. She twisted around, saw the Buck coming steadily on. Twenty strides distant he waved and shouted 'Start! Start!' but she stood there. He slid up beside her, threw her a withering look, and passed on.

Bodies surged around Ingrid. A few started after the racers. Three or four men flattened the snow with their thick moose-hide boots and their snowshoes. The spectators craned forward, blocking her path, ignoring her almost as if she were invisible. In a minute the race would be lost, Ingrid knew, and she burst from her trance and pushed forward.

They would not get out of the way – big lumbering men and sprawling children, a crowd of them falling in on the path

215

just before her, blocking her start like a herd of irresolute cattle. Ingrid could not contain herself; she shrieked at the top of her lungs. The Skraelings gazed at her with startled, wide eyes. She shrieked again and poled forward, slicing roughly past their heels. The racers were already tiny dark blots on the snow.

She picked up her stride, breaking out of the throng, gaining speed. She was angry, determined, her body began to respond. She could see the Buck looking round as he swept past the last group of wigwams then turned south, to the riverbed. Under her skis now, a good surface, a path worked up by the snowshoes, and Ingrid kicked forward in big striding motions, letting go with the full careless swing of her body.

She drove forward cleanly in the sharp windless air; the last wigwams stood up beside her. A small group of women and children appeared as if from nowhere; a boy jeered at her, flung out a handful of snow. Ingrid glanced back; the crowd in the village snaked along after her, brawling, excited, uncertain – a few seemed determined to catch her, though second by second, she pulled farther away. Up at the first turn, under a scrollwork of bare maple branches, the Buck leaned and drove; he had passed the council tent; nonetheless, she was gaining. And there, to the left, were the others, moving almost as one, some distance ahead of the Buck; with luck she could catch them in minutes.

She coasted into the space just south of the village, where the riverbed curved from the trees and the maple grove rose on a wide, low embankment. The council tent stood before her, a beehive of cut bark.

Here, something odd happened. She suddenly found herself struggling, as if physically bound, each thrust of her body requiring an effort that sapped more and more of her strength. She felt drugged, weighed down. One stride followed another at a leaden slow pace. Her eyes stung; she blinked away tears.

Endless minutes later, she had forced her way forward, as far as the back of the council house. She had walked here before without fear, though they told her that this was the spot where she first came in Windigo shape. Yet now every step had the slowness of nightmare. She swallowed again and again, tried to break the hard lump in her throat; then, through the blur of her tears she caught sight of an object hung up on a house pole: a white rabbit snared by the neck, with two red gaping holes at the eyesockets.

Ingrid bent over and retched; the lump in her throat would not dissolve. Her eyes stung so terribly she could barely open them on the harsh sunlight. She had to press forward, that she knew. She felt she was turning to stone.

Each movement now was an agony, an effort of will. She could hardly raise her arms; the ski-poles dragged behind her. She shuffled along, step by step. She knew that a trap had been set, that a spell had been cast, but she would not give up, she refused to collapse in the snow as her body desired.

Step by step; then at last it was easier. A little strength served her; the air seemed to lighten around her. She pushed a few paces forward, blinked hard and opened her eyes. Now she could see without pain; raising her arms she poled forward. A few yards more – it was better. A weight seemed to fall from her shoulders; strength flowed back into her legs. Stride by stride she came back to herself, back to her pace, holding speed.

On the lip of the bank, she glanced over her shoulder. The council house stood up in its starkness behind her. Shouting and chanting, a motley crowd swarmed down from the village, pushed out past the dwellings. Tracks stretched away towards the swamp; her rivals had gained while she struggled and were no longer in sight. Once again the race was slipping away from her grasp. But Shigak's terrible magic had not yet destroyed all her hope.

She poled up to speed on the bank, coursing away towards the swamp, riding close to the tracks of the others, alert for traps laid to snare her. Dead stumps and bare maples rose out of a thicket of stiff frozen scrub. Once again she felt her strength come, fixed her eyes on the trail: it ran round the outlying dwellings and on to the big stand of pines at the north, then back towards the river. Not yet in sight of the others, not yet, not yet, not yet . . .

217

Then at last the Buck hove in view, turning where Birch Tree's tent marked the flank of the camp, a moving shape seen and then gone. Ingrid's heart leapt – there was hope! Out of the corner of her eye she could see figures drift from the dwellings, women and children and a few braves – spectators who had chosen to stay in the camp and look out at the racers as they circled the settlement.

A small red flag at the edge of the pines marked the turning; she had reached the halfway point, even further, and was still in the race. She swept past Birch Tree's small tent – no sign of life there. She fought disappointment, bowed her head slightly, plunged forward.

Now came the loop towards the river. She broke into the open, ignoring the hostile faces, closing her ears to the taunts of lounging spectators, for there, straight before her, barely fifty yards distant, she saw the Buck running even with Amik and Wabooz.

The sight made Ingrid cry out for joy. She propelled herself forward with new energy; the rhythmical hiss of the skis made pure music. Here the surface was beautiful, the purchase quite perfect, and each stride seemed to carry her further and faster. She might have been riding her canoe, soaring across whitewater rapids, or dashing along on her skates where the Ice River ran beside Wayland. Her spirits lifted, she felt herself sail on the snow.

Second by second, the figures before her loomed larger. Three hunched slow-bobbing forms that seemed, as Ingrid drove forward, to hover and hesitate. The track led along by the riverbank, on the left the wigwams all gleaming in a dazzle of sunlight and smoke. And children frolicking down from the camp, tumbling and sliding and pointing with triumph to the men in the lead.

But Ingrid came on with big strides, leaning forward, in an effortless flow, almost bodiless, so that second by second, she closed the space between herself and the men. As she approached, they loomed larger, they filled up her whole sight.

There was the Buck, a few feet ahead of lean Wabooz, and

Amik, turning with a look of sheer panic, bending his head down and straining away at the heels of the other two. Ingrid saw she could pass on the left, and keep the men between her and the riverbed. The space straight ahead was smooth, flat and clear, and she angled a little, without losing ground, then forward she swept in an effort that brought her nearly even with Amik.

The Skraeling drove on in a slow pumping motion; the sway of his body betrayed his exhaustion, and Ingrid could hear how he talked to himself, unrelentingly forcing his stride, pushing the snowshoes with sharp little grunts, while his arms flailed.

Ingrid leaned forward, and with a few powerful thrusts, passed the struggling Amik, then in the same flowing motion she sailed on past Wabooz, who glanced at her darkly, but moved still with freshness and spring, his big snowshoes no match for her skis though. Another few yards, she came up on the Buck: he turned, tossed his head and bent into his stride, but she passed him as if he were hauling dead weights, ahead for the first time. Her confidence soared, she felt free, in control.

It was wonderful, having the clear track before her. Sunlight flashed on the snow. Her body relaxed, glowing warm in her clothes – she could go on forever, she thought, they would never catch her. Up ahead she could see the village folk waiting where the wigwams gave way to the clearing. They gazed down with round, amazed eyes – she had silenced their triumph and jeering. And there was the last of the dwellings, with bare maples rising behind the dome of the council tent.

Then she remembered the spell and the rabbit and her heart sank.

She was coming up fast on the place. In minutes she would enter the zone where the air clogged her soul, where the rabbit gazed down with its dead stare; the others would catch her and pass her. She would have to do it all over, find the strength to come from behind: did she have it?

Desperately, she tried to think of a way round the place. But she could not risk an evasion which might mean a judgement against her – to win she must go the route as laid out, or Shigak would question her victory. She cast a quick look behind her; the others had dropped back, diminished – the whole race lay in her power – but she could not bear the thought of the terror that waited ahead.

She passed the last dwelling, poling forward. There was nothing to do but go on. She had come through once, she could do so again. The council house loomed up. Now within seconds the dark power might take hold of her soul. The voices and cries of the spectators, far behind her, seemed to belong to a world that was drifting away. Within seconds, the intimate air would grow thick and enclose her.

Then she saw just ahead a black tufted object, about the size of a hat. It shivered and moved in the snow. She gasped, swerved and started to fall. The snow sprayed around her. She caught herself – her right hand grazed the crust, one pole flipped back against a ski, while her left hand shot up, clinging fiercely to the other pole.

She came to a stop no worse for the near-fall, crouching there on her skis, with the poles skewed around her. The black object, lying a few feet beyond the council house, burst apart: two crows, huddling together, cried sharply and sprang up. On dark beating wings, they made off for the depths of the swamp.

Then Ingrid saw the red-brown smear on the snow, what was left of the rabbit, a carcass picked over by the crows. Quickly, she pushed to her feet, shook herself off, glanced behind at the others. Two others, coming on slowly, but steadily.

Ingrid closed her eyes and breathed her quiet thanks to Odin, master of the dark birds, keeper of carrion, for sending the crows to destroy the power of Shigak's foul spell.

Then she sprang away past the house with a cry, feeling a new surge of power. Still she was first in the race, for Amik, who had disappeared, had already given up!

On the bank near the village the snow had melted off slightly. Once again, to the left, idle spectators hung in small groups – she could hear the ring of their voices as she poled

220

towards the swamp. Stealing a look, she saw that the Buck had not yet come out on the other side of the council house.

She was tired now, feeling the strain of the race, but she knew she had power in reserve. This was the quietest stretch of the track. The village was far to the left, the swamp just beside her. She slowed her pace slightly; there was still a long way to go.

Once again she swung round towards Birch Tree's lone dwelling, set there in the north of the camp, by the edge of the pine woods. The old man was nowhere in sight but a small group of children had appeared from the village, and stood on either side of the tent, watching the girl's steady run with fixed, frozen glances.

Something about their stiff manner made Ingrid alert. She noticed they were ranged in a row, with an even space (about twice the length of her skis) between each child. She wondered if Birch Tree had lined them up there for a purpose. Then, before she could think further, she was passing nearly in front of them.

The children moved suddenly. They wielded long curved notched sticks, at first holding them at arm's length, and then launching them along the snow. These were snowsticks, seemingly harmless playthings; the children had concealed them in the very trenches which now guided the slender missiles, with deadly sure aim, straight at Ingrid's feet!

She was too shocked to react. A missile slid towards her, striking her right ski and glancing off. She staggered and braked, pulled up short on the smooth track. Another came whizzing and struck her hard on the boot. She cried out in pain and fell sprawling.

Ingrid screamed at the children but already they were running, scampering away across the snow towards the village, not daring to look at her, but shouting, alarmed, at each other, as if they too were shocked at this sudden attack.

She lay sprawled on the snow and stared after them. The cold, seeping up, touched her fingertips. She peered back and saw Wabooz and the Buck in the distance, plodding on by the swamp. Slowly, she pushed herself up, stepping carefully, gingerly, testing her right foot, putting her full weight on the ski.

Her ankle was sore, as if bruised, but she felt no real pain, not even when she pushed sharply forward, bumping along on the last of the snake tracks. But anger poisoned her thoughts.

She cruised at a slow pace, past the red marker, coming out in the good snow. Far on her left the wigwams stood up in their simple tranquillity, clean shapes connected to the blue sky by innocent smoke trails.

It was all a deceit, Ingrid thought bitterly, the camp had been poisoned by Shigak, even the children set against her. For the first time she realized the full power of the Skraelings' hatred. To win she would have to defeat their conniving, their secret deceits; fair play was meaningless to them. They were caught up with the cruel trade of Loki the trickster.

Another glance back reassured her. Despite the attack, she was still far ahead of the Buck and Wabooz. They had gained on her, true, but her ankle did not seem to be swelling; the blow of the stick had not struck at the bone. It was luck, or fate, as she knew, but she bent slightly forward, set her jaw grimly and vowed she would beat them.

She coasted on down to the riverbed, keeping a sharp eye on the village, on the trail ahead of her. Near the dwellings the same motley bunches of spectators lounged, some quite ignoring her, others alert, pointing down, and many in furious discussion – about what she could hardly guess. This time she did not see any children and she wondered if shame or a secret command kept them back.

Short minutes later she made her approach to the council house. A spasm of tension, but her pace did not slacken; she sailed past the spot where the rabbit lay mauled and dismembered, coasted away up the bank, traversing until she could turn and make straight for the swamp-run. Only then did she steal a look back: she was now on the last lap round the village, and she wanted to pace herself; at the same time she must win by a margin that would put them to shame.

222

She looked back – only Wabooz pursued her. There was no sign at all of the Buck.

Impossible! Yet when she looked again Wabooz alone struggled on, a tall figure bent but not beaten, yet hopelessly out of the race. The bare white snow glittered around him. No-one else was in sight.

After all his proud boasting, the Buck had retired from the race. Ingrid shook her head sadly, drove forward. She thought perhaps he was injured; perhaps he had been tripped by the half-hidden snowsnakes. It did not seem likely; yet what could account for his absence? Ingrid pressed on, uncertain and nervous; she kept glancing around at the scrub in the deep swamp, at the clustering wigwams. Soon among the dark pines the red marker would flash into view; she would make her turn for the river and the race would be all but over!

Once again, Birch Tree's wigwam hove into sight. There was the flag set clear in the pines, at the end of a long channelled trail. No children this time, but Ingrid could make out the rough trampled place where their snowsnakes had struck her down. She bent low and poled hard ahead.

When she looked up the figure was there on the path, but far distant. Her heart skipped a beat – someone had come out of nowhere and was plunging along on the track by the river: a man so far ahead she might not be able to catch him. It was a joke, another trick of old Shigak. The man hunched down low, sliding along on his snowshoes, a dark hulking form whom she suddenly, angrily recognized. It was Amik!

Ingrid laughed grimly. She was tired now and the laughter came easily. So the scoundrel thought he could win the race by a short-cut!

Of course the whole village would know he had dropped out on the second lap round and retired from the race. Did he think he could fool everyone by pretending to beat her with so brazen a trick? Ingrid shook her head in amazement. She saw that already he had a good start towards the council house. Taking care, she picked up her pace towards the river.

Then a new thought assailed her, one that drove off amusement and set a nagging doubt in her mind. Perhaps it was only by her lights that Amik was cheating! Who could say what the elders would decide when the brave came in first at the finish? Already she knew that the ways of the tribe were not her ways. Perhaps this was Shigak's best trick: to make her look foolish, defeat her!

All through the race, with the skill of long years on the trail, Ingrid had paced herself well. She looked back and saw that Wabooz could not possibly catch her. There was only small risk, then, in sprinting away after Amik. Despite his great lead, she might just be able to catch him. She would make sure there was no chance at all of his stealing her victory.

With a shout, she drove herself forward, bent down and kicked out her legs, her body extended, her glance fixed ahead. She ate up the trail with her legs and her eyes. She did not look up, but held her head steady. She knew that on the far left a crowd had collected by the village. The voices came down to her, tempted her glance but she sailed on, not looking for Amik, but keeping the council house fixed in her mind.

She had never skied faster, for the surface was good, and the trail, broken in, seemed to lead her along as if tuned to her muscles, her stride. She might have been roaring down a nice slope near Wayland – indeed, had the earth here not tilted just now to send her winging on to her goal? Had the great mother not taken pity on this daughter of earth in her need?

Ingrid raced past the council house, up the slope near the maples and telemarked down towards the village, the final short run of the race. When she looked up and took note, Amik was approaching the first of the wigwams. Then she knew that she had him, for it seemed to her he stood still in her path.

If a powerful wind from the forest had lent speed to her motion, she could not have raced down the last stretch any faster. Her body seemed weightless yet was aimed like some arrow, launched by a desperate, skilled hand. She was hardly aware of the crowd that closed in on all sides, of the faces lined up by the wigwams, of the hoarse cries of triumph and pain that rose in the clear air around her. At the back of her mind, one small fear: that the path to the goal would be blocked, that she would crash at the end, spoil her finish.

When she was nearly upon him, only ten yards from the markers, Amik turned around. The look on his face she would never forget: the sheer hangdog terror of the male who, despite all conniving, is beaten. As she passed him, a figure stepped out of the crowd. In a faint fleeting second she saw the Buck spring at his rival and fling him down viciously in the black, trampled snow.

Then Ingrid went soaring and sailing to victory. She passed the three markers, gave a small whoop of joy, and braked herself down as she turned. The faces flew by, slowing down as she spun to a final true stop where the dwellings stood up in the sunlight.

When at last she took in the faces around her, she saw they were smiling – smiling broadly or shyly – but almost all smiling. The women of the village, lined up to welcome her.

Passion

Ingrid stood among the women. Exhausted, she raised one ski-pole aloft in a gesture of triumph. A few of them reached out to touch her, others smiled from unreachable distances, or bent aside whispering, as if already inventing together the story they would tell of her victory – her defeat of their own monstrous thoughts of her.

Just beyond the thick swirl of bodies Ingrid caught sight of Happy Tongue. The girl stood framed by a tent pole, motionless, watching her with eyes narrowed slightly in the blaze of the sunlight. In the heart of the village a drum started beating; the shouts of the men rose like a wild song; Happy Tongue came forward. She cut through the crowd straight to Ingrid, took hold of her sleeve and drew her away. A path opened up for the two women. They entered an enclave where the backs of four dwellings made a small private space.

'Take off your skis,' Happy Tongue told her. 'There is a sweat-bath ready for you. I will show you where.'

Ingrid bent down at once to her bindings. She touched her right ankle and winced – it had swollen more than she realized. Ignoring the pain she had gone on, determined to beat Amik. In the distance she could hear the men's voices, a confusion of shouting and chanting. She looked up enquiringly at Happy Tongue.

'There is argument,' the girl said quietly, 'but you have won the race. Amik and Shigak tried to provoke the judgement of the gods, but your power was greater than theirs. You have your freedom, of that there is no doubt.'

Ingrid stood up, leaning hard on her poles and her skis. She felt suddenly spent and longed for the ease of the sauna. Happy Tongue's close, wary glance never left her.

'When will the judgement be made, then?' Ingrid asked.

'After the sweat-bath you may rest and wait for Birch Tree to come to you. Shigak will send your possessions; there is nothing else he can do.

'For the time being, though, I will take charge of your skis,' the Skraeling girl added. 'I must return to the Way-Michi-Gooshi – he is already alarmed about what has happened.'

Ingrid felt stunned, as if in the excitement, the exhaustion of victory, she had forgotten something very important.

'Perhaps I should go with you,' she said. 'Perhaps it would be easier if I were to explain . . .'

'That is not necessary,' Happy Tongue interrupted. 'I told him that . . .' She hesitated and, taking hold of the skis, started to bundle them to her, but Ingrid, unthinking, held tight and swayed up against the girl, who drew back with a shivering movement.

'The Buck came out of the race to stop Amik,' Happy Tongue continued in a faint voice. 'No-one could have beaten you, but Wee-sa-kay-jac, the trickster, might have stolen your victory. I explained it to the Way-Michi-Gooshi as it was taking place, but his anger came up and he threatened me. He will not take me away with him now, for he thinks you have saved only yourself, that you intend to go north with the Buck.'

Both women let go of the skis and the poles at the same time. They clattered a little as they fell on the snow. Happy Tongue bent down and retrieved them.

'You must not go to him now,' she lowered her voice to a whisper. 'I still have power; I will make him see the truth. You must go to Birch Tree and prepare for your journey.'

With that she hoisted the skis on her shoulders and led the way through a maze of near dwellings.

Ingrid followed numbly behind, her thoughts in a turmoil. That Thorkel should think she had sacrificed him! That she might go north with the Buck! She must talk to Thorkel at once and set his mind at ease. He was jealous – with no cause whatever – for she had promised him nothing. They had been friends and companions and rivals since first they had met, but they had never been lovers. The very thought made her smile. She had known for a long time that Thorkel had ideas of marrying her, and that he was capable of real jealousy, of a feverish anger. But why this excessive hatred and fear of the Skraelings? Had Happy Tongue's potions and spells at last poisoned his mind? She must talk to him soon, calm his fears, and send him back to the village, with or without the Skraeling girl.

As for the Buck, she found herself imagining going north with him. Slowly, as a series of pictures, the idea took shape in her mind. She saw them on snowshoes in the heart of the woods; or watching the north lights together. Or at night in a small tent, all naked under the furs. She felt how his strong arms might enfold her, how she would welcome his clear smile, or his eager but uncertain glance when she talked of her past or her home . . .

The drumming and chanting continued but grew fainter as the two women moved slowly north through the village; from time to time a dog barked or a child cried, and a few women were seen at the customary tasks – beating out the skins, tending children, hauling sleds piled with burdens.

At last they came to a small tent at the north-east end of the camp; from there Ingrid could see the tracks they had cut in the snow during the race. It was not far away from Birch Tree's own dwelling by the pine woods, and there was no-one about. Happy Tongue stood and received Ingrid's clothes, warming them up outside in the glow of the fire as the Viking girl stripped in the tent. Using a stick, Ingrid pulled in the red hot stones, sprinkled water over them and crouched at her ease in the billowing warm clouds.

When she had been in the tent for some time her muscles began to relax; a new sense of ease came upon her. She was in good health despite all her trials; she had proved her skill and strength, even endured a temporary madness that wrenched her away from all she had known. Now at last she could begin to think of the difficult journey that lay before her. It was time to decide how best she could go after Glimir and Harg, recover the cup, and fulfil the hopes of her village. As she stood up and stretched in the steam, she felt a kind of well-being flow through her body, an energy that she knew would carry her forward.

She decided not to risk the chill that might come with a run in the snow, but signalled to Happy Tongue to bring over her clothes.

Ingrid dressed quickly and gratefully in the familiar jerkin and shirt, pulled on the buckskins, the hat and the leggings and boots and stepped out of the dim, cloudy space of the tent and into the luminous air of the very early afternoon.

Happy Tongue, it seemed, had vanished, but someone stood there to greet her: the Buck, looking fresh-faced and radiantly handsome in a thick gray fur coat that wrapped round his body like a fine, glossy skin.

For a moment they stood awkwardly facing each other, but Ingrid felt pleasure and smiled, and the young man responded by half-closing his eyes as if he too were enjoying the quiet understanding that seemed at that instant to flow between them.

'You have won the race,' the Buck said. 'It is the first time for a woman. They will make songs about you now.'

'You helped me – Amik would have stolen the victory. I'm so happy to be free.'

The Buck looked at her intently, as if he were trying to grasp the feelings behind her words.

'The Midewiwin is meeting even at this moment,' he explained. 'Birch Tree will recover the rest of your belongings and destroy the evil magic that clings to them. Happy Tongue will bring everything to you later. Now there is a feast in the village. If you will wait with me in Birch Tree's tent . . .'

A sudden shyness seemed to swallow up the invitation; the Buck turned away, not meeting Ingrid's quick gaze. A furious drumming rose up from the camp, voices chanted and shrill songs hung in the clear air.

The two walked together across the snow to the tent by the edge of the pine woods. As they came near, a young boy emerged and scampered away towards the village.

'The fire will be warm for us,' the Buck said in a quiet voice and touched her arm lightly. He pulled back the tent flap and beckoned her in. Ingrid felt excited, and a little afraid. She crawled into the warm space by the big fire and sprawled on the skins that were spread there.

She did not look at the Buck, but lay back with closed eyes, feeling all his quick motions: how he fastened up the entrance, stood for a minute above her, then crouched by the fire, stiff and silent.

'You are so beautiful,' she heard him say in a quiet voice. Pure desire made each breath, each slight gesture of thought like a tension between them. The snap of the wood in the fire was like the crackling of the very air. The daylight, unreal and remote now, shone through the tent walls around them.

She shivered and crouched by the fire. She looked in his eyes.

He slipped off his fur robe and stood bare to the waist, his body all golden with light. The flickering fire on his shoulders and chest she felt in herself like a soft flow.

His dark eyes were mirrors – they reflected her beauty. She had power to consume his desire. Yet she hesitated.

Then he reached out and took hold of the sleeve of her jacket. The garment slipped down. He gently undressed her, each movement dream-like and slow. His eyes never left her. She felt herself slowly revealed, but assured by the tenderness, awe, in his glance.

Then he too undressed; she gazed at his smooth thighs, his brown nipples hard as healed wounds. She could not hold back, but licked at his chest with her tongue. She felt him pressed hard against her; she was slowly enfolded, his strong arms came round, his warm beating body against her. She closed her eyes, shuddering, sighing. She heard his soft pleadings and moans as he kissed her repeatedly.

Gently, they wrestled down into the blankets. His strength, his flexed supple body, made her helpless. She lay back, her arms and legs weak with desire. Yet he too seemed powerless; he lay moaning beside her, stroking her breasts and her thighs, yet going no further, as if whirling round in a blind storm. Shivering, trembling, she reached out and took hold of his phallus; then he with a new surge of energy plunged it inside her; she was crammed with him, bursting. With a hoarse, strangled cry, he came nearly at once.

For a long time they lay there together. Then slid apart under the blankets. She wanted him now more than ever. She stroked him all over. He kissed her thighs and her armpits, stretched his tongue between her legs till she welled up with pleasure. He urged her around, his hands sliding slowly down the backs of her legs. Submissive, she crouched on her hands and knees, and he entered. She closed her eyes, her body shook, edged along further by each slow gentle stroke. Her heart beat wild in her throat; she felt herself slipping away. She could not endure it. Climbing a ladder in darkness and at each stroke the pleasure was greater. Upward and upward – she could not climb any more, she was bursting apart with sheer pleasure . . .

The fire burned down slowly beside them. Distant cries rose from the village, a dog howled, then another. Light angled up round the tent, an afternoon radiance. Ingrid sprawled under the blankets she had pulled up around them. The Buck hardly stirred; he lay sleeping beside her. She could not take her eyes from his body, from its shadowy contours. His compact and beautiful strength stirred her senses; she loved the way his dark hair had fallen across his forehead, the curve of his arm stretched across her, his slow-breathing warmth near her face. She lay there thinking to herself: this boy is so beautiful and so strong, yet helpless and tender in sleep. From the very first moment I saw him, my body belonged to him, though I shut it out of my mind. Loving him is no sorrow, oh yes, I *do* love him tenderly.

Ingrid leaned over gently, kissed the Buck's mouth. She felt his arm tighten behind her; then she closed her eyes and drifted away into sleep . . .

In her dream a great tree grew straight up from her body. It rose from between her spread legs, an oak stretching skywards, trunk, branch and leaf springing up towards the blue sky. With her long white hands she reached out and caressed the rough bark; she could feel how it swelled and burst into myriad branches. She gazed up, the sunlight flashed gold on the green leaves. Far out at the tips of the boughs she could hear the wind stir, a warm summer wind that touched her hair gently and ruffled the high grass at her fingertips. The birds sang, a thrush and a robin, and swallows soared out of sight past the low swaying branches. Then somehow she was no longer earthbound, but was climbing quickly up the tree, taking hold of the branches and swinging up, level by level, towards the blue sky. The tree began to move, turning round, revolving slowly in the heart of the earth. And the sky slowly whitened, as the great tree sought the light. She kept looking up through the branches, waiting for the light to appear, while the tree turned her ever closer to the radiant source. The sun filled up the spaces between the leaves, pouring out molten white light till the leaves burst suddenly into flame. Then at last came a great roaring around her, a sun-fall consumed her, she dissolved in a shower of pure light . . .

She woke up clinging to the man there beside her. 'Harg!'

she said softly. The man blinked and stared. His skin was smooth, golden, his embrace soft and warm. It was the Buck, and he smiled. He lay there erect, pressed against her, then pulled her close in and once again entered her. She ran her tongue on her lips and submitted, feeling the pleasure take hold of her body. She was lifted from sleep to a sharp, deep awareness. She clung to him, with a long sigh lay back. They dozed between spasms of love-making . . .

Ingrid opened her eyes, stark awake. Beside her, the Buck lay groaning and muttering – a whole string of incomprehensible phrases. His head moved in short vivid jerks; the sweat stood out on his brow. Between murmurs he gasped for air, as if choking or drowning.

It was dark in the tent, except for a tiny faint glow in the fire, and the cold lay upon them, though under the blankets was warmth, a fever of body heat. There were drums in the distance and chanting, high-pitched cries – the clear sounds of a feast.

Ingrid drew her hand across the forehead of the Buck. She leaned over and kissed him: the murmuring ceased and a slow even breathing succeeded. She turned around wriggling under the blankets so as not to expose her bare body to the cold, and threw a few sticks on the fire. She watched as slowly they kindled and flared up. Then she sat up abruptly, and tried to ignore the chill dampness as she rolled two large logs into the fire pit. She ducked back under the blanket, nestled in close to the Buck, who opened his eyes, blinked and listened.

Ingrid stretched up on one elbow and watched him. The chanting went on in the background.

'Did you hear something there in the darkness?' the Buck asked, sniffing and blinking, as if shaking off the cobwebs of sleep.

'You were dreaming,' Ingrid said quietly. 'I think you were hearing the sounds in your dreams.'

The Buck listened, sighed. 'I met a powerful dream-visitor. I am not sure what it means.'

'I, too, had a big dream,' Ingrid said. 'I will tell you what happened to me, but you must not forget your experience while I talk. You must share your dream with me.'

The Buck stretched and yawned, then lay back at his ease, staring up the light kindled fresh in the shadows above them. Ingrid started to tell him her dream. After a while he interrupted her, propping himself up on one elbow.

'Did you not hear a noise outside – the sound of an animal?'

Ingrid thought for a minute. 'Perhaps Birch Tree is returning,' she said with a look of alarm. She pulled the covers up around her shoulders and breasts.

The Buck shook his head. 'No – he will not come until morning. It was nothing. Go on with your story.'

Ingrid told him the rest of her dream. For a long time he lay back in thought. Then at last he said: 'I think it is good – there is nothing to harm you. Both the earth and the sun are your friends.'

'Tell me your dream, then,' Ingrid pleaded. She reached over and brushed a loose strand of hair from his eyes. The Buck looked at her tenderly, stroking her neck and her breasts. His expression grew thoughtful.

'Perhaps it is better I say nothing.'

Ingrid shook her head firmly. 'No, you must tell me. I have told you and you must tell me. It is only fair.'

The Buck seemed to struggle with his reluctance. 'It is not a pleasant dream,' he said, bowing his head in perplexity.

'Who was your dream-visitor?' Ingrid asked brusquely.

He looked at her shyly. 'It was you,' he said finally.

'Me?'

The Buck sat up on his haunches. The blankets fell away and Ingrid reached for her tunic and woollens, her glance fixed expectantly on the man.

'You came to me as the Windigo,' the Buck said. Ingrid, who had pulled on her tunic, stopped and stared at him.

The Buck bowed his head. 'You came to me, all covered with hair; it was terrifying. Somehow I loved you, even though you were the Windigo. Your claws and teeth tore at my flesh. Then you began to peel off your skin – you cast it away like a bearskin – but underneath, there was no flesh at all. There was only a skeleton, a skeleton that moved. I was frightened. I woke up.'

Ingrid shook her head sadly. 'Is that what I looked like when I was possessed by the Windigo? Did you see me all covered with hair?'

The Buck slowly rose, standing naked and tense in the firelight. Ingrid saw how he listened and she too bent her head and was still.

A soft wind stirred at the tent skins; the poles creaked gently outside. The fire flickered up and a log groaned. Ingrid turned round. She felt panicky. Had she heard, in between, the soft crunch of a footfall on snow?

The Buck reached across for his clothes. Ingrid, nearly dressed, crawled slowly across to the entrance. She drew back the tent-flap and peered out. Fitful lights played on the rounded far domes of the wigwams, twists of smoke curling in the darkness. Between lay a flat dim expanse of grey snow. The sound of the chanting and drums seemed to swell and expand round the space of the dwelling.

Ingrid turned back. In the firelight she saw the Buck stoop down to recover a boot half buried under the blankets. He smiled at her gently.

'There's no-one there,' she said. He started to get up. In an instant his face changed.

Before she could speak, a body in full stride charged through the entrance and flung itself past her. She was struck on the hip and went spinning away to one side. In shock she saw the Buck hurtled back by the thrust of a sword-blade, his hands thrown helplessly up, his face glazed and frozen, his sharp cry cut off by the force of the grip on his throat.

The next seconds pulsed by with the slow speed of nightmare. A familiar cloaked form seemed to engulf the young man. Ingrid screamed, struggled to her feet. A shining blade struck at him. He stood gazing at nothing; his attacker stepped back, allowing him to topple forward, bent double and clutching at his gashed chest. His fur robe slipped off his shoulders, but he clung to a part of it, blood pumping out through its thick folds. Face downwards, he squirmed by the fire, one hand stretched out, as if he were trying to crawl to her, then suddenly lay still. Blood ribboned his hands.

The man who had come through the door stared down at the blood-smeared sword in his hands, as if hardly believing its power. It was Thorkel. He looked up, his eyes fixed and shining with a wild, stricken passion.

Ingrid saw everything clearly, every notch of the tent's wooden frame, the separate orange and gold tongues of the fire, the Buck's bare-knuckled stained hand reaching out from the brown blood-matted fur. Her strength ran away as she looked. She stood frozen.

'Odin!' she cried out at last, 'Oh, God help me!'

She felt her legs buckle. The roof poles, the fire, Thorkel's sword blurred before her. She collapsed near the fire where the Buck lay. In her mind's eye she saw him struck down again and she cried out. A numbness crept over her, a deadening sorrow that pressed on her body like stone. There was blankness – the vision came back – she saw him struck down. She thought that the tent shook around her, as if his spirit, roused up, might be flying away.

But someone was embracing her, she felt herself lifted; strong hands held her up. A voice went on in Icelandic; for a minute she understood nothing. The words sounded foreign, and distant.

She opened her eyes, saw the Buck lying stiff and remote by the fire. She heard Thorkel's voice in her ear, urgent whispers, but his blood-spattered tunic pressed her shoulder and she shuddered and tried to pull free.

Thorkel held her. 'You must come with me, Ingrid,' he whispered. 'They have held you here under a spell, and now I have broken it. But we must hurry!'

She stared at his sword, thrust down through the skins on the floor. With an effort, she faced him. 'You killed him,' she murmured, her voice barely audible. His eyes were wild, and bloodshot, his face transformed. He shook his head, then said in a harsh voice:

'There is not much time. They will kill you for what I have done. We must go now, together!'

235

There was a clamour of voices in the distance. For the first time she noticed that the drumbeats had stopped, and the chanting.

Ingrid forced herself up. Thorkel's strong arms clasped her shoulders, but she shook herself free, and with two staggering steps, reached the Buck. She bent down to him; her whole body trembled. With an effort she turned him over. His body was heavy. His eyes stared sightlessly up. There was blood everywhere, the deep wound on his chest like a terrible mouth. Nausea and terror overcame her. 'I forgive you for loving him,' she heard Thorkel say from behind her. 'It was magic, I know. I was deceived by the girl, too. You must come with me now.'

Ingrid caught something in Thorkel's bare words – a confession. She turned round. 'You didn't hurt Happy Tongue?' She felt she would choke on her unspoken thoughts. 'You didn't hurt the girl . . .'

Thorkel started to speak, then took a step backwards. Outside, the shouts and the cries sounded closer.

'*She loved you,*' Ingrid burst out, through her tears. She was crying inconsolably, but she forced out the words. 'I loved *him* . . . Thorkel.' It was all she could say.

Again, he started to speak, then mopped at his brow with a gesture of helplessness. He plucked out the sword he had plunged in the skins of the floor. Outside the voices came nearer. He gazed at her for a moment, then turned and ran through the entrance.

Numbed with horror, Ingrid stood in the glow of the firelight. The Buck was not dead; he could not be dead. She crouched down beside him, cradling him up in her arms. His body felt drained and inert, but surely the gods would take pity; he could not really be dead. She began wiping away the blood from his chest with her tunic. The firelight shone luridly, coldly.

After a while she was aware of the movement outside, of the voices. Low murmuring voices, as if men were talking in soft tones together.

It came to her then that a man was standing above her, an

old man with a wrinkled quiet face, staring down at her with a tender, a compassionate gaze.

'You must come with me,' Birch Tree said. 'An evil spirit has led the Way-Michi-Gooshi to do this terrible thing. In his fury, too, he killed Happy Tongue, who loved him. There is anger and fear in the village. It is better that you come with me now.'

The Shaman

Now she must go north, Ingrid knew, with Birch Tree and a village boy serving as her guides, north through the desolate lands and, though one part of her mind in its misery longed to see her own village, she felt powerless to protest.

The Skraelings had buried the Buck and Happy Tongue at the edge of the maple woods, reverently placing their bodies, and a few treasured possessions in cedar-log cairns, after inscribing the clan marks, upside down, on the bare wood. Ingrid had stood with the boy while the men of the village chanted and the women raised a mournful cry. As the funeral procession wound back towards the wigwams, she had waited with bowed head among the trees.

Then Birch Tree came back and she followed him, resigned and unquestioning, for the strength of her will had been broken by the shock of the night, and by the effect of the shaman's soothing potions. Even so, she kept seeing Thorkel's face, twisted by fear and cold lust after killing: he must be in flight now, on his way through the deep woods, like an outlaw. To murder Skraelings – it had never been a serious crime among the Vikings. But in Ingrid's mind there were no Skraelings or Vikings – only Thorkel and Happy Tongue and the Buck. Yet she was truly spent now, and nothing arose in her heart as a claim; she drifted along through the woods without regret, though every step stretched the black cord that bound her numbed body to the body of her lover.

They walked on at a slow pace; the sun rose ever higher. Soon there were no tracks to guide them, only the gentle suggestion of pine-clad hills on both sides of the trail. Their path seemed to follow a riverbed; deep drifts, a virginal whiteness of snow, lay on both sides. The sharp green glint of the pines, almost hurtful in its brilliance, struck Ingrid's mind and roused it a little from lethargy. She watched the sunlight spill round the grey massing clouds, saw the quick distant wind lift white fingers of snow from the branches. She gazed at the rough-clad forms of the old man and the boy, moving always before her, like two tireless animals.

Hours passed; their path arched away from the riverbed; they stopped and put on snowshoes, and struck out through a bare stand of maples and birches. The sun's path, away to the left, and behind, was a dazzle of light; long shadows stretched through the grove. They crossed animal tracks and the low springing scrub of a long slope: the path led on up.

Their stops became ever more frequent. Ingrid had long ceased to think of her tiredness; mercifully, she had remained almost the whole time in a reverie, stumbling forward behind the old man and the boy. She wondered how Birch Tree could stand it; for his narrow shoulders slumped pitifully, and the lines on his face twitched with pain. At one point she thought the boy would say something in protest: he kept shifting the packs on his shoulders; he looked first at Ingrid, then at Birch Tree, and started to speak, but the old man forestalled him:

'Not much further,' he said in a dry, weary whisper. The boy bowed his head.

They pushed on; steep cliffs towered above them. Then came a gap in the cliffside and a small transverse valley running back into the hills. They entered this valley.

Ingrid looked up, caught her breath.

Between snow-mantled patches and sproutings of dwarf pines, the clear face of the cliff was all covered with carvings, figures in partial relief on the rock, images blurred and rubbed

238

out by the shadows, or blazoned to life by the spectacular sunlight.

Ingrid had never seen anything like it; it was a miracle of sunlight and stone: it was magical.

There were skyboats outlined in full sail; snakes twined together, uprearing with great fangs; a giant human handprint; the sun and the moon. There were huge bound sheaths of grain; sea-serpents swallowing a man; and, at either end of the cliff-wall, eaten away by time and the weather, the figure of a cat, crouching patiently with sly mouth and eyesockets winking precious light, as if the arrival of the travellers had rescued it from a long slow dream of ice.

When Birch Tree saw that Ingrid had stopped short and was gazing up at the carvings, he turned back, approached her and said in a low voice:

'It was the ancient ones who did it . . . They had more power, long ago.'

And Ingrid felt a vague thrill of connection; she knew then that the country which the Vikings had settled and claimed as new land, had been visited long before by others who had come, built and died, but left their marks on the cliffsides. And those marks revealed a profound connection with the earth and the sky, a grasp of magic deeper than anything she had dreamed possible, and also – as she realized with a shiver of terror, gazing at the cats – a sense of humour that echoed still with a sly, demonic laughter.

'We cannot stay longer: night is coming,' said Birch Tree. Ingrid pulled her mind back from the wild sea of figures. The old man stood close by, his round face all muffled in furs, and peered up at her.

She bent her head, and followed the shaman down the trail, awestruck and numbed by her vision. Then her mind gave way and she saw the Buck stretched out lifeless beside the faint glowing fire, the sword of Thorkel upraised, the wild glance of her lover. Events, like a great tide, swept over her; she could only go forward, one weary step at a time, trusting to fate and the powers that existed beyond her. The carved figures glinted in the dying light, and she remembered the words of the Wanderer (spoken, as it seemed, in long ages past) : *'The gods take pity on no-one!'*

They were in a deep cave, a cave that seemed to run far back into the heart of the mountain. The boy had already built a fire and, from a cache beneath some piled stones, Birch Tree drew fresh wood, which soon crackled and burned brightly. At Birch Tree's direction, and with a few awed looks and some hesitation, the boy moved back another large stone, dug roughly at the loose soil, and recovered a *mockuck*, a large tightly wrapped birch container, which, as Ingrid saw by the firelight, was decorated all over with a pattern of coiling snakes.

Birch Tree turned the object round then prised off the top, pulling out some parcels, which turned out to be thick blankets, wrapped tightly and bound in skins. When these had been removed he drew out an otterskin pouch, which he slipped quickly into the folds of his robe. The blankets they shook and warmed by the fire. Other packs were opened and their protective skins removed. Birch Tree distributed some dried fruits and nuts and Ingrid ate greedily.

She lay back for a few minutes, feeling dazed and exhausted, but warm. The old man and the boy gathered more wood, then assembled their own bedding near the fire, using the rock ledge as a shelter. Ingrid, stretched out, was already drifting down into sleep when Birch Tree touched her shoulder. He held out his hand and she saw what looked like some dried herbs.

'Eat these,' he ordered and she started to question him, but a weariness lay on her mind. She took the dry, sour-tasting morsels and swallowed them. Then she burrowed down into her blankets and fell, almost at once into a deep sleep.

A figure came out of the cave, a tall shaggy man-bear, with red, glowing eyes. A figure of dream, Ingrid sensed at once, and she was not frightened, but watching, felt a deep sense of awe as the shape moved and shifted. She thought of Harg, and the figure at once burst into fragments. Then she was out of the cave, in a blinding white light. She stood on a high cliff gazing down on a vast plain, on which, like a multiform beast, a great herd of caribou roamed. Their numbers seemed endless, a moving shoal spread out on the green ocean of grass and they surged with swift motion, tall antlers bobbing, heels flashing up, a wild swell of animals plunging forward as if driven by a single, wild impulse.

For some minutes, it seemed, Ingrid stood there, then in her dream she turned round. Beside her, on the bare rocky cliff, in the sunlight, sat Birch Tree. He was only a few feet away, and Ingrid saw at once that he was dead. His body had stiffened and mummified, his skin changed to parchment, but his eyes were wide open, and his arms folded peacefully. He seemed to be looking beyond her, far off towards the plain, towards the caribou.

Ingird started to speak, her voice stuck in her throat. She could not utter a word and she panicked. She stepped back too far on the cliff, lost her balance, and started to fall. The scream that she felt in her throat did not come . . .

She opened her eyes, found herself safe in the cave, the old man at her side, gently shaking her back into consciousness.

'It is morning,' he said, 'but there is no meal now for us. In a short while we must go. But first you must eat this.'

She looked down at what he held and shuddered – more of the dried herb-like stuff, only swollen and glazed, as if soaked in some liquid.

'What is it?' Ingrid asked. 'Why must I eat . . . ? I had a dream . . .'

'I know,' the old man interrupted. 'There will be more dreams and they will reveal the path, though the journey will be painful and strange. You cannot go back, nor can I. Only the boy may return. But the herbs will show you the way.' He pointed a bony hand towards the glittering roof. 'We must walk through the mountain,' he added. Then he coughed violently and spat in the fire. Ingrid thought she could see blood in the old man's spittle. She chewed the bitter herbs and forced them down.

The boy gave her water from a skin bag, and as soon as she

drank, she felt nauseated. She moved to the side of the cave, to the shadows, where she bent over, vomiting. She coughed and retched till it seemed that her stomach would turn itself inside out. She groped towards a stone shelf and held on, her hands trembling; tears ran down her cheeks. She thought she would die then. That was what she wanted.

Birch Tree came over to her, carrying the warm jacket she had taken off to sleep. He helped her put it on, took hold of her hand and led her towards the rear of the cave. The boy stood up and watched them. Ingrid noticed that the blankets had been put away, the caches set up as before, that only the boy's things lay near the fire, a small roll of bedding, a food pack, the snowshoes.

The old man and the boy looked at each other for some minutes. The boy picked up a brand from the fire and carried it over to the old man. Neither said a word. Birch Tree turned to Ingrid.

'We must go on,' he said, and took hold of her jacket.

Ingrid felt lightheaded, strange. She imagined that she could walk without touching the ground. Around her, the cave twisted and glowed, as if changing its shape. The old man's face seemed to have grown much larger. She could read every nuance of line, every stroke of old age on his cheeks and his forehead. She thought he looked beautiful, ancient. She followed his light through the cave. Neither looked back at the boy.

The path wound up steeply. It was easy to climb, like a river of shale that had frozen. At each step the stones gave a foothold. The old man breathed heavily; warm currents of air touched Ingrid's face, making the light quiver oddly. Flames licked the darkness to life. Yet the space all around them was bare and metallic; the mottled walls sloped off in shadow. The fire is a flower in the darkness, Ingrid thought. She stared at each petal of light as it shivered and danced, and she felt the light in her veins.

Then, without warning, the walls on both sides fell away – the light shrank and brightened. And Ingrid felt her whole body expand like a wave beyond the light. She could sense the great spaces that opened, felt the warm air swish down from somewhere, heard the faint, distant lapping of water, and the sound of their footsteps reverberating quietly around them.

They moved through a cavernous space, stirring shadows with each forward thrust of the torch. Between their harsh steps, when the slow echoes died, Ingrid heard rushing of water, then a vague flap of wings and a scampering as of small feet. Moving currents of air, or pebbles kicked up by her own boots? She did not feel frightened; the power of the herbs worked to slow up each sound and display it: as she listened the texture became part of her mind, and the light seemed to pulse in her veins like a signal.

At last, Birch Tree held up one hand and they stopped. A few feet away the rock seemed to split and beyond a deep vapour rose, like the breath of a river. The invisible waters gurgled and slapped at the low shelf of rock where the old man crouched down. From her reverie Ingrid saw that he scratched at the rock, shifting and shaping what looked like old embers from fires long abandoned.

Within a few minutes the old man had dug up some dry lumps of charred wood, disturbing some beetles and spiders and, with this wood, by means of the brand, he kindled a small fire. Ingrid stood still in the darkness, her eyes closed, the damp air like a soft wet kiss on her forehead. She stood there for what seemed a long time, then felt herself drawn to the fire, shielding her eyes from the harsh light with her cupped hands.

The old man, from his place on the other side of the fire, reached over and with tiny gnarled fingers gently stroked Ingrid's temples. She felt her mind sharpen; her eyes opened wide. She shivered, hunched up, looking around her.

'Do not be afraid,' the old man said. His dark eyes stared into hers; his hand trembled as he touched his thin wisp of beard. 'Only a short time is left to me – and to you, before your great trial. I promised to tell you of the mysteries that surrounded your coming to the village, to complete the story I began once before, so that you would understand at least one more part of your destiny. I must speak now, in order that your heart may be strengthened. You must listen first to what I say; then you will dream on my words. Now eat more of the blessed mushroom, so that your dreams may be fruitful.'

Birch Tree, with slow trembling hands, reached into his robe for the otterskin pouch that he had stowed there in the cave. Very carefully, he removed a few black shrivelled morsels from out of the small pouch and handed them over to Ingrid.

She took them and swallowed them without hesitation. The old man's eyes narrowed; he cleared his throat once and began to speak.

'Listen to me now. What I say concerns you very closely. I told you of Tindat, the brother of the Buck, who died after his fight with the evil bear spirit, but who saved the whole village. He came to me afterwards in dreams. He gave me the signs and showed me his power and told me of things that would happen. He told me that, during his wanderings, because she was brave and alone, he had taken pity on a white girl, and that he would bring her among us. He said she would come in the shape of a Windigo, but that she must not be destroyed, for she was under his care. She would change the village and it would change her and all would be different thereafter.'

Ingrid stared at the old man, whose burning eyes shone in the firelight. Slowly, her mind stretched out to encompass his words; hours passed, it seemed, as she thought of the Buck, of her lover . . . In the darkness, in the flickering light, she reached out to touch him. But behind was another face, the face of an unknown young man, who smiled on her. A numbness took hold; her tongue seemed to stick in her throat. From a distance, she heard Birch Tree's voice, faint but still audible.

'Through the sacrifice of Tindat, who found you and wanted to help you, you gained the power of our language. I did not interfere with your trials in the village, or with the contest.

244

Everything happened as destined. The Buck was to die and join his brother. I knew it. And he knew it also.'

The face of the old man seemed to float up before her; the fire sank away, far below. It had dwindled and now seemed no larger than a spark in a deep pit. Ingrid could not tell whether she sat there before him, or hovered high in the air. Yet a question kept riddling her mind, and she struggled to form it. Vaguely, she heard herself say:

'But Tindat . . . I saw nothing of Tindat.'

A voice quivered up, as if from inside her, speaking in the long-drawn-out phrases of the old man.

'Tindat found you and served you. His flesh gave you knowledge of our language and of what we feel in our hearts. His spirit was pure light, yet you knew him, for he took on the shape of a caribou, the beast that died for your sake.'

By the Great Northern Sea

The fire blazed up suddenly. Ingrid took a deep breath.

She remembered another cave, a cruel fire, the taste of burnt meat and a cold hunger and hurt that had driven her away from her lover: her first lover, Harg, whom she had injured and abandoned. How would she find him now? How could she explain? It had all been by design; the spirit of Tindat, her protector, had entered into the caribou: she had partaken of the sacrifice and had passed far beyond the boundaries of her familiar world to enter a new and unknown region. Was Harg, too, part of the sacrifice?

The old man reached out and touched her with his frail hands. I love Harg, she thought; in spirit I love Harg.

'We must go on,' Birch Tree whispered. She shivered; the

darkness beyond their firelight seemed infinite – where was there to go? Everywhere, nowhere . . .

The old man's grip tightened; she steadied. 'I have been chosen to show you the path,' he told her, 'but I cannot accompany you on the next stage of your journey. I can only take you to a frightening place: there you will find people even older than the Ice People among whom I was born, people older than the tribes and the Vikings. They hold a slender thread that may lead you back to the first dawn, to the origin. From there you will see much; you will know which way to go – unless the thread snaps and you perish – but that is in the hands of the gods.'

Ingrid swallowed; the after-taste of the herbs was bitter; swaying, she felt her body float away from the stone floor, but once again the old man's hand steadied her. Slowly, she found her footing, her centre.

'I don't know what to do.' She closed her eyes for a few seconds on the shivering light. 'I've brought evil to your village and no help to my family, to my people. I feel as if life will drown me before I can learn to find my course. I know nothing!'

Faintly, the old shaman smiled. 'Then you are like me, child, even though I am a *wabeno*, a master of the fire. But I have something to show you – one last thing – so gather your courage, and come now!'

The old man took a flaming brand from the fire, then he scattered the burning coals and trampled them down almost to blackness.

He led her through the cavern. All around them she sensed the cold stone, scaly and glittering, she heard the soft rushing water; the damp air lay on her cheek. Was it a lingering effect of the drugs that caused her nerves to fail her then? That made her imagine she could hear somewhere in the blackness behind them, the scuttling of clawed feet?

When they moved she heard it clearly; when they stopped – only silence. It became unbearable; she laid her hand on Birch Tree's shoulder: 'There is – something,' she said in a dry voice as he turned to her, the flames of the torch emphasized the strange curved folds of his eyelids.

'Small animals in the darkness,' he told her. 'Nothing else.'

She thought of the snake in Harg's cave. She had been near death, but Harg had nursed her and loved her, and now he was far away; perhaps he hated her. All her men should hate her; she brought them nothing but evil.

They walked on. The walls narrowed around them. She began to imagine that the cave was endless; they would never get out of it. It was like being buried alive – suppose that the torch should go out? It would be ultimate darkness, as if the world had not begun, as if the sun had been swallowed up on the last day of creation. A darkness to enclose and smother everything.

On and on. There was no path; the walls pressed in: only a vague track led up through the mist – she did not try to imagine who had walked it, but she thought of the carvings Birch Tree had shown them on the cliffs. Those ancient ones – had they walked here? Was this where they had buried their gods?

She had heard water; now all at once the water ran under their feet, a black stream that swirled beneath a stone bridge. If I fell into it, Ingrid thought, with a shudder, I would be washed away, far beneath the mountains, down to the roots of our earth, to the time before time when night ruled the pit by the world-tree, down in the cold well of Urd.

They walked on – and came to a rock face, almost perpendicular, but carved with deep steps; the old man began to climb up, slowly, stopping now and then for breath and chanting a song to the spirits of morning. And Ingrid, following, clinging desperately to the slippery crevices, saw, far above them, a smooth gray patch floating in the darkness.

They laboured up towards it, step by step, breath by breath. Cold ragged fingers of fog floated past them; Ingrid moved in a kind of terror now, shoving her boots into the step-holes, leaning her cheeks against the sharp face of the stone.

Craning her neck she could still see the grey patch of light. The air grew much colder, but the patch grew larger and brighter and, as they climbed higher, it was no longer a vague disc, but a sharp-boundaried gap in the rock far above them.

Her arms and legs ached; the old man did not pause. They climbed even higher; long minutes passed and, finally, she looked up – and saw through an opening in the cavern roof, an opening she blessed, a familiar dark velvet canopy, radiant with light: the night sky.

The cliff-facings in front of her shone with an icy smooth brightness; a few snowflakes touched her cheeks. Birch Tree gave a warning, then let the torch go. It whizzed away past her; Ingrid did not dare to look down.

Birch Tree reached the top, clambered over the edge and disappeared, and Ingrid, scrambling up eagerly behind him, almost lost her footing: she clutched at the rock, found a hand-hold and swung herself out of the shaft, away from the reach of that darkness that seemed to fill up all the cracks and crevices of the mountain.

She lay gasping for breath on a wide hard ledge; Birch Tree crouched beside her; his eyes were closed – he seemed almost to have fallen asleep.

Ingrid saw that they were high up on one side of a great rugged valley: in the cold bitter starlight everything was beautiful. It was all so perfect, a kind of death. But she felt such joy at being free of that cave that she knew she could lie there forever.

After a few minutes Birch Tree began to stir. Very slowly and painfully, he pulled himself up to his feet. Ingrid managed to scramble up and support him.

'You said it would be a frightening place,' she burst out, 'and it *was* – it was horrible.'

The old man looked at her strangely. 'The cave,' he pointed, 'down there? That is not the place I meant at all. That is nothing. The frightening place is still before us.'

After a while he led her along the path. It was a narrow ledge high up on the side of a cliff, overhung by a broad crumbling mantle of stone. The path curved around the flanks of the mountain.

The cold air filled her lungs, cleared her vision. She saw a bleak world, bleaker than anything she had ever imagined, a world of stone and frost and intangible light. She remembered the stories of her mother around the fireside; she had heard about Jotunheim, land of the giants, and now names came back to her: Ymir and Utgard, the emptiness of Ginnungagap.

She drew her cloak tightly around her and tried not to look over the edge of the cliff path; Birch Tree plodded on in front of her, a frail figure, limping a little, not stopping, never turning back.

It happened slowly, almost imperceptibly: the path turned and soon she became aware that they were emerging, ever so gradually, from a long narrow valley that was barely a cleft between bald, towering mountains. She noticed it first in a quickening of light: the rock facings began to glitter; one near ridge seemed to sink, revealing the expanded sky – and something else.

Then Birch Tree turned for the first time, his wrinkled face full of an excitement she had never before seen there. He was gesturing, gulping mouthfuls of air and pointing off at where the hills sloped down, opening up on a chasm that was as wide as the horizon. Out of this chasm drifted mist of a feathery lightness, delicate tatters of cloud, tiny plumes of pure light.

Ingrid sprang forward and made her way along the trail ahead of the old shaman.

She remembered as a child running in the moonlight through fields of shining wheat: now she was suspended above a field of light: what it was she could not tell, but it made her heart glad, and so happy was she to escape the cave's darkness, the cold bleakness of the near cliffs, that she ran recklessly forward, ignoring the great gulf that opened up beside her, just beyond the path's edge.

Behind her, the faint voice of the shaman cried a warning. She slowed down; the path ended suddenly, the hill fell away in a precipitous gulf at her feet, but this she ignored – her attention was elsewhere. Birch Tree finally came up, panting and coughing, to where she had stopped short. He pointed at the dangerously crumbling cliff, and admonished her quietly in his quiet voice.

'Oh, it's wonderful,' she whispered, 'so wonderful – is it the ocean?'

She could not turn her glance from the spectacle.

To her left, far away, all across the northern horizon, the magic lights gleamed: their shivering energy lit the fog-smoke that rolled south-westwards over a cold boiling sea. In the foreground, curving out beneath the ledge on which they stood, Ingrid saw a shoreline rimmed with ice dark as fish-scales: this ice, in its black silver depths seemed to mirror the sky's restlessness.

'Not the ocean,' Birch Tree told her, 'but the great northern sea. It lies near to the edge of the world. From across there, between floating mountains of ice' – he pointed to the north-east – 'the old people came long ago. Now they come no more, or seldom; only a few remain, but they have the secret; they are in touch with the grandfathers.'

Ingrid turned to him at last. 'The secret?'

'You will be tested, and if you are accepted, you may find that power you seek.'

'But where are they, these people?' Ingrid made a gesture encompassing the wild scene. 'This is the end of the earth, surely no human could survive in this place.'

Birch Tree cleared his throat and spat into the darkness.

'Not everyone thinks they are human.'

He groped, grasping her mittened fingers with his small hands. More than ever, he seemed to her childlike; or ageless. 'Now you must go on,' he told her, 'in order to reach the holy place before dawn. It is time to say goodbye, my child.'

She could not believe what she heard. She looked around at the vast night, at the glittering, ice-scummed sea.

'But surely, you don't mean to leave me here! How will you get back? You'll die here – and where will I go? – I know nothing about this land, absolutely nothing. I'll be lost here. We must go on together.'

Birch Tree shook his head slowly, but did not let go of her hands.

'You are still a girl,' he told her, his eyes full of a strange light. 'What you think of as death is not death. I will sit here and meditate and hold you in my mind for the rest of your journey, perhaps for your whole life. Is that what you call death? Now I must set up the rope.'

He let go of her hands, swung off his pack and brought out a length of rope.

'With the rope you can get down this cliff; there are steps and ridges – it will not be hard. Now I will show you where you must go. Look down there, at that island: on one side it is surrounded by dark ice, on the other the sea laps at its cliffs. That is where you will find the old people.'

Ingrid peered down and saw a bleak island, like a great boulder torn from the low ridges of the shore. She was about to complain that it was only a dead heap of stone when she noticed a vague glow, a dim light flickering in the heart of the rock. It was as if a hooded lantern shone out fitfully from behind a dark curtain.

She knew Birch Tree meant what he said: she must go on, down to that dark place, without him. The strength of his faith in her moved her. She took the rope from his hands and fastened it securely to a rock spur lying under a broad ledge.

'Hold the rope tight for me,' she told him, then observing the pride with which he looked at her, the humour and love in his old eyes, she flung her arms around him and hugged him until he protested. At the same time, without letting him see, she blinked away her tears, so that his pride in her would not be diminished.

For a few minutes, on her hands and knees, she leaned over, examining the sheer cliff below her, noting places where crude steps had been cut in the frozen rock.

She swung herself over the edge.

Birch Tree had already sat down under the rock shelf. The rope was snagged fast near his right hand.

'I will find you again some day,' Ingrid called out. Her voice sounded frail, yet there was no wind, only a great silence, the roar of the far lights.

Ingrid drifted down on the rope. The old man had begun to pray aloud.

She slipped lower, bumping softly against the dark cliff, then suddenly remembered a question – and with an effort, pulled herself up.

'But who should I ask for, what should I tell them?' she called out, clinging fast to the rope, her injured ankle buckling a little under the strain.

The old man's droning prayer continued for a while, then suddenly stopped.

'Tell them your name,' he called out. The murmured chant continued; he did not raise his head.

Ingrid slipped away into the darkness.

It was a steep cliff but not more than fifty feet high. Halfway down, still clinging to the rope, she thought: What a fool I am! I should have asked him more about the frightening place!

Then she stood on the beach – really a vast rocky ledge abutting the dark ice.

Far to the north, the white-capped mountains rose; the aurora caressed each peak and valley with tender violence. Smoke-frost poured up where the ice cracked and opened, giving birth to the sea. Down the long curving beach, to the south, one island glowed with a faint light.

This is the loneliest place in the world, Ingrid thought, yet surely there is nothing evil here. The sky, the air and sea, even the dark stone – everything is alive with light. But oh, I wish it were a warm light! Something like my dear home hearthfire and not this light, which is colder and stranger than the light of the full moon in winter.

She stood there, wanting to sing, to cry out, against the vastness, but she did not dare: it would be a kind of presumption to call attention to herself in that place.

She began her trek along the beach, threading her way among the stones, stepping carefully to save her still tender ankle. At one point she stopped and looked back, seeking the invisible ledge where the shaman must still be sitting in meditation and prayer. She remembered how Harg had watched her as, full of hunger and hatred, she had entered the forest. Now she was empty of all emotion, played out and exhausted; no-one was watching; she saw no-one.

She caught her breath, stopped. Something launched itself past her: quick beating wings, a flash of white feathers.

A great snowy owl rose up and circled, then flapped away across the ice fields.

It winged slowly towards the island, and disappeared into a port of shadows.

There is my way, she thought, and cut down across the barren rubble of the beach.

At one point, almost imperceptibly, the rubble smoothed out, the beach became the frozen sea. She had to step carefully on the queer level icepack. Very slippery it was, yet rutted and pockmarked, as glistening and oily smooth as the back of a great fish.

And gazing down through the murky skin of ice, she saw a myriad lights, a green and gold shimmer, as if sea-creatures with luminous shells swarmed there.

She walked on, wondering, but followed the faint track. The island loomed before her; stone ramparts revealed a structure cut and shaped to the contour of the rock. It was as if an ancient dwelling had sunk year by year into the very centre of the place. In the flickering light of the aurora, the dim starlight, she could trace the faint outlines of lintels and buttressings which, though man-made, seemed as old as the sea or the mountains.

She thought of the people Birch Tree had spoken of: those she was destined to meet. Of them, back in Wayland, she had heard not a single story. Yet the shaman had told her they had come from far away, they had sailed past the floating ice mountains, to make the markings on the cliffs – and what else?

At that moment Ingrid was struck by a thought that stopped her in her tracks – a thought fetched up from her deep mind.

The snake figures, the symbols carved high on the cliffs – they were like the shapes on the precious cup her father had given her at the beginning of the journey!

Her great grandfather Hannes had captured the cup from

the old ones, from the very people who still dwelt in this bleakness.

And Glimir, who had taken it from her, had she, perhaps with their help, escaped across this very sea?

Ingrid's nerves overcame her and she laughed, skidding forward across the ice until she was almost underneath the steep cliffs of the island. Glimir, she thought, I shall catch you! A breeze started up, bone-chilling, fitful. Then a curious, intimate sound – the sea slapping gently against ice-blocks or stone.

Ingrid edged forward; under her feet, the glow had vanished: she looked down at a black skin of ice. A hint of smoke tickled her nostrils: she had not seen any smoke trails, or else had confused them with the fog-smoke. It almost made her feel glad – that evidence of something human, a hearthfire.

She moved along the rockface; the cliffs were steep and much more irregular than she had thought from her first view. A very dim flickering light seemed to glow from somewhere high above her. She walked a little way; the ice beneath her feet felt oddly different – then she remembered that the sea was close by, and she stopped short. She did not want to step into that freezing black water.

She heard a fluttering of wings above her, looked up and saw the white owl hovering above a clean shaved wall of cliff. The bird, silent except for the flapping of its wings, drifted away along the cliffside.

She noticed that a kind of access had been cut into the cliff, a steep ramp running upwards to the smooth rock facing. Groping forward, she located the foot of this access. A pathway angled up, a rough-hewn way that led into a light-dazzled darkness.

Slowly, she began to work her way upwards. Although the rock was ice covered and slippery, there were many steps and handholds, and she made her way quite easily.

Only minutes later she found herself on a broad shelf that narrowed as it curved around the rock wall. Directly in front of her the cliffside was quite blank and smooth – though here and there shining with a thin skin of ice.

She stepped on to the ledge, groped along the rock facing, and turned the corner.

The path was very narrow – much narrower than the one she had climbed up on – and some twenty-five or thirty feet below she could see the icepack; then, due east, the black sea, plumed everywhere with fog-smoke.

The island rose around her, cliffs arching upward and, in the smooth wall of rock, fronted by another broad ledge, a few feet away from where she stood, she saw a door.

The door was of metal, very ancient, covered with intricate lines, which, as she looked, resolved themselves into the swirling shapes of birds, into a tracery of wings and sharp beaks, of claw-like feet and round, staring eyes.

She stepped forward, grasped hold of the ornate door-knocker (it was made in the shape of a swan taking wing), and announced herself by several sharp taps.

She waited. A shrill wind sounded across the icepack, water slapped faintly on stone.

She knocked again and waited. Close by, she heard a beating of wings; light glittered round her. Nothing happened.

Grasping the door-knocker firmly in her mittened hand, she knocked again.

A voice came, as if through a crack in the stone. It spoke her own Norse language, though harshly. 'Go away, fool!' said the voice.

'Let me in!' demanded Ingrid. 'I am just a poor girl who seeks shelter. I am tired and hungry,' she pleaded.

No answer came; she pounded on the door with her fists.

Silence once again – though she could hear the wind whistling through crevices, the low lapping water, the distant faint hiss of the lights.

'Birch Tree, the shaman, sent me. I am looking for Glimir, one of my sisters. Has she come this way?'

Still the silence.

Then she remembered what Birch Tree had told her. 'I am Ingrid, daughter of Einar,' she cried out in a loud voice. 'I seek the lost magic light to drive away the living dead.'

Once again, she waited for some moments, listening.

Finally, came a low creaking and a groaning of hinges; the wall moved slowly outwards. She drew herself up to her full height.

The door swung open.

The Shapeshifter

A hand reached out from the darkness, gesturing as if to welcome Ingrid within. It was a woman's hand, beautiful and slender. The girl hesitated: she could see nothing else – the woman's face and body were hidden; and around her was sheer blackness. There was a smell of dampness, of rotting wood, of moss or plants stored long ago in some cellar and forgotten, a strange smell, as of buried summers, that made Ingrid step back.

She looked around gratefully: the clear air, the bleak world became suddenly precious; the light on the ice, on the sea, seemed magnificent. Then, as if in answer to her wish, the cave itself became illuminated, a dim glow, but welcome: revealed was a passageway leading back into the heart of the rock, a narrow high tunnel whose smooth walls were beaded with moisture.

'Come in, Ingrid of Wayland,' said the woman who had opened the door. Her accent struck strangely on Ingrid's ear, but the voice was soft now, and melodious. Could this be the same voice that had told her, seconds before, to go away?

'Do not hesitate,' said the woman. 'The night is very cold.' She moved aside so that Ingrid could enter. The girl saw a tall figure, wrapped in heavy furs, and became aware of a bitter perfume, distinct from the warm sweet odour of the cave.

She stepped past the woman, without properly seeing her,

and entered the passageway. The door shut immediately with a loud clang that echoed for a moment in the hollow space.

She was trapped, she was inside: the walls pressed around her. Desperately, she fought against panic.

Ingrid touched the damp wall with a mittened hand. Then for the first time she got a good look at the woman.

She was youthful, and tall, taller even than Ingrid, with large dark eyes and high distinct cheekbones. A delicate pointed chin emphasized her long sombre face, and her skin was absolutely clear, almost translucent. She was wrapped round in a thick sable cloak, opened wide at the top, so that her long neck and the white skin of her upper body were strikingly evident. Ingrid had the impression that, underneath the coat, the woman was naked.

'I am happy to welcome you here, Ingrid,' said the other. 'Macha is who I am. Not many find this place.'

There was a kind of smile in her voice as she said this last phrase, but the woman did not smile. Ingrid noticed how wide and beautifully shaped her lips were, red as rowanberries. The girl allowed herself to be urged a little way along the passage, then turned to her guide.

'The shaman who led me here told me I would find the last of the ancient people who crossed the sea long ago. He told me you could help me on my journey. I must find the woman, Glimir, who stole a cup of my father's.'

Macha stopped and regarded Ingrid thoughtfully. Her dark bright eyes revealed nothing.

'My country is that of Brian, brother of Mathgamain; it is an ancient and beautiful country, beyond the floating ice, but not unreachable by sea. I know nothing of this Glimir, though perhaps I can help you find her.'

There was something veiled in the manner of her reply, though Ingrid could not be sure she was lying.

The woman pointed the way forward along the passage. A flickering light, apparently from tiny recesses along the walls, made the women's twinned shadows swell and mingle. Ingrid fought off the feeling that the rock walls were closing in around her.

They came without warning into a larger chamber. Here the walls were much darker, and trickling with moisture. On a narrow ledge, beside the entrance, a small fire burned brightly. Its flames made the corner shadows deeper. So deep in fact that Ingrid at first did not notice the bird.

The woman whirled round in front of her; something sprang up from a low ledge opposite the fire. Wings flapped, Ingrid jumped back: a black bird rose on a tether, cried sharply, settled.

It was a raven, croaking and clucking, in anger, as it seemed, its wedge-shaped tail wagging, its throat feathers ruffled.

Macha laughed. Her fur coat fell from her shoulders, slipped down. She was naked and her skin was so white it made Ingrid catch her breath. She had never seen a body so perfectly slender, but thin, almost starved in its perfection.

'My pet!' said the woman, and pretended to stroke the bird, which snapped at her ferociously with its black bill. She crooned a few lines of a song in a strange melodious language; the raven wagged its head from side to side, as if it were listening. Then it seemed to fall asleep. The woman pulled her coat around her shoulders, shuddering as if she had just felt a cold draught, though the air in the place had become stifling.

'This is a holy place, this island,' said the woman. 'It is here that a few of us wait for the great battle, the last battle, for the war that will tear the sun and the moon from the heavens, and hurl the seas upwards into the great bowl of the sky. We are prepared to wait a long time – but that is no concern of yours, Ingrid. If you wish to go further, to learn how to grow up and be a woman in this evil world, you must give me a gift offering. Otherwise – '

She stopped and pursed her red lips.

There was something disturbing, almost obscene, about Macha's gaunt beauty, but Ingrid was not physically afraid of the woman. What terrified her was the idea that Macha might go away, might leave her imprisoned in that chamber.

'What can I offer you?' Ingrid asked, thinking of how little she had in her pack.

Macha did not hesitate. 'I will take your food,' she said. 'All your earthly food, which is the food of death.'

Without hesitation, Ingrid searched out in her pack all the food they had collected for her in the village: dried meat, fruits, and nuts and some small cakes made of wild rice. It was good food and the sight of it woke Ingrid's hunger, but Macha immediately threw it into the fire.

The fire blazed up, revealing a narrow tunnel at the base of the rock wall, near the tethered bird.

'Go that way,' said Macha, pointing.

Ingrid hesitated. Crawl into that tunnel? She would have to go on her hands and knees, in the darkness!

Now she felt afraid; she started to protest, but Macha turned away, swinging her cloak and muttering a few incomprehensible words. The raven croaked; the fire began to dim. Ingrid hesitated no longer; she threw off her mittens and her heavy outer garments, swung her pack up over her shoulder, and made a rush for the tunnel. Closing her eyes, she crawled into the dark narrow space, scrambling forward as the angry bird beat its wings around her shoulders.

She wriggled forward, along a soft track of mud; her fingers poked unpleasantly into a shifting compost, her knees sank down in slime. Choked and nauseated, she endured the smell of deep earth rot and mud, mingled with a faint fishy odour. She crawled forward, with eyes closed, determined. All the while the roof pressed down on her; she feared it would cave in and trap her, bury her alive or break her spine. She kept crawling forward, gasping and choking back her fear. Then her pack caught on something; she cried out and panicked. Was this a trap, was it a trap, after all? The thongs on her pack broke; she tried to pull it along behind her but she could not. The tunnel had become even narrower. Her clothes began to rip and tear; it was as if the rock were flaying her alive. She could see nothing; she made her way by touch alone, by instinct, out of terror.

She screamed now. Again and again. She feared that the

tunnel would end, that she would come to an impassable barrier, a blank wall. She could never go back; she clawed forward, no better than an animal. Her clothes had been nearly torn away, clothes salvaged in the village, the last of her possessions from her own dear Wayland.

The thought brought her close to despair. But she did not stop, she could not. So it was above the sound of her clawing and scratching that she heard the strange voice.

It was a woman's voice keening, raising a harsh cry.

'Baaabd, Baaabd, Baaabd,' crooned the voice.

Ingrid wondered if it could be the echo of her own voice, a sound inside her skull.

'Baaabd, Baaabd, Baaabd,' crooned the voice. A voice from outside her, yet close in her ear.

I am going to die, Ingrid thought, this is the song of my death. But she crawled forward.

Her fingers touched emptiness; she lost her balance and tumbled suddenly through an opening.

Something dusty, prickly, yielding, broke her fall.

She blinked and rolled over. Half-blinded, she groped for a sense of where she had fallen. Her eyes stung; everything blurred, but she felt space, very welcome, all around her.

Her head bent slightly; she had started to rub her eyes to clear them. Then someone dashed cold water, icy cold water, in her face.

She jumped up, sputtering and choking. The water ran down from her forehead, down her cheeks; her eyes cleared.

A hideous old woman stood before her, laughing and holding up an empty wooden bucket.

'I am Morrigan,' she said.

Ingrid could not speak. She stared at the woman, a squat, white-haired crone, dressed in a ragged grey cloak. She had strange mismatched eyes, long crooked fingers, and a gap-toothed smile.

'Welcome to our humble little island,' said the crone. 'I trust my sisters took good care of you and made you welcome. You must be a strong soul, to come here all alone, to visit

Morrigan. Come to my table now, and refresh yourself after your journey.'

She led the way to a crude table. Ingrid, still dripping cold water, wiped off her face with her hands.

The girl saw a large rocky chamber, lighted by small lamps and a great blazing fire. The place resembled a crude stable (Ingrid had landed on some rotten old bales of hay); there were small niches like window-slits, along the wall, large double doors at the far end, a wooden table in the centre. To the right, a horned head rose out of the shadows, two mild eyes peered out at her. The air smelled of straw and dung. The cow (an ordinary milking cow, as it seemed) pulled its head up and bellowed: the sound was both mournful and stupid, and the animal, as if ashamed, bent away. Nearby, a slender white goat raised its sleek head and bleated. Tethered, like the cow, it stood on its thin wobbly legs not far from the big doors.

The old woman laughed, pointed a place, and Ingrid, shuddering a little, sat down on a bench. She thought of those 'sisters' – the thin girl at the entrance, the voice in the tunnel. Now she had to face this ugly old woman, with her vulgar turned-up nose and her strange mismatched eyes. Ingrid was fascinated by those eyes, the one fierce cornflower blue, the other grey, flecked with yellow. Yet she was also aware of a strange smell, slightly sulphurous and nasty, that emanated from the crone's person.

'Here, my dear, drink this. It will make you feel better.'

The crone poured some milk from a jug into a wooden cup. Ingrid drank it off: it had a sweetish taste, and made her a little dizzy. She closed her eyes and waited for her head to clear.

When she looked up again everything seemed brighter and sharper. It was an odd feeling, hard to define, as if everything in the room had jumped a little closer: yet the effect was not oppressive.

Morrigan, too, looked strangely different: she seemed thinner; her face somehow sharper and longer; her body not so plump, but thinner, almost scrawny.

'What kind of place is this?' asked Ingrid suspiciously. 'Why should the shaman have directed me to come here?'

Morrigan sprang around the table and gave a little shriek of laughter.

'This is a timeless place,' she whispered, 'where past, present and future meet. This is the place of all contraries, the shrine of birth and of death, of peace and of destruction, of male and of female!'

'It looks like a crude stable to me,' said Ingrid sarcastically. 'But at least there's a door to get out!'

'To see a door is one thing; to get it open is another,' said the crone. 'Have some more milk, dear.'

In spite of herself, Ingrid swallowed another cup of the milk. She felt better and better; everything looked almost cosy, inviting.

'You've come a long way,' said Morrigan. 'I hope you feel much better now.'

'I've come looking for the woman named Glimir, a witch who stole a cup from my father. It was an ancient cup, made by the ancient people – perhaps by your people.'

'Perhaps . . . who knows?' croaked Morrigan. 'Anyway, things are declining in this world – thievery, and murder and the marriage bed dishonoured. A wind-age, a wolf-age, till the world ruins! The old gods and goddesses, it seems, have forgotten mere mortals. And even those great ones, say the wise, may be doomed! The followers of the Christ talk of the end of creation. For a while they awaited it, and it didn't come – not even after a thousand years. What did they expect? A thousand years is nothing! I could have told them that. The end of the world will come between eyeblinks, quietly as a cat moves, or like the breath of a fish, and no one will be the wiser.'

Something in these words touched Ingrid's mind. Had she heard them before? In an old story perhaps? She peered more closely at the hag woman.

'I think I understand,' said Ingrid suddenly. 'Of course you belong to the ancient people! The people who made the magic cup, who wrote the strange signs on stone! The people who came to this land before the Vikings!'

'So many opinions,' said Morrigan. 'But what kind of host can I be? You're sitting there, nearly naked, shivering a little, and I've done not a thing about it.'

Before Ingrid could reply the crone moved across to the firepit. She picked up a large wooden bucket by the handle, and half-swung and half-dragged it back to the table.

Morrigan rolled up her sleeves, dipped her skinny hands into the bucket and brought out handfuls of mud dark as pitch, which she proceeded to slap gently on Ingrid's back and shoulders.

The girl was about to protest, but the mud felt warm and pleasant; she relaxed, and when Morrigan bade her to stand up, she did so.

The last bits of clothing were torn away from her body, and mud plastered all over her back, thighs, and shoulders.

She stood there, in a strange way moved, tears running down her cheeks.

The crone finished up by daubing her neck with the black stuff, then her forehead and even her earlobes.

At last Morrigan stood back and studied Ingrid with her crooked glance. She nodded her satisfaction, shook her hands vigorously, whereupon, to Ingrid's astonishment, the black mud ran off them.

'Come with me,' said the old woman.

Ingrid followed meekly; she felt eased, charmed; her body encased in a kind of quietness, though her mind was sharp enough.

Morrigan led her back towards the big doors, beyond the crackling fire.

After a few steps Ingrid stopped short. A tremor of fear, like a physical spasm, penetrated her calm. She started to speak but her throat was without moisture. The cow bellowed mournfully across the cavern, and the goat perked up its head and bleated.

Ingrid stared in horror and disbelief at the walls: the tiny niches she had thought might be windows seemed to have expanded and deepened; a faint light glowed from somewhere behind and to the side of them, illuminating the objects enshrined in each one.

She saw heads, human heads, set up and gaping, skulls, some old and shrunken, others peeling, as if cobwebs of flesh had fallen down and stuck to the broad stone ledge.

All Ingrid's terror of the dark woods, of the grey folk, flashed upon her. It was as if a blinding light had been thrust in her face as she stood in a dangerous, dark place. It left her helpless and paralysed. She could not even scream.

Morrigan's thin fingers touched her arm; she felt herself led forward, though her legs had gone weak and she stumbled. She was made to sit down beneath a skull that had been set in a high niche above the great wooden doorway.

It was an ancient dark skull, darker than amber, though not so black as the shining mud or pitch that encased Ingrid. She gazed up at the skull – two eyes seemed to float, like the blue flames of candles, in the shadowy sockets.

The voice of Morrigan squawked in the girl's ear.

'There shall be no triumph of the Christ while we hold the power. See, above you, the saint's head. He who sailed long ago to find a magic place in the West. St Brendan, locked forever in this island out of time!'

Ingrid could not speak, but Morrigan continued.

'And everyone who finds us shall die, unless he can read the deepest riddle of his own heart. Look before you, Ingrid of Wayland, and solve it if you can!'

There was a flat smooth rock floor in front of her. Ingrid gazed down at it, and saw, through a crack which opened suddenly, the dark swirling sea, its white waves tipped with light.

'There is an ocean to be crossed twice, once in sleep and once in sorrow. Cross it if you can, Ingrid of Wayland!'

Ingrid looked up slowly: was it the skull that had spoken? Or Morrigan, whispering in her ear? She could not turn; she could not get up.

The crack in the rock widened. A film came over her eyes: she saw Glimir lying naked on a ledge far below. The witch was very young and beautiful, her golden hair stirred softly in a faint breeze. A man came out of the shadows – he too was naked – he bent over and embraced Glimir. Ingrid could not see his face. Something stirred in her memory; she tried to stand up but a great weight pressed down on her shoulders.

The voice spoke again in her ear. 'The end of the world – if those Christians only knew! Brother will kill brother; the hatred between men and women will boil over into violence. Mothers and sons, sisters and brothers, will make love together. The winter of winters will come. Sun and moon will be devoured and the stars will vanish from the skies. The earth will be shaken and broken. All bonds will burst; the serpent will rise up from the depths and the gods and the giants enter battle. There will be no saints and no little Jesus to bless the world then!'

The crack in the rock widened. Ingrid looked down and saw her own village, the living image of her own dear Wayland. Her gaze swept past Horic's and Aun's, down past the blacksmith's and on towards the barn that fronted the Whispering Meadow. And there was Runolf's crooked chimney, and the widow Osk's bright yellow shutters. There was Ingolf's small weathered shack, and the little boy born with a hare lip sat beside it . . .

Tears ran down Ingrid's cheeks.

'Ingrid.' A voice came from where the skull sat. 'My sweet dear girl.' The crack in the rock closed at her feet. Like an eye winking shut.

That voice was familiar, a voice full of tenderness, one she had almost forgotten.

She looked up. It was no longer the skull of the saint; no longer the dark amber death's head. It was a man's head, and the face was familiar.

She jumped up.

'Father!' she screamed. 'Oh, my father!'

She heard laughter at her elbow; the mournful cry of the animals. She turned round.

Morrigan was gone. Instead there stood beside her an old man strangely youthful, his skin pink and fresh, his grey hair thick and lustrous. He was dressed in a curious motley garb, all patches and scraps, in a red and green jerkin, with a jewelled belt and a bright silver buckle on which the runic letter ᚠ appeared in dark inlay. His boots, sharp-toed and elegant, were a glittering mesh, as of woven silver, and his hands flashed with bright rings.

That much Ingrid saw at a glance, but what held her were his eyes: the strange mismatched eyes of Morrigan.

'A timeless place,' the man said. 'As I explained to you.'

'Who – who *are* you?' Ingrid asked warily, wrapping herself round with her arms. There were no skulls now; the niches were mere slits in the wall; the crack in the rock floor had vanished; there was only the smell of a stable and the restless stamping of the animals.

The man did not answer her question, but danced a little jig around her.

'What kind of trickery is this?' Ingrid turned on him. 'Is it Glimir then, who has sent you to do this?' She felt naked, exposed before the strange man, and at the same time very angry.

'Aha, a girl of some spirit, no ordinary flower of the country . . .'

The man had begun delicately to touch and press the wood of the great door, as if he were looking for a secret latch.

'How can a person be a woman and then a man?' Ingrid demanded. 'Is there no certainty in this place? I know there is some trickery here, either of Glimir or of – the Wanderer himself. Why have I been told to come here?'

'So many questions . . . Yes, I think I have the feel of this. Stand back, my dear, I want to do a trick for you.'

He waved her back towards the centre of the room, and Ingrid moved slowly away from the doorway and the central niche from which the dark skull of the saint had vanished. How ordinary the place looked now, how unfrightening, and that smell of the animals – it was almost like the farms in Wayland! Had she really seen her father's face above the doorway? It was a cruel trick. She had felt her love go out to him, overwhelmingly. She had seen Glimir and, yes, Harg lying together, as if they were lovers. And before that, this despicable old man, or young man, this changeling, he had touched her! It was horrible!

While she reflected, and grew increasingly bitter in her mind, Ingrid was watching him. She saw him touch the door repeatedly, then he cried out suddenly – a sharp terse command in a language she did not understand; he sprang back, his silver boots flashing. There was a creaking and several quick snaps. The great metal bolt in the door slid slowly back. Groaning like the wheels of a hundred wagons, the great doors swung in on their hinges.

Ingrid looked out upon space and the sky and the most beautiful sunrise she had ever seen.

Far away, and low on the vast horizon, the orange disc of the sun was swinging up on a dark bank of clouds, as if a light were being kindled, minute by minute, in the void left by an endless night. Stars sparkled softly in the high dome of heaven. A dark sea, streaked with the day's first bright beams, lay almost motionless and tamed, as if under the spell of both fire and ice. It was a moment as solemn as the end of the world; yet the day was clearly beginning.

Cool air rushed into the cavern. Far away, there was a gentle sound of waves lapping and the cry of a bird close at hand.

Ingrid was moved. She raised her hands and gave thanks with a single word: 'Odin!'

The strange man who had done this miracle turned to her and said in a voice that resembled a cackle: 'Odin, my dear, is an old brute. He loves power and war, but above all he loves suffering – so long as the suffering is that of others for him!'

Ingrid stood stunned. The man came back towards her and took her gently by the hand. His own hands seemed very cold; or was it the air that was making her shiver so?

He led her towards the open doorway, towards the sunrise.

'It's true that Odin once claimed to have tortured himself to gain knowledge, but I suspect he put out that story himself as a piece of self-flattery. More likely he stole the secret from someone else.'

As he spoke these words a powerful gust of wind from the clear air whirled into the space between the great doors and the chamber walls and set them rattling. They shook for a moment as if they would fly off their hinges. Then the wind stopped and there was silence.

The old man squeezed her fingers hard, looked around uneasily, then continued his discourse.

'As for the great goddess, the threefold – Macha, Babd, Morrigan – it's all so disgusting! She's a shadow, though her victims are legion. Who would want to be locked in her womb or nourished at her vegetative bosom! She is the great dark hollow underneath the mountain and you may wander there until doomsday and never see the light!'

As the old man spoke these words there was a shudder in the rock far below them, a rumbling like an earthquake, in the very centre of the island. They swayed for a moment, perilously close to the cliff's edge. A few small fragments of rock came tumbling down from the sides of the cavern. The cow and the goat set up a furious bellowing and bleating. This continued for some seconds, then the ground beneath them settled.

Ingrid stood gazing down at the smooth grey water. Minute by minute the sunrise was exploding among the grey clouds.

'What is important,' said the old man, who looked younger with each word, his eyes reflecting the sparkle of the first light. 'What is *really* important is to knock away the boundaries, and go forward. There is a spirit known by many names, among many peoples. Though some have professed to despise him, he alone furthers change. If you would find your true way, you must be prepared to name him, in the language of your people.'

Ingrid shivered in the fresh breeze. She gazed down at the gleaming cold sea.

'His name? You mean *your* name,' she asked quietly. 'Oh, that is no mystery – for at last I remember. It's like an old story from childhood; or a dream.'

'Then who am I?' asked the old man (though now he was looking younger, as in the first youth, his cheeks fresh and ruddy, his slender hands unwrinkling under Ingrid's very eyes). 'Who *am* I, dear Ingrid? Think carefully, for if you guess wrong, you lose everything!'

Calmly and thoughtfully, the girl's gaze encompassed the odd man's silver shoes, his piebald coat, the bright runic ᚠ at his ornate belt.

'Loki!' she cried out. 'The shapeshifter!'

'Yes, yes, yes,' he danced a few steps away, then leaned back and touched her lightly on the shoulder with his left hand. 'Now go forward!' he shouted.

And pushed her off the cliff.

Iceland

All morning Val had watched the sea. He lay on a flat rock beyond the marshes; the place overlooked the beach, itself no more than a rough shelf gouged in the low cliffs, but the boy knew it well. Many times he had gone there, pretending to be an outlaw, hiding in the pebbled crannies and ambushing his imaginary cousins, the lords of the high farms, who, because he had slain their father, were determined to hang him.

This day though, after a week of uneasy dreams and a surprise visit from his mother, he had no energy for games. Instead he had pretended he could speak and had sung a song that no-one would ever hear to the porpoises and seagulls.

Bored at last, he had rambled back along the path through the marshes to the mounds and the black river and watched the fish. He had bent over a little pool in the shallow stream and looked at himself in the water, touching his hair and his face, sticking out his tongue at his own voiceless image.

'Valgard,' he could almost hear Granny Falki's voice, see her lips move. 'Valgard, you must watch,' she must be saying.

He had watched, though, because of what he had dreamed, waiting at first with anxious joy and expectation, peering west and south, jumping at every shadow on the horizon, tensing at every flash of light that might signal a distant sail. He had seen the spring day become suddenly winter, observed the chill wind scour the scrub, watched a grey doom of clouds roar back towards the mountains.

A few times he had closed his eyes, and let the dreams wash over him – vivid dreams in which he was pursued by a cruel old man and a berserk, one of Odin's raging warriors, but a princess came out of the sea, and he led her to a homestead where she touched his lips and cured him, so that he could hear and speak.

Yesterday, when his mother had come, he had tried to tell her, drawing signs in the sand, gesturing and talking with his hands, and some of this she understood, but not everything. There were too many colours and shades, too many fine points, and she herself was obviously upset, speaking to Granny Falki and to him with her hands and eyes and pointing off to the rocky coast, which made him glad, because he sensed that she, too, knew about the coming princess. Granny Falki (she was not really his grandmother) had looked very worried, and kept glancing up beyond Thor's Way where the glacier streams ran down, as if she were afraid of a fire bursting out of the mountain, or of the ice expanding to swallow everything, the whole stormy island, in its cold jaws.

'There's no hope for any of us,' the old woman had begun to complain. (Val could almost imagine her old croaking voice as she bawled out the words.) 'There's killing everywhere on the island, and Christians ready to attack Trogheim. What can a granny and a deaf and dumb boy do against an army of Christians? If they find out who I am they might burn me! As for your sweet boy here, that's so handsome, who's to protect him? And you, who's to say they won't string you up as a witch? They won't give you credit, nor me either, for serving the great goddess. They won't understand that we took part

270

in the ceremonies to help the poor womenfolk ease their dying souls. Nobody knows how you live, coming and going like a ghost. Why don't you take the boy and me and go back to Eastland; the evil you talk about is a cloud of midges compared to what we have to bear!'

Then Val had seen his mother's firmness. 'Hold your tongue, old woman,' she had said. 'Leave such decisions to someone who knows what's important.'

So the boy had gone to keep watch. Now afternoon came on, the sun appeared suddenly, glumly, in the west. He saw a flock of snow buntings, a falcon, some seals sporting on a rocky shoal a short distance up the coast and a fishing boat, no doubt heading for Trogheim with the morning's catch.

He crawled out on the shelf, threw stones into the sea, found others which he pretended were Viking boats and set up a battle, pagan against Christian at the water's edge. If what Granny Falki had told him was true, they would all be forced on pain of death to worship the Christ. Of that god he knew nothing, though he had heard he had been hung up like Odin to gain wisdom, and that he had a loving mother.

The boy's own mother had insisted that during these troubles he stay right here at the little homestead, where he had grown up, and never go into Trogheim. She had never let him live in the town; everything he knew therefore he had learned from the farmers and the pedlars – though the most important things came sideways, from the wind and the sea and the birds, from the sight of the mountains and from his dreams. The farmers felt sorry for him, it seemed: 'Such a fine lad, with no voice and no hearing. It's a curse; there's good reason, but it's not his fault, after all.'

They would often say such things to each other, thinking he didn't understand.

But his mother knew how much he could gather from gestures and lips – she had taught him. Not only was she beautiful, but very clever and full of wisdom and craft. Mostly he didn't dare think of her because the sadness would overcome him; he couldn't bear it without her, and once she had left him for years, though he never forgot her slightest look or gesture.

Even Granny Falki, stern and grim, sometimes took him aside and hugged him, crying bitterly and telling him she knew things would change, that one day he and his mother would live together, like any mother and son.

Mostly, though, the old woman would desert him, without so much as a tear, going in to Trogheim to sell her eggs and chickens, or for one of the funerals, in which she had a part, but what it was she would never tell him.

At those times old Runolf came to look after him, a peasant with dirty fingernails and a running nose, who would beat the boy and make fun of his deafness, though not leave any mark on his skin, for he feared his mother. If Val told the blonde witch anything, Runolf warned him, he would kill him.

But when the boy felt persecuted and miserable he reminded himself that Runolf was not the only one who had secrets and power. For Runolf knew nothing about his mother's special treasure, the magic cup she had brought to the farm to show him one day, just a few months before, when she had come back to him after many blank years. It was by far the most beautiful thing he had ever seen, gleaming silver, all carved with strange, magical images. She explained that she was holding the cup for a time in safekeeping and they had hidden it together in a place by the sea, so that Granny Falki would never be able to sell it for food or steal it altogether and run away. Now and then they would take it out and look at it, and his mother would sigh and shake her head, as if uncertain, though sometimes she would smile in a way that made the boy afraid, because she looked then almost evil.

After learning how much his mother trusted him, Val was more than ever anxious to tell her about his vivid dreams. These came every night now. At first he thought everyone had such dreams, but when he understood more, he saw they were a special gift, probably conferred from his mother's womb – they were a special cleverness, a sharpness of eye during sleep.

So he remembered everything about them and drew images sometimes to show his mother; but even she did not always understand and urged him to be patient – her own life was sad and she could not help him, but she was going to see that he would have a new life. When he grew up, if he could not fight or tell stories perhaps he could draw or make tapestries – and she explained about all the rich things in the houses of Trogheim.

She explained something much more exciting too; she told him about another land in the west, where she and he had been born. But she had great sorrow there and while he was still a baby she had sailed here, to the old homeland, to escape the worst of her suffering. She was under a spell, the boy thought, though she never said so, perhaps it was one that might be broken by the princess; or else he himself would rescue his mother from her sorrow. Then they could live together and be happy forever. Or even find his father, whom he had never seen, whom his mother never spoke of, but when he asked her once, as much as he could dare, if he were still alive, she said 'yes.'

He tried to imagine himself, as a child, sailing over the great sea, but his mind stopped short of encompassing it. His first memories were of their poor little homestead, with the house hardly bigger than some others' sheds, and most of all the beautiful face of his mother leaning over his bed to tell him stories that he could never hear. When she learned how it was with him she began to teach him, drawing pictures and making gestures, speaking with a slow round mouth, so that he could connect the sight with some object or command.

He lived in a world of roaring silence and so, a few years before, when he was about ten, he had begun at last to dream, to fill up that silence with pictures. His mother told him his dreams would give him power.

That spring day, however, his dream was not fulfilled. When the sun began to sink down in the west and the wind grew stronger again along the shore, he picked his way home through the marsh. Granny Falki had porridge and mutton and some cow's milk for him at the table, but he went to see

Meadowsong, their only cow, and his favourite animal companion. He had cherished her clumsy presence for years, but he knew that some day she would die – that he, too, would die, passing away completely from the earth. So he went to her to make something happen between their eyes so that there would be a thread to catch hold of between them in the darkness of death.

That was the kind of thing he could not have explained to anyone, even had he been able to speak.

Granny Falki waved to him, standing at the house door and looking anxiously around at the dark clouds which by now had nearly blotted out the mountains.

The wind had gained strength and he saw that the boards of their only shed were flapping wildly. He felt a few drops of rain, ran towards the house and settled down to supper. He did not dare to ask when his mother might be coming back.

For a long time he lay in the warm loft not sleeping, feeling the straw at his head and feet and sensing Granny Falki nearby; he imagined the mice scratching and scampering around below, as he knew they always did. The dying fire cast a flickering light in the tiny chimney, which he could see beneath the ladder. He stared at it intensely and nearly drowsed into sleep.

Something told him that the storm was getting worse; the fire was springing up nervously, making shadows dance across the mud walls. Some raindrops sprinkled him. He got up, anxious to see the spectacle, and crept downstairs.

The door had blown open. Rain was pelting down in the yard which had turned into a mud-tarn. He could see the little shed, a vague dark outline, and knew the cow would be sitting down miserably underneath their one stunted tree. He decided to go and talk to her, to cheer her up, and pulled on his cloth boots and cloak. It must be noisy; he assumed Granny was sleeping, making deep breaths through her nose, and so could hear nothing. She would not wake and take alarm at his absence.

He crept across the yard, shielding his eyes from the fierce rain, but when he was about halfway to the shed he knew something was wrong – felt it suddenly in his throat – stopped and looked sharply around.

A shadowy figure stood in the doorway of the shed, the tall figure of a man whose presence was signalled to the boy in a strong wave of energy, as if a furnace of light had suddenly opened in the night's blackness.

Val knew that he could not retreat, that the energy was compelling him to go forward, step by step, though he could see nothing clearly. He was a little afraid, but it was not a fear that weakened him, but a feeling of awe that gave him strength, as if an eagle on a cliff had suddenly swooped down to address him and him alone, in recognition.

The figure did not move but the boy was drawn forward, and he wondered; could this be one of the Christians I have heard of, these folk with a new power?

He was only ten steps from the figure, not able to stop, when a flash of lightning illuminated the whole yard, and for an instant held everything in a magical suspension of half-light.

By the shed a tall old man stood waiting; he was dressed in a dark hooded cloak and remained motionless, leaning arrogantly forward on a great wooden staff, that was partially concealed by the folds of his overcoat. With one fierce burning eye, which reflected the lightning, he stared down at the boy, who at once felt impelled to walk up to him.

'Good evening,' said a voice in the boy's head. He would have jumped back, but some power held him rooted. He had heard his own voice like that and, very faintly, his mother's, but this was very different. It was as if a shaft of light had cleft darkness from darkness: could that be what it meant to *hear words*?

Before he could think further, he found his answer sounding clearly: 'Good evening, sir.'

'No I am not a Christian,' said the old man. The boy thought the voice had a rough edge of humour, though certainly the old man did not smile. 'I am far from that,' he added.

So the old fellow was answering his questions even before

he sounded them in his head! Surely, he must be a very great magician – unless this was only a dream.

'A dream of sorts, yet not a dream,' said the old man. 'Don't trouble about that. I have a command for you, one I am sure you are able to perform. You know of the young princess.' (The boy gave a jump and pictured her.) 'No, that is not a dream of yours only; she will come here in fact – very soon. When she does you must do as I command. You must give her the silver cup hidden by you and your mother. Your mother has sinned greatly; she had no right to take the cup; it must be restored to the princess. Do not let those feelings of rebellion stir you! MY WORD MUST BE OBEYED!'

With the first reference to his mother, the boy's mind had resisted the old man. Violently, he tried to push away the stranger's words; to throw them from his consciousness. He strained to break out of the vice of power in which the old man held him – he strained but was nonetheless held.

Anger came, the old man's, like a mountain exploding; it overwhelmed Val, made him stagger back under a violence of sound (silent sound) that was deafening. It was as if the boy's body was being shaken apart from within. It nearly tore his head from his shoulders; his eyes from his sockets. And yet he could not scream.

Then something happened, as if a bolt of lightning had first caught the boy, then thrown him suddenly aside. The old man, too, staggered. His cloak swirled out; the rain drove through its folds as if it were not there at all.

Meadowsong, the cow, had come lumbering out of the darkness to stand between the boy and the old man, switching her tail, opening her mouth in what must have been a terrific loud bellow. The rain ran in streams off her flanks; her hooves sank deep in the mud.

The boy was released.

He turned and ran out of the barnyard, his boots splashing mud, rain driving down in his face, almost blinding him before he found the narrow track through the marshes.

Could he really run away from that power? He half-expected some great flash of lightning, a thunderbolt from on high, to seek him out and kill him, but he ran, ever faster and step by step more surely along the path he had known since childhood, and no such violence came.

He felt terror then, thinking of Granny Falki in the house, of his poor cow, of the anger boiling in the man, an anger he had not thought possible on earth. He felt terror because of his mother. Now he was glad she was not here, but he must go and find her. Somehow he would have to explain to her what had happened: that the old man (who had not even told him his name) wanted to punish her, to take her one treasure, the precious thing they had shared between them, that cup.

His mother a sinner? Impossible! The boy had known her and clung to her since first opening his eyes. He had seen the beauty she could bring to ordinary things; he knew her tenderness to be a precious thing; his lips had tasted life from her breasts; his eyes had taken meaning from her lips.

It was a lie and, if the old man said otherwise, then despite all his power, he knew nothing!

The rain sliced down around him, beating against the black cliffs. He was approaching the shore and the boy knew he must rest. He could not see very far, but his sharp eyes easily picked up the trail. He wound his way among the rocks, bounding along, coming closer and closer to the sea. A plan was forming in his mind: he would rest on the beach where he had waited all day, then climb up a path he knew on the cliffs and circle back to the farm. He could spy out the buildings and see what the old man had done. Then he would get food and drink and go in search of his mother.

He stopped for a moment, breathing hard, and looked behind him. There was nothing, the marshes were dark. He plunged on.

The last part of the path wound among large boulders, balanced like stone eggs, above the little shelf where he liked to lie in the sun. These he approached warily; in the shining dark rain they looked almost like hunched figures, like the giants he had heard tell of from Granny Falki. He thought of the stranger: was he then a giant, a magician; or – something else?

Something, a faint recollection, some word of a figure with a hooded cloak and one eye had begun to form in the boy's mind. Runolf, he was sure, had spoken of such a man; and cautioned him not to mention this to his mother, for she had forbidden it. But Runolf had not called him a man . . .

The boy took a staggering step, caught up by a thought which raised him suddenly in the path like a fierce blast of gale, hurled him off his feet and sent him sprawling down among some loose wet stones.

Slowly, he got to his feet. His thoughts were in turmoil. He eased himself gently down on the rough shelf, wiped the dripping moisture from eyes and went no further.

Down on the beach was a light, a storm lantern. A small boat, a kind of coracle, sat rocking violently to and fro in the rough waves. Two men stood there in the driving rain; they were helping a third to step out on the beach. Farther out from the shore a faint light betrayed the presence of another, larger vessel. The boy, who had spent so many years watching ships sail past, could see at once that this latter was no Viking ship. The type in fact he recognized as belonging to their enemies, the ancient people, some of whom the Vikings held as slaves, though such wild people had visited his own stormy island even before the Vikings – or so said the old men who tilled the fields around their farm.

He crawled up behind one of the boulders and watched. This was no raid, not at night, with a single vessel anchored off the storm-racked coast.

No; it was clear they were putting someone ashore, that third figure even now standing, rather dumbfoundedly and alone on the shadowy beach, bent over in the driving rain, as the two others climbed back into the boat and began to paddle away into the near darkness.

The boy watched. Then a lightning flash illuminated the beach, the person standing there, the little boat pulling away from the shore, crossing the dark waters to the mother ship.

A moment before the lightning flash might have made Val think again of the old man, might have driven the boy in

278

terror far up along the rocky cliffs, into some hiding place there.

What he saw, however, transfixed him to the spot.

A girl, the tall white-faced princess of his dreams, was walking through the rain to where he waited.

The Hanged Man

They had left her there, on the island, an island that seemed as real, or as unreal, as the others. She could not be sure of very much in the rain and the darkness: was this at last the other world she knew they had been seeking?

A flash of lightning made her blink; in front of her, not far up the beach, she saw dark boulders, a rock wall, and steep cliffs. Water ran hissing in runnels, swallowed up by the sea. She sensed all around her the presence of a harsh violent land. Yet she prayed it would not vanish without warning, like so much she had known during the last days.

Her mind ranged away, climbing the bridge without breadth; she had climbed it before: she had seen the islands open up, one by one, then fade quickly like dreams only half-remembered.

They had sailed, in that frail boat of skins, to an island where four-footed creatures with huge antlers came down to the shore and watched them. She remembered their thin ribs, their starving eyes; and the mournful cries that pursued her across the water.

They had landed on an island where huge birds shrieked at them as they climbed high on the bare rocks, looking for eggs.

They had circled an island of fire, and watched great glowing embers hiss and vanish in the steaming waves.

They had sailed past an island of glass, in which the violent sunset glowed for a long time green, yellow and purple.

They had visited a grey empty island where their own wild laughter reverberated among the cliffs and hollows.

They had seen an island where an arch of water, like a rainbow full of gems, rose from one side and fell on the other.

They had found an island inhabited by dusky-skinned people but when some of them had tried to bed the women, a battle ensued; so they sailed away fewer than they came.

On the last island, strange people in skins ran out on the beach and shouted 'They are here!' But none of the voyagers had ever seen that place before, and they were frightened, and so sailed on.

All this Ingrid called up like events dreamed to life or half-remembered in fever. And these memories mingled with others: she saw an old woman who turned into a man; her own plummeting fall from a steep cliff into the icy water; strong hands gathering her up, wrapping her in furs like swaddling. Then the long voyage, a dream enclosing dreams, and the islands, stepping stones across a great void, like glimpses in a darkness in which she heard voices, felt hands touching her hot brow, and tasted sweet milk that made her sleep and forget.

Now she felt frail and worn; she might have aged a thousand years since her last sight of the shaman on that cliff by the far northern sea. She had been transformed; her body had been honed down, made wraith-like, so it might enter a web that stretched far beyond the crude world of her old seeing, the world of 'reality'. Yet she was she; her feet touched the ground, the hurt ankle still tender; she was aware of the strange clothing where it pressed against her familiar body; and this dizziness, this pain behind the eyes was real. Only now it was possible to understand a little what Birch Tree had said about her being held in his mind throughout her journey; even though she knew she had just stepped out of that world; and that another, a new human consciousness, drew her.

So she walked, step by step, up the stony beach, and the rain ran down across her eyes, and tickled her neck beneath the collar. Then she saw the great boulders, like dung droppings made of iron, and there, crouched behind the boulders, a boy stared up at her as if she were indeed a ghost, or had come from the Other World.

The boy stood up slowly. He was dressed in the rough clothes of a farm-lad; rained dripped from his shoulders, curled his hair. In the darkness she could not see him clearly, though his eyes gathered light. It had been so long, a long time without human touch; she wanted to hug him, to draw him to her, but she hesitated. The contact might be too much for her; she needed time, a few moments. So she waited for him to speak.

He did not speak, but in the next flash of lightning, she saw that he was signing to her with his hands, while his lips moved without sound. She also saw that he was very beautiful. She found her voice; it sounded strange; during her whole long voyage, she had not spoken.

'I have been asleep – sick for a long time,' she told him. 'A ship brought me from the west. Do you feel close to me as I feel close to you? Do you understand me?'

She sensed the boy's excitement; he nodded. She imagined she could hear him reaching out to her, as if threads spindled out from his mind.

'May I – ? May I take your hand?' she asked him, and a warm wave of feeling passed over to her, even before she touched him.

His slender hands were wet with rain. She took them and laid them on her cheek. It was as if the touch of human flesh burned through her skin. But she let the burning pass and soon felt only his hands, bathed in rainwater.

He pulled her away into a little hollow space where the cliff arched sharply over and the ground was dry. They crouched there together; she put an arm about his shoulder and it comforted her. They sat watching the rain.

Before the storm passed the boy made a fire, using flints and some dry wood he had concealed in a deep rock-cleft, behind a big log.

Then she could see him clearly, a boy of about thirteen,

with curling blond hair, blue eyes and smooth skin. There was something familiar about him; he did not look like a farm-boy; rather, with his sensitive hands, his thin and delicate lips, like an elf-child – like a waif cast up on the rocks. A quiet strength, she sensed though, behind that beauty.

She started to help him gather wood, reaching into his hiding place, only to have him spring up and with huge staring eyes, wave her back. Startled, she thought how unsure of her he was; how he kept looking out of the cave mouth as if he were fearful that someone might be stalking the place.

Finally, after the rain had stopped, he explained to her, using many gestures, and scratching on the floor, that he was going away a short distance, and would soon return.

So she lay back and waited; then dozed, finding that after her voyaging the land still rolled a little beneath her. It helped her almost sleep.

His return wakened her suddenly; she sensed that only minutes had passed, but his appearance shocked her. His face was streaked; he had been weeping.

She threw her arms around him and held him, feeling his resistance, his wariness.

'My name is Ingrid,' she whispered then. 'Don't be afraid, but tell me what has happened.'

He shook his head and pulled away from her, throwing out his hands in helplessness. He could not, or would not, tell her where he had been or what had upset him, but out of his ragged cloak he pulled a few pieces of cheese and some bread – these he offered her. It seemed to her she had not had any solid food for a long time, yet she ate.

When she had finished, the boy began scratching again at the rock floor. She could make out a kind of stick figure, seemingly a man with long legs, wearing a cloak, and leaning on a staff, while at his feet a dog or other animal lay prone and obedient.

'Your father?' Ingrid asked. 'Or your grandfather?'

The boy shook his head; tears ran down his cheeks, but he wiped them with his sleeve and wrote a single word on the rock. 'Trogheim,' it said: he pointed to himself and Ingrid and then outside where the rainless night was brightening slightly, as if before dawn.

'All right,' Ingrid told him, understanding everything at once. 'We shall to go Trogheim.'

They started immediately. The boy led the way along the cliff path. They walked for a long time, and the sky filled up with light. In the grey pre-dawn Ingrid could see birds far below them; gulls and ducks making a racket at the foot of the sea wall. The water stretched placidly to the horizon, not a ship to break its smooth surface with a ripple.

On the land side it was different: a great semicircle of black rocks; a grey glacier stream tumbling violently down a steep cliff and, beyond, an unimaginable range of mountains, a great mass of dark grey peaks worked into pyramids and shelves, like giant buildings ruined by some world cataclysm: at the very summits of these the sun spilled light, as from a cauldron, bursting through thin clouds and mist, illuminating endless jagged ridges and streaks of white snow.

For the first time Ingrid found herself in a landscape that induced a kind of hopelessness in her heart. The feeling overtook her that in the face of all this inhuman beauty, she counted for absolutely nothing.

Very well, then, I am nothing, she thought grimly, bowed her head and pressed on beside the boy.

Slowly, they made their way back inland, descending through a narrow valley full of loose shale and round grey boulders; then through a valley where old lava bed floors sprouted moss and flowers; then a great plain of grey sand, grey rocks sticking up, tufts of sea-pink and dwarf willows between two quick rushing streams.

They stopped to rest in the thin clump of willows; stream water, milk-white and sickly, flowed over the rough flat stones. Ingrid, puzzled and disappointed, drifted into memories of the clear streams of her own country.

That was when the first cry came, echoing harshly from the nearby cliffs.

She tensed and half-rose, hardly sure what it was. The boy did not move, but Ingrid saw him watching her. She waited.

Another cry followed – a wild roar, at first very deep-voiced and then shrill, a man's cry such as she had never heard before in her life. It was a little like the cries of the Skraelings – and the sound of those lost voices came back to her – but were instantly obliterated in her mind by the bellowing violence, the sheer mad rage of this outcry.

She could not tell how close the threat was. That it was a threat she never doubted. Thus the demons must cry as they were tortured, as they tortured in turn. It was a soul-cry, but demented.

Ingrid stood up, and the boy with her. He pointed excitedly along the rock-face to where spidery smoke drifted up out of a fault that might have been another valley.

Then she heard other cries, real human voices, women's voices's and men's, screaming in a panic that belied the calm of the clear day. These cries, she thought with a shudder, seemed to reverberate against the grim peaks like a fearful litany.

The sound of hoofbeats clattered along the trail. Ingrid pushed the boy down and they crouched there, waiting. More panicky screaming; then again the unbearable: a low sustained roar of pure violence that constricted her throat, twisted deep inside her and made her hands go limp at her belt.

A horse came galloping along the path from where the smoke rose. Its eyes rolled, as if in fear, its nostrils twitched wildly; part of the snaffle flapped crazily against its withers and back. The terrified beast dashed across the stream beyond the willow bed where Ingrid and the boy lay concealed, and clattered away into a neighbouring valley.

Alarmed human voices followed closely; a big farm wagon rolled by, drawn in haste by two galloping horses. Five or six men scrambled behind, shouting and pointing in the direction in which the frightened horse had just disappeared. Ingrid could see the huddled figures of a few women and children, crouched in the wagon among the baggage; the women moaned piteously; the cries of the children sounded painfully close.

284

She stared in numbed silence after the wagon; then realized that the boy was clutching at her and pointing.

Smoke clouds billowed thicker from the valley ahead.

'Is that Trogheim?' Ingrid asked him, speaking with round lips and pointing.

But the boy shook his head.

They crept out of the willow bush and made their way along the valley, keeping off the main track, making use of such cover as they found there.

The screams, the outcry had long ceased and they had almost reached the low collapsed shale cliffs that seemed to mark the entrance to the transverse valley when they saw the first body.

It was a burly man, lying half-pinned under a huge boulder, his bare feet embedded in mud, his body sprawled awkwardly across a trickle of water, as if he had been trying to dive beneath the rock for safety. It was not necessary to approach him closely to see that his head had been crushed beneath the stone.

Ingrid covered the boy's face gently with her arm.

But it was a useless gesture, as she soon saw, for the little valley was strewn with other horrors.

A dead man sat staring at them. A metal crucifix had been rammed so hard through his throat that part of it was visible at the back of his neck.

On the main trail they found a few severed limbs, which the wagon wheels had also run over.

A woman had been split nearly in half by some wagons and thrown up into a tree. Her arms were stretched stiffly across two twining branches, her long hair waved gently in the gentle wind.

Smoke trailed away overhead, temporarily dimming the sunlight, but concealing nothing of the carnage.

Convulsed with silent sobs, the boy stood beside the murky stream and vomited.

Ingrid, fighting back her own panic, spoke to him gently, and shielded his eyes from every odd-shaped stone; at the same time she questioned him softly: 'Who? . . . who?' she whispered, pointing, 'who might have done this?'

But the boy shook his head and could not answer.

They walked on and Ingrid wondered: could this really be the homeland of her people, the homeland she had heard of in stories, and pictured as a green place, where cattle grazed on pastures scant but beautiful? Could this be the island where great Nerthus rose up in magnificence to light the night sky, the distant place to which Glimir had fled carrying Einar's cup? Now some unweaving of fate had carried Ingrid herself across the broad sea, past islands fantastic as dreams, to touch these shores.

But to what purpose?

There was no light in these valleys, she reflected bitterly – no light despite the clear sky – only darkness and death, and a voiceless child to lead her to a town with an ugly name.

They walked almost blindly, not daring to look around them, then came on a farmstead, wreathed round with bitter smoke and in ruins. A few blackened beams stood up against the mocking blue sky; a dead dog lay beside a smashed trough. Wheel marks and a trail of ashes had half-obliterated numerous human tracks – possibly signs of the family that had fled past them in the rough wagon.

Ingrid had no stomach to linger at that place; she signalled to the boy that they must go on, but he pointed down the flank of the hill, where, from some spot concealed by a rough stone outcropping, more smoke twirled.

Ingrid bowed her head.

'Trogheim?' she asked quietly.

But the boy shook his head. Then he led the way, slipping between the boulders of a shale-washed slope, down through a little gully of red sand and loam, to where a birch grove spread a few scraggly trunks above a dark river.

As they descended, Ingrid could see the source of the new smoke: another farmstead, nestled in the hollow beneath the birch grove. It too had been burnt out, but only partially: the barn smouldered, a roofless ruin, and she smelled the singed hay, and saw loose slivers of black straw, like cut hair, drifting across the turf.

She and the boy crept forward. Two ponies grazed uneasily on the slope just below them. She heard male voices, talking excitedly as if in anger. A huge curved wall of rock, like one side of a tarn, concealed the speakers.

Then she heard it again, the roar of that voice, barely human, echoing from the high cliffs like a curse. It started out like an animal bellow, and ended in a shrill scream. Ingrid felt sick at heart.

She knew she was listening to a voice without pity, to the voice of a creature capable of crushing strong men under boulders and hurling women into trees.

She leaned over and touched the boy's hand. He brushed his head against her shoulder and pointed to where the ponies grazed on the hillside.

Two men ran out from the concealing earthwork, and struggled to mount the ponies, bumping against one another in their excitement and haste. The cries of a third man could be heard from the other side of the broken, dried-up tarn; he seemed to be in pain, but the two men ignored him, steadying themselves in the saddles and galloping away down the hill, disappearing beyond the farmstead.

Ingrid motioned to the boy to crawl along the right side of the earthworks, while she stole away towards the left. At the first cleft in the low wall she darted a glance towards the source of the outcry: what she saw brought her to her feet – then through the stone gap in an instant.

A man had been bound and strung upside down from a tree-branch. He twirled round slowly, his head wrapped tight in a black cloth. He hung not a foot above a fire whose bright flames were licking upward, feeding on a fresh pile of wood tossed there, apparently by the departing horsemen.

The man screamed repeatedly. Ingrid ran forward and kicked away the tinder in all directions.

Sparks crackled; one leg scorched, she stumbled back. The man tensed, tried to swing up, stopped screaming.

She groped for the knife at her belt and hacked at the rope, which frayed, split and parted.

The man fell in a heap on the black earth. He gave a shout, for the ground was still warm with the fire.

Ingrid seized him by the legs, and struggling a little, pulled him away from the glowing embers.

He lay, as if in a sack, his chest heaving, his arms tied behind him, muttering excited phrases she could not understand.

The semicircular wall was all battered and marked with the signs of a struggle. Not far away, a broadsword lay jammed beneath an old log. The boy was nowhere to be seen.

With the point of her knife, Ingrid began to cut away the cloth from the man's head. At first he resisted, then, sensing that he was being rescued, stopped.

She tore away bits of the strong cloth with her teeth.

All the while she had been pressing down on the man's body something had been crying out in her, some recognition. Her thoughts, however, had been elsewhere, with the boy.

Now, as she pulled away the black cloth from the man's face she saw that it was Harg.

'Water,' he whispered, then, recognizing her, he managed a wan smile.

'Harg,' she said softly.

She bent down and clung to him; she kissed his hot forehead.

'Ingrid – I was hoping you would come here. I . . .'

'Don't try to talk, Harg. We must get you up to the house. Only I don't know where the boy's gone.'

She half-rose; but there was no sign of him anywhere.

'The boy?'

She cut his bonds; Harg pushed himself up on one elbow. 'It's all right, Ingrid, they didn't hurt me. It seems that you frightened them off. They won't come back yet.

'But I must rest a while,' he added, his voice trembling a little. He nodded at the house. 'We'll be safe there for the time being.'

Ingrid helped him stand up. The bright flush on his face

faded; he looked suddenly pale and drained. He stood swaying beside her; the tattered, torn hood made a wreath of black skin around his neck.

'Who did this to you, Harg? There are . . . terrible things here . . . up in the valley there.' She looked anxiously round. 'And where can the boy have gone so suddenly?'

He leaned on her arm and they made their way up to the house; with each step Harg seemed to gather some strength.

The door of the place was ajar, and they pushed cautiously in. They found themselves in a dim room lined with bunk-like beds and lighted by a small lamp. Despite the smoky air, Harg collapsed gratefully on one of the beds. At the rear Ingrid found a large kitchen; there was a crude stone stove with a black kettle set on top. A few casks lay nearby and a bundle of peat-fuel. The kettle was warm and a thick stew bubbled within.

'We have shelter and food,' Ingrid declared. 'Now Harg, dear Harg, let me look at you.'

'I knew you would come here, Ingrid,' Harg said, his voice already stronger. 'I knew Glimir would not stop you.'

'Shhhh!'

She stripped off his jerkin and shirt. His shoulders and chest were bruised all over; a ragged raw gash marked his left arm. Ingrid tore some cloth strips, fetched hot water, and began, very gently, to wash him.

When she had cleaned off his wounds, she threw the rags out the door. She looked around anxiously but saw only the barn, still smoking, and the sunlight flashing on the loose shale of the hillside above. She realized she could not call the boy; she did not even know his name.

'The voice,' she asked suddenly, remembering. 'A terrible roaring voice, did you hear it? I think that was what frightened the men.'

He shook his head and looked troubled. 'I heard many voices. I'm confused now . . . I'm sorry.'

'Of course, you must rest!' She eased him back down on the bed, kissing him on the shoulders and neck and thinking how many white hairs had crept into his beard, how the lines on his smooth skin had deepened, her poor Harg!

'Tell me how you came here,' he asked her.

'No, tell me first about your journey.'

Harg closed his eyes and spoke in a low voice. 'This is the country they call Iceland. When you decided that you hated me – ' he smiled slightly on saying this ' – I took passage here in search of Glimir. I wanted to recover the cup for you. I was sure the gods would guide you to this island.'

He paused; Ingrid felt suddenly troubled.

'I don't know how I came here, Harg. I think it was through Loki, the trickster. I remember very little of the journey – it might have lasted minutes, or years. I feel like a wraith, like someone from the other side; I think I have lost all the flesh-lust you used to know in me.'

Harg reached out and drew her to him.

They lay side by side and he continued his story.

'Everything is in chaos here, the Christians beginning to war with the old believers. It is not like our country, where everyone may do as he pleases. They tolerate nothing here, no differences. The Christians are determined to exterminate the old gods.'

Ingrid shook her head in anxiety and puzzlement; he continued.

'I found Glimir in a village close to the foot of the great mountain, Nerthus. She spoke to me; it was the first time in years; she was not hostile, but humble and forgiving, though it was surely a trick. She told me that you must have perished in the wilderness, that if you did not come by winter, she would throw the cup into the volcano and return home. I refused to believe that you were dead. I planned to steal the cup for you, but she forestalled me.' (He laughed a bitter laugh.) 'She always forestalls me. She sent men to kill me before I could do what I planned, telling them I was an evil magician, and that they could gain great power if they sacrificed me, in the old style, to Odin. They would capture my magic, she promised, and perhaps through it help turn the tide against the Christ.'

290

He was silent then; Ingrid washed his clothes in hot water and hung them up by the fireplace. Then she brought him food, keeping an eye on the barnyard while he ate and talked.

'Glimir's men tracked me here. The farmer and his family fled when they attacked. I drove them off and would have killed them but slipped against the earth-wall. They did not kill me at once as I thought they would, but hung me there to burn. A cruel death, but you rescued me from it.'

'I think it was the beast's cry that saved you.'

Harg shook his head, looked away. 'This island is full of cries, full of bestial things, full of fear. It was your coming that saved me, Ingrid. For the second time you have saved me.'

She felt the tenderness in his voice, and hesitated. Then she got up, removed the plates to the kitchen, settled the fire, closed the door tight and turned down the lamp. She found a wool shift in the bedroom upstairs and undressed. The sight of her body surprised her, all aglow in the lamplight as she crouched in the doorway that led to the kitchen. She saw Harg sit up on the edge of the bed, then wince as he slipped off his trousers and boots. He pulled the blankets around him and waited.

Still, she did not move, thinking of another afternoon in a shut place, with violence threatening; she thought of the Buck. Violence and more violence – the Buck dead and Harg sore bruised and beaten. How Glimir must hate them – Ingrid could hardly fathom it. Must love always coil up with violence? Even the Christ, out of love, had been nailed on a tree.

But now she felt bodiless; without passion. She had died to her body; taken the long voyage through darkness, drunk the sweet milk of a life beyond passion. She could not go to Harg in his bed.

He called her softly, and longingly. She walked barefooted across the rough floor and lay down beside him.

'I can't bear it now, to be touched,' she told him quietly, not looking at him, aware of his body beside her.

'We must find Glimir quickly, then sail home together, with the cup. I will help you save your village.'

'Yes,' she said, though she knew it could not be the answer.

Harg was no longer capable of saving; something had taken all his strength – not the wounds of the assassins: something that fed on him, on which he brooded. 'We must sail back together,' she lied to him.

'But first Glimir,' he said, and his voice shook, it seemed with hatred.

She lay against him, feeling his hard body slowly relax. She too relaxed; he hardly touched her, but she slipped into sleep. She felt almost loved; but the thought came to her: there was something in Harg that could not love. As for her, she had loved him, and hated him; now she felt very close to him, but with no passion left, and little enough trust.

At one point she drifted into wakefulness, blinked her eyes and rolled over. Harg was beside her; asleep. Had she heard something else, something outside in the farm yard? Perhaps a falling timber, the crackle of the fire? Vaguely, she remembered the boy. Where had the boy gone? She did not even know his name . . .

Much later, it seemed, she awoke. She was alone in the bed. She sat up, rubbed her eyes, looked around in confusion.

A silence hung over everything, the thick impenetrable silence of a lonely farmstead, without animals; but daylight still lingered, a kind of dusk.

She climbed out of bed and wandered to the window. A round moon was rising, out of sight, though she could feel it, see its odd silver light on the black ruins of the barn and shed, on the dark lip of the old dried-out tarn; she could sense its presence in the glare of light and the deepening shadows that crept across the yard and beneath the few stark withered trees near the gatepost.

She saw the mist rolling down from the hills, a visible dampness, tumbling and swirling, drifting slowly down from the high valleys.

Then, in the shadow of the tarn, she saw two figures standing close together, leaning together in a conversation that was carried on without gestures, almost, it seemed, silently, in the silver darkness.

She recognized Harg and her first instinct was to tap on the window, to go straight out and join them, but something stopped her. Perhaps it was the furtive manner of her lover, who kept turning and casting glances back at the house, so that Ingrid had to draw away a little from the line of sight.

The second figure did not move at all. It was a tall man in a great hooded cloak and, after a moment's doubt and denial, the knowledge of who he was struck Ingrid like a blow.

'The Wanderer!' she whispered aloud, then clapped her hand to her lips.

She shrank back. She could almost feel that bright eye turn searchingly upon her; or did she, out of fear and awe, only imagine it, standing there on the bare floor, shivering, and wondering what Harg, her Harg, must be saying to the old man?

After some hesitation she crept back into the bed and pulled the covers around her. She lay there trembling, thinking how Harg would tell her everything. She herself had no power to face the old man; she would shrink away under the gaze of that bright eye.

She waited, listening for the sound of his footsteps, for the creak of the old door, but this she never heard.

Instead came a sound which shattered the calm night, and caused the windows in the farmhouse to vibrate.

A wild roar, an unearthly howl, flung out of the darkness, springing up from the deep earth.

Ingrid jumped straight from bed, tumbled across the room and tore open the door. Harg was there and she flung herself into his arms.

'We must go at once. We must leave this place!' he said and pushed her almost brutally back into the room.

She gasped for breath, clinging to him, her feet on the cold floor, moonlight in her eyes.

'That . . . what is it? Who were you . . .?'

'We must go, Ingrid! Gather up everything.'

She threw off her shift and fumbled for her clothes in the darkness. Harg was throwing some things in a knapsack.

They left within minutes. The mist had rolled down from the hills; a smell of stale smoke lay over everything. The road was barely visible. A few sheep had wandered from some-where and grazed quietly on the thin grass.

They slipped down to a broad stony track that was almost a road. Ingrid saw that Harg had buckled on his sword; he wore a bright yellow cloak, buttoned up with a brooch. The cloak she had grabbed in her haste was a deep blue.

They walked quickly, without speaking. Ingrid kept waiting for that terrible voice; she feared it would possess them from the mist, overwhelm them. Harg seemed very nervous, gloomy.

They came to a place where a stream bubbled up by the side of the road. Some distance away a hunched figure, like a great battered sack, lay sprawled out on the turf. They approached very slowly. Harg drew his sword.

When they were a few feet away they saw it was a horse, all coiled up and twisted. Its neck was snapped clean and its two forelegs broken. It lay with wide-open mouth and bulging eyes, its tongue drawn out like a pink ribbon, a litter of blood and vomit smearing the damp earth all around it.

Ingrid backed away slowly, overcome by horror and dis-gust; Harg began to draw her along the track.

'Harg,' she whispered, almost in anger, 'what is happening here? What was that terrible voice? You must tell me what you know!'

But Harg shook his head; he guided her along the road, his drawn sword bumping against her as they walked.

'You spoke to someone, Harg. I'm sure you spoke to someone.'

She was afraid to tell him what she had seen.

He sheathed his broadsword, put his arm around her and steered her forward.

'The voice has frightened you, Ingrid. You're imagining things. I was roused by the voice.'

'Whose voice is it then?' she demanded. 'It is the most terrible sound I have ever heard.'

Harg hunched his shoulders. 'I think it is the voice of a berserk, the killer who has no mercy. His cry sends fear into the hearts of his victims. I told you, it is war to the death in this country, the Christ against the old gods. It does not concern us, Ingrid. But we must get to the main road before the full night overtakes us!'

Ingrid let herself be drawn along. She saw how Harg would not look at her, how he concealed from her his meeting with the old man.

Another cry sounded, unmistakable, but this time far behind them, mercifully distant.

Ingrid found herself trembling, but it was not out of fear, for she knew they were ahead of their pursuer.

The berserks, she was thinking, the berserks, but are they not the violent, the fearless ones, the chosen warriors of Odin?

The thought made her tremble with new apprehension. But she followed where Harg led her through the thick mist.

Two Messages

And when the mist cleared a fine rain fell, damping the girl's cheeks, curling the man's beard and hair; they could taste the sea in it, a sharp, bitter taste. Clouds like grey sodden wool hid the mountains; the road wound on through the thick, curtained air. Farmhouses appeared in vague outline, afloat in the light, as if slightly unmoored from the green turf. From time to time a figure appeared in the path, a hunched wary traveller, or grim peasants struggling along behind a wagon, urging on the reluctant horses or cattle.

The road wound around a low hill; the stream disappeared in a boulder-strewn plain. There they saw the town. Dark steaming thatch, smooth shingled roofs rose, a crowd of them, wreathed by wayward smoke plumes from invisible hearthfires. Beyond, the shoreline curved like a sickle; and where the gauzy air split, the dark metal sea hove in view.

Ingrid and Harg stopped together. The girl gazed on Trogheim with sharp wonder and joy, a dim spectral place, but a town nonetheless, the first she had seen since leaving Wayland. There was even a town gate, a kind of portal in the low retaining wall that enclosed the whole place.

The wheels of a cart shrieked, a few voices rose; people and wagons full of goods lumbered in and out.

'This is the place the boy spoke of,' Ingrid told Harg. 'Perhaps we shall meet him here.'

'Trogheim,' he waved his arm. 'A happy town in normal times, but sad enough at the moment. The old believers control it, but the Christians are biding their time. Some townsfolk have fled, fearing a massacre. This is one of the last places where the old gods receive homage. It is not a good place to stay, so we must not linger here, whatever happens.'

They walked on past a few slow-moving carts, full-laden with cheeses and big jugs of milk; they met pedlars with combs, boots and beads, and fish wagons heading on up towards the hills. All the travellers seemed uneasy, peering from side to side sharply, as though sheathing their looks.

'Ingrid,' said Harg, 'We will pretend to be related. I have a cousin here, and it will make things easier. He is a merchant named Brodd, who has good connections; he will help us find Glimir.'

After a while they reached the gateway. They were able to satisfy the heavily armed guards and were allowed through.

Within minutes they were moving along a rain-slicked walkway, between high wooden houses. Because of the murky light lamps had been lit, and the buildings glowed from within like sanctuaries. The air mingled smoke, the odour of fish and the ripe smell of dung.

Ingrid found it odd to be walking on wood planks, unnatural after her long treks in the wilds. The townsfolk slipped by them with in-drawn tight faces; even so, she felt safer in Trogheim than she had on the road. Back there, in the stark hills, the sight of the mutilated bodies, the sense that someone pursued them, had begun to be daunting.

Yet her relief was only partial. Grim peaks, ice-capped towers, rose up, almost near enough to touch and, between the mountains and the grey sea, the town seemed almost insubstantial.

The travellers crossed over a low bridge spanning a sluggish, dark stream. They passed a weaver's and a shoemaker's where bright cloth and boots had been spread out before the doorways, protected from the rain by high canvas awnings. Nearby stood a temple, built all of wood, with a second-floor porch where the remains of the sacrificial animals had been laid out according to custom. Beyond, where the mist blew apart, Ingrid could see the beached ships, their stern posts curved high like the necks of great swans.

They stopped at a tall handsome house, with a fine roof of red thatch, its wattle and daub walls all fresh in the rain.

Harg tapped at the door with his sword. After a while they heard a faint stirring inside. Smoke drifted out of the gable hole.

The door opened and a young serving girl stood there; with a wide-eyed look she surveyed first Harg and then Ingrid.

'We are cousins to Brodd,' Harg told her. 'Perhaps you remember me? Is your master or mistress at home?'

Ingrid thought she detected a blush on the girl's cheek. She had obviously noticed Harg when he had first come to see Brodd. Am I going to be jealous? Ingrid asked herself, following Harg and the girl into the large kitchen. Before she could reflect further on this new experience a woman no older than the serving girl, but expensively clad, turned from the large loom where she had been working and greeted them.

She was tall – though not quite so tall as Ingrid – white-skinned and beautiful, with dark hair, bright smiling eyes and a body that moved with quiet flowing grace in her clothes. She wore a doeskin brown apron over her blue smock; it was fastened with large silver brooches. Her kerchief, set jauntily back, fell in bright silky folds – Ingrid had never seen the like.

'Harg, I am glad you are safe.' The lady came forward and

embraced him as if she was aware he had been in danger and had come through.

'Helga, Ingrid – my cousin, of whom I spoke.' Ingrid kissed Brodd's wife with warm admiration. She felt herself, at that moment stark and unpretty by comparison, yet Helga's pleasure in having her there was evident.

'Fetch some food and drink for the travellers,' Helga ordered the serving girl.

Brodd was busy with the funeral of a relative, a man named Knut, and would return later, Helga explained. Harg recounted the events at the farm with a tight, sombre face; his hostess' white hands moved nervously while he spoke. Ingrid half-expected him to speak of his conversation with the Wanderer – he seemed so at home here – but once again he passed by the subject.

'The cry of the berserk pursued us almost to the town gates,' he explained. 'There are terrible signs of slaughter everywhere. Yet we encountered no enemies. It was lucky for me that Ingrid appeared when she did.'

'I am so glad,' said Helga casually. 'We have had so many troubles. Townsfolk fleeing at every rumour. Shipments standing unloaded in the harbour. Brodd is half-frantic because trade has been so disrupted. Honey, wax, even the precious amber cargoes unaccounted for. And our fish stock rotting in a warehouse, even before it can be properly salted. How can one live with such misery? It is as my poor husband says, the settlements are on the verge of ruin. The gods do not want us to prosper! And yet we try to keep up the old ways. This funeral, I can tell you, is costing us a good deal! I just wish we could get out of this terrible town. Then at least we – '

A slave girl interrupted her, hurrying from an inner room with a message.

'The chosen one is asking for more wine,' the girl said.

'Give her whatever she wants, but do not let her be too sick,' Helga said with a sigh. 'Harg, I have something to tell you,' she broke in. Ingrid had started to ask about the chosen one, but bowed to the lady of the house, who continued:

'Glimir, your sister, was here in your absence. I did not see

298

her myself, and I was unaware of the terrible events you describe, but she left a message for you – it is surely important. I have kept it safely here, hoping for your early return.'

From a large oaken chest Helga drew a tiny parcel, close-sealed with wax. Noticing the imprint, a delicate five-pointed star, Harg breathed a deep sigh. Ingrid leaned forward; she had seen such a sign once before.

Without hesitation Harg broke the seal, spread the parchment. Inside was a small rounded stone with a mark on it. Ingrid at once recognized the rune: it was *berkana*, the birch tree, a large figure incised on the smooth face.

Helga looked puzzled. 'Nothing more then? No message?' Harg turned the parchment over: it was blank on both sides.

'The rune is the message,' he told her.

'What do you read in it?' Ingrid asked quietly.

'I must think.'

'There is an old man recently come here by ship,' Helga told them. 'A strange fellow, who camps by the harbour and trades with no-one, but watches everything. There are odd stories about him already, but it is said that he is a rune-master. I could send for him if you wish.'

Harg turned the stone round in his hands. 'I do not think that will be necessary,' he said quietly. He reached out and patted Ingrid's hand. 'I have some skill with the runes, even as my sister does. It is necessary to meditate on this. Even so I can tell you already, it is not as bad as I feared. You, Ingrid, will understand part of Glimir's intention. It is no accident, surely, that she refers us to the birch tree.'

Ingrid saw a wild sky, dark peaks, a cliff overlooking the sea. An old man sat praying: she trembled and the cold waters closed around her . . .

The slave girl stood in the doorway beside her, whispering frantic words to her mistress.

'I must go to the chosen one,' Helga explained to her guests. 'Please forgive – it is urgent business.'

'Who is the chosen one?' Ingrid could not contain her curiosity.

'Come with me, then, Ingrid, and see for yourself. Harg, in

the room there adjoining you can find a quiet space. I will have Skadi draw a bath for you shortly. Please be at home here; Brodd will return soon.'

Ingrid followed Helga and the slave girl into a narrow, dark passageway. The chattering laughter of women became audible; as they moved down the hallway, it seemed to grow more shrill. Outside a carved chamber door Helga turned to Ingrid and quickly explained.

'The girl, Geirhild, a slave and concubine of Knut's, has offered to die with him. She will be sacrificed tonight when the great ship is burned. She has become the chosen one, the chief victim. Many privileges are hers, the most important of which is to take part in the sacred rites. You may witness all that later, if you wish. Is it shock I see in your face, Ingrid? Well, remember, our customs are very old. You come from a new land. You will be surprised even more at how happy she is to die with her master.'

Skadi swung the door open and the mistress of the house strode in.

The room was windowless, but lit by a lamp, with a single long bunk and a table pushed against the far wall. On the table was a basket of cakes and two large common wine jugs. One of these had been tipped over; wine dripped from the spout, trickled across the thick boards and fell on the matted blonde hair of the woman who crouched there, half underneath the table, rocking back and forth on her haunches and crooning to herself.

'Disgusting,' said Helga with an angry look round. 'We must set things right quickly.'

With a stupefied, sad look, the blonde girl gagged once or twice and vomited on the floor.

Helga whirled round and shouted for Skadi to bring towels. The latter clapped her hands and a tiny red-headed girl came rushing into the room. Ingrid assisted Helga and between them they steered the victim across the room and settled her down amid the piled-up coverlets of a low bed.

'Bring water!' Helga commanded; the by-now-harried Skadi

made off once again. The red-headed girl was scrubbing away at the floor.

The blonde girl moaned softly. Ingrid drew her hands in a slow soothing motion across the woman's brow. She wore a glassy-eyed stare; her fat cheeks were reddened and blotchy; when she tried to smile Ingrid could see her yellowing teeth and the black line above her gums.

'How old are you?' Ingrid asked softly, ignoring Helga's disapproving look and her cautioning gesture.

The victim closed her eyes and murmured in a low voice: 'Seventeen.'

'The slaves should have watched her more closely,' Helga said, shaking her head in disapproval. 'It is a shameful thing when the chosen one loses all sense of decorum.'

'But I thought you said she was happy,' Ingrid protested.

'You will understand better when you witness the ceremony,' Helga told her firmly. 'It is the servants' fault that things have got out of hand here, and mine for being distracted. If you wish – '

'Mistress, the black priestess, the Angel of Death,' announced a tremulous voice from the doorway.

Ingrid turned in amazement. The red-headed girl, who had just spoken, stepped quickly aside as an old hag-like woman, thick-set and ugly, hobbled into the room.

Skadi jumped up, and Helga bowed quickly and attempted to conceal her discomfort, but the old woman ignored them and moved quickly to where Geirhild lay, half asleep now with stiff folded arms.

She fixed her sharp gaze on the bunk; then turned her beady eyes upon Helga.

'You have not done your duty, Mistress Helga – by no means! These slave-girls must be instructed. The chosen one must drink only for pleasure; she is to be kept happy at all times. There must be no excess.'

'I'm sorry, lady, truly. I have been derelict in my duty. I – ' Helga's voice trembled; she was obviously both frightened and ashamed. The old woman's glance did not waver. 'I ask pardon of the Angel of Death,' said the mistress of the house, blushing deeply, 'and I – I await my instructions.'

Ingrid thought she detected a gleam of amusement in the old woman's eyes. Helga had time to recover herself.

'Does your arrival, madam, mean that the chosen one should be brought to the ship? If so, I will see to it immediately.'

'Brought to the ship!' croaked the old woman. 'Brought to the ship like a drunken slut! Mistress, you will see that the girl is able to carry herself and with dignity, or she will be killed with no glimpse at all over the barrier. I will order that she be strangled like a common thief, and the disgrace that will attach to the house of Brodd will not be forgotten for a long time!'

The crone bent her glance down, as if indeed she were imagining the consequences of such dreadful things. Her tight black kerchief and the smoothly drawn line of her dark cloak gave her the look of a huge crow. She hobbled away towards the door, but at the threshold she stopped, turned and directed her fierce glance at Helga.

Helga bowed but the woman did not take her leave. Instead, she crossed the room and stood gazing at Ingrid with an enquiring glance.

'And you, young mistress. I do not recall seeing you before in Trogheim,' said the priestess.

Taken by surprise, Ingrid barely managed to stammer an answer. 'My name is Ingrid. I came recently from Markland, far across the sea.'

The crone smiled to herself. 'Let me look at your hands, dear. I will tell your fortune for you.'

Ingrid hesitated, but the old woman seized her left hand and stared at it intently for a few long seconds.

'A long life,' she said quietly, 'and many children. And many more blessings.'

She pressed Ingrid's fingers together. The girl stared at her. The crone had passed her a note, a secret message.

'An hour!' the priestess turned and croaked ostensibly at Helga, but perhaps really at both of the woman. 'One hour from now at the ship – and everything perfect. See that you manage that, at least!'

When she had swept from the room Helga collapsed in Ingrid's arms. 'She is impossible!' moaned the housewife. 'How I hate her!'

Ingrid slipped the note carefully into her bodice.

Helga continued in a whisper, as if she were afraid to criticize out loud. 'Her holy predecessor died a violent death a few years ago – one of the chiefs took offence at her service and had her strangled. They found this woman in the country at a rude farm. Granny Falki is her real name – an appropriate one, for she is truly a falcon, a dreadful old bird of prey!'

Then Helga vented her feelings on the two slave-girls. 'Now you see what happens when the customs are not followed! I gave you instructions, yet your carelessness has come near to disgracing the house of your master and mistress! You must prepare the girl in time for the ceremony, and tell her the consequences if anything goes wrong. Believe me, if there is any trouble from now on, both of you will be punished severely!'

Helga and Ingrid made their way slowly back to the kitchen.

In the shadowy corridor, Ingrid's mind was full of conflicting thoughts. What word had the old crone passed to her? And how could Helga deceive herself about Geirhild, the victim, who was not lucky at all, but pathetic, and monstrously used? She tried to imagine herself in Helga's place, but the scene was difficult to picture. Then she knew why: she would never submit to such a cruel role. She would rebel, no matter what the cost.

They entered the big kitchen, where Helga began to tend the central fire. Meanwhile she explained about the customs. Ingrid listened, but she was anxious to escape, to read the note the old woman had passed her.

'The old woman is herself a sacred person,' Helga said. 'She too is chosen, and gives up her own name for the title you heard. It is her duty to officiate at the ceremony and to make sure all is performed with due reverence. She has special charge of the victim, and slays her with her own hands. In all matters of ritual her word is law.'

'She seemed a bloodthirsty old crone to me,' said Ingrid with some passion.

Helga laid a finger to her lips. 'You must not talk like that. When you see the ceremony you will think differently.'

'But the girl was unhappy and probably terrified,' Ingrid protested.

'She was allowed too much to drink, that was the problem.'

Ingrid said nothing. She did not want to quarrel with Helga; she watched the other woman work at the loom, passing the skein from side to side and straightening the weft with a batten, a long carved wooden object, which she wielded with great skill. Then Harg appeared, very thoughtful, but seemingly in good spirits.

He took a seat by the fire, absently stirred up the embers, then turned to Ingrid.

'We must meet with my sister as soon as possible,' he said, turning over in his hand the runestone he had taken from the folds of his cloak. 'Her message must mean that she regrets her course of action. As for me, I am ready to forgive. I have always been ready for that! We must be wary, but to seek her out can do no harm.'

Helga turned from her weaving before Ingrid could speak.

'Brodd will help you to find her at once. As soon as the funeral is done with, the search should begin.'

But Ingrid could not contain herself. 'Harg,' she said excitedly, 'they are going to kill a girl at the funeral! An old hag presides over everything. It is a terrible custom, like the sacrifices of ancient times. How can we save our own people if we allow such a thing? The same doom will come here. It will infect all good people. The Christians will take over everything, but the curse will lie at the heart.' Helga threw up her hands, she moved to the fire beside Harg, and began stirring the hearthpot with a fury of constraint. Harg stood up and approached Ingrid, laying his hands on her shoulders. He said in a soft voice:

'Clearly, something has upset you. You must tell me about

it, and I will hear more from Helga. I have trust in your opinions. We will talk awhile and then decide on some action.'

'But, Harg – !'

They heard a banging and shuffling outside, a voice from the threshold.

The door was thrown open and a stout red-headed man with great shoulders and a short, well-trimmed beard stood before them. All at once the room seemed much smaller; Helga greeted her husband, then shrank away behind her loom.

Harg went across and embraced the man. 'Brodd, I'm glad you are here. We have just arrived and already need your strength of counsel!'

Brodd tossed his fur cloak to the red-headed serving girl. 'Harg! I am glad to see you safe! We have feared for you. These times we live in, these bloodiest of times! Things are in chaos indeed! I have been detained all day at the harbour – as for the funeral, you know we are occupied with burying Knut, a relative of mine. What a time to choose to die! It shows the worst kind of taste. I have just come from there now and preparations are not going well. Helga, we must talk . . .'

Helga bowed her head. Brodd swung his cloak back, looking from Helga to Ingrid. Then Harg burst in with the introduction, and presented Ingrid to their host.

'I'm sorry to bring so much bad news,' Brodd said at once, after embracing Ingrid and paying her the compliment of a favourable word and an approving look. 'But there has been trouble at the village gate, a skirmish. One guard killed, one wounded and the third driven off. A terrible uproar and confusion.'

'The Christians, the Christians have come at last,' Helga moaned, and covered her face with her hands.

'Not quite yet, my dear, though they are not far away. This was something quite different – a berserk of Odin, a warrior, full of death-power and rage, who forced his way past the guards, smashing everything in sight, then disappeared just as quickly as he had come. Now there is no certainty whether he has gone off, or hidden somewhere in Trogheim. And no-one cares to take over the guard-duty, until it is clear where he is and what he wants. It would be dreadful if he were waiting for darkness before he strikes.'

Brodd stood musing. 'The berserks . . . Odin's own warriors. In the chaos of these times they wander about, dealing death in the name of the god. They fear nothing, and can shut their minds on all pain. Ah, we are loyal to the old ways, but at what a price. Such times and such customs!'

'Brodd,' Harg said in a firm voice. 'I am sorry to bring this trouble upon you when you are heavily burdened with duties but we must have a talk. There are urgent plans to be made. It is myself that this beast seeks.'

Ingrid stared at him. The berserk pursuing Harg? But only a few hours before Harg had stood face to face conversing with the Wanderer and had escaped quite untouched. She had an overwhelming sense now that Harg was trying to conceal something: but what if she should be wrong?

She went over and laid a hand gently on his shoulder.

'You must take care, Harg,' she told him. 'Brodd will have men to protect you.'

He put his arm around her and drew her close. 'There's no need to worry about me, Ingrid. We shall be sailing back together, to Markland or Vinland, soon enough!'

But he did not look at her when he said this.

Ingrid excused herself, as if leaving the men to confer. She bowed to Helga and slipped away into one of the nearby empty chambers.

With trembling fingers she pulled the note from her bodice. On the yellowed parchment was written a simple message.

'I will speak with you at the funeral. But if you want to recover the cup, you must not tell Harg.'

Glimir herself, it seemed, had signed it.

The Angel of Death

Ingrid and Harg watched uneasily from halfway up the hillside. Two men armed with spears, friends of Brodd, attended them closely. Harg wore some light armour, and carried a sword. Ingrid, who wore a belt like a man, had borrowed a scabbard and sword. Just below them, a hundred or so mourners stood beneath the great Viking ship that had been dragged up from the harbour to serve as funeral pyre for the rich man, Knut.

A deep pit had been dug around the ship and, beside this, next to a half-dozen blazing bonfires, huddled a small group of the dead man's close relatives. On the ship's wide decks a life's treasure lay spread out: spears, swords and shields, great barrels and chests, all surrounding a small wooden structure like a hut, in which, some time before, with great ceremony, they had placed the body.

Ingrid had watched it all and had seen how they carried first, thick casks of ale, then big baskets of food, and had set them down there beside the dead man. She had shivered as they brought up a dog, killed it with a single blow and placed it in the ship. Afterwards, two horses had been forced to race up and down the hillside till the sweat ran in streams down their flanks. Then, several men with swords flailed away; raising terrible shrieks the animals went down, writhing and kicking, their blood poured out on the trampled-down, dung-littered turf. They were dragged to the boat and thrown in.

A thin, scrawny cow was led up, its throat slit, and the carcass hauled up on the deck. A cock and a hen, squawking madly, were quickly dispatched. They too became part of the cargo.

As the strange ritual went on before her, waylaying her attention, Ingrid had to remind herself that a threat might come, at any moment, from the gate that led to the town, or from the dark hillside behind them. For Glimir had promised to meet her at the funeral, and there were constant fearful rumours about the berserk.

From time to time she cast a nervous gaze around, probing into the deep mist and gloom of the sunless day that was bleaker than night; nor was Harg's touch at her elbow altogether reassuring: she responded to his closeness with no more than a wan smile.

Yet the ceremony was going well, and Ingrid could see that Helga had managed to regain her composure. The young housewife stood arm-in-arm with Brodd, and from time to time glanced back at Ingrid, as if to say: see, this is how the old customs should be fulfilled! Am I not a good wife indeed to have managed this?

Beside the ship itself, at the very edge of the pit, the old priestess paced, shouting instructions to her little entourage. Her face wore a rapt smile, her arms were spread wide, her black cloak lay on her smoothly as a crow's feathers – how well, Ingrid thought, she bore the ancient and fearful title of the Angel of Death. She was indeed the black Valkyrie, the comforter of fallen warriors – and in recent years of fat deceased merchants: one who made smooth the sometimes rough path to Valhalla.

Two handmaidens, also garbed in black, jumped at the very sound of the old woman's voice, while a small group of men trailed along, slowly and sullenly performing whatever she required. Yet sometimes, as they worked, they grinned sheepishly at one another as if they resented having to obey the old woman's orders.

After some preliminary chanting, the priestess jumped down upon the deck of the ship. She waved back the mourners, pointing to the front of the trench, where one of the bonfires blazed up. The handmaidens drew a large wooden frame from the ditch. They carried it to the lip of the trench, opposite to where the priestess had placed herself.

The priestess then signalled to her man-servants and they walked slowly across to where Geirhild stood motionless beside Helga's house-slaves. Two of them took hold of Geirhild and led her across to the lip of the trench. She walked in a stiff, helpless motion, as if without will of her own; Ingrid wondered if she had been given a drug.

At a gesture from the old woman the handmaidens propped up the frame near the trench. Ingrid now recognized it as a simple grave-frame, such as they used back in Westland to bury the dead. The deceased and all personal possessions were placed in the frame and then covered with earth – such was the custom.

At that moment, however, the frame was being held upright, and it looked like an ordinary door frame, a homely construction. The two men led Geirhild along and stood her just behind it, then, while the handmaidens held the frame upright, the men made a chair of the palms of their hands. They hoisted the girl up till her head stretched over the top of the wood.

The Angel of Death raised her right hand. Geirhild shouted some words which the mourners dutifully repeated, enabling Ingrid to understand them.

'Look!' she cried, 'Look now, I see them – my father and mother!'

The girl was set down, then quickly raised up, and as she peered over the frame, she cried out:

'Look! I see my dead brothers and sisters, my cousins, my uncles and aunts – now I see them!'

The crowd repeated these words in unison; then the girl was lifted up a third time:

'Look!' she cried out, 'I see my master, I see the deceased one in paradise! Paradise is green and fair; he sits there with his friends and shares all goods things. Let me go to him now, for he is calling me!'

Once again the crowd chanted, and as the chant still echoed, one of the male attendants produced a fluttering hen from a large sack. Using a long knife, he cut off its head – the hen flapped wildly, its blood spilled down on his hands.

He passed the quivering thing to the girl; she raised it up high.

The crowd gave a shout and she flung it up over the frame and on to the ship. It fell at the old woman's feet; she picked it up and carried it straight to the small wooden hut where the dead man lay. Next to this hut, a striped canvas tent had been pitched, and she set it down there, stopping to murmur some words – while her outstretched arms seemed to implore a blessing from the old, absent gods.

Then the handmaidens tumbled the frame in the ditch. The two men led Geirhild away, along the edge of the pit to a place opposite the bow of the ship, where a platform let her cross. The priestess met her, her black cloak trailing behind, and standing once again with the victim.

At a signal from the crone, Geirhild began stripping off her arm-rings and ankle-rings. These she handed over to the old woman. Meanwhile a few of the man-servants came up and began to examine the girl closely, touching her everywhere, laughing and making provocative gestures, which caused a few men in the crowd to guffaw and jeer.

A vague sense of disquiet took possession of Ingrid. She turned to one of the spearmen beside her: 'What is happening now?' she asked brusquely.

The man at first did not answer; he looked away, shrugged his shoulders, then said in a low voice:

'The friends of Master Knut, they may use her now – for their pleasure.'

Ingrid's hand strayed down to the hilt of her sword. She half-turned to Harg: his lips were set grimly, but to her questioning glance, he merely nodded. She took a few steps toward the ship.

The attendants had helped Geirhild strip off her cloak and her tunic, as well as all ornament. They had all crossed to the deck of the ship, near the tent, and the girl stood there in her shift, a round helpless figure, staring out at the flickering firelight, jostled about by the men who hung round her.

Ingrid's heart was full of pity for Geirhild. She moved step by step down through the centre of the crowd, thinking how

310

she had warned Harg that she could not remain aloof if they tortured the girl. 'You must do what you feel is right,' he had told her.

Ingrid drew closer; the spectators reluctantly parted; at last she stood directly across from the tent, and could hear the words of the ceremony much more clearly.

The Angel of Death held the girl by the shoulders. A burly man in a green tunic leaned over and touched her breasts. 'I do this for love of your master,' he said.

The priestess stepped aside. She pointed to the low canvas tent. The man put his arms around Geirhild.

Ingrid took a step forward; anger possessed her – then she stopped in her tracks. By the bright light of a nearby bonfire she got a clear glimpse of Geirhild, and saw that the girl's face, now upraised, had been transformed. Gone was the bland fearful look, the unknowing stare. She was radiant; she looked with joy on the man, who caressed her with an almost brutal intensity.

They regarded each other, as if enraptured. Then the priestess made a gesture.

They crawled into the tent – there came murmurs and a few suppressed laughs from the crowd. Ingrid could not connect what she had seen in the faces of the two people with the cynical cluckings that came from all sides. She turned back to try to catch Harg's eye, but at that moment the crowd hid him; at the same time she sensed that the Angel of Death had become aware of her presence. The old woman peered across at her sharply, then turned again to the tent.

From there came low groanings, cries of pleasure. A few feet from where Ingrid stood, the other male attendants had collected shields and staves from a pile. As the groanings and cries became louder, then men began to beat the staves upon the shields in a rhythmical fashion.

At once the crowd joined in, caught up in a frenzy.

Ingrid resisted the swell of emotion around her. The stronger its force (it was almost a physical thing, like an uncoiling wave), the more she walled herself up in her anger.

311

She felt cut off from the crowd, more hostile with every passing minute.

Suddenly, the tent flap was pushed back, and the burly man crawled out head first. He stood up, the broad smirk on his face only barely controlled; there was a kind of gasping cheer from the crowd, and his fellows came forward: a tall man handed him a stick and a shield and then bent down, and proceeded to crawl into the tent. The Angel of Death stood by, rubbing her hands and murmuring.

The attendants struck their shields and the audience responded with a clapping of hands.

After what seemed a long time, the second man emerged, crawling, on his hands and knees, into the firelight. He blinked, wiped his hand on his mouth, stood up, took a shield and a long stick and joined the other men in the circle.

Geirhild came out – her blonde hair hung tousled and loose; her shift had been torn away on one side. She drew up one ragged sleeve, ventured a few faltering steps and then paused as if uncertain.

Ingrid pushed quickly to the barrier, a short leap from the ship and the tent.

Geirhild stretched out her arms, and in a low, droning voice, began to speak.

'She is bidding farewell to all her friends,' said a woman's hushed voice from behind Ingrid.

'They will give her the potion and then finish her there in the tent,' said another.

Ingrid tore off her cloak, drew her sword, and with an agile, quick leap, landed on the deck of the ship.

She crossed the deck in haste, seized the sleeve of the blank-eyed victim and said loudly: 'You won't die. I've come here to save you.'

Geirhild did not move or turn her head. The crone, recovering from her initial surprise, leaned over and hissed at Ingrid: 'You're a young fool! Leave this girl and come with me, or you'll spoil everything. Can't you see that I've been trying to help her!'

And the old woman hobbled away toward Knut's death-hut in the centre of the ship.

Meanwhile, the guards had recovered from their surprise and were advancing cautiously, with lowered spears, towards Ingrid. The girl felt the powerful attention of the whole crowd turned on her: there were shouts from here and there, upraised angry fists.

She made her decision quickly, steering the dazed Geirhild towards the railing, then with a quick shove catapulted her forward and into the ditch.

Geirhild screamed and fell; the crowd dissolved in an uproar. One of the guards ran straight at Ingrid, brandishing a long knife.

Ingrid dodged away and ducked behind the tents and baggage; she tossed away her sword and on her hands and knees crawled between some large bags of household treasure and slipped into the death-hut.

There the old woman crouched, in obvious rage and frustration, atop the shut wooden box that was Knut's coffin. Seeing Ingrid, she waved her draped arms like crow's wings and cackled harshly.

A great roar arose from outside; then screams and a shaking of the ship as if all the guards were running at full speed up and down the deck.

Ingrid waited for them to burst in and take her, but no-one appeared. There was a moment of silence, followed by more screams and a faint rocking motion beneath the ship, as if all the spectators were jumping up and down at once across the hillside.

'What is this madness?' Ingrid asked aloud.

The crone tilted her head and listened, then sprang away to the entrance of the hut, and stood there exclaiming and muttering.

A woman stepped out of the shadows behind the coffin. It was Glimir.

Ingrid swayed on her feet and nearly fell.

From outside, from many voices, came a wild outcry,

followed by an unearthly and shattering howl, the howl of a madman, or a lost soul.

'The berserk!' said Glimir, then with a bitter scowl added: 'So you told Harg about my note!'

'I did not! And what has Harg to do with the berserk? Surely you don't think – '

Screams reverberated round her like some shrill wind of madness. She heard a clatter of weapons.

'Granny, fetch the boy at once!' Glimir ordered. 'Set the boat on fire. There is no hope for us here.'

'I did not bring the berserk with me; I fear him. He threatens us all,' Ingrid spoke at last. She felt troubled: all that was unspoken between her and the Viking seemed to haunt her. Yet here was Glimir, the object of her journey. She did not resemble the creature of Ingrid's fevered dreams; she looked older, more vulnerable. Had she lost all her magic?

Glimir laughed. 'Don't stare so at me, Ingrid. We were friends once. But you have mistaken everything. You and Harg have brought the berserk with you. He will kill me if he can – that is the Wanderer's wish. And also Harg's wish.'

Ingrid could not believe the brazenness of the woman.

'How can you say that, when even now Harg is sure to be fighting the creature? That monster pursued us all the way to Trogheim. Give me the cup, Glimir, I must learn how to save my village.'

'Villages are not saved by foolish girls!' cried Glimir. 'Harg has deceived you about everything.'

'*You* tried to kill Harg. Your thralls hung him up over the fire. You destroyed the caribou, vehicle of the spirit messenger! You tried to kill me, to entomb me on Moon Lake. Glimir, I would be a fool to listen to you. I will not be deceived again. But I must have the cup of my father!'

From somewhere came a crackling of flames. Ingrid looked around in sudden panic. Surely the boat was on fire? But where were the voices, the warriors? There was only silence, the crackling of flames, the acrid smell of smoke.

Glimir stepped forward and spoke.

'I return the cup to you gladly, Ingrid, for you are a brave

314

girl to have come so far. I hated you once, and was jealous, even of what I didn't wish. Now I ask only for my life. I do not want to have to kill my brother to stop him from killing me. Above all, I want the life of my son. You must persuade Harg to disobey the Wanderer; I have tried and failed.'

Ingrid could not speak. She stared at the other woman with new eyes.

'Your son . . .?'

Glimir bowed her head in silent acknowledgment. Then she reached up into a leather satchel that had been pegged on the wall behind Knut's coffin and brought forth the precious cup.

Ingrid took hold of it.

'Remember, you must not pursue me!' Glimir whispered fiercely, and slipped past Ingrid to the door. 'That is our bargain,' she added quietly.

'But your son . . . Who?'

A great roaring swallowed Ingrid's question. She felt the fire almost at her back, the heat pressing fiercely against the walls of the hut. Clutching the cup, she sprang away after Glimir, who had disappeared in the folds of the smoke that curled in through the narrow entrance.

Ingrid burst out on deck; choking, blinded by smoke, she could see nothing. Groping away towards the bow, she felt a wall of flames roar up behind her. She jumped down into the ditch and found Geirhild, the victim, wandering confusedly towards her.

She shouted at the girl and when she got no response, slapped her face. Geirhild began very quietly to weep.

Ingrid started to shove her bodily up the steep crumbling barrier. There was a danger that the burning ship would collapse and crush them.

But Geirhild did not want to climb; the smoke was thicker above them. She hung back, whimpering.

Hesitating, Ingrid took the cup and flung it gently up over the lip of the ditch. She scampered up behind it, clambering up the steep wall as the smoke rolled around her head. By digging her fingers into the smooth turf she managed to roll her body a few feet across the wet grass.

She tore off her jerkin, leaned over the barrier and screamed down at Geirhild to take hold.

The girl, like Ingrid, was now coughing and choking uncontrollably. She gazed up, round-faced, through wreaths of smoke. Ingrid waved the cloth at her. At last the girl's panic seemed to awaken her. She caught hold of the cloth. Ingrid pulled.

The cloth began to tear but the girl hung on, clawing wildly at the dirt facing and sobbing and whimpering, until with mud-smeared face and arms, she lay safe on the turf beside Ingrid.

A harsh male scream from the swirling mist above them brought them both to their feet. Ingrid recovered the cup, and with one arm around the faltering Geirhild, she led the way blindly, making as near as she could reckon for the town gates.

They stumbled along for a few feet before they found the old woman.

It was the Angel of Death, her thin body wrapped round by black vestments. Her head had been split open by the stroke of a sword or an axe; it looked as if she were trying to fly into the hillside.

Ingrid's heart sickened at the sight; and Geirhild kept murmuring 'No . . . no . . .'

After that, the two women ran.

Then hoofbeats, and the mist and smoke cleared and Ingrid saw Glimir, not twenty feet away, galloping full tilt across the hillside.

Glimir did not look at her, but another head turned with a wide-eyed stare, that of a young boy who sat mounted before her, clinging to the horse's mane for dear life. Ingrid recognized him at once; the farm-boy who had guided her to Harg and then disappeared.

The girl's thoughts whirled between confusion and light. She started to speak, to urge Geirhild forward. Then a man with drawn sword came out of the mist and she recognized Harg.

He walked excitedly towards her, calling her name, his eyes

alight with joy and relief, but everything overtook her at once and she swayed and then collapsed into the safe darkness at his feet.

Later, Ingrid woke up suddenly, as if from a powerful dream. She knew there was something she must fix in her memory; something she must never forget.

A fire burned low in the small room; she could hear voices in the passageway. Yet she forced her eyes tight shut, obliterating the attentive slave-girl, Skadi, who had smiled on her as she stirred and awakened: she snuffed out the room and the voices, and slipped down among the warm blankets which reminded her of Glimir's cabin, of her own grandmother's, of a childhood she had lost somewhere in the wilderness of her long journey.

The dream came back.

She was a white, lovely swan. 'What a fine neck you have!' cried an old crone, an ugly old woman who fell suddenly into a pit of ashes and was seen no more. Yet, swan though she was, Ingrid could not fly; she ran helter-skelter, pursued by stone-faced clutching things. She was terrified, to have no hands, only short ugly feet and wings that would not lift her into the safe sky. Then a boy, all naked and beautiful, rolled down a long glassy slope, and stood up proudly before her. 'He has stolen my body!' thought Ingrid (in her dream) and was angry. But the boy (who was the Buck, and yet not the Buck) approached her very gently. In his left hand he carried a fat ripe ear of Skraeling corn, with which he stroked her, so that she grew very calm. 'This is my child and my lover,' she said plainly (as if mute swans could speak) and the boy laughed very quietly, climbed up on her back, and then she stretched out her wings and as if by magic they flew up together, and the boy said: 'We're going home.'

'We're going home,' murmured a familiar voice close beside her. She opened her eyes and Harg sat there, by her bedside.

Ingrid was very confused; had she recollected her dream,

or had she just now dreamt it, flying away somehow backwards from Harg's simple statement?

She threw off the blankets and sat up.

'As soon as you feel better, we must find a ship for Markland,' Harg went on, peering at her anxiously, with his dark, uneasy eyes. 'Everything is in chaos here. And now you have the cup . . .'

'They killed the old woman,' Ingrid shook her head. She shuddered, remembering the sight.

'It was the berserk,' Harg told her, taking her hands in his cold hands. 'When he attacked, the crowd fled; the ship burst into flame and I could not find you anywhere. Then you walked out of the smoke with Geirhild.'

'She has a child,' said Ingrid starkly. 'Glimir has a son; the deaf-mute boy who led me to you. I wish – '

But Harg wrenched away, as if in pain, and paced across the room.

'No; there's no child. It's not possible!'

'I wish, oh how I wish, that you would tell me the truth, Harg! You must not conceal anything from me. Everyone, everyone has deceived me – from the very beginning!'

'It's some country foundling; a boy she's adopted. It's not Glimir's child.'

'You lied to me, Harg. You didn't tell me the truth about her lover, about Coyote. Ingrid had a child with her lover.'

'There was no child! I didn't lie to you!'

Ingrid sprang across the room and put her hands on Harg's shoulders, holding him fast.

'Then why have you concealed your meeting with the Wanderer, with the old man? Why haven't you told me the truth?'

'I didn't want to alarm you. He warned me about the berserk. He was trying to help me.'

'The berserks are the followers of Odin – why should the old man warn you? Why did the berserk not attack you when the ship burned, Harg? It is Glimir that the berserk is after, Glimir and her son! She told me so and I believe her. You have seen at Knut's ship how the old customs degrade all women – and who is behind them but Odin, god of battle, lord of the slain dead? But Glimir, like the dark priestess, is of the goddess – they have tried to soften the old ways. The old man cannot control such women, and that is why he hates and fears them!'

The door of the room swung open and Brodd entered, followed closely by Helga and Skadi.

'Excuse the interruption,' said the master of the house, with a slight bow, 'but the situation is desperate.' The sweat stood out on his white, drawn forehead.

'The Christians are on the move again. Most people are leaving the town, fearing that the berserk's attack means that the protection of Odin has been withdrawn. I have done my best by organizing the funeral. But the death of the old woman is ominous. I must think of my family. I have ordered all my portable goods and possessions to be put on board my largest ship. I am sailing north.'

'We have decided to become Christians,' said Helga. 'There is no other way.'

Brodd looked askance at his wife. 'It is not only that; we have been genuinely moved at the stories of the Christ. Besides, it is clear that the old gods are finished now. No-one respects them or fears them; every waif down in the harbour is repeating lewd rhymes about them.'

'I don't blame you for wanting to protect your family,' said Harg. 'We too intend to sail as soon as we can. There is no point in delaying now.'

'Not I,' said Ingrid. 'I am going to climb the mountain.'

She felt everyone stop, and catch breath, and regard her.

'Climb the mountain? You mean Nerthus?' Helga shook her head sadly. 'You must be out of your senses, Ingrid.'

'If I am, then Harg is too, for he is coming with me.'

Harg bowed his head but did not contradict her.

The red-headed slave-girl slipped quietly into the room, curtsied, and announced to her mistress: 'The old man has come again, with a message. He is waiting for a reply.'

She handed a small leather pouch across to Helga.

'He said – I mean the old man – he said it was for the Viking from the cave,' the girl stammered.

Harg looked from one to the other, hunching his shoulders as if the walls might be pressing in on him. Helga handed him the small pouch, and he made as if to leave them.

'Harg, read it here,' Ingrid asked. Her voice was unwavering.

There was a pause. Slowly, Harg unfastened the pouch. He removed a small flat white stone and held it uneasily between his fingers, not looking at it.

'A runestone,' said Brodd.

'A message,' his wife added.

'There is no message,' said Harg. His voice was faint and hollow. 'It's a blank rune. The sign of Odin, or . . .'

'Or what, Harg?' Ingrid could not bear the look on his face.

'Or of death.'

Ingrid slipped quickly past the others, ran down the hall to the front chamber. The fire blazed quietly in the hearth, a house cat jumped away as she sprang to the front door and flung it open.

It was night. The street was empty and dark. In the damp air hung a thin veil of smoke.

She waited for a moment, listening. Harg came up behind her.

'There's no-one,' Ingrid declared, and slowly closed the door.

He stood beside her, looking at her as if from far away.

'Tomorrow,' he said, 'we climb the mountain.'

The Mountain

Ingrid sat on the pony in the near-darkness, shivering.

Harg glanced over his shoulder from the door of the hut.
The farm woman, whom he had fetched out at last with his
thunderous knocking, stood babbling and pointing upwards
towards the bleakness beyond.

There was nothing friendly in her manner, nor in the looks
of the two children – dwarf-like, nimble, leering – who
clambered up on the tumbled-in roof of the hut and whispered
together, as Ingrid waited, and thought of the long way Glimir
must have come, of the fear that had driven her so far.

They had left Trogheim in the morning, she and Harg,
ridden away from a town from which many had already fled,
fearful of both the Christians and the old gods: a stream of
wagons flowing out of the unguarded gates; ships hoisting
sail in the harbour – signs of panic and hasty removal
everywhere, though some had stayed on – fixing crosses over
their doorways and counting on the Christ to save them from
the berserk – too old or too indifferent to pull up their roots
after so many years in the same place.

Indeed, many had nothing to lose, like this scrawny pinch-
faced farm-woman, with grey tangled hair, who lived high
above Trogheim, high above the last mountain village, on the
edge of the lava fields. No doubt she had never travelled up
the trail that led right past her very doorstep, to a world of
bare rock and sky, to the round rim of Nerthus, which, as
Ingrid knew, lay in the gloom far above, like a grim mouth.

Yet now the woman gestured strongly, waving a skinny
arm at the nearest high rim, which stood out in the gloom,
one peak among a crowd of grey shapes, a mere figment of

substance among those cones and bare towers that seemed, in the last minutes, to have sucked up all the world's sunlight.

What directions could she give, that skinny farm-woman, what could she say except what the others had said, drawing the words reluctantly forth, as if they were ashamed to tell: that a blonde woman and a boy had indeed come that way, not two days before, that there was a place on the mountain, up on Nerthus itself, where the blonde woman sometimes went, to practise magic, they said, to work her witchery; and who would think of seeking out such a one, if they were not as mad as she?

Slowly, Harg turned from the doorway, taking the reins of his pony and walking across the bare stony yard to where Ingrid waited.

The children slid down from the roof and tumbled away under his feet; the woman turned indifferently back to her dwelling. Harg tossed the children a few small coins and they shrieked with delight and ran screaming in after their mother.

Ingrid shivered again, and drew her cloak tighter. A sudden wind whirling down from a rock chasm made her pony stamp and turn its head.

'She has come this way,' Harg said. 'But we cannot stay here; it is an ugly place, and we are not far from the top.'

'I feel a bleakness inside me,' Ingrid said.

'Everything will be settled soon,' Harg said, and led the way upwards.

They rode out of the grim valley into an endless field of lava. It was like riding through a frozen grey sea, a sea struck by some great cataclysm that, ages before, had whirled up its surface, twisting everything into stark shapes – ridges, peaks and hillocks, all covered with grey moss, like a maze of fantastic barrows.

'The woman says there is a river that runs under the stone here,' Harg told her. 'Or perhaps many rivers. She says the water runs down from the high streams and that fish swim there, deep under these rocks, in the darkness.'

Ingrid shivered and drew her cloak tighter about her.

The stars had come out here and there in the darkness; the

waning moon climbed the sky. Far away thunder muttered; she could see flashes of lightning on the far peaks.

Within reach, in one of the saddlebags, was the precious cup which she had never thought she would carry up this mountain. It had vanished on Moon Lake; now she bore it here through another kind of wasteland, one ever further from home, even more bleak than the other.

And she thought of the strange markings on the cup, of the ancient people, of whom, now, she felt herself one, for she had travelled through all those islands and come out in a new world, with a new body and consciousness, with her mind tuned to new things.

She felt frail and strong, disembodied and yet anchored. Nothing, she felt, could surprise her. She hated no-one and loved no-one: her family, her village seemed to have fallen away, to have drifted down to the bottom of the sea, to a place where the failing light shone cold. It was a sea she could hardly descend through or return from, ever.

How could she bring light to her village from the dark place of her mind? She had managed to save Geirhild, to pull that dazed figure, shrouded in dark fire, from the wreck of the ship. But the old woman, Granny Falki, the Angel of Death, she had not saved. And now she was leading Harg on to Glimir, betraying her latest trust. How could the shapeshifter have thought she had a destiny? Or was this what he promised her: nothing; her fingers stiffening in the cold air, and everything out of reach?

Harg led the way onwards; a steep descent brought them to a chasm in the lava; they dismounted and led the ponies down the shelf-like trail. Then came a long narrow valley of grass shut in on one side by a green slope, and on the other by heaped-up mossy lava, quite straight and regular like a wall, but broken and jagged at the summit.

'We must make our way round, and come up the smooth cone on the other side,' Harg explained. 'It seems the mountain once burst apart here; something stirred in the depths and exploded outwards. Thank the gods it's quiet now.'

They could see well enough, moving swiftly along by the

starlight and moonlight. But the dismal rock clefts, opening here and there into the cliffs – blank streets that led into exitless chasms – seemed to Ingrid like passages to an under-world of darkness, and she passed each one, shuddering a little and pushing her pony forward, while the sense grew upon her that they were being followed – though this fancy she dared not mention to Harg, who, with bowed head, plodded on before her, plunged deep in his own thoughts.

They climbed upwards; the path grew steeper and steeper; the track disappeared underfoot. The turf shone with light, then gave way to smooth stone that glittered, grained a little by the uncertain moonlight.

It was cold; the wind spoke unceasingly, a long distant howl, then a close touch like needles penetrating cloak and leggings. Ingrid sipped a little of the brandy Harg had provided her with and the warmth flowed again in her veins.

After a while the trail narrowed; they rode over a valley slashed deep in the mountainside, treading a high narrow ledge that arched into a bridge, a precarious span between two slopes.

Ingrid felt her knees buckle a little, and hung on. She was vividly aware of the depth of the abysses that stretched below them, down past the long lava valley, past the bleak valley of the farm-woman's hut, beyond the low flanks of the moun-tains, down and down . . .

And miles past the villages of Nerthus, she imagined the faint fires of Trogheim, like a beacon in the darkness, but wavering, perhaps soon to be snuffed out . . .

They rode; she could hear bits of loose rock, struck by the feet of the ponies, spraying away into a nothingness of darkness; she could not hear them strike ground. But there were echoes – an echo – or was there a sound of something else, something moving very swiftly, very quietly along the trail behind them?

She was glad when they came off the stone bridge, when they approached a low outcropping, a cracked and scarred wall of rock, running like an ancient barrier across the bare moonlit hillside.

Harg turned from his dream, to force her from her own.

'This is what the farm-woman spoke of as "the boundary". For fear of the witch, she says, no-one dares pass it. The lip of the crater is up there.'

He dismounted and Ingrid followed. They sat together under the crumbling stone and shared some food and drink.

At first neither spoke. Then from a lower hidden valley came a deep rumbling sound, as if a high cliff face had suddenly collapsed into the void, or an ice mass sheered away.

Ingrid turned to Harg and started to speak. But there followed a long solemn cry, a cry that drove her to her feet; she stood beside the trembling, stirring ponies, her hand resting stiffly upon the saddle bag in which, long hours before, she had placed the precious cup.

'You heard it!' Ingrid whispered sharply. 'You heard it here on the mountain. Don't tell me it has nothing to do with us! Don't say it was merely the wind or the shriek of some night bird!'

Harg did not rise. He sat there, without looking at her, though she could see his face shining in the moonlight.

'I fear that the cliffs above the farmstead down below must have collapsed,' he told her quietly. 'I heard the scream of a woman, perhaps of her children too. It's very sad, but there is nothing to be done.'

Ingrid shook her head. She spoke quietly, as if from a great height above him.

'No, Harg, that's not so. You must stop lying to me now. And to yourself. There is someone – or something – down there on the trail; I have felt it for a while. It is what you are leading to poor Glimir.'

Harg looked up at her sharply.

'The woman you call "poor Glimir" tried to kill you; then she arranged to kill me. Why have you become so hard and cold to me, Ingrid? You once loved me. Since you ate the foul meat you have not loved me.'

'It bothers you still, Harg, doesn't it, that while I lay sick with fever you killed the sacred caribou? Did you do it to prove to Glimir that you loved her? Even though I saved you, though I gave myself to you to save you!'

Harg stood up.

Ingrid shrank back but he took a firm hold of her hands. His palms pressed hard against her knuckles; his eyes spilled a kind of reckless fear and rage.

'You made me come here, Ingrid. I didn't want to betray her!'

'We must see this through, Harg. We must see it through for the boy. I had a strange dream about the boy; he is no ordinary child!'

Harg's grip relaxed; he turned his face to the darkness.

'It cannot be her son. She is lying if she says so.'

'But *you* lied to me, Harg, from the beginning. I loved you, but when you killed the caribou your violence entered the meat. I tasted it there and learned to hate you. I even fell in love with another, one who was very different from you. But there was something else in the caribou, as I discovered: the food of a good spirit. I want to save you from your lies – and I think Glimir does too.'

Harg whirled round.

'Save me! How can a woman save me?' Ingrid felt the force of his scorn. He is jealous, she thought, despite everything, he is jealous. But then he added quietly: 'Yes, perhaps I believed that long ago, but now . . . now no-one can save me . . .'

He was silent; the ponies stamped and twisted in alarm; their eyes flashed blank white; they tossed their heads, as if trying to wriggle out of the harnesses.

'. . . Unless the Wanderer is right; unless her death frees me.'

Ingrid held her breath and listened, but she heard only the wind, like a shrill sigh, far below.

A black cloud drifted slowly across the face of the moon.

'Why do you need freeing, Harg? What is the terrible thing that binds you? Once I thought I knew. Now I'm not sure, and I fear for you.'

'We must go on up the mountain,' he told her quietly. He

326

patted the heads of the trembling ponies and began to lead them away around the barrier.

But Ingrid would not follow until she had her say, until she said the thing that was bursting within her.

'You blame Glimir for trying to kill you – that is what the Wanderer told you. But the boy who led me to the place where you were hanging – he had seen the Wanderer, for he drew the old man's image for me in the cave where we rested. It was no accident he took me to that farm – that we were driven there by the voice of the berserk. I was meant to find you, Harg! It was not Glimir who set the men on you, but the Wanderer himself!'

The white moon flew out from its thick nest of clouds. The shining hillside seemed suspended between heaven and earth.

Harg turned to Ingrid with a sickly, pale face.

Then a shriek tore away all the soft veils of silence: a bellowing roar that might have come, darkly laden, from a thousand dark places below them.

'Come,' Harg told her, and pushed the ponies quickly round the crumbling barrier.

They walked in silence, leading the ponies up the smooth steep flank of the mountain. Now there was nothing but the wind, nothing but their soft tread on that height, on the great bare turfed ramp that pointed them up to the stars.

And, though the going was easy, step by step, up that featureless incline, Ingrid felt fear, for the night stirred with forces – they were pursued by a voice – and there was nowhere to hide: all around them was blankness, and the smooth turf was treacherous: some powerful wind might blow them away into the endless space of the night, might lift them like leaves and whirl them away into darkness.

Ingrid had never felt so helpless as on those smooth and terrible heights.

And Harg, close beside her, whom she had never known to falter, was sobbing softly, as if catching breath from pain, gulping at the thin air as if he were drowning, as if some heavy sorrow pressed and crushed his strong chest – and this

327

pressure she too could feel as a tangible presence despite all that glitter of air, the beauty of those empty moonlit spaces.

At last Ingrid could stand it no longer.

'There is no hut in sight, Harg. We are walking straight up to the lip of the volcano and there is nothing!'

He stopped uncertainly, and looked at her with an odd, harried smile.

'This way, then.'

He slapped at the ponies and sent them off at a sharper angle to the right. They picked their way along an invisible trail, that nonetheless coiled upwards. Now Ingrid thought she saw a faint glow, like an aura, breathing out from the top of Nerthus, a film of light, like a ghostly projection against the background of stars. She blinked and rubbed her eyes in amazement, but it did not go away. And she wondered, awestruck, if this was the sleeping mountain's dream of light, a faint trace of the fire deep within.

All at once both ponies stopped together; Harg started to push them forward, then hesitated. He looked back down the trail, and Ingrid turned too, peering into the darkness, and listening. For a few seconds the whole mountainside lay breathlessly still.

Then the night was shattered by a sudden explosion, as if a huge fist had hammered through hard rock.

Ingrid thought the surface of the earth had burst apart: powerless, she stood with closed eyes, waiting.

But Harg touched her arm.

'Something has broken through the barrier,' he said quietly.

As Harg turned to Ingrid one terrified pony stopped whimpering, tossed its head and half-rolled and half-scrambled into the darkness, slipping away across the turf and loose stones and crying out, plunging downward as if it were being drawn by rein and strap back towards the unknown terror that was coming behind them.

Ingrid sprang after it, but Harg seized the other pony and shouted; the girl lost her footing, rolled over once and just sat there, her heart pounding wildly. The lost pony's cries hurt her soul, she could not bear it.

'The cup,' Harg cried out. 'The cup is not lost! We must go on quickly!'

Ingrid climbed to her feet and hesitated, remembering with terrible clear vision the mutilated body of the horse she and Harg had found near the farm.

Harg pulled her along the trail. 'We must hurry!' he whispered sharply.

She followed him meekly, mute and sorrowing, a kind of terror hanging over her: she did not look back, she could not, but she listened, though there was nothing, only the wind sighing fitfully across the bare turf and rock.

They struggled on, and when Ingrid next dared to look up at the heights she saw that the aura had vanished; its rosy glow condensed now to a single yellow point that hung in the darkness beneath the summit like a baleful eye.

Then Harg saw it and turned them upwards, back on the steep slope; there was a whinnying ahead in the darkness, and something, a dark outlined figure, moved fleetingly across the light.

'It is the place,' Harg murmured, and Ingrid felt a rush of terror and guilt, for she had insisted on this: it was her will that these two come together. And now she and Harg had found Glimir – but they had brought with them a force that could destroy everything, a power that could shatter the mountain and unleash a hellfire from the cold rock.

The moon went in and then out of the mottled clouds. Higher up, near the very rim of the crater, stood a small hut no bigger than a sentry post or a stall for a single animal. There was a tiny window where a light burned: it might have been a shrine, Ingrid thought, a shrine to great Nerthus, the mother.

A figure stood still in the shadowy doorway, barely visible in the eerie moonlight.

Ingrid walked upwards with slow, cautious steps, awe-struck by the grandeur of the scene, yet secretly wary; she listened, through the wind's folds and ripples, for the thing that pursued them.

Then a familiar voice spoke from the darkness, and at the

sound of it Harg groaned and stopped, his fingers reaching out like talons to hold Ingrid's arm.

'Oh Harg,' Glimir called down, 'you are cruel and relentless. But by the holy mother I will kill you if you lay hands on my son!'

Ingrid felt Harg's arm trembling in the darkness.

'I did not want to come here,' he called out, and his voice broke and quivered, 'but everything is ruined now. All chance of happiness is gone. Things must be settled at last.'

'Harg, dear, go away now; there is still time. You must go with the girl – think of our sad lives. You must take her far away and tell her everything.'

Then Harg released Ingrid's arm and spoke to his sister.

'What good is there in telling about evil? Who can understand it? Who can cure it? The Christians have a saying: if your eye offends you, pluck it out! Everything must be settled here at last.'

'You once thought that, Harg. And you killed to find peace. Have you found peace? No! Don't come any closer! An evil is stalking you. You must go!'

A pony stuck its head out from beside Glimir's hut and whinnied softly in the darkness. Then a strange slow tremor shook the earth; everything moved, as if the world had broken loose at its foundations. Glimir cried out; Harg gasped and Ingrid went tumbling down beside their own terrified pony: with one hand she reached up and clutched at the saddlebag which still held the precious cup.

This shaking lasted only a few seconds. Then the world settled.

Hoofbeats thumped on the turf. Their lost pony sprang into sight, came pounding up the hill past Ingrid's outstretched arms and continued its wild flight: on and on past the hut, as they gaped, as Glimir crouched in the shadows, on and on, until Ingrid stood up and screamed, but the pony went flying straight on, its little head tossing, its mane flying out. It reached the topmost crest of the mountain, the smooth lip, then was snuffed out in a faint flash of moonlight.

There was a terrible pause.

'It's gone over the edge,' Ingrid screamed.

Up the slope came a rushing of wind, like the breath of an iceberg. Ingrid grabbed hold of the reins and started to drag the other terrified pony towards the hut.

'Help me!' she cried out, swept along by the wild wind.

Harg stood as if paralysed, swaying and clutching at nothing.

The moon had gone suddenly dark.

Then came a low muttered growling that turned into a scream, a heart-sickening cry from the darkness just behind them.

At that moment the door opened, and in a blaze of light, she saw Glimir and the boy crouching low in the doorway.

Harg took a few steps, but Ingrid did not stop; she struggled forward to the doorway; the boy's eyes were round with terror.

Harg did not follow. He had turned and was peering down into the coalescing darkness, into that torrent of darkness that roared up the slope with a shrill voice.

'It's the berserk!' cried Ingrid. 'I can hear him!'

'I-can-do-nothing!' Harg cried out from where the darkness threatened to overwhelm him.

'Oh Harg, save your son!' cried Glimir, her voice shrill against the raving of the wind.

Ingrid fell down on the doorstep; the pony wrenched loose and galloped away in terror.

She felt the boy wind his arms about her and draw her forward slowly across the threshold.

Then she sensed the woman, too, bending down over her, and as she turned, before the wind snuffed the light out behind her, she saw Harg with drawn sword, standing guard, overtaken by a voice.

He stood aiming blow after blow at the darkness, at a bellowing wind, and then was bowled over, and sent flying across the smooth slope: he rolled violently upwards, towards the lip of the crater, and his body whirled round as he struggled to free himself from a shape that Ingrid remembered only in nightmares: a black beast or else a man, perhaps even a human warrior caught up in some frenzy and wrapped round with the skin of a bear.

Einar's Cup

Everything was silent for a long time.

Ingrid lay with clenched fists, exhausted, yet listening, half-afraid, until from almost beside her Glimir spoke quietly, though in a firm voice.

'He's gone,' she murmured, and Ingrid heard the swishing of the woman's garments. 'I can feel it in my blood – in my heart. O – my poor brother!'

Ingrid felt Glimir move in the darkness; then the boy, who had been leaning stiffly, shyly against her, drew away, his head uncradled from her side. And Ingrid thought: yes; Harg is gone; she would never see him again.

She pushed against the door of the hut. She crawled across the threshold and saw two ponies, their flanks gleaming dully, nuzzling together in the moonlight.

It was cold; the air seemed thin and weightless. Yet she was no longer afraid; the terror had gone – for a time.

She found herself standing alone in the faint light, shivering. And she remembered how sure she had been, despite everything, crawling from a similar hut, on another such night, on the edge of a wilderness even more desolate, for then she had a vision of the lights, and a magical beast had come out of the forest to guide her.

She pulled her cloak about her, edging close to the ponies, stroking their withers and backs, speaking soft words of reassurance, while in her mind a painful knowledge declared itself, like a sentence of judgement, and she knew that for the rest of her life, she would remember that moment – things could never be the same.

Harg and Glimir had been lovers – she had sensed it, secretly yet surely, from the beginning, but she had let the knowledge slip. Something in her had not wanted to believe it, and she had ignored the plain signs in Harg's cave: she had even refused to see the vision the shapeshifter had granted her. But she *had* known, and the image of those two naked bodies came back to her now and made her shudder.

And as she stood there, watching the moon sink down among the barring clouds, Ingrid felt herself a fool and, at the same time, she knew herself to be subtly tainted, as if she had been caught up in an evil she had secretly condoned.

She walked down the sloping summit. The turf was hard and firm; the air calm, though the wind stirred below, and a distant thundering could be faintly heard – avalanches crashing down in far, hidden valleys? Around her was magnificence: in the wavering moonlight she stood midway between earth and sky. The high slopes rose around her – she could see them across the intervening shadowy gulfs – smooth as grey glass, while the distant snow-capped peaks shivered in the starlight, only to dissolve, one by one, as a luminous mist crept out of the dark gulfs and hid them.

Harg had deceived her; he had died a foolish and heroic death, fighting against the very madness he himself had enlisted and invoked.

The Wanderer, the wise and cruel one, had shown his brutal power.

These things she knew, and could endure – and even challenge, for she was determined to face out the old man, who was the embodiment of a god, and defeat him.

Much harder to bear was the sense of her own complicity, the feeling that she had known more about everything than she had been able to acknowledge.

With slow deliberate steps she turned back, then stopped. Ragged edges of vapour floated across the very top of the volcano above her. She could not see the rim; only the suggestion of a curved lip of stone.

That way, in thundering fear, their first pony had gone; and then Harg had followed – in defence of his sister, and of their son.

It was as if Ingrid had been standing near him on a high plateau, on a platform suspended miles above the void, when a god's roaring voice and a god's breath blew him suddenly away, lifted him and, within the duration of a single cry, pitched him forever into a darkness that was unfathomable.

A light glowed suddenly in the hut, illuminating Ingrid's path. Two figures stirred and moved. The ponies called softly. Glimir came out and stood with her son, talking to him with slow, sad gestures.

When she had finished she stood waiting, her cloak pulled close about her, her blonde hair fringed with light. The boy watched Ingrid with his deep eyes.

'Come in out of the darkness, Ingrid,' said the older woman, and held back the flimsy door.

Ingrid remembered Moon Lake and anger took hold of her. Was she to be bound up with Glimir and her ways forever?

The room was completely bare, with a small window, and two pallets spread out on the turfed floor. A few cracks in the walls had been stopped up with turf, and when the door was pulled shut, the lamp gave off a strong heat.

Ingrid sat looking at the mother and son. Despite his strained, tired face, the boy's beauty was almost hurtful. His skin was whiter then ever, his hair soft and curly, and his blue eyes full of wonder and sadness. His thin hands kept restlessly moving, as if he wanted to speak something complicated through them.

Of course when she had first seen the boy he had reminded her of Glimir – or was it Harg? Yet she had not allowed herself to think it; she had shut all that out.

'You are looking changed, Ingrid,' said Glimir, 'I noticed it before.'

Glimir also looked different: she seemed much older; a weariness had crept into her movements; there was a heaviness in her eyes.

'I have been through much – as you have,' Ingrid replied. 'I have met the shapeshifter. I have sailed a long way, with little recollection of the voyage.'

'Ah, that is how you came here! Through the master of changes! That is why my son, Val, dreamt of you. He was the first to be sure how you would come. I made him watch the sea.'

'And he met me,' Ingrid recalled, thinking of that dark beach and of how the boy had welcomed her. 'He met me, and led me to where they held Harg – the old man directed him, I knew that later – but you, Val, you disappeared, though I tried to find you!'

The boy looked at her with serious eyes; he was watching her lips as she spoke.

Then his mother reached over and caressed him gently and said to him: 'Val, go out and take care of the ponies; be sure they don't wander too far off. I want to talk to Ingrid for a few minutes.'

The boy pushed open the door and slipped away into the darkness; Ingrid saw how outside the mist had gathered.

'Don't go far, Val,' Glimir called out after him. Then, as the lamp flared, she said to Ingrid: 'I will tell you now some things you may already know, and a few things you may have guessed. They are not very pleasant things.'

Ingrid bowed her head. She could listen to the other woman without looking at her: she thought it would make it easier for them both.

'I owe it to you to tell you everything,' said Glimir quietly. She hesitated, then continued in the same steady voice.

'I was only seventeen when Harg seduced me. We used to go riding together: he was strong and very handsome and I worshipped him. I knew he loved me, but I did not understand how. I should have guessed when I saw him change: he began to say strange things; to surprise me at odd moments with gifts. Our father was often away; our mother had died when I was born. One day during that summer of my seventeenth year we rode out; it was a hot stifling day. We bathed together in a river; we had done it before; this time it

335

was different. I did not want it that way, you must understand that!'

Ingrid did not reply but kept staring down at the hard turfed floor. She thought of the story Harg had told her, long ago, in a cave. After a while Glimir went on speaking.

'Later, I fell in love with Coyote, a lovely simple boy, half-Skraeling, and Harg grew very jealous. I was afraid he would give himself away; then my father would have blamed me, I know it, for he did not trust women. So I ran away with my lover. My father was outraged; but he was killed in a skirmish soon after. Then Harg became relentless: his guilt must have been terrible.

'I used all the skills I had learned to keep Harg away from us. But finally, all that failed. On Moon Lake he killed Coyote; then he raped me. Out of that union Val was born. With Coyote I had had a daughter. She died.

'I wanted to kill Harg after that, but I loved him. He was my husband, my brother – he was all I had in the world. But I would not submit to him. From the ancient people, I learned a deeper magic; I put him under a spell. If he could love someone else, and someone else loved him, the spell might be broken. When you came along I had wallowed too long in my hatred: I despised you because you were pure; you were the very age I had been when all that horror began. But I tried to warn you against them all – against those warriors, those mere men who know nothing of tenderness, or who are blinded by the power that the old man holds out to them.

'When you did not listen I stole the cup. It belonged to the wise ancient people who had taught me magic and I planned to restore it to the mountain, to the Mother.'

Ingrid heard the ponies stamping and stirring, almost at the door. She looked up and said to Glimir:

'But I found your anger overbearing; it frightened me. Then I fell in love with Harg.'

'You saved him,' Glimir's blue eyes fixed her. 'But he asked me to save him first. While you lay sick with the snakebite he came back to me, and to prove his love for me gave me the sacrifice of the caribou. I refused him, but you, in your love, did not.'

Ingrid closed her eyes.

'When I saw how it was,' Glimir said, 'I moved the caribou by magic and set it afire, and put a curse on it. I wanted to show Harg how I despised him. I was happy when you ate the foul meat.'

Ingrid shivered; once again she tasted the sweet burnt flesh of the animal; she smelled the thick smoke, saw the carcass hung up in the snow. She felt Harg's strong arms around her. Tears ran down her cheeks; quickly, she brushed them away.

'I had carried off my son to Iceland. From time to time I saw him, but I watched over Harg too: I hated and loved him. The journeys back and forth were wearying. Then he too crossed the ocean; after all, you had freed him. Oh, don't look so sad, Ingrid! I know he loved you – but he could not escape from the other thing. I never told him about his son – that was the punishment I relished most. He would have loved Val . . .'

She stopped, closed her eyes, took a deep breath.

Ingrid got up and went over to the other woman. She sat down beside her and took her hand. Memories came flooding back to her, memories of a cabin on a frozen lake.

'The boy began to have dreams of your coming. But Harg appeared first and I sent him away. I did not give him the cup because I was afraid of what he would tell you about me. I spoke to him only of forgiveness. I had been talking, you see, to the Christians. But the old man is relentless, he wanted to punish us. Perhaps in his arrogance he thought that after Harg killed me and my son you would still go with my brother, peacefully back to Wayland! Of course the high one rarely intervenes, though he rages. He works his will through others.

'I prepared for everything. But the old man had deceived Harg into thinking I would kill him, that he must kill me. He tried to force Val to give the cup back to you, but instead the boy brought it to me, but not before he was influenced to lead you to the very place Harg was. So you two came after me; and the excuse was the cup.'

337

Ingrid shook her head sadly. 'I told Harg as much; I suspected it – and I think he believed what I told him. But it was too late then, too late!'

'I gave you the cup, hoping that you and Harg would go away, but he was possessed by the berserk, he wanted to kill me. That is how one thinks when one suffers too much.'

Miserable now, Ingrid laid her head on Glimir's shoulder.

'But it was I who insisted that we come here! And he saved you! He destroyed the wild beast in himself!'

'Yes,' Glimir whispered, 'he did that.'

Ingrid stood up, her head nearly touching the roof of the tiny hut. Now she understood at last. She understood why she could never fulfil the task given her by the Wanderer. For Odin had asked her to capture the magic light – and that would be but to reaffirm the power of the sky god, to reassert the old ways of war and male dominance. Odin was powerful beyond imagining, but cold and indifferent to everything but his own power. And his reign was nearly over; it had begun nobly enough, no doubt, but had played itself out at last in violence and injustice, in an evil that had touched even the tiny village of Wayland, a mere outpost. For the coming of the grey folk had been but a warning of the corruption implicit in the old order. With a tragic doom upon him, the Wanderer had tried to perpetuate the old ways, using men and women as his instruments. Glimir, who had been hurt at such a young age by male violence, had understood this and resisted the old man; she knew that he had usurped and finally perverted the ancient power of Nerthus, the great mother. And so Odin had recognized Glimir as an enemy, and had used against her Harg's guilt about his incest, encouraging the murder of Coyote, freeing Harg from his spell by means of Ingrid herself, encouraging him to share the berserk's fury, and to sacrifice Glimir and her child. Yet at the last minute Harg too had rebelled, in the name of his new-found son, against the Wanderer . . .

Shadows danced as the little lamp flickered . . . Ingrid took a deep breath. Yes, she knew now that there were forces even greater than the great gods – those fates that caused her to be initiated, first through the caribou meat, then through their instrument, Loki. She had been given the chance to restore the power of the mother, to serve the great Christ – or perhaps – perhaps even to bring herself to a new birth . . .

She stood wondering; the door creaked and slowly opened. There stood Harg's son, the ponies nuzzling gently at his back.

'Val,' said Glimir tenderly, 'you must sleep now.'

Ingrid slipped past the mother and son, and stood for a moment watching the mist roll up the steep slope, her heart full of conflicting emotions. She was thinking back to her first meetings with Glimir and Harg, seeing everything differently in the light of what she now knew. She must seek out the Wanderer, and defeat him. But first there was something else to do. She had a debt to pay – to the mother.

She took hold of the reins of her pony, steadying the animal, then opened the saddlebag and drew out a carefully wrapped bundle that was not very heavy. In the background Glimir was singing a lullaby to her deaf son.

When the cup was unwrapped, Ingrid held it up in the lamplight. Its carved facets gleamed and, though she had examined it carefully at Brodd's in Trogheim, she saw it now with new eyes.

The figures on the cup had become her story. She had met the magic caribou, been bitten by the snake; she had run away from the wolf-pack in the forest, and gained a new vision of the living dead. Two warriors and the flesh-form of a Skraeling chief had been sacrificed because of her. She had met the shaman and eaten the sacred mushroom; he had shown her new visions and a path to the old lands. She had been stripped of everything, passed through the cauldron mouth of earth, and encountered the three goddesses, Morrigan, Macha and Babd. She had been tricked by the shapeshifter and had ridden the dolphin backs of ships to another country. She had found a child whose destiny, she knew, must be special.

Glimir stopped singing. Ingrid turned. It was all for a purpose. She had climbed the mountain to be with this mother

339

and child, the deaf-mute child of a forbidden love – for a purpose.

She took the cup in her hands and walked up through the mist towards the summit. The way was treacherous but she felt no fear, only a deep inner strength.

She climbed slowly, finding the clear path, step by step, thinking of how Harg had been driven this way in his battle with the violent one, his evil other self, his mad double.

He had hurt her, almost beyond her power to forgive, yet she would atone for his sacrifice, and remember his courage. After her initiation, her journey across the sea, it was as if her flesh had dissolved into a kind of light; she had been unable to make love to Harg, to touch him truly. She felt remote from her body; but her spirit had been honed fine: she imagined that she could penetrate all this mist and discern subtle eddies and currents of feeling, new contours in the landscape of the soul.

She walked upwards, so that the hut's glaring lamp became a candle-flicker in the grey gloom. The cup had been taken by violence from the ancient people; it must be restored as a free gift, to great Nerthus, to the mother.

Ingrid slowed her pace. She was approaching the summit, the very rim of the crater. Here, the smooth rock was fractured and scored with the marks of the long weathering years, the years of fire and ice, of an earth-time older than that of men and women.

Long ago the magma had poured out of the deeps of the mountain; now it lay hard-formed, almost smooth despite the myriad cracks and scorings; and she stepped over wrinkled folds, across ropelike twists in stone; and, as the mist drifted away from where she walked, she saw tiny bubbles marking how the mountain had struggled to breathe under the weight of its new skin.

And Ingrid thanked the great mother, Nerthus, for the boon of the mist, for the veiling of that terrifying central chasm which could swallow, or give birth to, a world.

She was grateful not to be cruelly exposed on that bare height, glad to be free of the buffeting winds that might threaten to pitch her away into the void; relieved not to look down on emptiness and blank rock, not to see the gleaming cold peaks that she knew rose everywhere about her in this bleak land.

She picked her way upwards, step by step, through a crudely gouged channel, treading carefully on the slippery rock. She tried not to think of Harg, wrestling with the berserk, hurled by a violent momentum, straight into the dark central cone.

At last she could climb up no further. She lay down in a hard hollow of rock and saw how the mist sailed across a jagged toothed rim just above her. That rim was like a barricade, a frail barrier that barely contained the unimaginable nothingness beyond.

Despite the cold mist, and though her gloved fingers felt numb, her body was drenched in sweat, and her breath came in gasps – as if the exertion of her climb had overtaken her only when she stopped. The air seemed to have been sucked away from her lungs as by some secret theft of her energy by the void just beyond her.

Ingrid closed her eyes.

Into her mind floated the image of her father, her own dear father, Einar, the healer, who had given her the cup. She had seen him in Loki's cave, a phantom who had spoken from a saint's skull, from above the deep rock fissure in which appeared the vision of Harg and Glimir, flagrant in their unlawful love.

Ingrid remembered how she had first taken the gift of the cup from him, in Wayland, long ago, centuries ago, as it seemed. She remembered how his hands shook, how she had felt the tremor that ran through his body as he had passed her the precious object and kissed her. Her tears had fallen into the cup. Innocent tears. But she was no longer an innocent.

She stood up, tensed her body, struggling to catch her breath.

Then, with a great swinging motion of her right arm, she flung the cup high, high up over the rim of rock and into the volcano.

The Rune Master

Trogheim was burning. The whole morning, as they descended from Nerthus, down through the pass that divided the two steepest outcroppings of the Arnajokul, they had seen white smoke-clouds billowing up. Now, as the two women and the boy rode across the high grassy mounds above the town, a harsh smell of smoke and charred wood filled the air.

Just below, they could see the black lines of Knut's burial ship, already nearly dissolved into the scorched earth. The eastern gate of Trogheim hung open; there was no-one in sight.

Ingrid spoke to Glimir and the boy. 'It will be safer if you wait for me just inside the walls. I will go to the house and find out if the old man has been seen in Trogheim. When I come back we can decide what action to take.'

They had been told in the nearest mountain village that there was looting in the town; and also that an old man, with a fierce, sullen look, had ridden down the mountain in the direction of Trogheim on the previous night.

Ingrid slipped away into the streets of the town. Everything seemed dream-like, uncertain: most of the doors were shut or barred, the windows covered up. She met no-one.

She made straight for Brodd's house, soon catching sight of the steep reed-thatched roof, then stood hammering again and again on the great wooden door. There was no answer from within; and she hesitated.

A woman stepped out of the alleyway, almost at her elbow. Ingrid recognized Geirhild.

'I've been waiting for you to come back,' the blonde girl said excitedly. 'You must hurry! Brodd and the mistress have shut up the house. They are already on the beach, preparing to depart. I did not want to leave without you.'

Ingrid hesitated. 'The old man . . . The one they call the Rune Master . . . Have you seen him?'

Geirhild looked puzzled. 'I have heard the servant girls talk of him, but I'm not sure . . . Wait! Yes, I remember now – there was a ship in the harbour . . .'

Ingrid sprang away. 'We must go there at once,' she said.

At the gate they came upon Glimir talking vividly by signs to her son.

Geirhild bowed low and said to Ingrid: 'You have brought the mistress of the ceremonies!'

'The ceremonies are finished, child,' Glimir told her. 'You were the last, but through Ingrid of Wayland the goddess saw fit to spare you. We must not forget to make an offering for Granny Falki, who did not survive to see the new order of things.'

'The black priestess!' whispered Geirhild. 'She gave me sweet drugs to make my heart sing in death.'

But Glimir explained to her: 'We tempered the harshness of the male gods as we could, though the custom itself was evil. The Christians will have none of it, for the Christ himself died for men and women, tended, they say, by his mother . . .'

The three women and the boy hurried away towards the masts that stood up like frail crosses above a nest of hulking warehouses.

A dog barked. The sky had grown even darker. Despite the acrid smoke Ingrid could smell the sea. She followed Geirhild around a dark-timbered house, shut up and boarded: a few smashed wooden boxes lay underneath a tangle of torn canvas. As they passed, a rat scurried away from the boxes and disappeared in a nearby heap of rubble.

They came out on the beach, a long span of dark sand, lapped at by the full wind-brushed tide. A rocky headland enclosed it on the west; to the east it was bordered by a few bleak low hillocks. The high strand was littered with the parts of beached trading ships, timbers and masts, and bits of old steering boards. Out in the harbour which was protected at either end by a long wooden jetty, a few trading vessels stood in various states of readiness for departure. Some of these were without masts and rolled gently in the wash of water, but at least one, a fine ship with striped sails furled and tilted, seemed ready to depart.

'There!' Geirhild pointed, 'That is Brodd's. But the master himself may not have gone aboard.'

Ingrid told Glimir. 'You must take Val and escape with Brodd's party. I will deal with the old man by myself.'

Glimir smiled. 'You are bold enough, Ingrid, but you are wrong if you think that fat merchant will welcome us!'

'He cannot refuse; he is your cousin, after all.'

Glimir shook her head and said nothing.

They walked slowly along the beach. A few men lounged on the nearby jetty, watching them. Others worked furiously, loading heavy packets on to small boats, casting nervous glances at the west gate of Trogheim. Small parties of armed men, strung out in groups from the headland, protected the beach from incursions from that side of the town.

Geirhild stopped and examined the trampled-down sand.

'The tent was here,' she said. 'I don't understand it.'

A stout man stepped out from behind a woodpile, where a filthy stream trickled down from the town to the sea. He was accompanied by two Vikings carrying axes. Three women trailed behind: Ingrid recognized Helga and her slave-girls.

'Here is the master,' said Geirhild.

Brodd strode up, dressed in a rich purple tunic, and bright yellow breeches; he wore high boots and a dark leather hat, which might have served also as a fighting cap. A heavy sword hung at his side; his jewelry – neckbands and bracelets and brooches – gleamed in the dull light. Ingrid saw that his boots had been scummed over by the mud of the stream.

'Thank the Christ,' said Brodd and made a clumsy effort at signing the cross on himself. 'I did not think you would come back from the mountain . . . But where is Harg?'

'Harg is dead,' said Ingrid bluntly. 'Killed by the berserk, whom he led on and at last destroyed. This boy is his son;

344

you must take him under your protection. I see you are about to sail from Trogheim.'

Brodd looked suddenly confused; he turned to his wife, who had come up beside him, nodding to her is if she should provide for him the proper emotion of grief he seemed incapable of showing.

And sure enough, at the word of Harg's death, Helga burst into tears. 'Now we've lost everything, everything!' she wailed, and her husband nervously signalled the serving maids to attend her.

'His son?' Brodd asked faintly, in his deep voice. 'I don't understand.' He laid a firm hand on the boy's shoulder.

'And I am the boy's mother.' Glimir spoke for the first time, staring hard at Brodd, who at her words had shrunk back, almost pushing Val away in his surprise and aversion.

'My God!' said the merchant, and then, after a short silence, added, 'If such things can happen no wonder the old gods are displeased. These times are terrible, terrible indeed.'

He coughed, cast a nervous look at the boy, then glanced away, as if to reassure himself that his ship still rode securely at anchor.

'You must take Glimir and her son with you when you sail,' said Ingrid boldly. 'This is no place for them, with the town burning and the Christians almost at hand.'

'The Christians – thank God for them!' said Brodd, stroking his well-trimmed beard. 'Speak nothing evil of the Christ, please! It is a time for forgiveness and for mercy.'

The Viking guards swung their axes restlessly from side to side. Helga was drinking something from a flask handed her by a serving maid.

'It is such a time indeed,' said Glimir.

'I beg your forgiveness, cousin, but I cannot take you with me.' Brodd spoke these words in a low voice; he did not look at Glimir. 'I would like to do so for Harg's sake, but there have been too many rumours – about witchcraft and other such, uh . . . unsavoury matters. And this poor boy, beautiful as he is, is the child of sin.'

'He is a poor helpless boy who cannot hear or speak!' cried

345

Ingrid, stepping forward. 'Do you mean to say you wil abandon him?'

Brodd shook his head slowly from side to side but did no answer.

Glimir took her son by the hand and led him over to where Ingrid stood. 'Do not excite yourself for this purpose, Ingrid I have something else in mind now.' She paused, and they al looked at her, even the impassive Viking guards.

Val crept into his mother's arms. It was as if he wer holding his breath, afraid of her next words.

'I want my son to go back to the land of his birth. I wan him to return to Markland, and it is you that must take him there, Ingrid.'

'As for you, Brodd,' and here Glimir smiled, 'I have no wish to presume upon the generosity of my dear cousin, far from it. I intend myself to take ship immediately for Ireland. Oh do not look so surprised, Ingrid, and Val, my precious one do not let that sadness come into your eyes! We have been parted before and this will be only for a short time. I have decided it. I too will try the way of Christ, though for differen reasons than those of my cousin. The time I have chosen i seven years. Seven years' penance. Remember, Val, after tha you must come and find me.'

Tears ran down her cheeks then; Val reached up and gentl touched his mother's lips with his fingertips.

'You see, I have something to expiate,' said Glimir, 'for kept this lovely boy from his father!'

Brodd rubbed his thick hands together, and cleared hi throat. 'This is a wise and beautiful decision,' he suggested He took a step forward, as if to embrace mother and son, bu at the last moment drew back. 'It grows late now . . .' h added, turning anxiously to his wife and the serving maids.

'But Glimir,' Ingrid cried, kicking at the sand in sudde frustration. 'There is no ship! How can I care for the boy How can I find my way back without your magic? I cannot d it, Glimir!'

'There is your ship and your guide,' said Glimir, an pointed out beyond the inner harbour.

Just beyond the far jetty, in the deep water beneath the high cliffs, a trading ship, called a knorr, had suddenly appeared, a low-riding vessel with a single mast and without special markings. Clearly visible on the foredeck was a tall figure, motionless as a pillar against the uncertain horizon of the sea.

'The Rune Master,' whispered Skadi, and the slave-girl crouched down beside her trembling mistress.

'We sail at once,' announced Brodd. He turned as if to bid farewell to his cousin and to Ingrid.

Glimir took her son in her arms. 'We will say our own farewell now. It is up to you, Ingrid, to win passage. But do not let the old man trick you.'

'Your mother is right,' Ingrid said quietly to Val. 'We must make the old man serve us. Are you afraid to sail with him?'

The boy shook his head.

Ingrid ran along the sand towards the jetty. A few men lounging on the landward side stirred, but made no attempt to interfere with her. She sprang up on the wooden platform and ran out above the dark waves.

The ship would pass close enough to the end of the jetty for her to hail it, she decided. The old man still had not moved but Ingrid felt that he had suddenly become aware of her. It was as if something in him tensed and strengthened, holding back the ship's motion, gripping it in a fierce will against its own momentum. By the time she stood there, at the end of the long jetty, the vessel, rocking gently from side to side, hung in a strange foaming eddy that resembled a whirlpool.

'Odin!' she cried out, and suddenly the water ceased its motion and the ship lay as if becalmed.

The tall man on the foredeck was wrapped round in a familiar dark blue cloak. He held a long staff in his right hand and his floppy hat tilted down over one side of his face.

'You! Slayer of men and of poor harmless beasts! You who gave the blank rune to Harg, your faithful follower. Can you do a favour for a girl who longs for home and for a poor orphan whose father you sacrificed?'

The sky had grown very dark, and there was a rumble of

347

thunder from the mountains, as if a storm were threatening to break.

The old man in the boat turned his head slowly round. He spoke and his voice reverberated strangely, as if he were speaking from beneath the water.

'I hear you, you do not need to raise your voice to me, child.'

'You must take us home now,' Ingrid called out. 'It is the wish of Harg's mother. I have done all I can for my village. I have returned the cup to the mother, to the one who forgives.'

'You have returned the cup. And yet there is no light. The great ancient mother has lost her power because of the sins of her daughters. It is women who lead men astray, thus the light is diminished. Then strange things come out of the deeps and everything falls to disorder. That is what your journey should have taught you.'

Ingrid looked back at the beach. She saw Glimir and her son kneeling rapt, their attention fixed on her. Geirhild stood a little way behind, hesitating. Brodd and his entourage were hurrying away in the other direction. Up in Trogheim flames had burst out again, flickering up against the dark sky.

'Admit it, old man,' Ingrid cried out, 'you were powerless to return the creatures to the dark bog. Because it was the violence of the old ways that served to rouse them. The mother of earth was forgotten – that is what I have learned on my journey.'

'You fear the father, girl, because you are drawn to him. Therefore you cannot truly admit him to your heart. Find your own way back to your childhood and your precious village!'

The old man turned away. The boat moved slightly in the water.

'Wait!' Ingrid cried. 'It is as Loki, the shapeshifter, told me. You possess no real wisdom. Everything you know has been stolen, taken over from others. You would not dare to match wits against a girl, not as the shapeshifter did once!'

The figure in the boat turned back. Waves slapped and broke on the hull of the long knorr. The harbour lay shrouded in a darkness that glittered with strange light.

Armed men were running up from the beach towards the town. Two small boats carried Brodd and his party out to his vessel. Ingrid saw Geirhild wave wildly and then she too vanished, leaving the beach almost empty. Only the mother and son had stayed behind; they crouched there in the sand and watched her.

'You dare to challenge me to a contest?' The voice roared up from the harbour, rattling the boards of the jetty. A thunderstorm was raging on the high knolls above the town. The old man's ship remained motionless.

Ingrid gathered up her courage and spoke.

'I do challenge you. But if I win you must take me and the boy to the new world. You must take us home!'

A pause; silence seemed to overflow her mind, then his voice came:

'I agree, on one condition. If you lose, you must still come on board. Then we will sail together truly, though I do not think you will like our destination!'

Ingrid shuddered. 'I am aware that you know all the best routes to hell!' she said quickly.

The Rune Master laughed. 'I will ask you three questions. You must answer all three, or I win the contest. Do you agree to that condition?'

Ingrid bowed her head.

The voice of the old man sounded again, but this time low and close, like a voice from her intimate mind.

'Answer me this,' it said quietly. *'What use is action on earth when the gods have planned everything?'*

Ingrid closed her eyes. She was no longer there, beside stormy Trogheim, but deep underground, in a great cavern sunk at the root of a tree. Three masked women sat beside a well, their gnarled old fingers forever weaving, and the trunk of the tree stretched up out of sight: it flowed onwards forever through all the worlds, known and unknown, and neither god nor man could chart its many branchings.

And Ingrid remembered that she was on the edge of an island that rose in the middle of a great ocean – the gods had decreed it; it was none of her doing. Long ago, she had ridden the back of a caribou into the dark wood. She had fallen in and out of love, eaten the foul meat and been transformed into a Windigo. Her triumph had been undermined; she had been driven away from the Skraeling village by the actions of Thorkel; and the Buck had been slain. She had been instructed by the shaman, carried across the ocean as the shapeshifter arranged it, and drawn into Harg and Glimir's strange web of love and hatred. And now she was being given care of a deaf-mute boy, who had once dreamed of her coming. How could she say that she controlled her own destiny? Was anything really hers? What use *was* action on earth when the gods had planned everything?

Ingrid felt that she had lost, that the old man, with his very first question, had defeated her!

She stared down at the cruel waves that slapped hard at the jetty.

Then she thought of the girl she had been, untried and innocent, eager but raw. She thought of the things that before had seemed important to her: how trivial now in the light of her journey! She thought of her transformation, of the power she had begun to feel in herself, a power of spirit, with which life seemed to have gifted her already.

'The use of action is experience,' she whispered, knowing full well the old man could hear everything. 'Though all may be planned, we know nothing until we live it through. And if nothing is planned and the gods are a mockery (as the shapeshifter might tell us) then my action gives me at least a sense of my own valid purpose.'

She saw a little rowing boat, one that had been secured by ropes to the larger ship, break suddenly free of its lashings and float gently towards the jetty.

The Rune Master shifted his staff in his hand and smiled across the water at her.

'Very well,' he said quietly, 'but that was my easiest question. Answer me this, then, out of your precious experience. *What use is love, when all loves are betrayed in the end*?'

Ingrid stood as if stunned. And in her heart she felt that it was true, all loves were betrayed, all loves compromised, in the end. Harg had seduced Glimir and perverted her sisterly love, betraying his father's love and trust. Her own family had loved her, yet given her up as a sacrifice. She had loved Harg, who had tried to deceive her. And had not she too deceived Thorkel, that simple trusting soul, and driven him to near madness because of her passion for the Buck? She had led Harg to Glimir, against her word, even after receiving the precious cup. And was not even Glimir, out of guilt, putting at risk her son's love, a love so faithful, so unquestioning?

She braced herself; the thunder cracked over her; mother and son moved slowly towards the jetty. The little boat stood still in the water.

Then it came to her.

Passion, she saw, was only a gleam of light on a fathomless sea. Love, however devious and strange, was much more. For love would at last seek forgiveness, and grow deeper with pardon and the yielding up of possession. *Love should teach selflessness, and betrayal itself must be a glimpse of how little we deserve from each other.*

Ingrid stood tall on the frail jetty, watching the waves roll in beneath the wooden pillars. She opened her arms as if to embrace everything, the sea, and the salt air, and the wild day.

But the Rune Master shook his head in anger, banging his great staff on the deck of the ship.

The little boat drifted quickly towards her.

'Very well,' said a quiet deep voice close beside her, 'but the contest still hangs on the last question.'

The old man drew himself up, his cloak like a dark flag of the storm. He raised his staff above his head and swung it three times round as the words came:

'Answer me this then, out of your precious forgiveness: *what use is life itself, when death closes all eyes?*'

Ingrid stared across the gap of water. In the old man's glittering eye, as if magnified in a giant mirror, she saw without solace the secret terrors of her childhood, and the grim shapes of Ragnarok.

The lights of a thousand stars shivered out in an infinite

darkness; the wolf, Skoll, seized the sun between its jaws and swallowed it. Gripped by the winter of winters, the world sank down in ice and snow, the mountains shook and cracked apart. She saw the trees fall, and waves tear the shore; the great serpent stirred in the deep.

And she found herself falling, hurtled down into darkness, into the bottomless pit beneath the mountains, where iron walls closed in. She fell ever faster, so that no-one, not even the All-Father, could save her . . .

The little boat flew up and down on the water. The storm broke. She had collapsed on the jetty, and with clumsy fingers sought a firm grip on the wet wood. The sky roared, lightning flashed, and a great bolt struck the ship's mast, illuminating the harbour, and the dark figure who stood like a thin blue shadow on the foredeck.

Ingrid rolled over and saw Val climbing up the jetty.

And she got up on her knees, and shouted hoarsely to the old man:

'You, old man, Rune Master – I call you the master of ruin! Cold and heartless, as all the gods must be, because you bear the curse of life eternal. You want to deny life because you stand outside it: nothing takes hold of you, as you take hold of nothing! *Your question is answered, your riddle is solved, whenever man, woman or child reaches out for a real thing and loves it!*'

At these words, which he could hardly have heard amid the tumult, the old man staggered back and disappeared in a flash beneath the knorr's forward deck.

Ingrid bent over. A great wave lifted the little boat easily, and swung it forward to the jetty. She reached down into the swirling water and took hold of the leader rope.

She was drenched, but ecstatic. For a thought came to her then, overwhelming: it was not magic that would bring Wayland back to the light, but the knowledge and experience she had gained on her journey, the power she could find in herself to make things better.

She held up the rope to show Glimir her triumph.

352

But Glimir had disappeared. Along its whole length, the beach lay deserted.

Then the rain began to fall in thick torrents.

The boy, Val, crawled across the jetty; Ingrid turned to him, helplessly laughing and weeping. He put a slender, wet arm around her shoulder.

She got up and held the rope, and young Val climbed into the boat.

So they rowed out together and boarded the Rune Master's ship.

The Return

The ship hurried on through the low coiling sea. For a while Ingrid slept beside the afterdeck, covered by hides that smelled of tar. When she awoke, it was darker; the old man crouched by the steerboard, his blue shadowed form swaying slightly, the brim of his broad floppy hat curled up by the wind. Near the mast the boy was bailing furiously, swinging a rough wooden bucket; the sea-spray, like tears, streaked his bright cheeks. Above him, the great square sail billowed; they were running off before a brisk southwesterly; the dinghy had been cut loose, and as Ingrid gazed back she saw the land like a grey silhouette, much shrunken now, as if it were slipping down through a chasm of ocean.

Ingrid pulled herself up and rubbed her eyes softly. How they had managed to raise the sail she did not know, though she could feel, even from where she lay, the old man's diminished power; no doubt he had used a spell to run the windlass and haul up the sail; now he was steering by will, attuning the inner space-map, the *husanotra*, to bring them in

353

towards the far shore, be it Greenland or Vinland itself, at the right place.

Slowly, she crept forward, pulling her woollen cloak about her, feeling the wind at her back, aware of the great banked dark clouds that stretched far away to the south-west. She approached the boy at the bailing hole, gently wrenched the bucket from his hands, and said to him, in a voice thrust out against the wind:

'We are safe with the old man now. He will not harm us, though his pride and indifference are cruel. You must forget the past and help him all you can.'

She turned, as if to address the Rune Master, but saw at once from the position of his body, his fixed downward gaze, and the way he held his staff, that he was sunk deep in trance and would not answer. At the same time she realized how glad she was that the boy had been sent with her, how much she had grown to like him in the strange hours they had spent together: and he was, after all, a witness to so much. Perhaps later he would serve to remind her of things she had forgotten, or might try to forget. Glimir had entrusted him to her; well then, perhaps he was destined to be hers, part of her family, in Wayland.

She motioned Val to the afterdeck, smiling at the way he did not answer, except with his eyes, which told her how impossible it was for him to leave her.

'Eat something, then, and rest. We have a hard trip before us, and worse things to face when we land.'

She slung the heavy bucket down and hauled up the water, watching him scurry away to where the tarpaulin and bales were piled up under the afterdeck. Then she pulled away with a will; after her sleep, she felt strong. She could think of her village, of her family, with tenderness unaccompanied by tears or by guilt. She would go there, she knew, she could bring them good sustenance. Her heart was open, her mind clear; the dark past was slipping away, like the faint silhouette of the island behind them.

Night came on little by little. The boy slept; the old man held course, hardly moving in his place at the steerboard.

Ingrid ate some dried fish and fruit, drank some water, and returned to her bailing.

It was a murky, deep night, without stars; the wind rose, the waves swelled but the ship ran along with the breeze. Ingrid could feel how the Rune Master's will controlled the rigging, how the ropes pulled taut at his silent command, forestays and backstays and shrouds, how the yard swung to measure, how the tarpaulins flattened and held, though the swift breeze tore at them. The ship ran light on the surface, like a great bird skimming the water, on and on through the darkness.

And Ingrid once again slept. Growing tired of her bailing, she slipped to the afterdeck, curled down with the boy, closed her eyes.

She awoke to a blazing bright morning, the first of three. It was a day of clouds that swirled and gathered in the great endless blue of the sky. The island behind them was almost gone now, reduced to a sharp beam of light, a needle of light, or a faint note of fire without substance.

She walked through the hold, stretching her stiff limbs. The Rune Master sat at the steerboard as if rigid with tension. The boy crouched at the bailing well, hauling up bucket after bucket of water. Ingrid smiled, yawned and stretched, inhaling the clear morning air, feeling her spirits rise ever higher, until her mind soared far beyond the bright fluffed-up peaks of the loftiest clouds.

All day the ship flew through the water. The sky was magnificent: clouds purled and ravelled; then made frail prints like bleached bones on a blue that turned to gold. Afterwards, the gold became pink, trailing fringes of green fire until darkness rolled in, a thick barring blackness that swallowed the last light.

Ingrid, as she moved about the ship, felt compelled to talk by discreet signals to the boy, because she could feel how the old man's power drained away with each hour, as he drove the ship forward towards a place that he held in his mind, an anchorage lost in the far western sunset.

They sailed on, day after day; the weather held clear. No

land rose in sight. The prow cleft the waves, the decks shone, the ship rolled and danced. The old man kept moving them forward, and Ingrid, a little alarmed, saw how quickly his strength waned.

Then one morning the storm broke. It was sullen and cold, the wind whistled out of the south-west, big drops of rain fell. Ingrid and the boy sat under a tarpaulin, shivering. The old man, she thought, this will finish him. She clung to the boy, trying to think of how she could save him.

A grim swelling darkness consumed the last light. The waves rose; deep troughs appeared, as if the sea itself were being sucked away beneath their ship. With a terrible lightness they slid down the side of the waves, swept up each mountainous crest, hung there for infinite seconds, then roared down. The ship groaned and twisted, as if slipping away from the storm's crushing love. They listed and threatened to capsize. The rain swept over them, lashing the deck like the tail of a great fish.

Ingrid pressed the boy under her cloak; with closed eyes she waited – this was surely the end.

Then she heard the old man's wild laughter, and looked up. He stood tall, his blue cape flowing out, his arms raised high as if he were saluting the storm. In one hand he held the tiller, in the other his old floppy hat, which he waved as he shouted, addressing the ship itself.

Before Ingrid's very eyes the great square sail came sliding down, the ropes flung about and secured themselves. The ship righted at once; they breasted the waves and ploughed on. She could feel how the old man's strength came, how the power swelled up in him, how the storm seemed to flow in his movements and gestures.

Minute by minute they swept clear of the darkness. Molten light ran in the sky. The wind died down, and, though the sea tossed the ship like a cork, they did not capsize. At last the rain thinned and then ceased. For a long time they drifted; the sky's leaden grey cracked: a dim yellow light veined the western horizon.

Night came, and calm seas, and a new stirring breeze.

Ingrid heard the ropes twisting and untwisting, the creak of the windlass and halyard, the flap of the great sail.

She awoke to a calm smiling sea. They drifted along in a light wind. The old man, untiring, stood fast at the tiller. Then the fish came and she and the boy clambered eagerly at the gunwales to watch them. With eager glances they gazed down into the blue-grey depths of the water, their eyes held by the flashing of silver, the glittering shoals like a single thought passing. Then emptiness, murky green depths, white foam and a dazzle of light at the surface.

From time to time dark shapes, like shadows, uncoiled, and were gone. In the distance a bald thumb thrust at the surface, a giant's thumb, the back of a great whale, running the sea in bright cascades of water, delicate spouts making fountains of light.

And at last the companions, the dolphins, criss-crossing the bow, breaking the surface with furious energy, poised for a moment in air, disappearing.

Ingrid gripped the boy's arm. She could feel a wild pulsing energy everywhere: the old man's fixed line of force stretching out, the disparate currents and eddies of life in the sea: how everything sang at the boundaries of air, water, light.

The birds came, gulls with black legs and wing tips, grey-mantled gulls with dark tail-feathers, then skuas with strong, beating motion, then falcon-like jaegers with white flashing wings. They flew in from the west, small flocks of them passing or diving, connecting the air and the sea with their dazzling flights.

At the sight of the birds, the Rune Master stirred in his place. As if awakening from a long sleep, he threw up his arms and yawned, pulled off his hat, and looked round.

'You!' he cried out, pointing a long, skinny finger at the boy where he stood by the scuppers. Trembling, but with firm step, Val crossed over to the starboard side of the vessel. The old man put on his hat, took hold of the staff which he had propped up beside him, and gestured to the boy to take over the steerboard. The boy grasped the tiller, the ship fluttered slightly and settled. The old man worked slowly along towards the foredeck, leaning down on his staff and advancing with stiff awkward steps. He stopped and pulled back a long tarpaulin cover, all punctured with holes, from one of the compartments beneath the foredeck. A leather mesh covered the opening, and, as Ingrid watched, the Rune Master lifted up the leather, at the same time muttering a few words very quickly in a language she could not understand.

A flutter of wings in the shadows, an explosion and, flapping and bawling, two ravens emerged, soared up once in the sunlight and landed as if with caped grace on the Rune Master's shoulders.

The old man reached up and stroked each in turn, their beaks touched his ears; from out of the folds of his cloak he drew a fistful of food, which he offered them. Screaming and gobbling, they fluttered around him, devouring their meal.

The old man held out his staff like a lance; they perched there a moment; he swung his arm up and whiplashed them free. They flapped away awkwardly, gaining height with fierce wingbeats, soared out away from the ship, wheeled and sailed back.

Not landing, they skirted the foredeck, then with strong wingbeats rose steadily, pulling slowly away, heading westward.

The Rune Master watched them until they were two wavering black specks on the shining horizon. He made his way back to the wheelboard, grabbed the tiller from the boy and turned the ship slightly to follow the line of the birds' flight.

Ingrid watched all this, then quietly set about preparing some food for herself and the boy. She was thinking of the Rune Master's power, and how, for all its strange magic, it was bound up with the real facts of nature. He was following the birds to the near shore; soon they would come there, to Vinland or Markland – and from the coast how far to her village? She closed her eyes and let the delicate breeze caress her face.

Towards evening of the next day, the ravens returned. They flew straight to their master, who let the boy take the tiller while he shut the birds away under the foredeck. Ingrid watched him, then looking casually out across the molten gold fire, she saw a black ragged outline of coast, thin and wavering, where the sky met the sea.

That night she tossed fitfully, consumed with excitement. Was it Vinland or Markland at last? The boy slept beside her; from time to time wriggling free of the covers, he groaned quietly, as if from cruel dreams; she stroked his pale forehead, and soothed him, then lay watching the old man at the steerboard, a stark figure in the soft moonlight.

She awoke after sunrise, shivering with the cold. The sight that answered her impatient, and questioning gaze was disturbing. They had come in to the coast through the night, but what lay before them was no bountiful shore but a grim land of mountains and glaciers, peak after peak stretching up to the bleak heights. Not a tree, not a green thing, but barren bald rock, steep cliffs on the shore and, behind, raw jagged peaks of the mountains, snow-capped and glittering.

Overcome with disappointment and indignation, Ingrid pulled her heavy cloak about her and swept through the hold to confront the old man.

'What is this terrible place you have brought us to?' she cried out, wanting badly to shake him but not daring to touch his blue cloak. 'Is this Vinland or Markland – this wilderness? How will I ever get home through those mountains? You've steered us to the end of the world, old man – you and your ravens!'

The Rune Master looked at her calmly, his grey eye glittering with humour.

'Your wisdom has not made you trusting,' he said, in his strange, creaking voice. 'But a bargain is a bargain, when I make it. Be silent now for a moment and listen. I did not wish to meet strangers along the way. Therefore we have sailed first to the south-west, then north-west, so as to come to the country the Vikings call Helluland, the place of stones. From there we can follow the snow back to Wayland. Some day, I believe, you will make your own journey to Vinland. Go now, and prepare for the landing, and do not let the boy see your

359

disappointment, for he will need all the courage he can muster.'

All day they sailed in towards the grim coast. The sky remained grey and faint silver; the slate-grey cliffs towered. It grew colder and colder. Waves battered the granite, great fists of water striking at gates that would never open. The only sign of life was the seabirds, vast whirring flocks of them, darting and tumbling on the face of the cliffs. As they sailed close, they heard a wild shrieking and crying, pitched against the booming voice of the surf. And at the foot of the cliffs, and in the steep gashes that split the cliff-walls everywhere into shrunken fjords, they saw the giant slab-like stones, sliced by time and the frost from the granite, that gave the coast its name.

'Helluland?' she said to the boy, moving her lips slowly, so that he could understand, 'or Hell-Land?' He laughed, and she hugged him to her.

But the old man seemed sure of the coast. He steered them in closer and closer; and at last they swept round a small island, smooth as the egg of a giant bird. On both sides the cliffs rose up steeply. No white peaks were visible now; only the gashed jagged facings, the beetling black sides of the sea walls. The square sail had been struck, and they rode a swift current past cyclopean platforms; the squealing birds leapt as they coursed by.

Angling in sharply above them, the cliffs nearly shut out the sky. Ingrid had the feeling that they were sailing straight into the land-mass, sucked down by the current into some fathomless cavern in the heart of the mountains. The eddying water, churned up into spray, hissed about them. A giddiness seized her as she gazed up; she fancied the peak of the cliffs moved above her. She wanted to cry out, to question the old man, but then, through the spray, she made out a low shelf of beach dead ahead. They were running aground up the channel.

The old man was waving instructions at the boy, who bounded around between foredeck and hold, securing and coiling the lines. There was a low rumbling and scraping, a shuddering all through the ship. The tilted-up rudder was clear, but the low keel took hold and steadied their roll as they shot off the crest of a long powerful wave and came up on the beach.

Ingrid clapped her hands together with pleasure. They had run aground snugly, the bow notched up on the shelf, though the churning water threatened to turn the ship and so float it awkwardly free when they needed it steady. There was not a moment to lose, and she began piling up on the foredeck the small skins containing the food, clothing and water they would need for the journey overland. The old man, with surprising agility, had climbed over the side and dropped down on the wet pebbled shore. The boy paused a moment, responding to some signal from the Rune Master, who did not look back. With a few frantic motions Val stripped away the leather covering from the compartment under the foredeck and let the two ravens step free. They strutted on deck, then wheeled up and followed the old man.

Ingrid signalled to the boy, who leapt down from the ship and hauled away the sacks as she tossed them in his direction. But after he had shifted a few sacks, Val suddenly bent down and kissed the cold wet stone, and Ingrid knew he was thinking of how he had been born in this harsh land.

Then she too leapt down, touching land for the first time in days, with a few wobbling steps coming up on the beach.

Yet her heart sank as she looked around at the bleak shelf of rock they had run aground on. She was furious at the old man until she noticed how, just at a point beyond where he stood, speaking quietly to companion ravens, the valley walls sundered. Opening out at the back of the low shelf, was a narrow cleft angling to one side, at the mouth of which several large flat rocks lay shattered and riven together. It was as if, at some primeval time, the whole rocky headland itself had split, creating a passage running inland.

As Ingrid's eyes fixed on the cliff, she heard the old man begin a chanting. He stood with upraised arms and his voice rose suddenly, icily high, echoing coldly and sharply around them. Then Ingrid realized how ancient that voice was, how like the keening of the wind and the hiss of the sea-spume it sounded, mingling and blending with the song of the elements.

There was a pause. She and the boy stood expectantly. Then came a yelping and snarling, a low whining issuing forth from the cleft in the rock face. One after another, a dozen grey shapes leapt into sight, as if springing from the ancient cliff wall itself, twelve timber wolves hauling a long sled, straining and tugging against the thick dark leather thongs that bound them together.

The sled-runners struck fire on the pebbles; then the strange team pulled round, and came tumbling and snarling at the feet of the old man.

The Rune Master raised up his staff with two hands and at the same time shouted a command. The ravens sprang from his shoulders, flapped away through the air, gathered speed and flew up. Circling the beach once, they vanished, swallowed up by the gap in the cliffs where the wolves had come out.

Ingrid and Val stood amazed at the sight, but the old man, without hesitation, led the wolves down the long pebbled strand to where the skin bags lay on the damp shelf. He motioned to the still-gaping boy to load up the sled, wheeled round, and strode up towards the long narrow cleft where the ravens had vanished.

The Rune Master had just reached the mouth of the narrow valley as Val threw the last sack on the sled. The old man shouted, the wolves sprang in motion, the sled rattled and scraped up the beach. Ingrid and Val hurried after it.

They sprang in together, laughing a little, content to let the sharp-eyed wolves carry them along: those lean bodies pumped and strained, while the old man with unfailing stride, walked beside the team . . .

So their long trek began, and Ingrid fell into a calm dreamlike state. She lay on the sled, dozing, or else sat wide awake – but only the alternating light and darkness gave hint of how much time had passed. It seemed to her sometimes that the great empty world revolved around her; the same low bleak hills coming back into sight, the same boulders piled up with snow, the same frosty nights glittering around her.

The chill wind might rise, or the snow fall in thick blinding sheets, but the Wanderer plunged on, the wolves never baulked – they drove on as if tireless, first north and then westward, across the great trackless barrens beyond Helluland.

On and on they went. There was no speech and no rest; the nights seemed to fly by, the days drifted past. From time to time Ingrid would attempt to talk by signs to the boy, but Val simply stared at her, his empty round eyes full of amazement, as if it were a strange thing that a human being should want to talk in such a place. Ingrid imagined, or dreamed, that the seasons changed swiftly. She saw the land magically rise from the grip of the ice: great bays and rivers appearing, the cold barren plain fuzzed with lichen, with sedges and shrubs. She saw rare moths and butterflies everywhere, heard the hum of mosquitoes, watched the murre chicks go leaping from steep cliffs to the water, heard the geese trumpeting high overhead.

They had followed the low frozen riverbeds across mile after mile of the barrens, through the endless bleak days, when they finally emerged on the edge of a great body of water, still solid and passable, in spite of the oncoming spring. And something touched Ingrid, and she remembered a great sea, with frost smoke rising up, and an island where the ancient folk's magic still lingered.

Now everything was touched by clear sunlight, made lovely, but as they traversed the rough ice, some hours on the way, Ingrid seemed to wake up as from a day-dream. She became aware of Val's ragged breathing, of his slumped, helpless body. Quickly, she pulled off her mittens and touched his brow with her fingertips: he was fevered, burning hot to the touch. When she soothed him, he stirred, murmuring quietly.

'Val is ill; we must stop,' she cried out at once to the old man, startled by the sound of her own voice. But the Rune Master did not even turn; he strode on, with the same powerful steps; the wolves plunged along, the steam of their breathing rising up in the chill air.

'You must stop! He's ill. Don't you understand?'

She threw off the blankets, swung her feet off the sled and tumbled down in the snow. She scrambled a little way, her body unused to the motion, felt drained of all strength. She stood up, took a wobbling step, and fell down. The sled pulled away as she stood there.

She started to panic, but got hold of herself. Fists clenched, she took one step, then another, moving gingerly forward, feeling the strength come back into her limbs.

The sled was some distance ahead and she walked on, suffering it to pull farther away, as she regained the use of her body. The sled topped a low ridge and vanished. The old man had not even looked round.

But Ingrid could move now and started a slow jog behind it. She sighted it quickly, and jogged on. Her body found strength by the minute. She jogged on, and was starting to gain on the sled.

Soon she could run at full speed. The sled seemed to stand still; she ran forward and flung herself in, hanging on to a skin bag wedged in at the rear of the sled.

She rested a few seconds, her breath coming quickly, and saw that Val's eyes were open, though his head drooped weakly to one side. The old man, she knew, would do nothing; he knew little of pity and, to him, in such matters, there existed no kind of appeal. It was up to her to save the boy.

A thought struck her then, the image of her own father and of a beautiful woman searching the woods for rare herbs. She turned and pulled open a small skin bag they had brought all the way from Iceland, a bag she had been given by Glimir on the morning after Harg's death. It was Glimir's healing pouch, and from it she took a tiny stoppered jar, and poured out some thin yellow oil into the palm of her hand. After brushing back the boy's hair, and settling him comfortably down in the sled, she massaged his burning hot forehead with the substance, finally scooping up snow with her hand and rubbing this too on his temples.

The sled careened on through the endless white country. But Ingrid bent over the boy soothing him, encouraging him, holding his hand, until, after endless hours, she heard his steady breathing beside her and felt how the fever had left him at last, his forehead all silken and cool to the touch, his eyes closed in sleep.

She too drifted into sleep, a long sleep in which she dreamed of Glimir and her father walking hand in hand through a lovely broad meadow where grew all manner of herbs and rare flowers: aloe and amaranth, dragon's blood, poppy and lemongrass. And the meadow was radiant with light. And she thought: the true light comes in helping, in love and forgiveness and in tending the poor and the sick.

Though the dream seemed so short, almost as if the vision had flashed only once to her eyes and then faded, her sleep seemed to go on forever. She remembered once waking, feeling the boy press against her; she heard the sharp yelping of the wolves, and caught sight of the endless green sweep of the forests, the evergreens rising on all sides, the tundra long vanished behind her . . .

Then she did wake, and saw the boy's hands sign excitedly beside her.

'The trees, Princess Ingrid, just look at all the trees!'

With her knuckles she rubbed at her eyes, as if she were rubbing away a dream of blank emptiness, pressing a white unformed world into sharp coloured shapes.

They had stopped in the midst of a great wood, and row after row of dark evergreens swayed in the light breeze. In the glitter of sunlight she could see it was real, it was all real!

The Wanderer stood by the sled, his blue cloak drawn round him, his floppy hat raked down across his blind eye. Beside him stood the boy, smiling up at her – with one hand he idly caressed the lean silver wolf by his side. The rest of the team lolled and played close beside him.

As Ingrid slowly climbed out of the sled, the old man came forward.

'Quick! We have no time to lose. You must come to the river!'

Ingrid took the old man's proferred hand, and accompanied him, still blinking and rubbing her eyes, towards a shallow depression, all covered with fresh snow, that ran like a soft curving road through the trees.

They clambered down the bank and she could feel her boots sink through the snow until they touched ice. She took a few steps, than came a crackling and sagging of the ice underfoot. She stopped and looked questioningly at the Rune Master.

'Hurry!' he urged her, drawing her out towards the centre of the frozen river.

The ice went on cracking beneath them. She could see how a few tufts of bush had sprung out through the snow on the opposite bank.

'Here!' said the Rune Master.

Ingrid reached down: it was as if she had thrust her hand into a blazing fire: pain seared her fingers, her palm and her wrist. A throbbing pain shot up her arm. She wanted to cry out, to pull back, but the old man said, 'Push!'

Suddenly, her hand struck the water, the pain vanished. Her fingers thrust into a niche in a large sunken stone; they closed on a small piece of metal. The cold began numbing her hand. She felt the quick rush of water.

'Now away!' said the old man, already striding full tilt towards the near bank.

Ingrid heard the roaring on all sides, and ran after the old man. The ice was very slippery. The roaring and rushing filled up the woods all around them.

She saw the boy jump towards her, the old man step up on the bank. The river was melting beneath her feet!

Two steps and her boots touched a boulder on the edge of the river. From there she sprang forward and came down in a quick sprawling dive on the bank.

She rolled over and saw the river, suddenly released from winter's grip, in a torrent, engorged its whole length with thick chunks of ice. The ice turned and glittered. Then while the wolf-team yelped and whined at her feet, Ingrid opened

366

her right fist and looked at the small piece of metal pressed in the palm of her hand.

It was the whistle her brothers had given her at the start of her journey, the whistle that had summoned the grey folk. Harg had placed it in the ice (how many ages ago?) with his own hands.

There were tears in Ingrid's eyes as she slowly turned the precious object in her hand. Val stood gazing with pride and love at Ingrid, as if no feat of hers could surprise him.

'In our contest you were sure of your knowledge,' the Rune Master said in a quiet voice. 'Do you have the courage now to face the dead ones, in the name of your new power?'

Ingrid looked around in the woods, remembering with a shudder the ancient nightmare, the slow treading forms of the undead. The old man raised his staff high and fixed his single penetrating eye upon her. The boy came slowly forward and with his right hand delicately touched her lips.

She held the whistle in her mouth and blew a long piercing note.

A silence followed, as if the wind's furtive breathing had been stopped by a spell. Then the wolves began howling together, each cry succeeding the other, in a mournful slow song.

The Rune Master lowered his staff, touched the brim of his hat, and strode off down a trail that ran south through the forest. Ingrid and the boy climbed slowly back on the sled. The team started up, and the runners, though deep in the soft snow, took hold.

They followed the old man along the track. And as Ingrid gazed anxiously round, the landscape grew slowly familiar: vivid memories possessed her. Her thoughts drifted back to a lonely hut, to a caribou plunging through darkness, to a glittering house made of ice on Moon Lake.

But as they entered a valley where evergreens clung to the chill steepening cliffs and a wind stirred the low thickets, all such thoughts fled away. Ingrid stood in a clearing, in the cold, vivid sunshine, and saw, to the right and the left, a legion of slow drifting shadows take shape among the trees.

Wayland

Bjorn reached down into the cool shining stream and scooped up handful after handful of the clear and delicious water. Then, with a groan, he sat down on the dry, rough stump of an aged fallen oak, spat once in the stream and mopped his brow.

Spring had come again to Wayland – that was clear, anyway. Well, even a town cursed by the gods and shunned by all sensible men, must have a change of the seasons to cheer it. Bjorn shook his head and gently rubbed his swollen legs. What use was spring to him, with his gams gone all rheumy and useless, and he a pedlar by trade, the greatest traveller in Westland, except for the Wise One himself, and nobody saw much of him anymore? What use was anything, for that matter, when old age got a grip on a man's poor body? May as well turn up your toes and be done with it, if the girls looked away when you passed and you had no children to cheer you in front of a blazing hearthside, the home brew gone sour in your mouth.

The morning sun rose higher, a small clump of blossoming willows stirred in the wind, and bees hummed and droned without ceasing. A cottonwood stretched its long branches, the buds pink and tender as young nipples. A pair of robins were gathering twigs for a nest on the opposite bank.

Bjorn saw that his collecting bag lay a little too close to the fast-running water, and he reached down and, with some difficulty, pulled it closer to the stump where he rested. He had just about finished his morning's gathering for old Einar and he certainly didn't want to lose his specimens now, after all the trouble he had gone to get them. *Cedar-bark, at first light, on the west side of a quick running stream*! The healer had amazing requirements, but then he claimed that the plants just wouldn't work properly unless they were collected in a certain way. The pedlar shook his head. What would Einar think if he knew that Bjorn sometimes cheated a little – after all, who in his right mind would go out at midnight to find hemlock leaves to reduce the size of his member – you could get hemlock leaves just as well at noon, couldn't you, and the point anyway was to make it larger, not reduce it?

Bjorn spat expertly at the stream. As usual, he was chewing on roots and on leaves, trying out a few of Einar's choice specimens, just on the chance that they would make the damned rheumatism go away once and for all. But none of Einar's treatments seemed to do that; only the sauna, which Einar of course hadn't invented, seemed to help. But that was the way of things, after all; nothing came easy in this life – folk talked of magic and some believed, and there might now and then be something in it, but mostly it was all just a thick wad that you chewed and spat out, so as to get on with the real business of living.

With a sigh, Bjorn reached for his bag, carefully drew the mouth shut, and eased himself up to his feet. He looked at the deep shining woods stretching around him. He had come far today, almost to the path that led on after a few miles to Skuld Lake, and even in the bright sunlight, and after all these years, he found himself shivering a little when he thought of the night of his last trip north from Eastland.

He remembered it all, every detail. How he had come upon Floki and the woman in the clearing and had seen the grey ones drag them away to the swamp. How he had run to the town with the news, half-afraid of not being believed, though they had believed him all right, when all the misfortunes, one after another, had descended on the place. And Floki's relatives had made a prayer to Odin, and the Wanderer had come (though only the gods knew who he might really be). Also the priest had run away, and the town was given over to the old gods entirely, which was to Einar's liking, but to almost nobody else's.

But then Einar, too, had paid the price. His own youngest daughter had been sent away as an offering for the village, and though there were some who said she had been spirited away to save her, when Thorkel returned with his story, they knew the truth: that she had become a savage and lived in the far north woods with the Skraelings. Well, Einar could believe what he wanted, but they would never see that girl again, and perhaps it was better that way.

Bjorn tied the collecting bag carefully to his belt and hobbled away down the path. There was no need for more collecting this day. Einar would pay him well enough for what he had gathered already. The old man had been good to him, especially since his misfortune, those bad legs that had stuck him here in this cursed village, probably for life. Of course, Einar didn't know he had a bit put away from his former trading in trinkets and skins, but that was his nest-egg, and he had a dream after all. He wanted to see Eastland and Vinland once more before he died! He could still remember the golden fields full of corn, the great houses, the rich tables – not to mention the willing wenches a man could buy for a pittance – by the gods, *that* was living!

The pedlar brushed the side of a thicket. Some pheasants flapped up from beneath and he jumped back, alarmed. He felt his heart pounding – his fingers touched the hilt of his knife.

He stood there a moment, feeling the sweat run over his face, choking down as he could the hard knotted fear in his throat. The pleasant field stretched out before him, all lazy in the sunshine; the sky was a clear cloudless blue. There was nothing to fear.

Bjorn looked behind him, took a deep breath and walked on. It was no use deceiving himself, it was fear that had done it. It was not really his bad legs, but his terror of the deep woods that had forced him to stay here. After that night three years ago he had found he could not face the woods, not ever in darkness, and sometimes even in sunshine on the brightest clear day the terror would seize him. The pedlar watched a hawk circling round in the distance – no fear there! He spat, mopped his brow, and continued his slow hobbling march.

That was the problem for the whole town, for all of Wayland, he was thinking, the terror. The crops had gone bad, some monstrous bad births had occurred, the priest couldn't save the town and he knew it and had fled, and the old gods, if they answered the prayers at all, spoke in riddles. If Thorkel hadn't frightened Floki's relatives away, it might even be worse, but look at Thorkel, taken with the melancholia after his trip north, sitting all day in a dark room, and Einar, no leader, just managing to hold things together. God, how they needed a strong man, someone to finish the fear!

He thought of the village in its isolation, how rumours had spread and the trade had finally stopped, how the hunting and fishing and a few little gardens had kept things together, though many had run away, and probably perished on their way to the south, for the grey folk still roamed at will in the woods, and no-one dared face them. Well, maybe the end of the world was in sight, if things were as bad as this everywhere. Of course no-one knew.

The pedlar trudged on, and had crossed the broad field and was entering the path beneath the trees, still some miles from the village, when he heard the first cry. It stopped him dead in his tracks; in an instant he had ducked off the path and held his long knife at the ready, though his hand shook with terror and he crouched down with trembling weak limbs.

As he huddled there, sweating, hardly daring to look, his first thought was that some fool had wandered out from the village and fallen into the river. That voice, a man's voice it seemed, sounded human, there was no doubt of that – so he thought – then the cry sounded again, this time closer, a man's voice raised up in a cry of alarm.

A crashing and beating noise followed, as if branches were being thrust back – then the crunch of urgent footsteps along the path. Bjorn mopped his brow, and with a great effort stood up. He peered round the trunk of the elm tree that concealed him and saw a sight that surprised him.

A foppish young man wearing baggy mauve trousers, a red

tunic and a mauve cape, came sprawling and scrambling down the path. He seemed to have lost his sword, for his scabbard hung empty, and he was bareheaded, his dark locks falling down like a boy's on his shoulders.

As he pitched headlong down the path, the man slipped on the damp earth and crashed down. He lay there a moment, as if stunned, casting anxious glances back down the path in the direction he had come. He did not seem able to move, but stroked his small moustache and shook his head violently, as if he were about to speak.

Bjorn laughed, and his amusement overcame his fear. He stepped from his place of concealment.

The young man turned, gave a yelp and sprang to his feet.

'In Christ's name, who are you?' he shot out in a thin high-pitched voice. It seemed to Bjorn that the fellow might swoon on the spot.

'Christ left us long before this,' the pedlar said wryly, glancing up the path at the deep woods. 'Who's after you, lad? We'd best hide if they're near.'

The young man, brushing himself off, looked rather crestfallen. He sniffed and fingered his empty scabbard with obvious embarrassment. 'Well, no-one is really after me, as a matter of fact . . .'

Bjorn shrugged his shoulders and spat, his own fears forgotten. 'Just taking a morning run in the woods belike?'

'No . . . ,' the young man frowned at the sarcasm. 'I'm looking for the village of Wayland.'

'Is that so? Well then what are we waiting for?' In truth Bjorn was not anxious to stand there much longer. He stole a look at the woods, listened carefully, and was relieved to hear nothing.

They walked along the path as quickly as Bjorn's lame legs would allow, the young man trying hard to conceal his impatience.

'You don't mean to tell me a coxcomb like yourself has trekked through the forest all the way from Eastland?' Bjorn asked him brusquely, sniffing some perfume that was not in his herb bag.

The young man shook his head. 'Oh no,' he said quickly. 'Not exactly. I accompanied traders. They were going far west, but they said things were worse here than anywhere, and they wanted to stay clear of Wayland.'

'And you didn't?'

The young man laughed. He seemed more at ease now. 'I have a taste for adventure.'

Bjorn's laugh rang through the woods.

'Oh, it may be hard to believe, having observed . . . my panic. But you don't know what happened back there! You see, the old man never told me that I'd meet the princess like that.'

The pedlar pulled up short, turned and grabbed the young man by the shoulders. Sniffling loudly, he fixed his squinting gaze on the fellow's dark eyes.

'Now just a minute! What old man are you talking about? And who is this princess? What kind of story is this? You haven't been drinking, but you don't make any sense to me. Did you leave your wits back there in the woods?'

The young man very gently disengaged the pedlar's grip from his shoulders. 'If you don't mind please, sir, this is very expensive cloth, and your hands *are* rather dirty . . .'

Bjorn stood back speechless – the peacock!

'The old man – I met after I parted with the traders. They told me it was an easy journey north to Wayland. How could I know they were making fun of me and leading me on? After all, I'm only a poet . . .'

(Ahaa, Bjorn was thinking, that would explain it.)

'Anyway, the old man helped me. He told me that I had come at the right time, and that if I went on to Wayland I should find the princess, and that I would instruct her, and teach her the art of song, and maybe even some day I would write a great poem about her. And she would reward me of course. That's the way it goes, you know, when one is lucky.'

Bjorn laughed despite himself. He was beginning to like this young fellow. It was too bad to have to bring him back to reality. But the truth couldn't hurt.

'Well,' he said quietly, 'that's a nice story. But *I* come from

Wayland – at least I live there. And I can tell you, there isn't any princess. And what's more – '

'Oh, there is a princess all right,' the young man interrupted. 'It's just that she hasn't arrived at the village yet.'

Bjorn decided it was time to stop the nonsense. 'And how in blazes do you know there's a princess, my lad?'

'I met her just now in the woods. At the edge of the lake. But it wasn't the princess that scared me. I mean, I wasn't really very scared, you know, just a bit startled. It was the other ones . . .'

Bjorn felt his scalp prickle and his chest tighten. 'The other ones?'

The young man's eyes widened and he cast a glance down the path. 'The grey folk,' he whispered. 'The old stories tell of them.'

The pedlar took hold of his sleeve and drew him off towards the trees. 'We must get to Wayland at once – this is news for the village. But the princess, you must describe her to me . . .'

The young man pulled back and did not answer. He stepped in the path and faced round, staring back down the trail, saying nothing, one arm slowly raised, pointing hesitantly at the trees.

A tall girl walked out of the woods into the sunlight. With long easy strides she moved down the path towards the men. Beside her, a boy jogged along, a small pack on his back, his arms swinging loose at his sides. The girl wore dark leggings and a green tunic like a man; from her belt hung a long knife. She wore a leather skull cap and her short hair, almost like a man's, hardly touched her shoulders. Her expression was clear and direct, and as she approached, Bjorn could see her elegant white neck, and the sharp humorous glint of her blue eyes. It was with something of a shock that he recognized, in this tall-striding woman, a girl he had seen in the past, none other than Einar's youngest daughter.

'Princess Ingrid!' said the poet, stepping forward as the girl came near. 'Let me introduce myself properly. My name is Skallgrim, and I've come all the way from Eastland to teach you a song.'

*   *   *

374

So they called her a princess. First the boy, then the strange poet and now, as if by common consent and revelation, the whole village of Wayland had adopted the title.

She stood for a while in the small central square, alone for nearly the first time since she had returned (was it nearly a week now?) and watched the sparrows flutter and dance on the brown roof of Aun's little house. She noted with pleasure the bright yellow shutters on the widow Osk's cottage. The old woman had never let them fade, despite all the troubles, though Runolf's crooked chimney had fallen down, the blacksmith had boarded up his windows before he departed, and Horic's place had burned to the ground – all in that first dreadful winter of her absence.

How sad it had been, on that first walk around Wayland with her father, to see how the town had been ravaged by the years of famine and despair. (For she soon found that Wayland in its suffering and isolation had become an island out of time. What to her had been the events of months merely, the villagers reckoned in years, and everyone seemed to have aged correspondingly.) Old friends had vanished – they had fled during the period of troubles, striking out for the east and the south, and had not been heard from thereafter. Their houses had been boarded up, or had been given to the sick and the poor; some were left empty and soon started to fall down. As usual, the very old and the very young and those who were impulsive and foolish, had suffered most. Kari, the beggarwoman, had been found under the snow near the barn that fronted the Whispering Meadow; Senta, whose daughter years before had been raped by Floki and then run away, had hanged herself because she had no food. A few of the young men, friends of Ingrid's brothers, feeling powerless at the turn of events, had armed themselves and gone into the woods near Skuld Lake to challenge the grey folk. But they had not returned. During that time several babies were stillborn, and one or two children, who had been born with deformities, were exposed, after the ancient custom.

Einar had told her of these things in a sad voice, as they walked hand in hand through the scenes of her childhood.

They had ended up at the Ice River, where she used to canoe, and sat watching the sunlight on the water, the swallows in ceaseless swift flight, the corn just beginning to come up in the nearby fields.

'I did my best to hold things together,' he told her. 'There was a system we had of distributing food from the gardens; of course some hoarded what they had, and I had no power to force them to contribute.

'The winters were terrible because of lack of food, and we were cold because the horses died and people were afraid to cut the trees on the edge of the wood. I had trouble restraining your brothers – you know how young Vikings are: they think everything can be cured by violent action. They wanted to attempt the trek to Eastland. But how could your mother have made the journey? And besides, this is our home. So I made them my deputies; but nothing went well. There was squandering of food, and sacrifices to the gods that were a disgrace to men. I had reason to suspect that even a baby was . . .'

His voice had trailed away, and he shuddered, his wrinkled old hands pressed together. Ingrid had looked at him and thought how much he had aged during her absence; he seemed so frail in person and, when he spoke, his glance was often averted. She had not remembered his voice as so trembling and distant. It was as if he had at some point fallen into a dream, and had not yet found a way out.

'You're tired, father,' Ingrid had told him, gently touching his forehead with her fingertips. 'You sacrificed yourself for the village. You tried to heal. Now, see how the corn is coming up, the grey folk have vanished – everything will be well again. Wayland will flourish.'

He had fixed his grey eyes on her then, almost coming out of his dream.

'It's you who has brought the light back, Ingrid, you, my own daughter. We owe you everything. You have the healing power and everyone feels it. Somehow you have discovered the mysteries I have sought all my life, in my books and my herbs. Yes, I tried to heal as I could; but you have saved us. And now . . .' (here his voice had sunk down to the soft

purling note of the water that rushed along at their feet) . . .
'and now you must, the gods help you, assume the responsibility that comes with power. They call you a princess, Ingrid.
Well, our family descends from a noble line, and the times
remain troubled. Men such as Floki, the merchants and greedy
fat traders, the exploiters, have made mockery of the common
rule of the chiefs. You must be prepared to lead us. Otherwise
Wayland cannot survive.'

They had walked back through the fields: how green and
smiling the land looked, Ingrid thought. And yet, if she were
to be the new head of the village, some things would have to
change.

There would be new ways of planting and new crops – she
would learn from the Skraelings, hunters though they were,
for during her time in their village she had noticed how they
could make do with little, treasuring the woods and the
streams for their riches. The Vikings must understand this
new land better, both in its wealth and its terrible power to
withhold. When the harvest was in or the following year, she
might think of returning north, and make an alliance with the
tribes. When she finally sent scouts north to enquire after the
shaman – for visions of the old man on that desolate cliff by
the great inland sea still perturbed her – she would have them
seek out the boy, Birch Tree's young helper, and try to bring
him back to Wayland. If he and Val could grow up together,
perhaps become blood brothers, then peace might be assured
between the two races for a long time.

She smiled at the thought of Val, who at first followed her
about Wayland like a shadow, for almost at once there had
been cruel jokes about his affliction. How her heart went out
to him then – because she could understand him, and knew
how much he missed his mother. Yet she was happy that
Harald and Eric, her brothers, seemed to take him under their
protection. Awestruck by some of the things she had dared to
tell them of her adventures, and perhaps a little jealous, they
needed a bridge back to the closeness with Ingrid they had
taken for granted before. And Val would become that bridge.

As for her sisters, Lina and Helsa and Kristiana, they

welcomed her with many tears and a little understanding and tried to conceal their shock at the changes that were evident in her person.

Asta in fact spoke for them (and for most of the women of the village) when she blurted out simply at first meeting 'Why Ingrid, you look like a man!' Poor Asta, Ingrid thought. She was more changed and shaken by events than Einar, but her way of escape had been to lose herself in the little details of housekeeping. Also, her memory was failing, especially for the painful things, of which her mind seemed to be swept clean. Now life was beginning to return to something like normal, yet when someone ventured to mention a terrible event of the near past, Asta would look at them doubtfully, as if they had suddenly started speaking in an unknown language. Then quietly, without a word, she would return to whatever small domestic task she might have in hand.

Ingrid did not take the references to her changed appearance too seriously, but she did have one burning desire, one small frustration connected with her great journey that she soon ritually assuaged. On her travels she had often dressed in the simplest: trousers, shirts and tunic, buckskins, a wool cloak – the rough clothes of the traveller, designed for a man's body and very suited to her lean frame. But just a few days after her arrival, she ransacked her knapsack, as well as the clothes chest of her girlhood, and dressed herself up with almost sumptuous splendour: she was costumed for once like the princess they wanted her to be.

She put on the softest undergarments, and a beautiful yellow silk chemise, which Bjorn had acquired for her in Vinland. It was very finely pleated and closed at the neck by white ribbons. Over this she wore a blue tunic of the finest light wool, fastened by matching brooches of silver, handed down from her mother's mother. Her cloak was a very rare brocade in dark blue, fastened at the neck by a horsehead pin of fine silver. She wore stockings and garters and long boots of the softest, most pliable pigskin. Having fluffed up her hair (there was little else she could do with it), she daubed herself

378

lightly with musk, and then applied a few touches of dark eyeshadow.

With innocent vanity, and a certain air of smiling humour, she proceeded to inspect the results in the family's best mirror of polished metal. She was agape with astonishment, and when she made her appearance that evening there were cries of amazement through the house with three chimneys. The whole family, once again happy, sat for a long time around the fire, and Ingrid reflected to herself, not without irony, that her mother seemed to think that her youngest daughter had at last become human again.

The next day, dressed in the rough clothes of her journey, Ingrid had gone to see Thorkel.

He had been staying, Einar explained, with Bergthora, his mother, in her tiny log house on the eastern edge of the village. The place had been built by Hoskuld, Thorkel's father, many years before, and was one of the oldest in the settlement. While Thorkel was still a boy his father had been buried near there, having drowned after falling through thin ice on Skuld Lake one spring morning. Ingrid had visited the house many times, but as she walked there that morning she felt nervous and vulnerable – she did not know if she had the strength to deal with Thorkel, or to face the memories he would arouse in her. And to make matters worse, just as she was fastening her cloak in her room, prior to departure, her sister Lina had appeared, and had shyly confessed that she had been visiting Thorkel regularly, 'in order to try to help him,' for many months now.

Ingrid had walked along, remembering the intensity in Lina's dark eyes, and the gesture with which she had brushed back her shining dark hair: it was almost a salute, as if she were resigning herself to Ingrid's superior claims on Thorkel, though she herself was older and had every right to see him or whatever purpose.

Bergthora, a gentle old woman who showed her teeth when she smiled, embraced Ingrid at the door of the cabin. She said little, but took the girl's cloak and pointed to a door, hung with a small fox skin, that led to the inner chamber.

379

Ingrid held her breath for a few seconds, knocked once then pushed the door slowly open, at the muffled command 'Come!'

The room was very dark, and the air nearly stifling, for the fire had been lit, though the windows were closed up and hung with heavy curtains. Thorkel sat facing the fire, his blond hair long and scraggly, but gleaming with light. He did not turn round or move to get up when Ingrid greeted him with his name.

She walked slowly over to where he sat. There was a bench piled up with skins by the fire. She seated herself on the bench. There was a pause; Ingrid said, 'Thorkel, I've come back!'

Then she sprang up. The pale bloated face, those eyes full of sadness, his hands clasped tight in his lap – she could not sit there and let these hide from her the young spirit, the warrior. *Her* Thorkel was present, she could feel it, and she knelt down and kissed him, took his limp hands in her hands and squeezed them, touched his shining mop of hair.

'It's all right, Ingrid, it's all right,' she heard him say softly. 'I've had some hard times, but I'm better now. I'm very glad you've come back to us.'

'Thorkel, they told me how you've been, but it's over now. The village is coming back to life, and we need you. You must get strong now – to help us rebuild.'

She fought back the tears; she did not want to corrupt him with her seeming pity. She could feel the strength that was in him. She knew he would recover. Had she cried then it would have been for joy.

'Ingrid, I told you this once before: you've changed. It's nice to see you smile. You look different to me somehow, though. Lina was here yesterday – she comes to talk to me sometimes – and she told me a few things. But some day want to hear about your journey from your own lips.'

Ingrid slowly nodded her head. 'You, Thorkel,' she said, reaching out to take one of his hands. 'You must tell me too about yourself.'

They were silent for a while. Thorkel stared at the slow

crackling wood in the fire. Then he spoke in a very soft voice, almost a whisper.

'When I came back here I thought about – our last meeting. I thought about your words to me then, about what I had done. It was a hard journey back – there were sights not pleasant to tell. Our old home seemed a place of the damned. There were things I knew I could do, but I had no power to act. My whole body seemed weighted and burdened, all passion was gone. I sank down, as you see me – just to raise my arm seemed a torture.

'It was easier to sit here, to do nothing: for a while I could barely speak. Your father tried to help me, but I spat up the herbs. They reminded me of you – of my crime against you. I thought you were dead, or lost forever to me – that I would never see you face to face, and be able to tell you – how sorry I am . . . that I love you, forever – with no claim, and no hope.'

Slowly, Thorkel bowed his head.

Then Ingrid had a vision. She was standing with a tall gaunt old man by the side of a lake. Nearby a boy sat, holding the reins of a team of grey slinking wolves. Ingrid put to her lips a small copper whistle; she remembered the feel of the metal, quite cold. A thin piercing sound came, not the silence she recalled from a dream long ago, but true sound, a summons. After a while, from the deep woods, in the shining clear sunlight, came the rustle and thrashing of branches, the soft tread of footsteps on the spring earth. She listened at first, then she saw them, shape after shape, coming out of the woods, so many with beautiful features, lines etched on dark skin, bodies brocaded with outline of clothing or hair; wisps, strands and loops spun round into delicate patterns, coiled braids and rope at the neck; eyes closed or sockets filled up with light – they came one after another – singly, in groups, hand in hand, and slipped, without breaking the surface of the water, into the blue lake.

And as they passed, Ingrid saw many strange faces, though she knew them for the faces of her own people. And from Wayland itself there were many faces that she knew: Thorgeir son of Flosi, Hrap, son of Atli the blacksmith, Thorunn, daughter of Ketil, and many, many more. She watched them all vanish into the blue morning lake . . .

Then Ingrid's vision faded, though she knew she would remember it always. She looked up into Thorkel's blue eyes.

'I forgive you, Thorkel,' she said quietly.

She bent down and rested her head in his lap for a moment and he stroked her hair; then slowly she rose and stood by the fire.

'As you have heard, Thorkel, I am to lead the village, to change things, to bring a new peace.' She laughed a light laugh and held her hands out before her. 'To tell you the truth I am already suspicious of whatever is in me that inspires and accepts such a task. I think we must soon get rid of our princess, and let everyone share in the rule. It's much better that way.'

Thorkel looked at her with something of his old astonishment at her surprises.

'Oh, I don't mean I want the mob to take over, or the fat merchants, but only that I'd like some help with my burdens. I'm already backing out, you see,' she added with a laugh.

'But you are going to accept – for now.'

'Yes – for now.'

'And – what of the Wanderer, of the ancient gods of our people, what of them?'

'The old man has said he will never come back,' Ingrid told him. 'As for the gods, I don't know. Now the Christ has the power in the old country, yet his teaching too will be perverted and mocked like the old one, no doubt. The great mother's nurture, Odin's power of rule, the saving vision of the Christ – everything at last goes out of balance, and that is where the trouble starts. Even so, there are things that the Christians proclaim that I want to remember.'

Ingrid gazed thoughtfully at Thorkel; she was happy to see the liveliness in him – how intently he looked at her, how the colour had returned to his cheeks.

'One of them is forgiveness,' she went on quietly. 'Forgiveness. The other is peace, never to use violence at all. And that I am just beginning to understand.'

There was a pause. Then, slowly, and with a great effort, Thorkel got to his feet.

'I will help you, Princess Ingrid,' he said, and reached out his hand . . .

So Ingrid, much later, walked through the village, thinking of all that had taken place since her return. And when at last she stood alone in the small central square, feeling the sunlight on her face, she had a deep longing to go on, alone, all the way to the Whispering Meadow. And as she made her way there, she was happy to see that the townspeople, the elders, her own friends, did not trouble her, so that she could enjoy a little peace and the fine spring day that was blooming around her.

She walked on, beyond the last of the houses, out where the long grass ran back to the deep woods, and she remembered young Skallgrim, the poet. He would compose for her surely, but perhaps also teach her, so that she too could master the art and someday recite her own story.

Blackbirds went winging away across the cornfields; insects hummed in the grass, and the swallows were building. Yet a wind stirred, a sudden chill gust of the spring.

And Ingrid looked north.

She imagined her own story. She thought of how, much later, she might have children of her own, and they would be her best audience. They would sit there wide-eyed, listening to her speak of the strangest and most wonderful things: of Moon Lake and its hidden terrors, of a girl who raced on skis for her life, of the marvellous untellable beauty of the Northern Lights. And sometimes, caught up in her tale, and wishing to make sure of their attention, she might bend down, bringing her head close to theirs, and they would, with the idolatry of children, admire their mother's long fine white neck.

And then, all of a sudden, because of the magic that lies in the gift of song, they would see before their eyes a tall woman standing by a town in a far land, matching wits with a grim old man who had power to destroy her. And, though storms might rage and threaten, they would know finally, as she knew, that a young girl can transform her whole life and draw from herself enough knowledge and courage to return from the darkest regions of the soul with a gift of light.

Here ends Skallgrim's Tale

EPILOGUE

All through the dwindling lazy summer, I, Skallgrim, a captive, fashioned my story of Princess Ingrid for Gunnar the bandit and his village. Each evening bonfires were lighted, and a motley crowd of men, women and children gathered by the river to hear yet another episode in Ingrid's journey. So the year waned; great Thor climbed up in the southern sky, while to the north, on many an evening, the lights shone, unfathomable and icily distant, illusory, like a fabric of dreams.

As my story unfolded I began to forget that I was, after all, a thrall of the bandits, that my tale was covertly the plea of a prisoner for honour and well-being. In fact, our relations soon changed. They grew more and more fascinated by what they heard, so that they, and not I, became the captives! How I relished those moments when those thieves and murderers, unable to control their curiosity, would sidle up to me in the village, and beg for a preview of my recitation of the coming evening! They had no idea whether what I told was true or invented (nor am I sure I can myself distinguish between history and invention, though perhaps readers still to come, now that everything is written down, will have their sharp opinions on the matter).

'Just a hint,' those bandits would beg of me. 'Is it really possible that Thorkel, that handsome fine warrior, could die without issue?' (Their questions were always so obvious, ridiculous even; they were like children hungering after sweets; even so, I was flattered at their interest.)

But if they became my thralls and if, at some moments, it seemed that I myself was chief in that Thule beyond Thule, it was their power that conquered in the end. For I had nothing material and they had everything. So they fed me, and I became a little too fat; they gave me a comfortable bed-closet, and I spent much time snoozing; they supplied fine clothing – soft linen underthings, a blue kirtle, dark brown breeches, new leather shoes, arm rings of silver and a rare turquoise neck-ring – and I grew quite vain of my dress; and Gunnar even provided me with my own concubine, Inga, whose slatternly ways of seduction began to arouse me, so that I forgot love was anything but lewd jokes, drunken fondling, caresses accompanied by giggles and followed by a blank snoring sleep.

When the first frosts heralded snow, and my tale about winter wound away in a beating of wings, and the sinister shapes I had evoked were ready to be submerged again in the element from which they had crawled up – I grew bored. God help me, yes, I grew bored. I did not want, in the current fashion, to commit my tale to writing, I did not want to think of another story, as Gunnar was already urging. I had recited to save my skin, and to satisfy the guilt I felt about my wasted life – yet what had it brought me? I was none the wiser; no more at home in the mysteries. I did not feel transformed by my visions, though they were given form by my voice. My only reward seemed to be a life of comfortable blankness; days that were dissipated in foolish trivia; nights full of strange dreams in which I often became a witness to disturbing visions. How many times did shapes rise up from the swamp-mud to drag me under? How many times did I wake up, drenched in sweat, to discover I had not, after all, been buried alive in some ice-fall?

It was just such thoughts that assailed me, one warm fall afternoon, when I lingered by the river, fishing. Gunnar and the men had gone off on a caribou drive, and I sat near the great oak, half-heartedly casting for trout, day-dreaming about my earlier days at Wayland, and wondering if Princess Ingrid – the real Princess Ingrid – would approve of my much embroidered tale of her girlhood. I doubted it – for how often does the muse approve of a poet's ravings? – but she was much older now, with some grown-up sons and daughters, and no doubt would be telling them the tale as she conceived it, from a very different perspective than mine.

I sat there, thus bemused – if I may make a pun of it – and watched the red-gold leaves stir in the gentlest of breezes. The river ran sparkling on, winding in among the spruce trees and chokecherry bushes, darting and dancing out of sight where the edge of the settlement merged with the deep forest thickets that stretched far away to the south. I dozed in the sunshine, closing my eyes, letting the soft stir enfold me, while nearby the birds sang consolingly, flies droned and the bees hovered over the wild sunflowers.

After a short while – I could not tell how long – something made me open my eyes; I sat up, blinking and yawning, my fishing pole fell from my unclasped hands. Coming straight towards me, directly across the stream, was a girl, long-limbed and beautiful, leaping from stone to stone with quick airy strides, approaching the rock where I sat – and before I could shake myself fully awake or gasp any greeting, she had crossed over and flung herself right down beside me, smiling up at me brightly with her clear dark-blue eyes.

'You're Skallgrim,' she said in a voice that was musical. 'I've counted on finding you. I've been sent here to talk to you.'

Was this a dream, I wondered? I was held by the perfect soft glow of her skin, by the curve of her white neck rising out of the buckskin jacket; dark hair fell to her shoulders: I longed to touch it, but something restrained me. At the same time I was thinking, with a thrill of fear and wonder, that this girl somehow resembled the Princess Ingrid of my story. I had lately ceased to trust my memory of the exact appearance, in youth, of the real Ingrid, but here at my feet was a girl who resembled at least her youngest daughter; here was the perfect embodiment of my own made-up princess, tall and bold, and fresh as a young doe in spring.

'What . . . What's your name, my dear?' I remember stammering, wondering why I had to sound so timid and incompetent in the face of beauty. I sat down beside her, rubbing the sleep-daze from my eyes, half-expecting the vision to vanish, but she leaned towards me, a flesh-and-blood girl, and said boldly:

'My name is Kara. I am one of Gunnar's bondwomen and I am risking my life to speak to you. You must listen carefully and make up your mind quickly; there are spies among the women of the village.'

She looked around nervously, then suggested:

'Put your arms around me; pretend it is a love-tryst. If anyone is watching they will carry the wrong message to Gunnar.'

I embraced her quickly and with enthusiasm; such luck comes rarely in a man's life! I closed my eyes with joy and listened, as we bundled down together on the soft grass.

'I come from Lokasenna in the south – exactly as the Glimir and Harg of your story. All summer long, I listened with joy to your tale. I want you to teach me the art of the story-teller – but that can come later. The story I have to tell you now is more important. Listen carefully!

'I was captured in spring and brought here to be Gunnar's mistress: to say I hate him would be too mild, an understatement. I have long planned to run away, but feared the consequences. Last week, however, everything changed. I was picking berries near the ash tree in the great clearing that narrows and becomes the main track leading south. I saw a man hiding in the bushes and was about to report him to our guardian, Haldor, for I was afraid he was going to ambush and murder us. Then I saw that I knew him – he was a man from my own village! I managed to slip over and talk to him and he explained that a hunting party was nearby: they would help me escape if I wished, but in turn I must help them capture the poet, Skallgrim, whom they had been trying to buy for some months from Gunnar.'

Oh yes, I was listening, though fearfully distracted by her trembling body, the sweet scent of her hair, but at this point I drew back. I held her at arm's length without speaking.

'You must believe me,' she went on. 'The fame of your story-telling has spread south, but Gunnar has decided to

390

keep you here forever. If you try to resist or run away, he plans to kill you. It is part of his perversity.'

Looking into her clear blue eyes I could not doubt that she was speaking the truth.

'What shall we do?' I asked, making her sit up beside me, keeping my arm around her shoulder, my lips close to her delicate ear. 'True, I am tired of this place, and want badly to escape – but my absence will be noticed; they'll pursue us. And who must I be bound to in the south – some shadow-brother of Gunnar who lords it over your home village? Perhaps I should take my chances and make straight for Wayland.'

'I love you,' she said. 'If you come with me I will be your woman and no-one will oppress you. My family is very powerful in Lokasenna. Someday we can go together to Wayland.'

A wonderful vision opened up in my mind, but I must confess that the main part of it involved us lying naked together in a tent. Was my imagination really so enchained by immediate, by instantly to be gratified desire? (As it turned out, we loved each other well, Kara and I, though we never had children and never made the journey back to Wayland.)

'I must go now,' she whispered, pulling slightly away. 'We will wait for you tonight under the ash by the boundary line, where the southern track opens. Gunnar's absence will serve our purpose. Even if you don't come, they may take me with them – though in anger they may kill me, and invent some excuse for my brothers. But I will risk anything to get away from here – especially if you can come with me. Don't miss this chance, Skallgrim. Gunnar will not serve you well, in the end.'

She had slipped out of my arms and taken two steps back towards the riverbank. I felt my heart pounding wildly, and murmured my promise. Oh, yes, I would join her!

I watched as she made her way along through the willows, then cut back north towards the village.

For a long time I sat there, and saw my future branching

away down long, unseen trails, quite divergent. But of course I would join her.

I returned to the village.

Without the young men it was a strange place. I strolled past dozing sentries, down the dusty beaten tracks between the houses, where a few children played dice and horse-games; I nodded to old Aun, who sat under a tree nursing the arm he had broken in a hunting accident. I reached my lodge without exchanging more than casual greetings with anyone along the way.

I spent the afternoon lying low, gathering a few possessions and stowing away clothes and trinkets on my person. I pretended to sleep. After a while Inga came and started making fun of me – the usual prelude to our nightly carousing and love-violence. I slipped away, saying I had a debt to pay to Gnorre the cripple.

It was only a half-hour's walk to the clearing that the girl had mentioned. I had to be careful; there were sentries, though not many, here and there in the woods. I crossed the river, found a good broad branch in an old oak and rested. I remembered how Gunnar, that sly pig, had strung me up to make me sing for him. When it got dark I crept away south, on the lookout for guards or pursuers.

After a while I began to trust the sounds of the woods. The wind blew up stray leaves, a few birds called softly, a fox barked. The branches above me seemed to glow with a strange light. I thought how wonderful it was to be free, to enjoy these precious moments, between master and master.

I approached the great clearing with due caution. It was quite dark, some time before moonrise. I could see where the trail led south, a thin dark cleft in the deep woods just opposite. A light flashed, more than once, on the topmost branches of the trees across from where I lay.

Then something moved in the branches of the ash tree. A figure slipped down and dropped on the turf. It was Kara. I hesitated a moment, then stepped out into the clearing.

Two mounted men emerged from the south trail. I heard padded footsteps behind me and turned. A Viking with drawn

392

sword walked up behind me. Kara came towards me from beside the tree.

I approached her swiftly, not wanting to stop, with that man right behind me. We met at the foot of the ash tree. She looked beautiful. Then for the first time I noticed what was causing the miraculous shimmer on the treetops. It was the lights, the Northern Lights, occupying the whole sky behind me. I had never seen them so wonderfully bright and various.

'Are you Skallgrim the poet?' asked one of the men on horseback – a good-looking youth with a blond moustache. I nodded. 'It's all right,' said the man with the sword. 'I followed him through the woods. He hasn't betrayed us.'

Kara, who had said nothing, squeezed my hand.

'Would you like to come to Lokasenna?' asked the blond youth. 'We can offer you protection, and Kara is willing to marry you.'

I was startled. She had not mentioned marriage. I thought of everything I had missed in life, of what I had run away from.

'I would like to come with you,' I said, then added, 'in five minutes.'

'Touch a poet and find a fool,' said the man with the sword. 'Does he want us to squander our time? The whole village may be turned out to find us.'

'I want five minutes with Kara while all of you wait for us there.' I pointed to the far side of the clearing, near the trail mouth.

'Make it much longer and we may kill you both,' said the young man and pulled his horse round.

The lights in the north had grown incredible. I drew Kara close to me and we stood there, not far from the flickering ash tree, gazing upward, in silence.

All the beauty I had sought after and tried to capture and express seemed at that moment within my grasp, as close as my pulse, as intimately present as my heartbeat. I had never felt such a thing before, neither in love nor in story-making.

'Do you really want to marry me?' I asked softly, and she told me that indeed it was her wish.

Then, on that spot, in that clearing aglow with white light, I had an insight such as I had never dreamed of. I suddenly knew that despite its hidden terrors, despite even its obvious boredom and nullity, life could reveal a spirit of beauty – a light that would sometimes shine forth from the most common thing. This spirit was like a hawk that might break free and soar high, without scorching its wings: it might be swallowed up, but not consumed, by the ever-shifting clouds, or vanish in a flash of sunlight, to be reborn, strong-winged and dazzling, in the clear blue light of day.

That moment my senses shook, for I could see that spirit, that clear light, shining in the far sky and in the eyes of my wife-to-be, Kara.

Such an energy would sustain me through the years and, though I never returned to Wayland, when I wrote of the journey of Ingrid, the memory of that night and the figure of Kara, finally entered my story.

So I walked with my princess towards the dark trail, where the Vikings were impatiently waiting.

They had a horse for me there.

Then I, Skallgrim, poet and story-teller, bowed to the strangers, my new masters, because I wished to, climbed up on the mare, and keeping the fair form of the girl in sight as in mind, rode with all of them south in search of a new home for my inspiration.

Stephen Donaldson

The Chronicles of Thomas Covenant, the Unbeliever

'Comparable to Tolkien at his best . . . will certainly find a place on the small list of true classics.' *Washington Post*

'An irresistible epic.' *Chicago Daily News*

'The most original fantasy since *Lord of the Rings* and an outstanding novel to boot.' *Time Out*, London

'Intricate, absorbing, these volumes create a whole new world.' *Sunday Press*, Dublin

The First Chronicles of Thomas Covenant, the Unbeliever

LORD FOUL'S BANE
THE ILLEARTH WAR
THE POWER THAT PRESERVES

The Second Chronicles of Thomas Covenant

THE WOUNDED LAND
THE ONE TREE
WHITE GOLD WIELDER

FONTANA PAPERBACKS

The Winter King's War

The Ring of Allaire
The Sword of Calandra
The Mountains of Channadran

An exciting new fantasy trilogy by
SUSAN DEXTER

To save the land of Calandra from the greed of the evil ice-lord Nímir, Tristan, a mere apprentice, begins a perilous quest where a thousand master magicians have failed . . .

FONTANA PAPERBACKS

Fontana Paperbacks
Fiction

Fontana is a leading paperback publisher of both non-fiction, popular and academic, and fiction. Below are some recent fiction titles.

You can buy Fontana paperbacks at your local bookshop or newsagent. Or you can order them from Fontana Paperbacks, Cash Sales Department, Box 29, Douglas, Isle of Man. Please send a cheque, postal or money order (not currency) worth the purchase price plus 22p per book for postage (maximum postage required is £3.00 for orders within the UK).

NAME (Block letters) _____

ADDRESS _____

_____

_____